BREAKERS

ACADEMY OF STARDOM - BOOK THREE

BEA PAIGE

Kelly Stock writing as Bea Paige to be identified as author of this work has been asserted by her in accordance with sections 77 and 78 of the Copyright, Designs and Patents Act 1988.

All rights reserved. No part of this publication may be reproduced, stored in retrieval system, copied in any form or by any means, electronic, mechanical, photocopying, recording or otherwise transmitted without written permission from the publisher. You must not circulate this book in any format.

This book is licensed for your personal enjoyment only. This e-book may not be resold or given away to other people. If you would like to share this book with another person, please purchase an additional copy for each recipient. Thank you for respecting the hard work of this author.

Copyright © Kelly Stock writing as Bea Paige

First published: 11th Jan 2021

Alternate cover design by Cover Couture.

www.bookcovercouture.com

This book is dedicated to 2020. I'm glad we're through. 2021, you better not fuck us over.

Bea Paige

I want to break free

~ *Queen*

PLAYLIST

Dear Reader,

By now you'll know that music plays an integral part in Pen and the Breakers' story. Like Lyrical, Breakers has specific songs to go with critical dance scenes.

For a more immersive reading experience I recommend listening to the songs as you read.

Each scene will be prompted with the title of the song.

You can find the *Breakers* Spotify playlist by searching for Bea Paige.

Bea Paige x

PROLOGUE

York

I'VE ALWAYS BEEN good at reading people. Call it a gift. Intuition, if you will.

Pen was always so easy to read. She could never hide her innermost thoughts from me.

I'd known, before she'd admitted it to herself, that she loved us. I saw it in the way she'd held back, in the way her emotions played across her face like a love poem trapped beneath her skin. Her eyes would flash with intensity, her mouth would part, her cheeks would pink up, her eyelashes would flutter, her brows would pull together in a frown as though trying to contain the love within her eyes. But I saw it. She'd watch us with all these secret words fluttering across her face, this secret love hidden inside.

Love words. Words of love.

I read them all.

Unspoken. Kept secret. Contained.

In the beginning she'd held them back, that truth, that love.

Perhaps it was from fear of rejection. That ache that comes with loving someone who may never love you in return. She'd been so badly hurt by her own mother's cruelty and her brother's brutality that it was little wonder she was so fucking cautious. I don't blame her. It's hard enough to love one person, but four? She was so fucking brave.

Yes, *brave*.

To love us. Four boys broken in their own way. Each of us carried a burden. Dax's was his father's hate. Zayn's was his family ties. Xeno's was the darkness he held inside from some past trauma he never shared. And me? I came from a home where my parents didn't even know I existed. I lived with parents who barely cared where I was from one moment to the next. So to have her look at me with *love* was scary. I didn't believe I deserved it.

But she loved us anyway. All of us. Every broken, jagged part.

During the early years of our friendship we'd placed her firmly in the friendzone, and we were all happy there. We laughed. We danced. We spent hours together. It was natural. She fit into the Breakers perfectly. She became the organ that pumped us with blood, that kept us alive, vibrant. She became the pulse that gave us purpose, focus. A reason to be better.

Then things changed. She evolved from this scrappy, little kid, into a beautiful young woman. It was as though a lightbulb had flicked on inside of her, lighting her up from the inside out. I wasn't the only one who'd noticed.

We all did. Even Xeno. *Especially* him. Though he'd never admit it. He couldn't deal with it. That light that poured out of her. That love.

I knew he had demons, but I never really understood back then why he reacted so badly to her love. Why he pushed her away. Why he gave her an ultimatum. Because I *saw* what he refused to believe. He loved her too. Just like the rest of us.

She was our best friend. Our Titch. Our Tiny. Our Kid. Our Pen. Our lucky penny.

Until she became so much more than that.

It scared the shit out of Xeno. All of us to a certain extent.

Frankly, I was a dick. I can admit that now. Before I acknowledged how she felt, I'd flirted with other girls in front of her. I'd kissed them and touched them knowing deep down that she'd be watching, hurting. It was wrong. So fucking wrong. But, like I said, I was broken too.

Then she kissed Dax. Then she admitted how she felt about all of us.

I'd never felt happier. She was so fucking brave opening herself up like that.

Finally. *Finally* someone noticed me. Noticed *us*.

Four boys who hurt.

And what did we ultimately do?

She gave us her love, and we threw it back in her face.

That night when she walked away, we proved to ourselves that we were unworthy of her love, her light, because there wasn't one of us who'd noticed how it'd gone out.

How, in the space of a couple of hours, Pen's light disappeared.

Even me. The one person who could always read her better than the rest.

We were all fucking blind to it.

Maybe it was because we'd knocked back too many drinks that night.

Maybe it was because we were too high from the joint we'd smoked celebrating our win.

Maybe it was because by the time she'd finished breaking our hearts, we were too busy bleeding out from the rejection that we didn't stop to look at how *she'd* died inside.

All the broken parts she'd smoothed out with her love, suddenly became sharp once more.

It fucking hurt, her rejection. It hurt so fucking bad.

That night I'd failed her. We *all* did.

We failed her every day that followed for not questioning what happened. For being so fucking self-centered. We'd lived off each other's pain, and we'd wallowed in it like a bunch of fucking selfish cunts. We didn't fight the darkness that took over.

We threw ourselves into the Skins. We became the very epitome of everything we hated. We did bad things. *Terrible* things.

Then a year ago something happened. Something that would change the course of our lives forever. Something that eventually led us back to our beating heart even when we still refused to believe that's all we ever really wanted.

We lost sight of the girl we loved once before. We lost sight of ourselves. Then we returned and we still couldn't see the truth that was right in front of our faces.

But she made us *see*. She made me see once more. Titch pulled away the veil of hate and pain that had blinded us for years by dancing her way back into our lives, into our motherfucking souls. Now that the Breakers' heart is beating again, we will do everything, *anything* to keep it safe.

1

Pen

MY EYELIDS FLICKER OPEN, and I blink back the heavy fog of unconsciousness. My muscles feel weak, my throat is dry, and a headache already blooms across my forehead. It takes me another few minutes to have enough strength to sit upright. I groan loudly, my gaze flitting around the dimly lit room as my hands slide over my body. I'm dressed in a loose t-shirt and sweatpants. Something about that doesn't seem right, but I can't gather my thoughts enough to figure out why. My fingers creep across the bedding, which is surprisingly soft beneath my hands. The room itself is warmly decorated in jewelled tones, there are canvases covering the walls with art that looks vaguely familiar in my foggy brain. Even though I feel like I'm drunk or high, I know this isn't a dream just like I know that this isn't my flat.

Where the hell am I? What am I doing here?

Then, like a spotlight being switched on inside my dark and cloudy thoughts, I remember.

I remember being in the cage at Grim's club.

I remember dancing.

I remember the girls.

I remember Xeno.

Xeno.

Xeno who told me to trust him, who told me he loved me then stabbed a needle in my fucking neck! My hand lifts automatically to the spot, my fingers pressing against my skin where he'd injected me, and I wince at the phantom pain. Adrenaline rushes through my veins at the memory, followed swiftly by betrayal and anger.

Flipping my legs over the side of the bed, I sit upright. My head goes woozy at the sudden movement and I have to squeeze my eyes shut to force my brain to stop thinking I'm on a rollercoaster. When the feeling passes, I open my eyes and take another good look around me. On the side table next to me is a glass of water and a packet of headache pills with a sticky note fixed to them.

Take these, it will help.

Fuck that. I don't trust the note or the person who fucking wrote it.

Speaking of which.

A familiar voice draws my attention to the slightly ajar door. Gingerly, I creep forward, my feet padding over the soft carpet. With the side of my body pressed against the wall, I peer out through the crack. At the end of the hallway is an open plan living room. Sitting at a table that separates the kitchen area from the lounge, is Xeno. He's talking in hushed tones into his phone.

I see red.

Anger like I've never felt before courses through my veins as betrayal clogs my throat.

I yank open the door and storm down the hallway into the room ignoring the way my head spins, ignoring the fact that my balance is still off. Thank fuck for adrenaline, otherwise I'd be on the floor in a fucking heap.

Xeno's eyes widen and he bites out a terse reply before placing his phone onto the table and rushing towards me. "Tiny, fuck, you need to sit down before you fall down," he says, reaching for me, concern rippling across his traitorous face.

"Don't you fucking touch me!" I shout, holding my arms out as I stagger sideways, gripping hold of the back of the sofa to steady myself.

"Tiny, let me explain..." His hands drop to his sides and he steps back.

Tears prick my eyes. "Let you explain? Let you fucking explain?! You drugged me. You stabbed me with a needle and knocked me the fuck out, Xeno! You stole hours of my life. Why would you do that? Why would you fucking *hurt* me like that?"

My body shakes so hard that my teeth start to chatter, and my skin covers in a sheen of sweat, instantly cooling my heated, enraged heart until it's ice cold. I want to throw up. But there's nothing in my stomach, so I just heave and gag instead. I double over, retching, with nothing to show for it but a burn in the back of my throat that matches the sting in my eyes.

"It's okay, you're safe," Xeno says softly, but there's the slightest hint of an edge to his voice as though he doesn't quite believe that either. It's as though the softness of his tone is covering up how he truly feels. When he presses his hand against my lower back, I feel the tension he holds, and the lies burn a tattoo into my skin.

"*Safe?*" I hiss, forcing myself upright and backing away from him even though a small part of me wants to step towards him, but *fuck that*. Just because he says I'm safe doesn't mean it's true. Xeno asked me to trust him, and then knocked me out. How can I trust him now? Who the fuck does that to someone they supposedly care about? "Don't you dare lie to me!"

"Sit down. Let me explain." There's a pained look on his face, and I see how his hands shake, how he curls his fingers into fists trying to suppress whatever's eating him up inside. "I won't hurt you."

I bark out a laugh. It sounds thready, broken. "Again, lies! I see you. I fucking see you, Xeno," I shout, my gaze falling on his fists, at the veins bulging beneath his forearms like any minute now he's going to lose his cool and show me the man underneath the mask.

He shakes his head, his nostrils flaring as he uncurls his fingers and shakes out his hands. "Don't make this harder than it already is. Sit down," he orders, pulling out a chair at the table.

"Where am I?" I snap, ignoring his request and looking wildly around me. Hanging on the wall above the fireplace is another huge painting similar in style to the one in the bedroom, the bold colours and style familiar even though I don't know why that is right now. My head's still too foggy, my thoughts disjointed.

"If you calm down, I'll tell you."

"Don't fucking patronise me, Xeno," I snap, forcing myself to look at him.

He watches me carefully, his bottle-green eyes glinting like cut glass. The shards deep enough to cut. He always knew how to make me bleed, this is no different. Without even saying a word he hurts me, and I'm done with it.

"Tell me where the fuck I am!" I shout, my hands grabbing hold of the beige sofa behind me, a fine-knit throw chucked across it. My fingers curl into it and I have the urge to pick it up and wrap it around my shoulders. This place is luxurious, homely, warm, but I just feel cold, afraid, uncertain. I let go of the material. "Did you think that bringing me here would lull me into a false sense of security? That I would lower my guard because I hadn't just woken up in some dingy cellar somewhere tied to a fucking bed? Did you assume that I would relax because there are photos of happy, smiling people I don't recognise lined up across that fireplace?" Even the familiar smell of coffee feels like a trap. My eyes track across the kitchen countertop behind him where four mugs are sitting, heat rising.

"No, that isn't what I thought, but if you want, I can take you to a fucking basement and tie you to a bed if that would make you fucking listen to me!" he snaps back, forcing me to look at him once more.

"I bet you'd like that wouldn't you, huh? I'd bet you'd like me at your mercy."

He growls at that. A deep rumble rising up his throat. "You have no idea what you're saying."

"No? Then why are you looking at me that way? Why do I get the feeling that you're a second away from proving me right, that I'm *not* safe? That I'll *never* be safe with you."

Xeno sucks in a breath through his teeth as he takes another step closer. "Because I *love* you that's why," he roars. His fingers curl into a fist as he thumps his chest. It makes me jump a little at the ferocity of it. "Tiny, I fucking *love* you."

His voice is gravelly, coarse, as though saying those words is difficult, agonising. I guess I have to agree because they're just as painful to hear. My stupid treasonous heart squeezes inside my chest, and my body sways towards him. It would be so easy to walk into his arms, but self-preservation kicks in and I listen to my head instead this time.

"Love me?" I scoff. "Don't tell me that you love me after what you did."

He scrapes a hand over his face. "I did it to keep you *safe*," he repeats, firmly, without an ounce of apology or regret. He widens his stance as though he expects my anger to turn physical, like he's preparing for it. "You were in danger, Pen, and you can bet your arse that I'd do it again in a heartbeat."

"Tell me something I don't already know, *Xeno*." I hiss, my stupid fucking heart hating that he's stopped calling me Tiny. "When have I *not* been in danger? I've spent my whole life as a target for people who want to hurt me. *You* included. You could've fucking warned me about this sudden danger. You could've called me and told me something was up. You could have told one of the others if you didn't want to speak to me. I spilled my guts to you, Xeno. I trusted you with my truth and you *disappeared* without a word and with no fucking explanation." He opens his mouth to respond, but I hold my hand up preventing him from speaking. "Then you turned up out of the blue and *danced* with me. You gave me *hope* that we could fix us, only to do what you did. You. Hurt. Me."

He flinches. "I deserve that. I deserve your mistrust and your anger but there wasn't time to explain. I thought..." His voice trails off as he looks away, a sudden shame burning his cheeks. I know what he's thinking, and I'd laugh if I wasn't so angry.

"You thought that by dancing with me it would cancel out what you *then* did? That I'd be so fucking grateful that you finally deemed me worthy of dancing with that I'd forgive you for knocking me out?"

"No, that's not what I thought. I wasn't trying to soften you up, so you'd forgive me the second you woke up. I'm used to making hard decisions, Pen. The fact of the matter is, I wasn't *supposed* to do anything until the lights went out. I was supposed to wait, but I let my fucking emotions get the better of me. You were so fucking beautiful, so powerful up on that stage. I was fucking entranced, drawn to you like a motherfucking moth to a flame. Before I knew what I was doing, I was holding you in my arms. I *thought* I'd be strong enough to keep myself in check, but I couldn't fight it anymore. I couldn't fucking fight it anymore, Tiny."

"Couldn't fight what?"

"Your *pull*. Jesus fucking Christ! Don't you get it. I've been battling for years now," he exclaims, pulling at his hair as though the truth is too much to bear. Maybe it is. Maybe that's always been the problem. I make him feel things he never wanted to feel. Love shouldn't be this difficult, should it? Only between us, it is. It always has been.

"Why fight it?" I whisper. It's a question he doesn't hear, or if he does, he can't answer right now. I've never understood why he's always held back. Nothing is any clearer now that he's admitted his love for me. It doesn't make me feel any better knowing that he loves me.

"Even before when we were kids, I fought against my need to have you until the others persuaded me to give *us* a chance. I did that, then you ran off, and I felt my whole fucking world give way. Everything went to shit because of—"

"*Me?*" I interrupt, feeling as though he's just stabbed that fucking needle straight into my heart and pumped a syringe of air into me, the organ ready to burst under the pressure. I need to get away from him. It's suddenly hard to breathe. "Unbelievable. I'm fucking out of here," I say, choking on the words. Spinning on my feet, I head towards a set of stairs that appear to lead downwards and hopefully to the exit. I'm torn up inside. His words make me want to both hold him and slap him. I don't know what the fuck to do, or where the fuck I am, but I don't give a shit. I want out. I will fight him to get out of wherever the hell I am.

I don't get very far.

Xeno grabs my arm and spins me around, hauling me up against him roughly. My hands press against his chest automatically and I can feel the frantic thump of his heart beneath my palms. Raising my hand, I slap him hard against his cheek, the biting sting on my palm doing nothing to tame the anger I feel.

Heat flares in his gaze and his grip tightens. Despite his bruising touch, I can't help but remember how it felt to finally dance with him. How perfect we moved together. How *right* it was. This anger between us now feels wrong and yet, I can't stop feeling this way. I swallow hard and square my shoulders, pushing off his chest and straining against his hold as my fingers curl into fists, scrunching his t-shirt in my palms. He won't let me go though. He slides one arm around my back whilst the other clasps the back of my head. Tugging on my hair, he urges me to look up at him. Our gazes clash, my heated one crashing against the sizzling passion in his.

"You've got it wrong. Everything went to shit because of *me*. I'm not blaming you," he says through gritted teeth.

"Let me go, Xeno!"

"No!" he responds, almost manic. "Not until you understand. You weren't responsible for how we've turned out. We used you as an excuse to fall deeper into the Skins, but you were right all along, Tiny. We had one foot in the crew way before that night. No one is to blame for that apart from our-motherfucking-selves."

Narrowing my eyes at him, I refuse to acknowledge the dark circles beneath his eyes or the haggard way he looks. I refuse to see the concern written plainly across his face, or the *love*. Because what kind of person disappears for a week after you empty your soul, dances with you as though you're the only person that truly fits—*then* hurts you that way? Xeno flinches, and it's only then I realise I actually said that last part out loud.

"I had to do it, and I would do it again. I will *not* apologise for that." He proclaims, dropping his gaze from my eyes to my lips. His mouth parts, and for a second I swear he's going to kiss me. I'm almost ninety-five percent sure I don't want him to. The other five percent is ruled by my heart, which is currently begging me to lean in and press my mouth against his. "You were in danger, Pen."

I bark out a laugh, trying not to allow myself to be affected by the fact that he's referring to me as Pen once again. It's as though he's having an internal battle within himself to keep me at arm's length, by calling me Pen, or hold me close and never let go and calling me Tiny. Given the torn up look in his eyes I'm not certain which side of him is winning. "Yeah, from you!" Pushing at his chest, I force him away. This time he lets me go as his attention focuses on something behind me. *Someone.*

"You weren't in danger from Xeno, Penelope."

2

Pen

I SNAP my head around to find a man I don't recognise walking into the room. He's older than us both by at least ten years, maybe more. He's good looking in a clean-cut way and is wearing a grey suit as though he's just come home from the office. I watch as he runs his hand through his dark hair as his serious, penetrating, green eyes stare back at me.

"My name is *Pen*."

"Apologies, Pen," Mr. *Suited-and-booted* replies with a tight smile.

"Who the fuck are you anyway?" I snap, backing away. My arse hits the back of the sofa once again, but that's not what makes my knees give way, it's the fact that Grim has just climbed up the stairs and stepped onto the floor behind him. "You!" I accuse, jabbing my finger at her.

She heaves out a sigh, lights up a cigarette and blows out a steady stream of smoke before strolling over to the table and taking a seat. "Sit down, Pen, before you fall the fuck down. This isn't what you think."

"Isn't what I think?" I shout, vibrating with betrayal. "You're in on this! It wasn't Jeb and David, or even Malik-fucking-Brov that I should've been afraid of all this time. It was you. Him," I rage pointing at Xeno who is glaring at Grim.

"What the fuck are you doing here? I asked for time to explain," Xeno exclaims, his jaw gritting in anger.

"Looks like you're doing a shit job at it," she replies, with a shrug.

"What did you need time to explain? Because it seems pretty fucking clear to me. You both betrayed me, and now I'm being sold off to this motherfucker?" I shout, jabbing my finger at the stranger whilst glaring at Xeno.

Said motherfucker, Mr. Suited-and-booted, raises his eyebrows and glances at Grim who shakes her head. "That is not what's going on. Despite his royal fuck-up, Xeno saved your arse tonight. If it wasn't for him and *this motherfucker* you'd be waking up in The Collector's castle as his new possession, with no fucking hope of ever escaping that place. Fortunately for you, Beast shot the bastard."

My mouth drops open as I stare at Grim. "*What?* He saved my arse..." All the blood drains from my face as another kind of panic slides like poison into my veins, taking over that thought and blurring it with another. "Beast shot The Collector?"

"Yep. Bullet between the motherfucking eyes. Jeb's face was a fucking picture, given most of Brov's brains were splattered across him." Grim chuckles darkly.

"Wait—" I sway on my feet, my fingers curling into the back of the sofa to keep me steady. "Malik Brov is *dead*?"

"That's right. Dead as a fucking doornail. The cunt should never have tried to fuck with me," Grim says.

"Oh, God...."

Grim pulls on her cigarette, and for a second I'm mesmerised by the glowing red tip. "What, Pen?"

"What do you mean, *what*?" I blurt out. "A man's dead. A dangerous man. Before, when Dax jumped to my defence in the cage you said that Malik was the leader of a Polish crime family. You said there would be repercussions after Dax *threatened* his life that night... What's going to happen now that Beast has fucking *killed* him?"

Grim shrugs, like it's no big deal. "Malik started this war by trying to take you when you weren't for fucking sale. He's lucky Beast took him out quickly. Usually he isn't so kind."

"Damn right she's not for fucking sale. Just because you gave Jeb information in exchange for Pen working at Tales it doesn't mean to say that she's your fucking property either. She's ours. She belongs with the Breakers," Xeno warns possessively.

He steps towards me, but I hold my hands out, shaking my head as I try to get my head around everything I've been told. Grim said Xeno saved my arse. So he wasn't lying when he said he was protecting me? "Don't. I need to think."

"Pen's my *employee*, arsehole, and as far as I'm concerned, the only person she belongs to is herself. Correct me if I'm wrong, but until very recently you didn't even want her, right?" Grim takes a deep draw on her cigarette, challenging Xeno with her stare. I watch as her chest expands, drawing the cancerous smoke into her lungs before she blows it out again in his direction.

Xeno grits his teeth, a muscle ticking beneath the stubble that shadows his jaw. "You don't know a fucking thing about our relationship, so stay the fuck out of it."

"Or what?" she taunts.

Mr. Suited-and-booted places a hand on Grim's shoulder and squeezes. "Enough, Grim—"

"No," she shakes him off. "I'm not done," Grim retorts, and whilst I appreciate her sticking up for me. I don't need her to. It's not her place.

"Yeah, you are," Xeno says before I'm able to. "Your relationship with Beast is private. It has fuck all to do with anyone else, so unless Pen wants your advice or your opinion, I'd *respectfully* ask that you keep it to your goddamn self!"

Grim holds Xeno's stare for a moment before leaning back in her chair and smiling slowly in that assessing way of hers. "Fine," she concedes, and the tension in the room dials down a notch. At that moment I wonder whether her provoking Xeno was to get him to open up rather than piss him off. Either way, I'm not sure it matters, because he's both pissed off and saying things that surprise me.

"So what happens now?" I ask, rubbing at my temple as a headache forms.

"Right now, The Collector's body and what remains of his head, are currently being dissolved in acid," Grim says, as though this is a normal, everyday occurrence for her. It probably is.

"Jesus Christ," I mutter, feeling nauseous.

"Look, Pen. Malik made a huge error trying to take you. I had to send a message. No one tries to fuck me over, *ever*. Besides, I like you. There's no fucking way I would've let that creep get his hands on you. Employee or otherwise."

"Fuck—" It's about all I can manage to say right now.

"Fuck indeed," the mysterious stranger, Mr. Suited-and-booted, says. I glance at him, frowning, but I'm too desperate to know what went on to question who the fuck he is, why he's here or even where *here* is, right now.

"How did you know Malik was coming for me? Did that bastard Jeb make a deal with him after all?"

"Jeb might be a prick, but he's not a fool. He wouldn't double-cross Grim and have the audacity to sit in her club and expect to live. Though that fucker Malik sure as hell had some balls thinking he could take you just like that. That we'd *let* him," Xeno bites out.

"I still don't understand *how* you knew?" I say, frowning. Xeno eyes Mr. Suited-and-booted and they exchange looks. Xeno tips his chin up, almost imperceptibly, as though giving this man permission to talk. It strikes me as odd, but I don't question it.

"One of my men intercepted some correspondence between Malik Brov and another criminal we've been watching—" Mr. Suited-and-booted remarks casually, like he's talking about the weather. "Xeno was with me when I got the intel. We were able to inform Grim just in time and get a plan in place. It was with Jeb's approval that Xeno be the one to get you to safety."

"*Intercepted?* Wait... What do you mean by that? Who *are you* exactly?"

"We'll get to that in a minute," Grim says, waving her hand as though that piece of information is insignificant.

I let that go for now because I'm equally confused about the fact that Jeb agreed to Xeno getting me to safety. Why? It makes no sense. The man couldn't give two shits about me. "What do you mean *with Jeb's approval?*"

Grim draws in another nicotine cloud of smoke then blows it

out before answering. "Well, retrospective agreement anyway... We dealt with the threat and informed Jeb after the fact. He's lucky Beast didn't shoot him, too. He didn't because we need Jeb for this plan to work," Grim continues.

"What?" I shake my head, confused. The lingering effects of the drug are still blurring my ability to think straight.

"We found out that Malik had planted one of his men at the club for the sole purpose of stealing you out right from under our fucking nose," Grim continues. "This thief came into *my* club with a new crew. Most likely Malik paid them off to keep quiet that this man wasn't actually one of theirs. Needless to say, those fuckers are going to have a long and torturous weekend ahead of them."

"What happened to the man who—"

"Dead," Xeno says coldly. He flicks his gaze away when I stare at him open-mouthed, that infuriating muscle still ticking in his jaw.

"Yes, Xeno dealt with the little prick then took his place. Jeb didn't really have much choice but to agree that it was the best course of action given he wants to keep me sweet. Besides, he's currently holed up in a suite in my hotel in Mayfair getting the best pussy money can buy."

I laugh at that statement for two reasons. One he fucking hates pussy, and two why would Jeb want to keep anyone sweet besides himself? "Keep *you* sweet?"

"Yes. Jeb wants information that I have, and he knows if he were to double-cross me or disagree with anything I choose to do, then frankly, he'd be dead at worst or without information at best. Of course, Jeb has plans to take over Tales, but he doesn't know *I'm* aware of that. When the time comes, that prick will die too.

Xeno here played the part of the thief to save your arse from a life of sexual servitude."

"You were playing a part?" I parrot back.

"Yes," he replies, watching me closely to see how I react.

Grim shakes her head, scowling at Xeno. "*But* he fucked up."

"Fucked up how?" I ask, looking between them. Xeno's face darkens. Then I remember what Xeno said earlier before Grim and the stranger arrived. "You *danced* with me..." My voice trails off as realisation dawns on me.

"The second Malik saw you together in the cage he knew he'd been found out and attempted to leave. Fortunately for all of us, he didn't get very far," Grim explains.

Xeno grits his jaw. "It was an error in judgement. A mistake I won't make again."

"Dancing with me was an error in judgement, a *mistake*...?" I whisper. My chest heaves as his words strike me again, stabbing my skin just like that motherfucking needle. Before I know what I'm doing, I spin on my feet and walk away.

"Smooth, fucking smooth," I hear Grim say behind me.

"Shut the fuck up!" Xeno retorts. "Pen, wait!"

Tears fill my eyes, and I blink them back as I push open the door to the bedroom. Two steps inside the room, I turn around and try to shut the door, but Xeno forces his way through.

"That's *not* what I meant," he says.

"Get out!" I swipe at my eyes, forcing the familiar feeling of unworthiness away. One minute he's professing his love, the next he's saying that dancing with me was a mistake. I don't know what to believe. My head is fucking spinning and my heart, I'm not sure it even knows how to beat anymore.

Xeno shuts the door behind him, locking it. On the other side,

Grim slams her fist against the wood. "Pen, give us the word, and we'll break this door down."

"Fuck off, Grim!" Xeno shouts over his shoulder. "Just give us some privacy. If we're not back in a couple of minutes, you're welcome to break the fucking door down."

"You scream if you need us, Pen," Grim says, and I can hear her footsteps as she walks away. The fact that she concedes to Xeno's request is telling. What's going on?

Xeno presses his back against the door, leaning his head against the wood as he studies me from beneath hooded eyes, as though looking at me is difficult. I raise my chin, drawing strength from deep inside. If I can go through what I have, then I sure as fuck can look him in the eyes when he breaks my heart again.

"I wasn't lying when I said it was an error in judgement dancing with you last night, because it was. Dancing with you last night *was* a mistake. I shouldn't have done it."

"Well, that makes me feel a whole lot better. Thanks for that..." A huge part of me wants to look away, but even though tears pool in my eyes and I hate the weakness I'm showing him, I don't. For a while we stand in silence, facing off against each other. His gaze feels like a too hot sun on a midsummer's day. It burns my skin as he drinks me in, as he quenches his thirst.

"That doesn't mean that I didn't want to," he says eventually, heaving out a sigh. "In that moment I didn't think past my own needs and desires. I didn't think beyond my need to finally fucking dance with you. Just you and me. Just us. Like I've *always* wanted. For once, I was selfish."

I meet his gaze and see the honesty in them. He means every word he just said, and it stings, because in denying himself he's caused so much unnecessary hurt. "Then why have you always held back? Why keep away all this time? You claim you love me—"

"I don't claim. I *do*. So fucking much—"

"And yet it's as though that love is a curse. I don't understand you, Xeno." The truth is, I'm not sure I ever have. He's always been an enigma, a mystery. There's something fundamentally different about him, something that I've never been able to put my finger on. Only letting me in so far. Keeping me at arm's length. Denying what he wants, what I want, what we *all* wanted and for what?

He barks out a laugh at that. "Try living in my shoes. It ain't easy being *that* man."

"What man?"

"The man who has to make all the hard decisions. I *can't* afford to make a mistake. I can't afford to indulge myself like the others do. They can, and have, made mistakes because there is always someone else who can clean up after them. *Me*." He pushes off the door, unlocking it. "You gave me your truth, Pen, now it's time you finally hear mine, *ours*. Will you hear me out?" Pulling open the door, he waits.

And honestly, what choice do I have?

3

Pen

GRIM AND MR. Suited-and-booted look up as Xeno guides me to a seat at the table. He doesn't try to touch me; he simply pulls out a chair and sits down on my left.

"Beast called. He said it's going to take a few more hours to get shit cleared up at the club," Grim says, eyeing me as she talks.

"I thought you said Malik was being dissolved in acid," I say, shocked at my own ability to talk about such a heinous act without feeling nauseous this time. I feel disconnected from the horror of it. Numb. I'm not sure that's a good thing. In fact, I know it's not. I only have to look at my Breakers to know that.

"Malik wasn't the only one who was put down last night. His bodyguards and the dozen soldiers Malik sent to storm Tales were also taken care of. The fucking pricks thought they'd get past my security, fuck us all up and take you. Stupid. It was a bloody fight. Your Breakers did good dealing with them."

"*Bloody*! Are they in the hospital? Why didn't you—" I can feel my heart thumping in my throat as my words are lost beneath the frantic beat that makes my head spin. "You didn't tell me they were hurt!" I accuse, my teeth clacking as a sudden onset of shivers wrack my body.

"They're okay, Pen," Xeno reassures me. "I spoke to Dax earlier. York has a surface wound on his arm where a stray bullet caught him, but he's good. Nothing that a few stitches won't sort out. He's getting sewn up by Joey as we speak. Zayn and Dax are helping Beast clean up. They'll be on their way here as soon as they can."

"York was hurt because of me..." I mumble, trying to wrap my head around everything.

Opposite, Grim watches me closely. "York was shot because of Malik Brov. This isn't on you, so don't even go the fuck there. You're in shock, Pen. Frankly, I don't blame you. Despite Xeno's fuck-up, you *are* safe, and we will continue to keep you safe."

"I want to believe what you're saying, Grim..." My voice trails off as I try and wrap my head around everything they've told me. Xeno hadn't lied when he said he was trying to protect me, except he put *everyone* in danger by stepping in the ring and dancing with me. I have mixed feelings about that now. That moment of pure joy has been sullied by the fact that his decision could've cost everyone their lives, that he acted on a whim and regrets it. Now I understand what he meant by it being a mistake and I hate that.

"I get your caution, I really do, but I also need you to understand that if I wanted to hurt you I would've let that prick, Jeb, sell you to Malik that first night you danced at Tales. I would've said no when you asked me to protect your sister. I didn't."

"I know, and I appreciate that. It's just I've—"

"You've always had to rely on yourself. You've had to fight your own battles. You've been let down by the people who promised to look out for you before. You don't trust easily," she fills in, glancing at Xeno who stiffens by my side.

"Yes," I whisper.

"Look, Pen, I'm gonna give you a little insight into my past. I'm trusting you with this information. Xeno, too. Maybe then you'll understand where I'm coming from and will trust that I'm on your side. Me and Xeno might have our differences, but we're both on the same page when it comes to the goal we all have."

"Goal you all have?" I ask, frowning. I look between the three of them wondering how the hell this all fits together.

"Yeah. I'm sure you've gathered by now, but there's more to this than meets the eye."

"Grim...?" Mr. Suited-and-booted questions. He's been silent, listening, watching this all unfold.

"It's cool. I trust them both. Actually, I trust Pen. I'm still on the fence about Xeno," she admits, giving him a sweet smile that I would've laughed at if I had the energy to do so. "But *you* trust him—"

"I do," Mr. Suited-and-booted agrees.

"Besides, Xeno knows if he betrays me, *us*, he's dead. I think that's a pretty good incentive not to fuck up. Right?"

"Likewise," Xeno retorts, glaring at Grim.

Mr. Suited-and-booted sighs, but he doesn't prevent Grim from sharing whatever it is that she wishes to say. Her pretty eyes meet mine and I can see her shore up her defences just like I'm prone to doing.

"You're not the only one with shitty fucking parents, Pen. My father turned out to be a first-class bastard." She laughs bitterly, and I hear her pain, recognise it. "For a long time I believed he was a good man. Don't get me wrong, I *knew* he was dangerous. But dangerous was normal for me. I grew up surrounded by dangerous people, in an environment that wasn't fit for a girl who spent most of her time with her head in a book dreaming about ivory towers and knights in shining fucking armour. Despite that, I believed my father loved me." She laughs at that, shaking her head at the child she was. "I realised pretty fucking quick that my father wasn't the man I believed him to be when he attempted to exchange me in lieu of payment of a debt. I was *seventeen*. He was prepared to give me up to live a life as a sex slave to get himself out of a spot of trouble. So let's just say, I'm a little sensitive about the subject." Her voice trails off and for a brief moment I see the sadness and deep pain she holds.

"I'm sorry," I say, meaning it. Understanding her betrayal.

"Don't be. It all worked out in the end because when it came down to it, the person I didn't think had the strength to protect me was the only one who could."

"Beast?"

"No, Pen. *Me*. I realised that the only hero in my story would be me. You and I are alike in that respect. You don't need anyone to save you because you're strong enough to save yourself. I admire that, respect it. You trust your instincts. You fight for the people you love. You don't take any shit. It's hard for you and me to trust because we've both been let down in the worst possible way by our parents, by people we care about. Like I said, Beast and I weren't always this close. He let me down too, and he's been making up for that ever since. So, I get it. I get what you've been through, what you're going through now. You're uncertain. It's understandable." She flicks her gaze to Xeno and when I look at him, I can see a flash of shame pass across his face before he slips his mask back on.

"Why are you telling me this?" I ask.

"A little while ago you asked me what I'd want in return for protecting your sister. I told you that I wouldn't ask anything of you that you wouldn't be willing to give."

"Yes, I remember—" I stiffen, waiting for the blow. Waiting for the price I'm going to have to pay so they continue to keep Lena safe.

"I'm asking you to go against your natural instincts and *trust* me, trust the Breakers not to hurt you anymore, because believe me Pen, if they so much as make another damn tear fall out of your eyes, I will personally castrate them," she says fiercely.

Xeno barks out a laugh. "Fucking try it."

"More importantly," she continues, ignoring Xeno. "I'm asking you to trust my best friend. I'm asking you to listen to him." I watch her stub out her cigarette in an ashtray that's already overflowing.

"Beast?" I frown.

Grim chuckles. "Beast winds me up way too much to be my best friend. No, I'm talking about this man here." Then she looks over at Mr. Suited-and-booted and smiles. It's a warm, genuine smile, and I can't help but wonder how Beast feels about their relationship. I can't imagine he'd be all that happy about it.

"Beast isn't going to like you saying that," he replies as though reading my thoughts.

Grim shrugs. "Beast knows how I feel about you. He deals

with it. Besides, he's my whole fucking universe, and he happens to know that too."

"Yeah, yeah. We all know how much you love that brute."

I look between the two of them. Like, what the actual fuck? These two are best friends? They couldn't be any more different if they tried. Grim is edgy, dangerous. This guy looks like he'd be better off sitting in some office in the city with his crisp suit and fucking handkerchief sticking out of his pocket.

"You must be wondering what the hell is going on. I can see the questions in your gaze. None of this is making a lick of sense, right?" he asks me.

I nod. "Yeah, you could say that I have *a lot* of questions."

"Then between us we'll answer anything you wish to know." He flicks his gaze to Xeno and nods. "Xeno can tell you how we came to meet a year ago, and then together we'll fill you in on everything else."

I look between them all, my throat drying. "Okay."

"But first I think it's only polite that I should introduce myself seeing as neither of these two have the manners to do that. My name isn't *motherfucker*, though on occasion my brothers might tend to agree with that evaluation of me..." His top lip twitches in mirth, but my face remains deadpan.

"I'm guessing it's not Mr. Suited-and-booted either?" I ask, perhaps a little too sarcastically.

His smile grows, those green eyes of his lighting up. "No, Pen," he says, offering his hand for me to shake, I take it and he grins broadly. "My name's Hudson. Hudson Freed. It's a pleasure to meet you."

4

Xeno - A Year Ago

"WHAT ARE WE DOING HERE, DAX?" I ask, scowling at my best friend. My gaze flicks around the dingy pub situated on a backstreet in Hammersmith that's frequented by old geezers who look like they've got one foot in the grave already. None of these arseholes care that they're drinking piss-water so long as they get the kick they need to satisfy their alcoholic selves.

It's the perfect spot for secret meetings. None of the Skins would come here, and Jeb definitely wouldn't, but I'm guessing that's the point. Despite that, I'm on edge, just like I am most days. I can't even remember the last time I ever felt relaxed enough to chill out, to crack a fucking smile even, and this shit they pass off as brandy ain't helping me to feel any better.

"I told you, we're meeting someone important," Dax replies flippantly, like we're not here doing something we shouldn't, given

Jeb knows fuck all about this meet up. Really, I don't give a shit about Jeb or what he would think, but I am pissed that Dax is keeping things from *me*.

"Meeting with *who*, Dax?" I give him a look that tells him I'm about two seconds away from walking out and spending the night with some random woman to ease the constant pain in my chest. The pain we all carry, because of *her*. I need this bullshit, today of all days, like a fucking hole in the head. "Dax, I ain't fucking around."

"Eastern called me," he replies, picking up his pint of beer and necking it back in one go, like it doesn't taste like shit, making my eyes bug out of my head.

"Eastern's coming to London? Has he got a fucking death wish? Jeb might've stepped in and taken over the Hackney's Hackers crew after the King died, but you know as well as I that those cunts are still after his head," I hiss.

"No, he ain't stupid. Eastern, Asia and the rest of them ain't coming back to London anytime soon. Besides, I never said we were meeting him. I said he *called* me."

"If we're not meeting Eastern, then who the fuck are we actually here for then?"

Dax's eyes flick from my face to someone entering the pub. He jerks his chin and I follow his gaze which lands on a man who—despite wearing a pair of scuffed trainers, jeans and hoodie—has all the hallmarks of someone with a lot of money. He might be dressed down to blend in, but even from over here I can see the expensive haircut, the bright white teeth and clean-shaven face that tells me he's more than just some punk off the street. In fact, I know he is because I recognise this man.

"You've got to be fucking kidding me," I mutter. "That's Hudson Freed."

"Yep. Got it in one, mate."

I watch as Hudson, businessman and co-owner of Freed Corporation—alongside his brothers Max and Bryce—catches my gaze and walks towards us. Their story is the stuff fairy tales are made of. Anyone who's grown up on the streets of London has heard about them. They're legendary. Street kids turned multi-millionaires who've got that way cleanly, buying and selling property. Now they own holiday resorts all over the world. There are no shady deals with dodgy crews for the Freed brothers.

Until now, it would seem.

"Fuck sake, Dax. What the fuck could he possibly want with us? More to the point, what the fuck are *you* getting us into?" I grind out under my breath. Jeb would have no qualms with loading a bullet into our brains for meeting like this without his knowledge or fucking approval. Again, I don't give a shit Dax is keeping this meet on the down low, I just need to know what it's about so that I can do some damage control if it all goes to shit. That's what I do, I protect my best friends, even from themselves.

"Behave, Xeno," Dax warns me like I'm some fucking delinquent child.

"Behave?" I scoff, ready to throw a punch at his meaty head, the dick. "Being a good boy hasn't been part of my repertoire for a long, long time. You'd do well to remember that."

Dax rolls his eyes at my threat. Fucker. He's lucky he's my best mate and a punch is all I'm threatening.

"You must be Xeno," Hudson says, holding his hand out to me the moment he reaches the table. I look from his hand to his face and back again.

"That's right," I respond, not bothering to ask how he knows who I am or shake his hand that appears as smooth as his words. I'm pretty sure he's had a fucking manicure given there's not a scrap of dirt under his nails. Still, I can tell by the way he holds himself that he's no stranger to slumming it. He doesn't flinch at the revolting state of this pub or the fact that the carpet stuck to the bottom of his trainers with every step towards us. He simply pulls out a chair and takes a seat. "What do you want?"

"Thank you for agreeing to see me," he responds, avoiding my question and sizing us up instead.

"I didn't agree to shit. You'll need to thank Dax for this meet." Whatever he wants from us, I'm pretty sure it's gonna cost him. Either in blood or cash. I ain't decided which way this is gonna go just yet.

"Well, then, thank you, Dax. It's a pleasure to meet you both..." Hudson holds his hand out to Dax who takes it and gives him what I know will be a bone-crushing handshake. The motherfucker doesn't even flinch. Interesting.

"So, what the fuck is this all about?" I ask, picking up my shot of brandy and knocking it back all the while keeping my eyes fixed on Hudson.

"I'm Hud—"

"I *know* who you are," I interrupt, leaning forward in my seat. "But do you know who *we* are?"

"I do, yes. You're one half of the Breakers," he starts, resting his unflinching gaze on me. "You once danced together, though these days rather than battling opposing dance crews you're more likely breaking bones—amongst other violent acts—in the name of the Skins."

Dax glances over at me and I have another urge to punch him

in the face for bringing me here today. I'm in a bad fucking mood as it is, which has now been made worse by this arsehole. So what if he's aware of the violence we dish out. I'm guessing whatever the fuck this is about is more to do with the Breakers' specialist skills than his need to point out the fact that we're violent bastards past saving.

"Well done, you did your homework," I say, slow clapping him. "Want a gold star or can we get to the fucking point already?"

"I've not finished—"

"So hurry the fuck up," I snap, already disliking the arrogant bastard. The fucker should watch his step, I'm still buzzing from last night's kill. Lingering violence ripples beneath my skin and the edgy feeling after a kill remains. Normally I'd fuck a woman to rid myself of the restless energy, but I'm up for feeding the violence if that's the way this is gonna go down.

"Your crew," he continues, not in the least bit concerned, "Is headed up by Jeb Bernard. Who, a few months ago, took over what was left of the Hackney's Hackers crew, otherwise known as the HH crew. A crew made up mostly of *kids*. I think their youngest member is sixteen. Wait, *your* youngest member is sixteen given they're Skins now too."

The accusation and judgement in his eyes pisses me the fuck off. I'm well aware that the youngest kid in the Skins is sixteen, I don't need him to remind me of that fact. "And your point is?"

But the smug bastard ignores my question and looks at Dax instead. "And you're Dax, an old friend of Eastern's. You know Asia too, and a couple years back you asked her to draw some graffiti art for a girl you once hung out with. Penelope Scott, I believe that's her name? She must've been very special to you?"

At the mention of her name I lose the last shred of patience I was holding onto. "What the fuck is this exactly?" I snarl, slamming my clenched fist on the table. My reaction is loud enough to warrant looks from several of the drunk patrons who, wisely, look away when I tell them to fuck off.

"I'll get to the point shortly." He smirks and I snap, launching myself across the table at him. Lucky for the prick, Dax gets to me before I can knock that smirk off his face.

"Sit the fuck down," Dax orders, getting in my face.

"Are you telling *me* what to do?" I snarl, my nose pressed against his. Me and Dax have fought before over the years, but never over something like this. I don't like his fucking attitude. Then again, of all the Breakers, Dax has always challenged my decisions. It's why, despite it all, I respect and love the fucker. He reminds me that I'm not impenetrable, and he reels me in when it's warranted.

"Come on, man. Sit down and hear him out," Dax says once he realises I'm not gonna take this any further.

Straightening up my jacket, I take a seat. "Go on," I say calmly, as though this meeting wasn't about to go to shit. What can I say, I'm fucking unpredictable like that?

"Zayn is the nephew of Jeb Bernard and York is quite the fighter in the ring. Like Dax, he's never lost a fight—"

"All of this is common knowledge on the street. So if you think I'm impressed you're sadly mistaken."

"But that's not the best part. I also happen to know that the four of you have been putting money away for years now, and you've built up quite a small fortune. All of it blood money, of course, but a tidy sum, nonetheless. Lately you've been looking at properties overseas, far, far away from London and, more importantly, out of reach of the Skins."

"How the—" I start, only for the fucker to interrupt me again.

"I also know you've heard of Camden, Sonny and Ford given Eastern's their best friend. As you know Camden was once the leader of the HH crew until he decided to change his life for the better and get the fuck out for good. Alongside my brothers and some other friends, I helped him do that. We helped the five of them get the fuck out and start fresh somewhere new."

"Ohhhh, so this is some kind of intervention?" I laugh, rolling my eyes. "You found out we put away money and want a fucking *holiday home* and decide we want out? Are you a closet missionary or something? Did you find Jesus in your climb up the rich ladder and now want to absolve your past sins by helping the *sinful?*" I laugh, shaking my head at the absurdity of it, not to mention the fucking audacity. How the fuck he found out about our money or our plans is beyond me. It's also a big fucking worry because the dickhead is right, we do want out. But I thought we'd been careful.

Dax snorts at my snide remark to cover his own shock, but if he thinks he's getting in my good graces just because he hasn't told me to shut the fuck up again, he's got another thing coming. Ignoring him, I pull out my gun—which until now has been tucked discreetly into the back of my jeans—place it on the table and rest my finger against the trigger. "Lucky for you today I'm feeling generous, so I'll give you a piece of advice, unless you want to do business with the *Skins*, I suggest you take your manicured hands and couple hundred-pound hairdo and get the fuck out of my face before I splatter yours against the wall for digging into our personal shit."

"Woah," Dax exclaims, the smile falling from his face as he places his hand on my arm. He's worried. He fucking should be. I could kill this motherfucker without so much as flinching.

"Xeno, don't start something here... This is on me. I agreed to meet Hudson."

"You know as well as I do that I don't start shit, I just *end* it."

"Just hear him out. That's all I'm asking," Dax says, eying the gun and, more specifically, my finger on the trigger.

I smile slowly. "Fine. I don't much feel like putting a bullet in all these drunk motherfuckers heads anyway. Which is what I'd have to do if I put a bullet in your brain," I casually remark, releasing my finger from the trigger and clicking on the safety before tucking the gun away.

Hudson watches me with a confidence that pisses me off. He's got balls of steel, I'll give him that. I lean back in my chair, keeping eye contact with him. "You're quite an interesting man, *Hud*."

"Hudson," he corrects me, folding his arms across his chest and holding my gaze like a true fucking pro. If he wasn't such an arrogant cunt, I could like him. "Tell me what you think you know." And even though I've just pulled a gun on him, there's a calmness that settles across his features that I begrudgingly respect. Anyone else would've shit themselves at the sight of a gun. He didn't even flinch.

"I know you're some hotshot millionaire. I know you once lived in a care home with your business partners because your parents were all worthless pieces of shit. I know you now live in some fuck-off, great big house in the suburbs just outside of London with your two point four kids, and your *brothers*. Oh, and the most exciting part is that you and your brothers *all* fuck the same woman—"

Hudson slams his palm against the table, his calm facade slipping at the mention of his family. The look he's giving me now tells me that, despite appearances, Hudson ain't so different from the rest of us. You can take the kid out of the street but you sure as fuck can't take the street out of the kid. We're loyal to a fault and disrespecting people we care about is a cardinal sin. Looks like I just found his Achilles heel. I file that away should I ever need it.

"Do not speak of my wife or my kids. Do not fucking mention them again—" Hudson says darkly, his lip curling up over his teeth as a little of the smooth calm he came in with disappears and is replaced with someone I think I could admire. You don't get to be where he is without having balls of fucking steel, street smarts and intelligence to match. He's what we could've been if we hadn't joined the fucking Skins, and that pisses me the fuck off.

"Fair enough," I shrug, enjoying the fact I've made a dent in his cool exterior. I can tell he's pissed off at himself for reacting. He recovers quickly though. "So can we stop with the bullshit now and get to the fucking point. I got shit to do, and a woman to fuck."

Hudson shakes off his anger enough to nod tightly. "This is really very simple. I need your help."

"Help?" I would laugh if he wasn't deadly serious.

Dax glances at me. "With what exactly?"

"Someone wronged me a long time ago. Hurt someone I cared about—"

"Ah, so you want *us* to put a hit on this person, is that it?" I grin, how the mighty fall. Perhaps there's more to this arsehole than meets the eye. Let's face it, we've all got a dark stain on our souls. Some are just better at hiding it. This fucker wants to knock someone off without staining his own hands with blood. Figures.

Hudson shakes his head. "No. I want revenge. I want his businesses dissolved. I want his fucking life destroyed and then when he's lost everything, I want him to rot in jail."

"And why the fuck would we help you to do that?" I ask.

Hudson stares at me, his finger tapping against the tabletop. "Because you and I have the same goal."

"Is that so? What goal is that?"

"To be free from what haunts us," Hudson replies, deadly fucking serious as he looks between me and Dax. It makes me wonder what the fuck else he knows. Is he aware of the significance of today? It's two years to the day when Pen walked away from us and it still hurts like a bitch. I shake my head. There's no way. No one but us Breakers know what eats away at us every second of every fucking day since she left.

"Get the fuck out of here." I tip my head back and laugh. A deep belly laugh that normally proceeds me losing my shit. I'm feeling particularly unhinged today. "Are you fucking hearing this shit, Dax?"

"Listen, Hudson. You're talking in riddles. We ain't got time for no bullshit," Dax says hurriedly, intervening before my trigger finger gets happy. "I'm here because Eastern is an old friend. Xeno's here because he's my brother, but we ain't no fools and we ain't got time to dance around the truth. Tell us what you want, or we're gone."

"I want you to help me take down Santiago Garcia," Hudson says, calm as a fucking cucumber.

"You fucking *what*?" I hiss. *Fuck me.* This is not what I expected. Not the fuck at all. The colour drains from Dax's skin whilst red hot anger bleeds into mine.

"I said, I want you to help me take down Santiago Garcia."

"Why the *fuck* would we do that? He's our boss's, boss. The main man. You know that, right...?" I hiss, reaching for my gun. My fingers press against the cool metal. Looks like I'm gonna be putting a bullet in this fucker's brain after all.

"I know that," Hudson responds tightly.

"Yeah, of course you fucking do. Then you'll also know you ain't got a hope in hell in taking that man down." I drag my gaze away from Hudson and glare at Dax. Over the years Dax and I have fought, but I swear to fuck I've never wanted to beat him unconscious until now. We are not getting mixed up in this. "What the fuck, Dax?"

Dax holds his hands up. "I swear, this wasn't what I was expecting either."

I take a deep breath, then lean forward, my forearms resting on the table as I concentrate on the clueless motherfucker in front of me once more. He might be some hotshot businessman, but he doesn't know shit about the circles we walk in or how fucking dangerous that man is. If Jeb is a shark in the food chain, that motherfucker Santiago is a killer fucking whale and you do not take a punt at the biggest predator in the sea if you want to stay alive.

"Let me get this straight. You want us to help you take out Santiago Garcia? The same Santiago Garcia who supplies London, the whole fucking UK, with cocaine and heroin. The Cuban crime lord of the fucking century and the Skins' *real* fucking boss?"

"Precisely."

"You're fucking insane." Internally, I'm cursing Eastern. The little prick. What the fuck was *he* thinking dragging us into this? "There's no way you'll be able to pull this off."

"I can with your help," he insists, leaning forward on his elbows.

"No. It's a suicide mission. Why the fuck would we sign our

own death certificates for you? Because that's what we'd be doing." I point out.

"Because we wouldn't just be taking out Santiago, we'd be taking out Jeb too. I have the money to fund whatever you need to get this done. I have the contacts. I know people who can help. We can do this."

"No." I shake my head, and move to stand, but Dax rests his hand on my arm. I recognise that look in his eyes and I don't fucking like it one little bit.

"What's in it for us?" Dax asks after a beat, and I swear I almost swallow my fucking tongue. He can't seriously be considering this. No one fucks with Santiago Garcia. No. Fucking. One.

"You help me take him down and I can promise that you get immunity from the law. You get enough money to do whatever the hell you want, but more than that you get what you desire the most."

"And what the fuck is that?" I snap.

"To be out from underneath Jeb, to be *free* of the Skins. You get the life you should've had. All four of you," Hudson says vehemently.

"That's a bit fucking presumptuous, don't you think? You're assuming we want out of the Skins. Tell me Hudson, what makes you think we're not gonna just take *you* out now? Who the fuck do you think you are coming in here like some fictional fucking superhero? The world doesn't work like that."

"Believe me when I tell you that I have enough money and enough contacts in the right places to ensure that it does."

"Why us?" Dax asks.

"Because you're already on the inside. Because Eastern tells me that, despite your namesake, you're good people."

"This is bullshit. You don't know the first thing about us or the kind of men we are."

Dax rests his hand on my arm. "This might be our only fucking chance, Xeno."

I see the look in his eyes, and I swallow hard. Dax never wanted to be a part of the Skins. Both he and York only joined because of their loyalty to the Breakers. Zayn had no fucking choice, and I joined because who the fuck else would look out for them, if not me? Maybe I've settled into my role all too easily, but every decision I make is for my brothers. Every last one. They fucking deserve a chance to live a normal life.

Turning my attention back to Hudson, I nod once. "What do you need us to do?"

5

Pen - Present Day

I TAKE the proffered drink from Grim and swallow back the contents in one go. It's whisky, and the fiery liquid burns the whole way down my throat. "Another," I state, pushing the glass back across the table.

"You need to slow down. You still have anaesthesia in your bloodstream," Xeno warns.

"I said, give me another." My fingers clasp firmly around the glass as I glare at Xeno. Grim nods, pouring me a second generous shot. This time I sip it slowly, relishing the burn. Loving the way my legs feel heavy and everything Xeno's just told me is a little less difficult to absorb.

"It's a lot to take in," Hudson says.

"A lot to take in? That's the understatement of the century." I shake my head, trying to make sense of everything. Right now, I just feel numb. This is all so much bigger than I had ever anticipated. I knew they were keeping secrets, but this? I had no fucking idea. "So you were hired to take down this Santiago Garcia guy in return for riches and freedom from the Skins, is that right?" I ask Xeno, but it's Hudson who answers.

"Yes," he confirms. "For the past year the Breakers have been working undercover, gathering information and feeding it back to me. In turn, myself and my brothers have been passing that information on to Interpol who are gathering a case together."

"So you can get your revenge?" I spit, narrowing my eyes at Hudson, and I can feel it, that anger boiling inside of me. How dare he use my Breakers like this? How dare he put them in *danger* like this. I'm not stupid, I know how this shit works. Fuck, Jeb put a bullet in his security guard's brain right in front of me without a second thought because he failed to do his job and keep his secret from being found out. I'll never forget walking in on Jeb getting his dick sucked by a man, but this is nothing compared to that. I can't bear to think what could happen to them if Jeb, if Santiago, finds out what they're doing. I'm betting whatever they'd do, a bullet to the brain would be the better option.

"Pen, it's not as simple as that," Grim says, noticing my sudden change in mood. I've gone from shocked to pissed off in under a second.

"No? It seems pretty fucking simple to me. Your best friend here, the man you're asking me to trust, is using my Breakers, then men *I* love to mete out his revenge. He's put them in danger, Grim, and you're asking me to listen to what he says? I can't fucking believe it."

"Do you think we can't handle ourselves? Is that it, Pen?" Xeno asks me in a tone of voice that pisses me the fuck off.

"That's not what I said—"

"Do you think we're weak fools who follow Hudson's lead because we can't think for ourselves? Stop looking at us like we're those boys you knew and start seeing us for what we *really* are. Maybe then you wouldn't be so blinded by your love," Xeno snaps.

I scowl, every word coming out through gritted teeth. "I'm *not* blinded by my love, Xeno. Don't throw that back in my face as though you're somehow allergic to it. I might not know what you've been doing these past three years exactly, but I can fucking guess. But right now, all I see is someone with a different kind of power using you to get what he wants," I say, narrowing my eyes at Hudson. "If you're offended by what I've just said, that's because I want you to be."

Hudson nods, but he doesn't try to deny it. "Understood."

Xeno shakes his head in frustration. "Maybe that was true when we were kids. Maybe we were led by the nose by Jeb. Not anymore. Hudson doesn't own the Breakers, and he sure as fuck isn't the boss of me, though at times he fucking acts like it," Xeno states, casting a scathing look at Hudson and daring him to object. "We're doing this for *us*. We're doing this because we fucking *can*. Jeb's a piece of shit. Santiago is a dangerous man, granted, but a piece of shit nonetheless. We help Hudson, he helps us. It's a win-win. A partnership," he points out.

"Not to mention your Breakers have already done pretty well out of this deal, and will continue to do so," Grim interjects, then cants her head at me. "I understand you've already had an evening at Jewels Nightclub…"

I snap my head around to look at Xeno. "*You* own Jewels Nightclub? Rag 'n' Bone man played there. How did you manage—"

Xeno shrugs, like it's no big deal. "It's a cool club, singers want to perform there. We own Chastity Nightclub too."

"The *sex club*?" I choke out.

"Why do you think I was so angry you were there? I know exactly what goes on in that club because I fucking own it."

"Jesus Christ. Are there any other clubs you own that I should know about?" I ask, my head spinning.

"No. Just those two."

"And what does Jeb think about your little side venture? Is he skimming the profit from your clubs just like he does with The Pink Albatross? When I ran into Jeb there, he basically said he owned the place even though D-Neath's name is on the deeds."

"Jeb doesn't know shit about our clubs and that's the way it's gonna stay," Xeno says, his words brooking no arguments.

"So you're telling me that Jeb doesn't have a clue that you're double-crossing him? That you're owners of not one but two exclusive clubs in his city and he doesn't know about it," I ask, doubtful.

"As far as he's concerned, we're his most trustworthy soldiers and that's the way it's going to stay until the time comes to pull the fucking rug out from under him. We own those clubs, but if anyone were to go digging, they'd see Grim's name on the deeds."

"So *that's* where you come in," I say, barking out a laugh, even more pissed off than before.

"You're set to gain an awful lot if this goes tits up, right? Fuck, you really are smart." It's not a compliment and she knows it.

Grim flinches, but she doesn't rise to the bait. "Whether you choose to believe it or not, I'm not helping Hud and your boys just on the off chance they fail, Pen. Though I completely understand why you would assume that. You're right, I *am* smart, smart enough to keep those who've shown me loyalty and friendship close. Unlike some of the criminals I mix with, I happen to have a conscience, a moral fucking compass. Last year I helped Hudson get Asia, Eastern, Ford—my half-brother, by the way—Camden and Sonny out of a tricky situation with the King because it was the *right* thing to do.

"That guy who picked up the phone when you called Asia was your brother?"

"Half, and yes."

"Wow."

"Anyway, Hud filled me in on his history with Santiago and told me about that sick bastard's new business venture. Given my past experience and what could've happened to me, I wanted to help."

"What new venture?" I ask.

"Sex trafficking, Pen. Women, girls mainly. Santiago sells them into the sex trade. Most of the girls are under the age of eighteen. A high proportion under the age of fifteen. His operation was stopped in its tracks when the King was killed but now he's taking up business again," Grim explains.

"Jesus fucking Christ!" I exclaim. "And Jeb's involved in that? The sick fuck!"

"Actually, no. Jeb deals purely with the drug side of the business here in the UK. Though I don't think it'd take much to push him in that direction," Xeno clarifies. "We do have reason to believe that David, however, is more than happy to step up."

"David?" I retort sharply. "What are you saying?"

"We found out very recently that your brother is heavily involved in the sex trade. He is the go-to man in Mexico," Hudson informs me, a dark look flitting across his face. "Santiago is already doing business with him. As far as we can tell, Jeb isn't involved, and if he's aware of their relationship, he doesn't give two fucks."

"I feel sick." Nausea rises up my throat, but I swallow it down. "Why is David so evil? Sex trafficking... Fuck!"

"I know this is a lot to deal with. Take a deep breath, okay?" Grim says gently, reaching for my free hand that's curled up into a fist on the table. They give me a moment to absorb all the information, and it's the first time all evening that I wished I was still out cold.

"I still don't understand why you're at Stardom Academy. What has being there got to do with anything?" I ask.

Xeno sighs. "Jeb sent us to Stardom Academy to work with D-Neath."

"D-Neath?" My mouth drops open. I don't know why I'm so shocked given his history, but I am.

"Yes. Santiago has developed a very dangerous drug that he wants to bring to the UK club scene. He needed an opportunity to test it out. Duncan was the perfect person for Jeb to choose to help make that happen because of his past experience, his club, and his access to a readily available market. You've heard of Molly, right?" Hudson asks.

"Yes," I nod, glancing at Xeno.

"Molly is essentially the powder form of ecstasy," Xeno continues, "A drug that was at its height in the late eighties and early nineties in the rave scene. Add in speed, a dash of cocaine— and a secret ingredient that even we don't know about, to the mix—and you have a very powerful narcotic."

"And potentially, a very deadly one," Grim adds.

"So, D-Neath hasn't turned over a new leaf then? He's at the

Academy to supply the dancers and distribute through The Pink Albatross, is that what you're saying?"

"Precisely," Hudson agrees.

"But he's Madame Tuillard's boyfriend and she has a zero drugs policy at the Academy..." I say, in disbelief. "*Wait*. Please don't tell me she's in on this too?" Then I remember the conversation I'd overheard that day Sebastian sent me to her office, and I share it with them. "A couple of weeks ago I overheard D-Neath assuring Madame Tuillard that he had a solid plan. She was pissed off, she said that she hadn't built the Academy for some arsehole she didn't know to destroy it. She'd said she didn't need the police on her doorstep either. Fuck, this is what she meant!"

Grim's head snaps around as she pins her gaze on Hudson. "Do you think she's losing her nerve?"

"Wait, what?" I exclaim, looking between them both. I feel like the stupidest person in the room. Nothing's making sense. "I don't understand."

"Tuillard's aware of what's going on, to a certain extent at least. D-Neath isn't working for Jeb. He's working with *us*. He's an informant, just like we are. Jeb and D-Neath go way back," Xeno explains. "When D-Neath was released from prison, Jeb contacted him, bringing him into the crew, having no idea about the deal he secured a few months before with Interpol to lessen his sentence."

My mouth drops open as I try to process everything. "And you trust him? This is insane." I rub my fingers against my forehead, trying to subdue a headache I can feel coming on.

"In answer to your first question, I trust him now. I didn't at first, but he's proved himself loyal, and in answer to your earlier question, Jeb began to get suspicious of D-Neath," Xeno explains. "He started to think that D-Neath had gone rogue and was trying to cut a better deal with Santiago. That's why Jeb sent us in. He wanted to make sure D-Neath wasn't fucking him over. Little does he know *we're* the ones who are doing that. We've managed to convince Jeb that D-Neath is still trustworthy when really none of us are. At least not to him."

"Fucking hell. I literally can't wrap my head around any of this."

"Jeb's instincts were on point," Xeno explains tiredly. Exhaustion pulls at his features as he swipes at his face. "We believe your brother's suspicions were roused because we were back in your orbit. He knows we're still part of the Skins so he knew we wouldn't be at the Academy to pursue a career in dance. What better way for him to find out why we're at the Academy than use you."

I look at Xeno for a long time until both Grim and Hudson become just blurred images in my peripheral vision. "Now I understand what you meant by returning to reclaim what's yours. At one point I'd convinced myself that was me. It wasn't though, was it? You came back to take down Jeb and Santiago in exchange for riches, for your freedom. This was never, *ever* about me... The fact I'm at the Academy is purely coincidental."

"Tiny—" he begins, the shadows in his eyes growing darker.

"I'm such an *idiot*," I mutter, taking another sip of the whisky and closing my eyes against the heat of everyone's stare. It hurts to know Xeno wasn't lying when he said that they hadn't returned to the Academy for me. It hurts so much more than I ever thought it could.

"No! *Fuck that*. You're not an idiot. You're everything. You're everything to us!" Xeno exclaims, drawing a surprised look from

Grim at his sudden passionate outburst, but I can't look at him right now. I just can't.

"You've known all along..." I say, focusing my attention on Grim as I push away from the table and stand. I walk over to the other side of the room needing to put some space between us. "You've known about the Breakers and what they were doing at the Academy."

"I didn't know who you were to the Breakers until that night Jeb brought you to my club. I'd believed you were just his side-piece for the night. I judged you based on that prick. It was wrong and I'm sorry for it. Then you danced and I knew you were something special. I saw how the Breakers reacted to you and it didn't take a genius to work out that you meant something to them too. Dax's reaction to Malik touching you and Zayn's need to protect you from him were pretty fucking big clues. Why do you think Beast didn't shoot Dax? It wasn't because he was feeling generous, it was because we're working together."

"Why didn't you say anything?" I ask.

Grim sighs. "It wasn't my place to interfere, Pen. Your relationship is your own. Don't get me wrong, I would've stepped in eventually if they didn't fucking pull their heads out of their arses. Not because I think they deserve you— because the jury is still out on that— but because you deserve to be treated better. As it turns out, they got there in the end." She smiles knowingly, then nudges Hudson. "Come on, let's go. I have a club to clean up and the leader of the Skins to entertain."

"What about The Masks?" Xeno asks.

"We'll cross that bridge when we come to it. Besides, that really isn't on you guys. Beast shot him in *my* club, after all. They won't act right away. Taking out their father is a blow, and it will take them time to recover and get a plan in place before they make their move," Grim says. "And by that time, I'll be ready."

"Shit, Lena!" I blurt out, panic suddenly returning. I've been so consumed by everything that's happened tonight and all that they've told me that I haven't stopped to consider how Lena is. I've been a shit fucking sister. "This will just make her even more of a target, surely?"

"She's safe. Beast called me just before I got here. He knew you'd worry. She's staying at her friend's house this weekend by the looks of it. My men are watching her twenty-four seven," Grim reminds me, immediately putting my mind at ease. "No one will get near her. I promise."

"Thank you, Grim, for keeping her safe," I say, a lump forming in my throat. Despite some of the revelations tonight, I do believe she's a good person underneath it all.

She frowns, then moves around the table and across the room. In a couple of strides has her arms around me. "You listen to me, Pen," she says, whispering in my ear. "You've got a friend in me. I like you, so I'm going to give you a piece of unsolicited advice despite Xeno's warning. Don't forgive him easily. Fuck him, sure, but make Xeno work for your heart. If he loves you like he says he does, he'll win you over." Then she steps back and winks at me before giving Xeno the once-over. If I wasn't so shattered, I'd laugh at the scathing look she just gave him. It must've been a monumental task for Beast to win *her* over.

"I'll call you in a few days. We'll meet soon. Catch up and discuss next steps," Xeno says to them both. "I'll also fill D-Neath in on what's gone down."

"Good. Keep me apprised with anything else that comes up," Hudson replies.

Xeno nods, pushing up from the table. "Of course."

"Come on, these two need to sort some shit out, and you need to go home to your family," Grim says, winding her arm through Hudson's.

"This isn't your house?" I blurt out.

"It's one of them. My brothers and I take turns to stay here when we're working at the office in the city. Max and Bryce are at our family home with Louisa and the kids. I'm heading back there now. Max will return here Monday. You're welcome to stay until then. There's food in the fridge, so help yourself to whatever you need. Our housekeeper has cleaned the house and changed the sheets too, just avoid the largest bedroom upstairs. Otherwise, make yourself at home."

"I appreciate it," Xeno says.

"Goodnight, Pen. It was good to meet you, though I do apologise for the circumstances."

I smile tightly, still pissed at the man. "Goodnight."

Xeno follows them both out. By the time he returns I'm standing at the fireplace looking at a photograph of a beautiful woman with long blonde hair and a pretty smile. "They look so happy," I say softly, my fingers running over the photograph. The woman—who is surrounded by three men, one of which is Hudson—is holding a newborn baby in her arms. Clutching hold of her leg is a toddler whose face is covered in ice-cream. All of them are smiling. They're happy.

"That's Hudson's wife, his brothers and their two kids."

"His brothers?"

"Yeah. By choice, not by blood. They grew up in a care home together. Hudson took Max and Bryce under his wing. Looked out for them... Or so the story goes. They built their business from the ground up. I'm surprised you've never heard of Freed Corporation."

"She's with all three of them." I say, focusing on the part of their story that most intrigues me. I don't really care that the Freed's are hotshot businessmen, what I care about is this family they've created. A family I've always wanted.

"Yes. She is. Her name's Louisa. Hudson's very protective of her."

"They make it work."

"It looks that way," Xeno says roughly.

Placing the photo I'm holding back on the mantle I pick up another one where Louisa's kissing Hudson passionately as a guy with a beard looks on adoringly. "They don't care what anyone thinks, Xeno. All I see here is love. So much love..." My voice trails off as I try to wrap my head around what I'm feeling. There's this pang of longing deep inside my chest. I want what they have so much. Placing the photo back on the mantle, I turn around to face him.

Xeno sighs heavily, his eyes tracing over every inch of my skin like flames licking up a pyre. The heat makes me breathless. "Love is dangerous."

"You truly believe that?"

"I do. It's a weakness other people will exploit. Love can be used against you. You know that better than anyone."

"Yet you love me. So where does that leave us?"

"In a very dangerous position." Xeno rocks on his feet, his fingers flexing and curling into his palm. He swallows hard and I watch his Adam's apple bob up and down as he battles with himself.

"What is it? Aren't we past all the secrets and lies, Xeno?" I ask. He remains stubbornly quiet watching me with his assessing gaze for far longer than is comfortable. I wish I could get inside his head. Understand him better.

"Loving you makes us vulnerable. It makes you a target... Jeb was suspicious enough that he tested us. When we were kids, he knew that you were the one thing we cared about more than the Skins. You were a threat. You were the reason we held back—"

"Until I walked away."

"It was a trigger, I can't deny that, but being in the Skins was always an inevitability. Zayn had to join the crew, and we wouldn't let him do that on his own. Like I said, you *weren't* to blame. It was just a hell of a lot easier to do that."

"Must be nice..." I say, feeling jealous of the loyalty and the brotherhood they share. At least they had each other.

"Nice?"

"Yes, to have that kind of bond. You would do anything for each other, even join a crew you hated."

"Tiny..." The sound of my nickname on his tongue feels bittersweet. Every time he refers to me that way, my heart squeezes. If only that was enough. "We let you down."

"I missed you all so much." I meet his gaze with a sad smile. "I never once stopped thinking about you, worrying for you, *loving* you." I heave out a sigh, but my lungs just refill with all the past mistakes we made, clogging them up with regret that starves me of oxygen. My head begins to spin, and I'm not sure whether it's the lingering effects of the anesthesia and alcohol or the emotional drain of this evening's events, but either way I suddenly feel exhausted. Xeno takes a step towards me but stills when he sees the look on my face. "When you returned, do you know what hurt the most, Xeno? More than your rejection, your harsh words and your hate?"

He shakes his head and keeps his gaze fixed on me. I see him drag in a breath and straighten his spine as though expecting to be felled by my last and final truth. "Tell me," he demands, stoic.

"It was the family you'd created with each other, *without* me. That hurt more than anything, because whilst I was mourning your loss— dying a little inside every day, living with a woman who despised me, struggling to survive in the absence of affection — you were living a life *together*. You were brothers. Inseparable. We'll never get those years back. The only person I had was Lena. Thank God for her." My eyes fill with tears, and this time when they spill over, I don't try to stop them. I let them trickle down my face, needing the release. Needing to let this final shard of pain out. "So, yes, I agree, Xeno. Love is dangerous, but the alternative, to live without love, to feel the cold absence of it... *That*, that is so much worse. I know because I've lived it."

He gives me a pained look, and for a moment I think he's going to stride over and fold me in his arms. I want him to do that more than anything. Instead, he turns his back to me, presses his palms against the table and drops his head. "You should rest. I'll wake you up as soon as the boys arrive."

His dismissal doesn't surprise me, I expected it. He's still holding back. It's that restraint that will ruin us in the end, that will keep us from having what Hudson clearly has with his family.

As I head back to the room I woke up in a few hours ago, I can't help but wonder if we'll ever be able to get over the mistakes of our past or if this brief reconnection is just an interlude for more agony yet to come.

6

Xeno

STANDING before the wall of mirrors in the Freed's home gym, I look at the man I've become. I see someone who's dangerous, violent, cruel. I see someone who has taken life and barely flinched. I'm *that* person.

I do what others find intolerable.

Last night we came close to losing Pen forever.

If he'd gotten away with it, Malik Brov would've had her locked up in his fucking castle dancing for him like a goddamn puppet on a string. Once inside, there's no getting out again. She would've been lost to us. They would've *broken* her.

Pen is strong. There's no fucking doubt about that, but to survive that place…? I've heard the rumours about the Brov family, and if they're true then they really are twisted fucks. Cruelty, violence, torture, degradation, sexual exploitation, sadism, it all happens behind the walls of that remote castle.

According to Grim, only one of The Masks is Brov's natural son, the other two were stolen. Malik Brov— a real life fucking Rumpelstiltskin—took those families firstborn sons in payment of a long-held debt. Rumour has it he brainwashed those boys, including his own son, using torture to bring them to heel. He twisted them up good and proper. Put it this way, the whole family is a Brothers Grimm fairytale come true. There's no *happy ever after* shit up at that castle. It's the real fucking deal.

Knowing all of that, knowing how close we were to losing Pen, hits me like a bad high. My knees give way, and I have to press my clenched fists against the mirror to keep myself upright. My head drops between my shoulders and I force myself to breathe. To inhale precious oxygen before I drown in my own guilt.

I fucked up dancing with her. I fucked up so bad.

Of all the stupid, selfish things I've done, stepping into the cage and dancing with Pen tops them all. There are no excuses. None. I don't deserve her love.

I let my emotions take over, and it could've cost her life.

Thank fuck for Grim, for Beast. Thank fuck for my brothers because the truth is, she's safe because of *them*. Not me. Upstairs she's sleeping off her ordeal and all I want to do is go into her room, lay down beside her and fold her into my arms. I want to comfort her. I want to fucking protect her. *Love* her. Fuck her. I want to fuck her.

Jesus. My need to bury myself inside of her is torturous. It's taking every last drop of self-restraint to hold back because touching her is dangerous.

Truth be known, dancing with Pen has unleashed the savage within. There's this dark energy right in the pit of my stomach that feels like a goddamn cyclone.

I can barely contain it.

Dancing with her has opened the door to its cage. This beast, this untameable, fearsome fucking monster of emotion writhes in the pit of my stomach. It lives and breathes. No longer dormant.

Now that it's out, there's no locking it back inside.

And I will tear the fucking world apart to keep her safe.

The thought of anyone hurting Pen has me wanting to break out of my own skin; it makes me wanna go fucking psycho.

I almost did.

I had every intention of flying out to Mexico and putting a bullet in the head of that sick fuck, David. I would've done it too if Hudson hadn't talked me down from making a fatal fucking mistake. It wasn't time. We're not ready. Not yet. He convinced me to stay. He convinced me to keep my shit together, so I spent the last week in this house getting a hold of myself, getting my head straight and my emotions in check, only to lose my shit again the second I found out what Malik had planned. You see, there is something fundamentally wrong with me.

Something I've been protecting Pen from all this time.

My mum always said that I was a sensitive kid. That I *felt* too much. That I *loved* too hard. It was overwhelming feeling everything so intensely, so much so that I would hurt myself.

I was ten the first time I hit myself.

I slapped myself across the cheek so hard that my mum had to cover up the red handprint for fear my teachers would send around social services. Over time the slapping wasn't enough, and

I would resort to punching myself, learning that I should hit myself on parts of my body that could be hidden beneath clothes. Then I began to cut my skin to relieve the pressure. Just tiny little nicks in places where no one would see because I needed release, relief. It was blissful, cathartic. I used to watch the blood slide down my leg, dripping from my skin. It would numb the emotions enough to get through another day. The tattoo on my arm covers some of them, the others are close to my crotch, high up on my thigh, hidden by more tattoos. The Breakers never knew. I kept that part of my past hidden. My dark, dirty little secret.

My mother always feared that my inability to curb my emotions would be the ruin of me. So she taught me to keep everything contained, under wraps. She taught me how to funnel that passion, those emotions, into something else. Into dance. Into Bachata.

That's why I never asked Pen to partner with me. It's why I kept her at arm's length for so long. I was safe dancing with her in a group but partnering with her would've changed things. It would've unleashed all the dormant emotions inside. I could keep them in check with girls I didn't really give a shit about. I could even keep them in check around my best friends because the way I feel about them, though powerful, isn't a patch on what I feel for her.

Pen. *My* Tiny.

Dancing with Tiny intimately like that would've made me volatile in a way I couldn't control, but now that I have danced with her, these long-trapped emotions are dying to find a way out and keeping them inside is killing me.

Love shouldn't fucking hurt. It shouldn't pull you to pieces. It shouldn't shred you. It shouldn't fucking ruin you. When I said that love was dangerous, I meant it was dangerous for *me*.

I'm wired differently.

When I love *it hurts*. It really fucking hurts.

It's a physical pain. An all-consuming sickness. A wild-heartness. A soul-searing blindness.

And I have to keep it in check because right now I'm literally seconds away from barging into the room Pen's sleeping in and taking her, just like I wanted to do that night at Grim's club. I wanted her so bad that I'd convinced myself that she meant nothing, that I fucking hated her, because even though hating passionately hurts me too, it has nothing on how loving someone makes me feel. I pushed her away, made her feel like shit and convinced myself that what I felt wasn't real.

It was safer that way. For the both of us.

But now my emotions are becoming untethered. Now that I've held her in my arms and danced with her, she has become every damn thing, and I *can't* see clearly. This savage fucking monster within me is ready to tear up the world to keep her safe. I'm going to kill every last motherfucker who's threatened her and fucking smile whilst I do it.

I. Will. Gut. Them.

Pushing off the mirror, I step backwards. My chest is heaving with exertion as though I've run a marathon when all I've done is kept myself in this damn room and away from her. Striding over to the panel on the wall, I tap on the screen that's connected to the internal sound system and scroll through the selection of songs. Unsurprisingly, the Freed brothers have a state-of-the-art music system with speakers in every room that's voice activated. The whole house is rigged up with tech way beyond anything I've ever experienced. Even the fucking blinds open and close on command. Last week Hudson had a space in the gym cleared for me so I could dance. He saw very quickly that was what I needed to release my stress and to get control of my emotions.

Maybe in a different life I could've been like him. Selfless. *Good*.

He's a good man whilst I'm... *not*.

Pressing my forearm against the wall, I scroll through the selection of songs and choose *Silence* by Marshmello, featuring Khalid, then walk into the centre of the space. My skin is already covered in a sheen of sweat, my t-shirt sticking to my chest and back. A heavy feeling of claustrophobia surrounds me, and I have a desperate need to be free from the heaviness. Stripping off my clothes and shoes, I stand in the middle of the space wearing just my boxer shorts, but the temperate air of the gym does nothing to cool my blood. Only dancing will take the edge off this feeling. It will help me release some of the pent-up emotion, get it under some semblance of control.

Rolling my head on my shoulders, I narrow my eyes at my reflection. "Play music."

The opening piano chords begin to sound out around the gym, and I grasp my head in my hands, gripping the strands of my hair, revelling in the sting to my scalp. Jerking my torso forward, I bend at my waist, stepping into the movement, then stumble. As though I can't hold myself upright.

But I have to keep moving.

Being the way I am means I can't linger in a moment, a mood, a feeling. It's too much to take otherwise, too fucking overwhelming. I subdue, damp down, suppress.

Like Khalid sings, I would rather be a lover than someone who is constantly fighting.

Fighting these emotions.

Fighting to keep my boys safe.

Fighting to keep away from Tiny.

Fighting to be normal.

Fuck knows that's all I've ever wanted. To be able to love like a normal person.

I didn't. I couldn't.

So I danced instead, or at least I did until I began to kill.

Drawing my fists up to my chin, I punch at the air like a boxer in a ring, battling an invisible enemy. I move my body in staccato beats, my left foot rising then dropping, my right leg kicking out, dragging me forward. I lash out with my arms, my legs, as the cyclone within me twists up and expands, threatening to break free of my rib cage. It wants to detonate my heart. It wants to destroy.

I can't let it.

Turning on my feet in a spin, I funnel the momentum within and mimic it on the outside. I become the cyclone, letting a little of it out to release the pressure only to feel it drag me down like gravity would a stone. My legs slide out across the hardwood beneath me as I fall to the floor, my forearms resting against the coldness, my fists curled, my toes tucked up beneath my feet. This close, I can see the faint scars on my forearm hidden beneath my shattered heart tattoo and the cracked penny with Tiny's name inked onto the surface.

Looking at it, my fucking heart expands to the point of bursting. This isn't some metaphorical bullshit. I suffer an uncontrollable physical reaction to overwhelming emotion. I *feel* my heart bulging, swelling, aching.

It hurts.

Sweat slides off my forehead, my pulse jumps erratically and as the beat drops, I feel a very real need to just fucking move. Pushing up off my knees, I put all my weight on my right hand and lift my legs off the ground in a floor leap before transitioning into an aerial cartwheel. As the floor passes beneath me in a blurred rush, and my body cuts through the air, I feel peace.

But it's short-lived.

I land on heavy feet and a rush of emotions floods my chest trying to crush me.

"No!" I grunt, refusing to give in.

Jerking my torso to the right, I continue to dance as though my fucking life depends on it. I suppose in some ways it does. Because if I don't dance, I will seek Pen out and do something I'll regret. I won't hurt her that way. I've done enough of that already. But what I can say with absolute conviction, is that if Jeb was here now I would kill him with my bare hands. Like the song suggests, I'd find peace in violence. I'd find peace in murdering that motherfucking cunt.

Because I *have* found peace in violence before.

After Pen walked away, I used violence to control my emotions. The act of violence calmed me, it made me feel numb.

I could live with numbness.

But living like this is torturous, and I need to control this emotion within me before it does even more damage to the one person I need to protect from myself. Lifting my right leg up, I kick out to the side before slamming my foot back down. Sweeping my arms out in a wide arc, I allow my body to follow the motion until I kick off the floor and flip forwards into a series of tumbles. Air rushes past me as the room blurs.

I feel like a leaf dragged up into the vortex of a tornado, twisting, turning, tumbling.

But still it's not enough.

Reality stills my feet. It drags me back down into the clutches of my emotions that swell, consuming me. My hands rise up my body, my nails digging into the sweaty skin of my chest, my neck, my face, until my fingers curl into my hair and tug. This time a few strands of my hair fall away, dropping from my fingers.

I let out an anguished cry, doubling over as I heave and choke on these feelings.

There's no peace, no contentment.

"Xeno?"

My whole body stiffens.

Her voice is no more than a soft whisper, a cautionary tale. I hear it. I feel it like a motherfucking bullet to my heart.

The concern. The fear. The empathy. The *love*.

"I've never seen you dance like that before," she says, stepping towards me. I straighten up. Every single part of me pulled taut to the point of snapping.

"Get the fuck out of here, Pen." I grind out, choking on the words as I glare at the floor. They feel like fucking shards of glass in my throat, slicing my gullet open. They hurt me because they hurt her. Before, I could be cruel because I believed she was my enemy. The words that caused her pain didn't cut me so deep because I'd convinced myself that she meant nothing to me. It's different now. All I know is that if she stays in the room, I will lose every last shred of my resolve to hold back, to keep it all in. I have to contain it. I *have* to. "I need you to go. You're not safe around me right now."

"No," she replies firmly. "You're hurting."

"I can't stop it." It's a warning, one I hope to fuck she hears.

"Then *don't*. Let it go, Xeno. Whatever this is, let it go."

And that's when I feel them, the fucking tears. They slide down my face. They aren't cathartic. They're not a release. They're fucking painful, like acid burning into my skin. I'm ashamed of them. I don't cry.

I. Don't. Motherfucking. Cry.

The next track begins to play and Emeli Sandé's song *Hurts* sounds over the speaker system.

Fuck. The beat matches the pounding of my heart and the words fucking speak to my soul.

Loving Tiny *hurts*. It fucking hurts.

"Don't," I snap, holding my hand up and stumbling backwards as she takes a tentative step towards me. This girl. This brave, strong, gutsy, reckless, courageous girl refuses to leave me whilst I fucking break. She loves me despite all the shit I put her through.

"I don't deserve you."

"Maybe that's true, maybe it isn't. Grim said I should make you work for my love. She wants me to punish you."

"You should." I swipe at my face. "You fucking should."

Pen smiles softly. "See, here's the thing. I don't want to punish you. I'm done with that. Haven't we all suffered enough?"

"Not me. *I* haven't."

She laughs softly at that. "You especially. Look at you…"

"Don't pity me."

"I don't pity you. This is purely selfish, Xeno, because I *want* your love. I've always wanted it. Whatever that looks like."

And with those words the thin shred of my restraint breaks.

I rush towards her.

No, I fucking sprint.

But instead of being afraid, instead of running the fuck away, she squares her shoulders, looks me in the eye and opens her arms. She opens her arms and the fucking cyclone within me rips out of my chest, taking my heart with it.

7

Pen

THE FORCE of Xeno's passion lifts me off my feet as he grasps the back of my thighs and smashes his lips against mine. There's no tenderness as his fingers curl roughly around the back of my neck and he forces his tongue into my willing mouth. There's no warmth as he crushes my body between his and the wall. He isn't gentle when he grasps my breast in his rough palm and squeezes.

This is fire.

This is pain.

This is a suffocating kind of anguish.

This is a combustible explosion.

This is a stripping of every bad fucking decision, of every cruel word, every act of hate and replacing it with something infinitely more dangerous for our hearts.

It's a crushing, crashing, bruising pain.

It's the breaking apart of what we had as kids and reforming it into something new.

It's overwhelming.

I've never been kissed, touched, so... so *desperately*.

He's wild. Unhinged. Raw.

This is the true Xeno.

And I understand why he held back. Why he was so afraid to let himself love me.

Because this right here is the real beating heart of a man who's finally let go of his restraint. Who's given in to his true emotions, and it's clear he's suffering for it.

I don't think he could stop himself even if he wanted to.

And I *don't* want him to. As selfish as that sounds, I don't want him to stop.

If this is who he truly is, then I must love that part too. I won't pick and choose. I have to accept him for who he is *now*, no matter how bitter the taste of leaving those boys behind leaves in my mouth. He was right when he accused me of seeing them all as they once were. They aren't those boys anymore, and I *have* to accept who they are now and not mourn a past I can't change.

Maybe I should be afraid. Maybe this is the worst thing that could happen between us. Or maybe this is exactly what we've needed to happen to finally break down that last wall keeping us apart, crash it to the fucking ground and crush it until it's nothing but dust.

We've been building up to this moment for years. This is a culmination of all the fervent glances, the heated arguments, the raucous laughter, the flirtatious jokes, the angry glares, the dances, the hate, the pain, the friendship, the love.

This is us.

This is me and Xeno.

This is everything.

His kiss robs me of my breath.

His grip bruises.

His hands fly over my body, grasping and squeezing in his insatiable need to fulfil the deep cavernous hole in his heart. He rips my t-shirt up over my head, removing my bra with ease, and leaving my tits bare before him. Xeno's chest heaves as he takes me in. The *hunger* in his gaze has me gasping, and when he ducks his head and sucks my nipple into his mouth, I writhe in his arms.

"Fucking beautiful," he utters against my skin, his voice guttural.

Kissing across my chest, he draws my other nipple between his teeth, sucking in some of the plump flesh surrounding it, and bites me hard enough to leave little indents of his teeth. I let out a shriek of sudden pain before he soothes the bite with the gentle caress of his lips. Then he fucking *licks* me, and the heat between my legs combusts, causing my body to soak it with wetness until my knickers are drenched with lust.

Sliding his hot tongue and mouth across the globes of my flushed breasts, Xeno kisses and licks up the center of my chest and neck before finding my lips once more and kissing me deeply.

This kiss comes from a desperate man who's searching for redemption, seeking atonement. What's happening between us now goes beyond his need for me to forgive him. This is so much more than that, and I know, without a doubt, that I'm the *only* woman strong enough to weather his dangerous expression of love.

"Tiny, Tiny, Tiny," he laments, and the sound of my nickname on his lips has my heart swelling as his cock thrusts against my core through the joggers I'm wearing, dragging out an illicit moan from my bruised lips. Every part of my body lights up beneath his touch. I'm on fire.

My clit pulses, my nipples tighten, my pussy floods with more heat.

I come alive beneath his touch. Every part of me is sensitive to him.

I *ache*. I *burn*. I *yearn*.

His touch is painful, yet pleasurable.

His kiss is suffocating, yet freeing.

Xeno's fingers slide into my hair as he grasps me to him, as though he's afraid that I'm not real, that I'm just a phantom and I'll slip through his fingers if he doesn't hold on tightly enough.

"I'm here. I'm here," I reassure him, clutching him tighter.

My legs tighten around his waist. My fingers dig into his flesh as I grasp at him. His heart is pounding out of control beneath my palms. It feels like a ticking bomb. Turbulent. Dangerous. Fragile. So very, very fragile.

"Xeno," I mutter against his mouth, my nails digging into his too hot skin as he takes and takes and takes.

But he can't hear me.

He's lost in his emotions, and I have a feeling if I break him out of this, it will hurt him in a way I don't yet understand. So when he pushes on my thighs, urging my legs to drop to the floor, I follow his lead. I return every kiss, every bruising grip, every desperate, hungry moan.

Because I'm not afraid.

I want this. I want him.

Every dark part. All of it.

"Tiny... I need, I need..."

He can barely get the words out. It's as though touching me, kissing me, is the only thing keeping him sane. As though fucking me, sinking inside of me, getting release, is the difference between him losing his mind and keeping it intact.

That thought makes me reckless.

So when he twists me around and shoves me against the wall, his hot, hungry mouth sucking on my neck, his hand cupping my throat as his thumb presses against the thumping pulse in my neck, I moan with lust and arch my spine.

When his free hand skates over my stomach and slides beneath the waistband of my jogging pants, I beg him to touch me.

When his fingers find my drenched core, and slide between my swollen pussy lips, I widen my stance, and rock my hips, encouraging him.

When he twists and pinches my nipples, sending lightning bolts to my clit, I scream at the agony and growing ecstasy.

When he enters me with two thick fingers and a deep, hungry growl escapes his throat, I push my joggers and knickers down, kicking them away, and bare my arse to him.

"I want you," I say, my voice thready, *needy*.

"Fuck!" he exclaims, before biting down on my shoulder.

He removes his fingers, yanks me by my hips whilst simultaneously pushing between my shoulder blades so that I'm bent over at an angle, then drops down behind me and buries his face in my pussy.

He fucks me with his tongue, his saliva mixing with the heat of my dripping cunt.

I'm so fucking wet.

So turned on.

I grind against his face, rocking my hips in a rolling wave as he tongues me expertly. The noises he makes as he eats me out are nothing short of erotic, and the slippery, wet sound of his licks and his kisses make my legs shake uncontrollably. I feel his thick thumb slide into my entrance as he flicks my clit with his tongue. The intrusion is welcomed, my internal walls squeeze his thumb tightly. When his plump lips suck on my clit, stars blur my vision.

"I'm going to come. Fuck, Xeno!" I scream.

A powerful orgasm bursts out from my core and forces my spine to arch unnaturally. I scramble at the wall, trying to keep myself from collapsing, but I don't get time to come down from the billowing storm of my orgasm before Xeno stands, flips me around and pushes me back against the wall hard enough for the air to burst out of my lungs.

Blinking back the blurred vision from the most powerful orgasm I've ever experienced, Xeno rips off his boxer shorts, kicking them away before he smashes his lips against mine and grips me by the arse, hauling me back up in his arms. I taste myself on his lips and it's so fucking dirty that when I feel his cock sliding between my folds, his thick head slick with my wetness, I groan with need. *Fuck.*

"Condom," I manage to blurt out. Common sense breaking this moment of passion and preventing us from doing something stupid.

"Fuck!" The mention of a condom seems to snap Xeno out of his passionate haze and he pulls back enough to stare at me with panicked, lust-crazed eyes.

Given the circumstances, I don't have a condom on me, and I've no idea whether the Freed brothers would have need of them anymore, let alone know where some may be kept in this huge house. "I don't have anything," I manage to articulate, my words breathy beneath the dying embers of my orgasm.

"Wait," he says suddenly, planting a rough kiss against my lips before striding across the room to where his discarded trousers are lying. I watch him as he pulls a wallet free from the pocket, trembling at the frantic, desperate way he snatches at the leather. I've never seen him so on edge.

Never.

When he pulls out a silver foil packet, drops his wallet and stalks back towards me, I let out a breath of anxiety, not because I'm afraid of him, but because I'm afraid *for* him. Everything about this is so intense, and he seems almost pained by it.

I can't explain it, all I know is that I want him as badly as he wants me. He's so fucking beautiful. My core aches at the sight of his beautiful erect cock bobbing between his legs as he strides towards me.

So fucking male.

So. Damn. Sexy.

So... *damaged*. Knowing that, seeing it, hurts, and all I want to do is heal him somehow.

When he reaches me, a hungry smile glides across his face and a heart-stuttering darkness glints in his eyes that speaks of hidden needs I've yet to discover. I mean, the Breakers own a sex club, so it's not too much of a stretch that they may have grown up to be sexually liberated men.

Despite my heart skipping a beat, and goosebumps covering my skin, I'm *not* afraid. Just like the still, silence of night, there's something alluring about the unknown, the unseen. I've never been afraid of the dark. There's something so peaceful about it, at least to me.

"Look at me," he snarls dangerously, and I snap my gaze up.

There are no stars in Xeno's eyes like I might find in Zayn's.

There isn't the kind of deep understanding that I see in York's or even an overwhelming protectiveness that would be present in Dax's. No, Xeno's gaze is just a gateway to everything hidden inside, and just like Alice in Wonderland, I willingly fall right into his depths.

Without taking his eyes off of me, Xeno rips the foil with his teeth and pulls the condom free.

I follow his hands, watching him as he rolls the latex over his beautiful cock. When Xeno grasps my hips once more, and he slides his cock teasingly between my folds, I place my hands on his shoulders and let him lift me up, crossing my legs over his firm arse.

"Tiny..." he laments, the sound coming from a place deep within. It's vulnerable in a way that would break my heart if I let it.

Grasping his head in my hands, I kiss him with every last ounce of love I hold inside. I kiss him with forgiveness, with hope, with a fierce protectiveness. I kiss him knowing that his love might not be the most straightforward, but it's just as worthy as the others. I can no more live without him than I can the rest of my Breakers.

"Xeno, don't hold back," I demand, the roughness and emotion in my voice calling to the darkest parts within him. "I want *all* of you, even the parts you're afraid to share."

He lets out a strangled cry before entering me with one hard thrust, sending a scream of agony and ecstasy ripping out of my throat. His eyes widen as my nails dig into his skin, drawing blood. We're panting, both of us shocked momentarily by the significance of this moment.

It's... *powerful.*

There's no other word to describe it.

Xeno locks his gaze with mine and the darkness within his eyes glint with those familiar shards of green, still sharp enough to cut. "I love you, Tiny."

Then he lets go.

Xeno *fucks* me.

He uses the wall to keep me upright as he slams his cock into me. Not once does he stop kissing me and every swipe of his tongue, every press of his lips is an apology. But I don't want an apology, because this is *everything* I've always wanted, and I love every last knee-shaking, core-trembling, pussy-creaming moment of it.

What's happening between us is a basic need. A joining of two people who've lost themselves in the frenetic need to fuck. To lay waste to everything that was painful between them and replace it with something else.

Something fulfilling.

Something life-affirming.

Something edged in delicious pain.

This is love wrapped up in abandon. This is our three-year absence brought into stark existence.

Our kisses turn into desperate gulps of air as my head falls to his shoulder and my arse cheeks slam against the top of his thighs. He spears me with every thrust of his hips, hitting deep inside. I cup the back of his neck with one hand, holding on whilst my fingers slide over the taut tendons of his shoulders. Pressing open-mouthed kisses against his skin, I soothe away the scratches I've inflicted. With my other hand I reach between us and palm the slickness of his chest. I can feel how his heart hammers against his rib cage so strongly that I fear it's going to give out if he doesn't find his release soon.

"Xeno," I say breathlessly, pressing my lips against the crook of his neck, tasting him on my tongue.

He grows thicker in response, and my body reacts to the telltale sign of his imminent release by clamping around him tighter. My internal muscles squeeze him like a fist as the tendrils of an orgasm build and swirl inside us both. My lips slide up his neck, my tongue glides across his jaw before I swallow down his cries with my lips.

I'm so *full* of him.

My pussy is full of his cock, my mouth is full of his groans, and my heart is full of his love. My heart isn't afraid of the danger, it's brave enough for the both of us and it welcomes the onslaught of emotions, absorbs them, holds them close and keeps them safe.

"I love you, Xeno."

And with those words, I throw back my head and scream, my orgasm drawing out Xeno's until he's coming so hard that his hips buck in quick, short thrusts, his seed spilling deep inside.

I go boneless, the roaring thump of my pulse lost beneath our frantic breaths.

Xeno's knees buckle and he reaches for the wall behind me, collapsing to the floor, bringing me down with him. We hold onto one another for long minutes, neither of us able to move, let alone speak.

Eventually, as the heat of my skin begins to cool and our breaths even out, I pull back, cupping Xeno's face in my hands. His hair is lying in damp curls against his head. His eyes are wide with shock and his lips are as puffy and as swollen as my own. He seems lost somehow, almost in a trance like state, and that scares me.

"Xeno, where are you right now? Come back to me," I say gently, pushing his hair back off his face and pressing a tender kiss against his forehead. He moans at my gentleness, with every kiss, as I gently pull myself off his cock, which is still hard despite his orgasm. He slides out of me, my release wet against my thighs and his. Adjusting myself in his lap, I smooth my hands over his shoulders, gently touching the marks I've made.

"I hurt you," I say apologetically.

"No," he shakes his head, capturing my gaze with his. "You didn't."

He brings his hands up, his fingers sliding over my cheeks as his eyes rove over every inch of my face. He presses a delicate kiss against my parted lips, sensually sweeping his tongue into my mouth. I try to deepen the kiss, but he pulls back and the pain I see in his eyes is like a hammer to my heart.

"Don't do that. Don't you *dare* regret this," I warn.

He strokes my skin, his fingers slipping lower as they run over my damp neck, across my collarbone and between my breasts. He rests his palm over my heart, feeling it thump. I know what he's thinking, feeling, as his fingers caress my skin, because I feel it too.

"I don't regret this. I will never regret this. Fuck, Tiny..."

"What, Xeno? What is it?" I ask, brushing a sweet kiss to the tip of his nose.

"All this time I was so fucking afraid."

"Afraid?"

"Of feeling. Of *letting* myself feel."

"Are you still afraid?" I ask, smoothing my hand over his hair and swiping at the bead of sweat that slides down his cheek.

"More than ever," he breathes out.

My face must drop at his honesty because he smiles then. A genuine, warm smile that takes my breath away. "Come with me," he says softly, holding out his hand.

I take it and he leads me out of the gym, snatching up his t-shirt as we pass it by. When we reach the hallway, he stops and takes care of the condom before dropping to his knees before me and wiping at my damp thighs with his t-shirt. He's gentle, reverent, a far cry from the absolute wildness of our coming together. For some reason that makes my throat tighten with tears.

When he stands, he notices them glistening on my lashes. "You're not afraid," he says, gently taking my hand once again.

"You're wrong. I'm afraid of everything. I'm afraid of David, of Jeb. I'm afraid of what The Masks will do now. I'm afraid for my sister. I'm afraid what will happen to the men I love. I'm afraid that tomorrow I'll wake up and this will all be a dream, that you'll go back to hating me again."

"I meant you're not afraid of showing how you feel. It's your greatest strength, Tiny, and one I envy. Everything else you're afraid of is understandable, but I swear to you we will make this right. I will never go back to hating you. *Never*," he says vehemently. "Come on, come with me."

I follow him silently back upstairs, lost to my own thoughts as he guides me past the room I was sleeping in, and pushes open another door along the hallway. It opens out into a huge bathroom. A roll top bath sits in the center of the room. He kisses my knuckles then lets my hand go and busies himself turning on the taps, adding bubble bath to the rising water.

Xeno swirls the water with his fingertips, making the bubbles grow in size. I watch as the muscles of his shoulders and arms tense and flex, my gaze lingering on the tattoo on his forearm before lowering down the curve of his back and focusing on the tight muscles of his arse and legs. A tribal print tattoo wraps around both thighs, a thick black line darkening the skin.

"Tiny...?" My eyes snap up as he catches me staring and I give him a small smile. "It shouldn't be too hot." He offers me his hand and I take it, stepping into the bath and sliding beneath the water. It's the perfect temperature and despite myself, I let out a sigh, my muscles instantly relaxing.

"Aren't you getting in?" I ask him as he stares down at me.

He shakes his head. "No. I've got something I need to do."

"Where are you going?"

He leans over and presses a lingering kiss against my forehead, then pulls back and walks away.

"Xeno, wait!" I say, sitting up, the water sloshing over the lip of the bath. He stops at the door and gives me the most beautiful, heartfelt smile.

"Just relax, okay. I'm not going anywhere."

"I have no regrets, Xeno. None. Hear me?"

"I hear you, and now that you're mine, I don't plan on having any either," he replies softly, then shuts the door behind him with a gentle click.

8

Pen

AN HOUR later I hear the sound of raised voices. Climbing out of the bath, I dry off quickly and grab a towelling robe from the back of the bathroom door. Stepping out into the hallway, my wet hair dripping down my back, I follow the sound, my feet padding silently over the heated floor.

"You piece of fucking shit. What were you thinking?" Dax yells, shoving at Xeno's chest as I step into the open space. Both are too busy getting in each other's faces to notice me enter.

Xeno grits his jaw. "I *wasn't* thinking Dax, that's the issue."

"Tell me something I don't already know, dickhead!" Dax's left eye is completely swollen shut now and a trail of blood trickles down his face from his split eyebrow, aggravated by his anger. Beast certainly did a number on him. That fight, and our conversation at Tale's, seems like a lifetime ago, not just a few short hours.

"I asked Beast to send York and Zayn back too, where are they?"

"Don't change the fucking subject! I could fucking murder you!" Dax shoves Xeno again, and I see the familiar anger that Xeno tries his hardest to keep under wraps, flare to life.

"Just do it. Just hit me! Get it out of your system so we can move the fuck on," Xeno growls, squaring his shoulders, the muscle in his jaw ticking. He doesn't even try to fight back when Dax grabs him by his jumper and fists the material in his hand, before raising a clenched fist.

"Dax, stop!" I shout, snapping out of my inertia and rushing forward. I get how he's feeling. I understand he's pissed at Xeno, but I'm done with all the bullshit fighting. The only way we're going to get through this is together. That starts right the fuck now.

Dax lets Xeno go with a shove the moment he hears me and turns, capturing me in his arms.

"Kid, thank fuck!" he exclaims, sweeping me up against his chest and lifting me off my feet. He steps away from Xeno, still holding me close as he rains down kisses over my face. Behind us, Xeno strides into the kitchen area and clutches onto the sink, dropping his head between his shoulders. I feel torn between them. It's not a feeling I like or want. The easy way we used to be with each other when we were kids seems so out of reach. That needs to change.

"Kid, are you okay?" Dax releases his hold enough for me to look up at him.

"I'm doing fine, Dax." I don't tell him that up until a few hours ago I was a complete mess, or that Xeno and I fucked away our past hurt. I'm not sure that will help the situation right now.

After another bone crushing hug, Dax drops me to my feet.

Lowering me slowly down his body before capturing my cheeks in his hands, his good eye searching my face. "You sure you're okay? I came back the second I could get away. I've been going fucking insane needing to get back to you."

"I really *am*, but are you?" I ask, my fingers gently hovering over his bruised and battered face. Lifting up onto my tiptoes, I press a gentle kiss against his swollen cheek. "It's worse."

"I'll live," he mutters, as my mouth slides lower and I gently press a kiss on his lips, not wanting to hurt him. Grabbing my arse and hauling me close, Dax kisses me back passionately. "No need to be gentle with me, Kid," he mutters after I pull back and drag in a breath. God, how these men make me lightheaded.

I'm pretty sure I hear Xeno growl, which only makes Dax lean back in and kiss me harder. I'm not complaining.

"Ah, so that's why you left us to bring the bags up. Nice man, nice."

York.

Dax chuckles against my mouth, but he lets me go and I wiggle out of his arms, running into York's, who drops a rucksack on the floor. Like Dax, he hauls me up against his body and kisses me thoroughly. By the time I pull back, we're both flushed, and York has a sheen of sweat across his forehead.

"I've got to be honest, I wasn't expecting such a warm welcome, Titch," he remarks, with a wink. "Just so you know, I'm partial to a spanking in case you come to your senses and wanna give me a slap for keeping secrets from you." He's referring to the whole Hudson, Santiago thing and I realise Xeno called them whilst I was in the bath to fill them in.

"You're sweating!" I exclaim, swatting at his chest because he's got a point. He *did* keep things from me, they all did, but I'm prevented from fulfilling his fantasies when I see just how pale he looks. He's more ghostly than vampish in the early morning light that feathers between the gaps in the blinds.

"That's because you're so damn hot," he retorts with a wink.

"York, you should sit down," I say worriedly.

"What a fucking wimp. Anyone would think he was shot." Dax scoffs with a smile in his voice and a warm, brotherly kind of love in his eyes.

"Fuck off, you prick. At least I'm not giving Frankenstein's monster a run for his money. Have you seen the state of your face?" York retorts with a smirk.

"Ha ha ha, you little prick! Do as Kid says and sit the fuck down." Dax is chuckling now, and the sound warms my heart. I've felt so cold and alone for so long, and now I feel as though I'm beginning to thaw out just being with them *all* again like this.

"Nice to know you've all still got banter after the fucking night we've had. I don't think I could face cleaning up another shitstorm," Zayn says, climbing up the stairs. He's carrying an overnight bag too and drops it to the floor as I rush for him.

"Zayn!"

"Hey, Pen." He gives me a tired smile, then meets me in a couple of strides, grabs my face and kisses me stupid. After a long indulgent kiss, I break free from his hold then grab his hand and lead him to the table where the others are waiting for us to join them. Xeno is making coffee, avoiding the angry glares from Dax and Zayn. When he's poured five mugs and added some milk, he places them on the table with a bowl of sugar and a spoon then takes a seat at the head of the table.

"How was the bath?" he asks, looking at me with guarded eyes.

"Relaxing, thank you." I reach for his hand, squeezing gently, trying to reassure him that I meant what I said earlier. I have no regrets. Not one. He looks at my fingers wrapped around his palm then back up at me. I think he's shocked at my outward show of affection around the others, not to mention my forgiveness. I'm not. This is it for me. This is the start of our new future and if we can't show our love and affection in front of each other then when can we?

York whistles softly. "Fucking *finally*," he says, giving me an encouraging smile when I meet his gaze. Thank God for York. "You know I'm pretty sure you two dancing together was the hottest form of foreplay I've ever had the pleasure of witnessing. No wonder you stayed away from Titch for so long, man. You totally would've jizzed your pants if you'd allowed yourself to give in when we were younger," he jokes, winking.

Dax snorts, and my cheeks flush.

Xeno, however, doesn't crack a smile. "Shut the fuck up."

"Jeez, take a fucking joke. Clearly you're not at the bantering stage quite yet." York rolls his eyes and leans back in his seat, taking a gulp of coffee but he smirks at me above the rim of the cup. He's such a wind-up merchant and right now I adore him for trying to make light of a tenuous situation.

"Shame the rest of the fucking warehouse witnessed it too," Zayn says pointedly, bringing the tentative truce crashing back to the ground. I would scowl at him if I didn't want to make this any worse than it already is. Besides, he has a right to be angry. I can't prevent him from feeling the way he does.

Dax grunts his agreement, folding his bulky arms across his chest. "Fucking stupid arse move." He cuts a scathing look at Xeno. "What the *fuck* were you thinking?"

"I told you. I wasn't."

"What kind of explanation is that?!" Zayn cuts in. "Pen could've been killed!"

"Do you think I don't know that?" Xeno exclaims. "Every time I shut my goddamn eyes; I see what could've happened to Tiny. To you *all*. I acted on impulse. It's not an excuse, just a fact. I can't change it. I won't fuck up again. I give you my word." Xeno gives me a meaningful look and my stomach tightens at the dangerous promise within them.

"What's done is done," York states, always the peacekeeper. "The Collector is dead. I call that a motherfucking win."

"Where the fuck did you disappear to?" Zayn asks, ignoring York's attempt at smoothing over the cracks.

"I guess we really are doing this now," Xeno mutters.

"You better have a good explanation for disappearing for a week then wreaking havoc the second you're back." He swipes a hand over his face, trailing his gaze from our clasped hands back up to Xeno.

"You know why that had to happen," Xeno retorts heavily. "Hudson and I intercepted—"

"Don't fucking patronise us. We're fully aware why last night went the way it did, but I'm talking about the fact you fucking disappeared for a week with no fucking word. Where the fuck were you?" Anger and hurt clear in Zayn's gaze.

All three of them wait for an explanation, and I understand in that moment that Xeno's absence cut a lot deeper than any of them care to admit. They're not just angry with how Xeno handled things, but also because he left without a word.

"I was here," Xeno admits.

"You were here? Fucking unbelievable," Zayn shakes his head. "So whilst we were covering for you with Jeb, trying to stop Pen from losing her damn mind, you were chilling here without a care in the goddamn world? You fucking prick."

"I deserve that."

"You deserve a throat punch too," Dax mutters, scowling. "I'm happy to oblige."

"Hey! Enough. If I can forgive Xeno, you three sure as hell can," I say, stepping in. "I'm sure he had his reasons for leaving the way he did, but he's here now. We *all* are. That means something." I smile, more tears welling in my eyes. "That means something to *me*. I have you back, all of you, and I will not let anger tear us apart again. *I won't*."

"Titch has a point," York says looking at me with pride in his eyes. "I say we listen."

I look between Dax and Zayn, both of them have their arms folded stubbornly across their chests. "I know you're angry. You should've seen me earlier," I say, a light laugh bursting out of my lips. Xeno glances at me and gives me a puzzled shake of his head, like he can't believe how lucky he is to gain my forgiveness so easily. "But we're beyond this now."

"Agreed," Dax grinds out. "But I swear to fuck, Xeno, I will kick your arse to Timbuktu if you ever put Kid's life at risk like that again. Hear me?"

"I'm counting on it, brother," Xeno responds, giving him a tight nod. "I *need* you to keep me in check. I need all of you to remind me every day what's important. If that means a throat punch, or a kick up the arse, then I accept the punishment. I'll fucking take it willingly."

"Done." Dax picks up his coffee and swallows a mouthful, some of the stress leaving his shoulders.

"Zayn?" I ask, watching him carefully. He seems the most

reluctant to let go of his anger. I squeeze Xeno's hand and get up, circling the table to reach him. "Zayn, I need you to look at me. Turn your chair around and face me," I say, echoing those words I said to him that night at Grim's club when Jeb offered me up as a prize. It has the desired effect, and he looks up at me with pain-filled eyes as he makes room for me. I step between him and the table, resting my arse on the edge.

"You really know how to hit where it hurts, Pen," he says, swallowing hard.

"I'm just reminding you that we're all capable of making mistakes. It's how we deal with them after the fact that counts. It's easy to hate, to hold onto anger. It's far, far harder to forgive."

Zayn sighs, pinching his nose. "Okay, but if that fucker walks out on us without a word one more time, I will throw a knife in his goddamn back and not even flinch."

"Fair enough," I hear Xeno say behind me.

I glance over my shoulder. My smile broadens when his gaze zeroes in on Zayn's hands that have found my hips and are dragging me towards him. Xeno's eyebrows pull together when Zayn hugs me close. There's no mistaking the jealousy and propriety in his gaze, but he keeps himself in check. I'm thinking we're going to need to discuss *us* as a fivesome and how we move forward from here. But I bench that thought for now. There's only so much I can expect of them for one night and, honestly, I'm tired.

"Bed?" Zayn asks, drawing my attention back to him and reading my thoughts perfectly. He peers up at me from under a swathe of dark hair, and whilst the innuendo is clear, I can see the sheer exhaustion in his eyes.

"That sounds like a really, *really* good idea."

Taking my hand in his, Zayn stands.

"Bagsy first," York interrupts, winking at Zayn who laughs.

"You prick."

"Don't think you're getting first dibs because you're acting like a sensitive little bitch," York says, standing too.

"Erm," I mutter, not sure how to handle this situation. I glance at Dax who just grins.

"We've got all the time in the world, Kid. Take these two to bed. Me and Xeno need to talk through some business anyway." He cuts a look at Xeno who presses his lips together in a tight line.

"Anything I can help with?" I ask, my gaze flicking to Xeno who is currently glaring at Zayn and York like he wants to do some damage.

"They love her too, Xeno. Let them be," Dax says, resting his hand on Xeno's arm.

"Yeah, man. I know," Xeno replies nodding his approval. He looks at me then. "We just got things to discuss, nothing urgent that I can't fill you in on later. Go rest. All of you," Xeno says, reassuring me that there'll be no more secrets between us.

"Would you look at that, are you sure this is the same Xeno we know and love?" York jokes, as

Zayn slides his arm around my back and presses a kiss against my temple. York flanks my other side, sliding his hand into mine. I daren't look at him, because I just know he's got a shit-eating grin on his face.

"You know, you could always come watch," Zayn offers with a smirk.

"Fucking get out of here," Xeno snaps, but we all see his lip twitching with mirth and that, that is just the kind of tonic we all need.

9

Pen

I LEAD York and Zayn back to the room I woke up in earlier today with my heart pounding in my chest. The last time I was alone with just the two of them, I was angry at them both for being overbearing bastards. They were jealous that Beast dropped me off back at the Academy, and they metaphorically thumped their chests like a couple of gorillas before conceding they were acting like twats.

"So what now?" York asks, a twinkle in his eye as he shuts the bedroom door behind us.

Zayn chuckles. "Mate, you were shot tonight. You need to sleep; you look like shit."

"I was shot *at*. I wasn't shot. There's a big difference. Like Dax said, it's only a scratch."

"Yeah, but you still lost a shitload of blood. Look at you, you're practically see-through. I'm not sure you'll have enough blood left to fill your cock."

I cover my mouth with my hand stifling a laugh. York narrows his eyes at me in challenge. "Believe me, Tiny, I have *plenty* of blood left." He cups his cock, and I see the outline of his erection beneath his trousers. He's not lying.

"Fucking hell, mate," Zayn exclaims, shaking his head in amusement.

"What is it, are you afraid of a little competition?"

Zayn chuckles. "I'm game if Pen is," he says, eying me, and despite the dark circles beneath his eyes I can't help but notice the sudden change in energy. You wouldn't think they've just been involved in a firefight.

York grins. "Fuck, yeah."

"I think sleep is what's needed," I say firmly, biting on my lip as York unzips his trousers and slides them off. Kicking them away alongside his shoes. His dick tents his boxers, and I have to force myself not to drool.

"You sure about that, Titch?" he asks, removing his top, and making my mouth dry out at his beautiful body.

I point at the bandage wrapped around his left bicep where a little blood seeps into the white. "You'll aggravate the stitches."

"Shit! That old fucker, Joey, better not have sewn me up ugly. I've got a reputation to keep," he remarks, fingering the bandage.

"What reputation is that?" Zayn questions with a smirk.

He too starts removing his clothes until he's standing in his boxer shorts. I'm trying hard not to salivate like some sex craved addict. I've just had sex with Xeno an hour or so ago, and whilst the bath soothed all sorts of aches and pains, I'm still tender down there. My poor, inexperienced pussy. I smile internally at that thought.

"Being the best-looking Breaker, of course!" York quips.

"Shut the fuck up, you prat." Zayn rolls his eyes and takes my hand. "I don't know about this fucker here, but I need a shower. I've got blood under my nails, and God knows what else. The quick shower at Tales hadn't exactly done the job at getting squeaky clean, and there's no way I'm getting into bed with Pen until I am."

"Yeah, agreed. Let's shower," York says, striding towards the ensuite and the large walk-in shower that's big enough to fit all of us comfortably.

"You fucker. I wasn't inviting you!"

"Hey, I'm all in. I'm not afraid to share, ask Dax..." York chuckles at the look on Zayn's face and my cheeks heat when Zayn turns his attention to me.

"What did I miss?" he asks.

"That was *before*," I mutter, internally cursing York as he laughs out loud. He turns on the faucet and strips off his boxers, not in the least bit embarrassed by his nakedness or his growing erection.

"Before?"

"Yeah, when we were kids..."

"Fuck sake," Zayn curses. "You kept *that* a secret."

"Hey, a gentleman never tells," York calls out from the shower. "Though tonight I'm feeling far from gentlemanly. Want to see how ungentlemanly I'm feeling, Titch?" He winks at me through the glass. The bastard.

"Should you be getting your bandage wet?" I ask, totally changing the subject, determined to keep my gaze level with his and not stare at his cock. I'm slightly concerned that I've become a little unhinged after last night and all the revelations that followed. I'm not normally this... this, I don't know... *free* with my loving. Then again, I've only ever loved these boys and we've got a lot of catching up to do. So why the fuck does it matter?

"Fuck the bandage. I know what needs wetting, and it ain't these motherfucking stitches."

Zayn squeezes my hand, giving me a knowing look. "He's being fucking extra tonight. You'll have to forgive him, York gets a bit hyper after a little bloodshed."

"A little?"

"Okay, a lot."

"I see." I frown and Zayn winces, his eyes darkening as he lowers his voice.

"Sarcasm, bravado, and laughter is his way of coping."

My heart squeezes. "And how do *you* cope?"

"Sleep mainly. Not that I get much fucking respite where that's concerned. Nightmares," he explains with a shrug, looking more like the boy I met when we were kids than the man he is today.

I nod my head, understanding in the moment what he needs, what they both need. Distraction. *Love.* I can give them that in abundance. There are other ways to get off without full penetration, right? I'm more than happy to fulfil another one of my fantasies right here and now.

Cupping Zayn's face in my hands, I press a gentle kiss against his lips. "Come on, let's join York."

"You sure about this? It's been tough on you too. Despite how this fucker is behaving, we don't expect anything from you, Pen. Not a damn thing."

"I know that, Zayn. The thing is, even if I wanted to, we can't anyway..."

"Can't what?" York asks, his head peering around the entrance of the walk-in shower.

"No condoms," I say with a shrug.

"Shit!" York looks down at his engorged cock then back up, laughing a little hysterically. "Zayn, please tell me—"

"Sorry man, didn't really cross my mind whilst we were shooting holes in those bastards ..." he shrugs.

York leans his head against the glass which is rapidly steaming up. "Fuck me," he exclaims.

I can't help but laugh. "Hey, we've got the rest of our lives to indulge in each other," I say, meaning every word. I don't intend to ever let them go.

Zayn smiles his chipped-tooth smile, and my heart does a little flip-flop. "I like the sound of that, Pen," he says.

Taking his hand in mine, I pull him into the bathroom, shutting the door behind us. I can feel York's eyes on me as I untie the cord at my waist and slide the robe from my shoulders, letting it fall to my feet.

"Jesus, fuck," York mutters and out of the corner of my eye I see him fist his cock.

Smiling at the powerful way I feel right now, I run my hands over Zayn's chest, my fingers lingering on the scars that crisscross his skin. "You have so many scars," I say, a lump forming in my throat.

"It doesn't matter."

"It matters. *You* matter," I retort, pressing a gentle kiss against his lips. My fingers trail lower, hooking beneath the band of his boxers. I pull them down, sliding them over his hips and thighs. He kicks them away, standing naked before me. Entwining my fingers with his, I pull him towards the shower cubicle. As we step inside York steps out of the stream and backs up against the wall opposite, an intense look on his face as droplets of water drip from his hair and glide over his beautiful body.

"Hey," I say softly, giving him a soft smile.

"Hey," he replies, pressing a gentle kiss against my lips.

"Fuck, let me at least get clean first..." Zayn grumbles and I grin, nodding towards the bottle of body wash that's sitting on a shelf beside York.

"Pass that to me, please," I request. York hands it to me with another kiss.

Behind me Zayn steps under the water and tips his head backwards. I watch as he brings up his hands to swipe the droplets off his face, slicking his hair back. He lets out a low moan as the water runs over his skin, wetting him thoroughly. The tattoos on his upper arms glisten under the spray and my chest pangs at just how beautiful he is, how beautifully damaged by his scars, by his uncle and this life he's been forced to live.

Wanting to smooth away some of the memories that he must have from every one of those scars, I pour some body wash into my hands, and hand the bottle back to York who's looking at me intently. A sexy smile pulls up his lips and he pours some of the body wash into his hands.

"You wash Zayn, I'll wash you."

"Sounds good to me," Zayn agrees.

Biting my lip, my cheeks flushing with heat, I turn around and place my hands on Zayn's chest, sucking in a breath when I feel the scarred and bumped skin. Tears prick my eyes, but I refuse to let them fall. Instead, I touch him with care, making sure that I'm gentle. My fingers run over his collarbone, over his scarred pecs and abs, before working their way back up again. When my fingers stroke over his nipples he lets out a moan, and his mouth pops open. Behind me York is massaging my shoulders, his expert fingers running over my skin as his thumbs move down my spine, the sensation drawing a groan from my lips.

"Like that, Titch?" York asks, stepping closer behind me. I feel his cock press against my lower back and this time it's York who lets out a groan.

"I hate that he hurt you," I say quietly, as I take in Zayn's ravaged chest and the relatively new scar from the cut Jeb had made that night Zayn had persuaded him to let Grim hire me.

York's hand still on my hips. "Who hurt Zayn?"

"Shit, I—"

Zayn flicks his gaze from me to York standing behind me. "Some of these are from Jeb," he explains, and I can't help but see a flicker of shame in his eyes that he covers quickly. "Every time one of us fucked up, I took the punishment so none of you had to."

York's fingers dig into my hips involuntarily. "That motherfucking cunt. Why the fuck didn't you say anything?!"

My fingers are still on Zayn's chest as he answers. "What good would it have done?"

"Fuck man, I always knew he was a cunt, but that's messed up," York exclaims. For a second he drops his head to my shoulder as though needing to steady himself.

"I did what I had to do. I don't regret it," Zayn says, then coughs trying to cover the break in his voice.

Over my shoulder, York reaches for Zayn and cups the back of his head, bringing him in closer so that I truly am sandwiched between them. My hands slide around Zayn's waist, and my cheek presses against his chest as York hugs us both. "Thank you, brother. Thank you for protecting us, for stepping up, but know this, from this moment on it stops. Understand?"

"Yeah, understood," Zayn agrees, his voice scratchy as their foreheads touch above me in the cutest bro-hug ever.

"As much as I'm loving this," I say, wiggling my hips provocatively, fully aware of their nakedness pressing against me, "A girl really needs to breathe."

York pulls back with a laugh. "Shit, sorry Titch."

Zayn grins down at me and presses a kiss against my forehead. "I think it's York's turn."

Over my head an intense look passes between them and my heart warms at the thoughtfulness between them. God, I love them both so fucking much.

"I think you're right," I agree, twisting in their arms.

York already has the body wash bottle at the ready, and he squeezes some into my palms, and Zayn's. Behind me Zayn wraps his arms around my waist as he presses a hot kiss against my bare shoulder.

"You're too much of a fucking temptation," he grumbles, holding me close, before he slowly starts rubbing his soaped-up hands over my stomach. I let out a breathy laugh as he slides his lips up my neck and gently nibbles on my earlobe, sliding his erection along the crease of my arse. "Wash York, make him come," he whispers into my ear.

York meets Zayn's gaze over my head and behind the grin I see the love between them. It's not sexual, just pure. The kind of love we all dream of. I don't need to be told twice. Focusing my attention back on York, I rub my hands together to foam up the body wash, then press my hands against his chest. He lets out a low groan as my warm hands caress his pecs and stroke over his hardened nipples. Leaning back against the shower wall, York watches me with his icy-blue eyes as I gently wash him down.

I run my hands over his chest, shoulders and arms, tracing his tattoo as I go and avoiding the bandage wrapped around his upper arm. Stroking my fingers down his arms, I massage each hand in turn, taking my time to loosen up the tension. My touch has him moaning with pleasure that gets louder as I run my hands over the trail of hair leading to his cock. He jerks in my hand when I wrap my fingers around the base of his thick length.

"Fuck, Titch," he grinds out, his hooded eyelids dropping shut as my other hand clasps the mushroom head of his cock, and gently slides down his thickening shaft.

"That's it, Pen, stroke his cock. Can you see how hard he is for you? Can you feel how hard I am for you?" Zayn asks, his own words needy and oh so fucking sexy.

With one hand running over my stomach, he removes the other and it doesn't take a genius to work out that he's stroking his own cock, soaping it up good. I glance over my shoulder at him and bite on my lip at the sight.

"Zayn," I say, breathily, my clit pulsing with need as I pump York's dick, loving the feel of him, loving the way his breaths are coming quickly with every firm stroke.

"Eyes forward, Pen. I got you," Zayn replies, stepping closer as he slides his lips over my shoulder once more. Then it's my turn to moan when he rocks his cock up and down my arse crack, his fingers sliding lower, inching towards the place I want him to touch most of all. With a groan, he finally parts my pussy lips with his finger and finds me wet and wanting.

"You're so goddamn slick for us," he grinds out, circling his finger over my clit and drawing a low moan out of my throat. I rock my hips, the motion creating delicious friction for his cock as he presses into my back until I'm sandwiched between them both, only leaving enough space for me to jerk off York.

"Look at her," Zayn demands, and York's eyes snap open. His gaze flares with heat before dropping lower, trailing a blaze over my slick skin, lingering on my tits then focusing on my hands sliding up and down his dick.

"Fuck, Titch, that's so damn hot."

With one hand, Zayn continues to pleasure me, whilst the other hand wraps around my throat and squeezes gently. I whimper as he circles my clit with the perfect amount of pressure, matching the grip he has on my throat. For a brief, lust-fueled moment, I wonder whether York can feel Zayn's hand between us, but if he does, he doesn't appear to mind. Right now York is burning a hole in my chest with his heated gaze, and when he cups my breasts in his hands and runs his thumb over my peaked nipples, I jerk in their hands.

"Pen, keep doing that and I'm going to come all over your back," Zayn chuckles, his voice full of love and lust.

"I thought that was the point," York retorts, his mouth going slack as I run the pad of my thumb over his slit. "Titch, you're killing me."

"At least you'll die a happy man," I giggle, swallowing down my laugh and replacing it with a groan when York squeezes my tits and Zayn sucks on my neck.

"No, Titch, that will only happen when I'm buried deep inside your cunt and my best mate here has his cock filling your arse," York replies with a devious smile before crashing his lips against mine and kissing me with firm lips and a promise. My responding moan is swallowed by his hungry mouth as the lust building in my core expands and grows to breaking point.

As hot water slides over us all, we move against each other in another kind of dance that has our hearts beating in unison, our breaths mingling with every movement and our love expanding around us in a bliss-filled hug.

The mounting pleasure of York fucking my mouth with his tongue and Zayn's fingers between my legs has me gasping for breath and shattering first. York releases my mouth so I can cry out and a few seconds later, York roars as his hot cum spurts in thready strings all over my stomach. Behind us, Zayn swears under his breath as his cock slides faster between the crack of my arse. I arch my back into him, pressing my tits against York's chest and kissing him half-blinded by my orgasm. For a brief moment, Zayn slips his cock between my pussy lips, the tip of his cock rubbing through my folds and over my too sensitive clit. I cry out, wanting to feel him slip inside of me, but fortunately for me, Zayn has enough self-restraint for the both of us and pulls back, wrapping his arms back around me.

"York, get on your damn knees and fuck our girl's beautiful pussy with your mouth, before I lose my mind and slide my dick inside her cunt," Zayn grinds out.

"Lucky that's exactly what I was planning on doing, you overbearing shit," York grumbles, but he grins devilishly as he sinks to his knees, hooks both of my legs over his shoulders and fucks me with his tongue just like Zayn ordered him to do.

"That's it, Pen, ride his face," Zayn whispers in a sexy-as-fuck drawl that makes my toes curl just as much as York's expert tongue. Zayn's thick arms support my weight so that I'm literally sitting on York's shoulder's in a reverse cowgirl move and York secures me in place grabbing my arse cheeks in his large hands as he encourages me to ride his face, growling in appreciation as I follow his lead and do exactly that. I've never experienced anything so fucking hot. Actually, that's a lie, because every sexual encounter with my men so far has been fucking molten-lava, volcanic, *hot*.

Whilst York strives to bring me to another mind-blowing orgasm with his expert tongue, Zayn uses my lower back and the flat of his palm to create the perfect friction for his cock.

"Kiss me," he orders, before reaching around to cup my face and dragging my head to the side, claiming my mouth just as much as York claims my pussy. Seconds later I fall apart, my pussy convulsing and pulsing as York laps at my juices and Zayn's hot seed spurts over my lower back.

Ten minutes later, we climb under the bed covers, clean, satiated and utterly exhausted in the best possible way. Lying down in the centre of the bed, York climbs in behind me wrapping his body around me as he presses a kiss against my cheek, snuggling in close.

"I fucking love you, Titch."

My fingers slide over his forearm, tangling with his fingers as I draw his arm tighter around me. "I love you too, York."

He sighs, buries his face in my hair and in less than a minute has fallen into a deep sleep.

"Hey, you prick. I wanted to be the big spoon," Zayn complains, but quickly quietens when I raise my finger and press it against my lips indicating that York has passed out cold. "Look at him, sleeping like a baby."

"Shhh. He was shot, you know," I say with a soft smile.

"He was shot *at*. Big difference," Zayn quips, climbing into bed.

I reach up with my free hand and encourage him to come closer, pressing a soft kiss against his lips. "There will be plenty of opportunities for you to be the big spoon," I offer with a sweet smile, relishing the thought.

He pulls a face. "You reckon? I think we're gonna need a fucking rota or something because these bastards are gonna test my patience with their alpha bullshit. You were always *mine* first," he grumbles with a slanted smile.

"Yeah, but she's *ours* now," York mutters, half asleep. I smother Zayn's response with another kiss and York's soft snore tells us both that he's fallen back under.

"See. Even in his sleep the bastard has to have the last word."

"We'll figure this out... together. *All* of us," I say.

Zayn flicks his gaze to York and grins. "Yeah, together," he agrees.

And that's how I fall asleep, with York's arms wrapped around my back, Zayn's soft breaths feathering against my skin and hope blooming in my heart.

10

Pen

THE REST of our time at the Freed's house passes in a blur of laughter, heated kisses, and a deepening friendship. Making love to each of my Breakers was on my mind constantly, and I don't doubt it plagued their thoughts too, but despite feeling horny as fuck we seemed to come to an unspoken agreement that the rest of our time together in the Freed's home would be better spent on reforming our relationship and just being friends again. It's been the best kind of tonic and exactly what we've all needed to cement our bond. Yet despite this brief moment of bliss, I've vowed to never forget the hurt we put each other through to get here. Not because I want to hold onto it but because I need to remind myself what we must avoid at all costs.

I won't survive another separation. I won't.

That's not to say that I'm under any illusions that our relationship is going to be straightforward from here on out. I *know* it will be difficult. It's going to be hard enough to juggle this new status quo we've found ourselves in, let alone outside pressures and everything else stacked against us. But my relationship with the Breakers has never been easy, and I don't expect that to change any time soon. Together we'll figure this out. I have to have faith in that even though my stomach turns over every time I think about the precarious situation we're in.

"Kid, you smell heavenly," Dax says, snuggling against me in the back of Xeno's car as he drives us all back to the Academy. It's Sunday night and Madame Tuillard has asked me to meet with her tomorrow morning about the end of year show. I'm going to take the opportunity to request that Dax and I are paired back up again. I love River as a friend and respect him as a dancer, but we've got no chemistry whatsoever. It's the right move to put us back together, I think she knows that. At least, I hope so.

"You don't smell too bad yourself," I joke back, tucking my nose into the crook of his neck and drawing in a deep breath. Honestly, he smells fucking delicious, and if it wasn't for the fact that we're in a moving car and we've put ourselves on a self-inflicted sex ban, however unspoken, I probably would've jumped his bones way before this point. Remembering how we made love has my legs squeezing together and me pressing my lips against his skin in an open-mouthed kiss.

"Stop snuggling up to that fucker. I'm getting jealous over here," York says, sliding his hand over my thigh and squeezing. The warmth of his palm seeps into my skin through Zayn's joggers that I borrowed, heating me up from the inside out.

"Shut the fuck up, York, need I remind you that you spent the best part of ten hours wrapped around our girl *again* last night. It's *my* turn for a bit of Pen lovin'."

York leans around me and cuffs the back of Dax's head. "Fuck you, I was asleep. It doesn't fucking count."

"It fucking does," Xeno, Zayn and Dax all say simultaneously. I grin. Sometimes they're so in sync it scares me.

"Oy, shithead, do that again and I'll mess up that pretty face of yours with some bruises. Besides, you *chose* to sleep," Dax points out.

"I was shot," he grumbles.

"*At*," the three of them chorus in return, before bursting out laughing. A grin spreads across my face and it feels so good to be surrounded by their happiness. It warms me up from the inside out.

"Fuck you, you bastards. Don't expect any damn sympathy from me anytime in the future. I wouldn't piss on any of you if you were on fire," York mutters, causing another round of laughter.

"Hey," I say, taking York's hand and replacing it on my thigh, "Enough of that. You know they love you."

"Yeah, I know." He turns and smiles at me, his eyes twinkling with mirth. "I love these cunts too." Winking, he squeezes my thigh before trailing his hands up higher.

Dax growls, the sound rumbling through his chest. "Hands off, motherfucker. I'm happy to share, Kid. But I'm not happy to share, share. Comprende?"

"That's *not* true and you know it. I distinctly remember you having no problem sharing Titch, *big boy*," York chuckles and my cheeks flush at the memory of us as kids on Xeno's bed the night I was covered in bruises, and they touched me with gentleness I'd never experienced before. It was the first time I'd felt truly loved and adored. It was also the first time I'd come by someone else's hand.

"You fucker—" Dax laughs, shaking his head.

"Shit!" Xeno exclaims as the front dash lights up with an incoming call. "It's Jeb."

I stiffen in my seat. Dax presses a gentle kiss against my forehead and tightens his arm around my shoulder, attempting to reassure me. Zayn, who's sitting in the passenger seat up front, reacts much the same as I do. He looks over his shoulder and gives me a tight smile, the tension obvious. The phone continues to ring and for a moment I think Xeno's going to ignore it until he meets my gaze in the mirror. Thank fuck we've stopped at a traffic light, because I'm certain that Xeno's ability to drive this car safely would be hampered by his attention fixed solely on me.

"Tiny, as far as Jeb's concerned you mean nothing to us and as such, we have to act a certain way. He needs to believe you still mean nothing to us, that you're a toy, nothing more. It's the only way to protect you. Whatever we say about you, however we refer to you, believe me when I say it will hurt us just as much, but none of that is true. None of it. Understand?"

"Yeah, I get it," I respond, dropping my gaze, my heart sinking despite his reassurance. I know how this conversation is going to go and I know I'm not going to like it.

"Jeb, what can I do for you?" Xeno asks casually the second he accepts the call.

"You taking the fucking piss?" Jeb snarls, his voice loud through the speakers. I cringe. I fucking hate this guy.

Xeno holds his voice steady even though I can see his knuckles turn white from how hard he's holding onto the steering wheel. "I don't follow you, Boss."

"Don't play that shit with me! When I said I had everything handled, I did not mean you could go fucking AWOL and spend the weekend shagging whores and avoiding my calls!! Was your head so far up some skanks pussy that you couldn't answer me? When I call, I expect you to fucking answer!"

"Duly noted. It won't happen again." The car lurches forward, Xeno's anger making itself known even though his voice is steady.

"Where's Zayn? Is he with you? In fact, where are the rest of the motherfucking Breakers? I should fucking shoot every last one of you pieces of shit."

"Here, with me now," Xeno replies, not rising to the bait. I can't say the same for Zayn, however. He's currently making very aggressive motions with a knife that he pulled from his leather boot a second ago. My eyes pop open in shock at the way he plays with the blade, flipping it from hand to hand and rolling it through his fingers like some kind of expert knife-thrower you might find at the fucking circus. I look from Zayn back to Dax.

"*What the fuck?*" I mouth. He just shakes his head and gives me an intense look.

"You're on loudspeaker, Boss. We're just driving back to the Academy. What's up?"

"*What's up?*" Jeb shouts. "What's motherfucking up is that I've spent the best part of this weekend holed up with that fucking bitch Grim and her sidekick Beast. The fuckers' said they had business to discuss after Friday night's fuck up and then spent most of the time I was with them interrogating every member of that two-bit crew. I mean I'm partial to a bit of torture, and I appreciated the pussy and the cocaine, but what I wanted was more fucking information and she was sorely lacking in that department."

Pussy? Yeah, right. I roll my eyes, the man's fucking delusional. Again, why the fuck doesn't he come out already. Who gives a fuck?

"Yeah? So, they didn't talk at all?" Xeno asks, humouring him and completely ignoring his complaint.

"Turns out the cunts were nothing more than a bunch of roadmen playing gangsters. Squealed like pigs before Beast cut their balls off and shoved them down their motherfucking throats. Remind me never to do that. The fucking blood..."

My mouth drops open in shock when I realise Jeb isn't talking metaphorically. Beast really is a beast and a force to be reckoned with. Knowing he's on our side makes me feel a hell of a lot better about things even if the thought of him cutting off a man's balls makes my stomach lurch.

"So, they *did* talk?" Xeno persists.

"Only to confirm that they're nobodies, and Malik paid them a tidy sum to bring his man in. Otherwise, nothing of importance. I only fucking agreed to humour Grim and stay at their hotel in Mayfair because I thought she might have some more information for *me*. Fucking wasted weekend."

"Grim certainly was pissed someone went after her property," Xeno says without an ounce of emotion in his voice. It doesn't take a genius to work out that *I'm* the property he's referring to. He gives me a brief, apologetic look in the rearview mirror that I accept with a terse nod of my head.

"She's a fucking crazy bitch. The second we get what we need, I'm going to put a bullet in her skull, but not before riddling her fucking boyfriend with holes first. Let her watch that twisted fuck bleed out before she dies."

I suck in a shocked breath, covering my mouth when I realise my mistake. York squeezes my thigh and I catch his sharp gaze. He holds his finger up to his lips, warning me with his eyes to keep quiet. "She sure is a crazy bitch," York agrees, knowing as well as I do that Jeb won't get the chance to take out Beast, let alone Grim. He's an arrogant cock for thinking he could.

"York, you fuck. I'm surprised you haven't tried it on with Grim yourself. You like your bitches a little unhinged, ain't that right?"

I keep my gaze fixed on York and catch the slight tick of annoyance in his jaw before he covers it up with a laugh. "Yeah, you got me there, Boss."

"Did you get *anything* worthwhile from Grim?" Xeno asks, steering the conversation back to less personal ground. Next to him Zayn's currently balancing the knife blade on the pad of his forefinger. I watch entranced, silently praying he doesn't suddenly drop it and impale the blade into his thigh. It seems to calm him, playing with the blade that way. Funny, when we were kids, *dance* did that. It used to be the only thing to calm him down after an altercation with Jeb. Looks like knife handling has the same effect these days. I'm not sure I like it.

"What do you think? She's a shrewd bitch and plays her cards close to her chest. Though she did tell me that The Belladonnas are going to make a move on The Cobras' turf up north. Looks like those bitches are getting a little too big for their boots."

"Best to stay out of it," Xeno advises.

"Yeah, let them take each other out then I can step in. Nothing like a good, clean takeover," Jeb says with a chuckle, and I'm reminded of how he swept in and claimed the Hackney's Hackers crew after the King was murdered. Figures, he's the type of guy to let other people do the dirty work before claiming leadership. Dickhead.

"Sounds like a solid plan," Zayn says, suddenly flipping his knife and catching it by the handle.

"Ah, I wondered when *you'd* speak up. Did all that pussy tire out your tongue," Jeb asks, the sneer in his voice making me vibrate with anger. How fucking dare he speak to Zayn like that!? York squeezes my thigh and my mouth slams shut.

"I think we deserved the entertainment, don't you? Pretty sure me and the boys took most of Malik's men out whilst you disappeared to clean his brains off your clothes..." Zayn retorts, the insinuation clear, Jeb's a fucking piece of shit coward.

Clearing his throat and not cursing Zayn out like I expect him to do, Jeb simply changes the subject. "What the fuck happened to Penelope anyway? That little slut is way too close with Grim for my liking."

"I knocked her out with anaesthesia and dumped her back at the Academy just like Grim asked me to do. She probably woke up with one hell of a headache and is most likely scared shitless. I'll let Grim deal with the aftermath. Though I sure had fun playing with her," Xeno says, all blasé and heartless sounding like he really doesn't give a fuck. If I didn't know any better, I'd assume he hated me still.

"Yeah, nice touch dancing with her like that. You're a sick fuck," Jeb chuckles and I want to throw up.

"She got what she deserved." Xeno glances at me once again, and I swallow hard at the fear in his eyes. I know he's playing a part, I *know* that, but it doesn't make it any easier to hear. Being together again is so new and given what we've been through it would be easy to fall back into all the mistrust if we allowed ourselves to. Breathing in deeply, I give Xeno a small smile.

"Penelope's fucking lucky I didn't let Malik take her that first time. Zayn was right, she's way too valuable to me as Grim's new toy. Grim looks out for her own and given she likes the little whore it works as a nice bit of leverage for later, don't you think? Besides, you stepping in like that at the last minute secured our newly formed relationship nicely. It was a win-win." Jeb laughs raucously like he's some villain from a fucking Marvel movie. A sudden anger rushes beneath my skin. He's such a fucking prick.

"Yeah, it worked out perfectly. Though we gotta tread carefully with Grim. I'm surprised she let Xeno get up on that stage," Zayn adds.

"Don't I fucking know it. She drove a hard fucking bargain when it came to that little whore but the fact she let Xeno do the job tells me she's more trusting than I gave her credit for, and that is just fucking *perfect*. She's playing right into our hands..." His voice trails off as he quietens for a moment.

"What?" Xeno asks, and I can hear the tension in his voice. I can feel it. It's as though all the Breakers are taking a collective breath. The car swerves suddenly and Xeno narrowly misses a cyclist. He palms the horn, and curses loudly.

"What the fuck are you doing?" Jeb snaps, his patience wearing thin.

"Cyclist," Xeno bites out.

"Anyway, I was thinking. Maybe it's time you all start acting like you're interested in the little slut again. Grim needs convincing of our loyalty and what better way than to use Penelope to do just that? Perhaps she'll come in useful after all."

I tense in Dax's arms, and in response he just pulls me closer and presses a kiss on top of my head whilst York strokes my thigh reassuringly.

"If you think it would work, I'm game," Xeno replies tightly.

"So long as you boys remember our code."

"Skins before whores," the four say in unison and I cringe, hating every damn word.

"That's it boys, Skins before whores."

"What did you make of the show, Jeb?" Zayn asks casually, moving the conversation on.

Jeb scoffs. "Really who the fuck cares? Tales is successful because of the *fighting*. A bunch of whores prancing around ain't befitting of such an establishment. Not that I give a shit what Grim chooses to do with the club right now because as soon as it's mine, I will own every member of staff, including Penelope *pretty-girl* Scott, and she will be doing way more than dancing to earn her fucking keep."

A sudden dread slides down my spine, and despite the fact Dax's arm is wrapped around me in that protective way of his, I still can't help but be fearful. Dax lowers his mouth to my ear. "Don't. We got this. He will never own you. I'll kill him first. Okay?" he whispers.

I nod, telling him that I believe him, but that doesn't stop the sick feeling in my stomach when all I keep hearing is the four of them saying 'Skins before whores' in my head over and over again.

"Well, I've got to fucking go. I want a catch-up meeting at Rocks before our first shipment is due to go over the finer details. Make sure D-Neath comes along. It might be fun if you bring Penelope along with you. She could entertain the club with her *dancing* whilst we talk business. She owes me a show, perhaps we could loan her for the night. Know what I'm saying?" Jeb suggests, laughing cruelly. He really is a spiteful bastard.

"Grim ain't gonna go for that. Besides, she's working every weekend at Tales now. Best not piss Grim off by stealing her prized possession," Zayn reminds him.

"Yeah, point taken. Maybe you're good for more than just a knife fight," Jeb says, taking every chance he can to belittle Zayn. My fingers curl into the seat as I try to dampen my anger. How the fuck any of them, especially Zayn, have kept his cool with the prick I'll never know. York rests his hand over mine and squeezes it gently. I relax a little, his touch calming me.

"Now fuck-off and get on with your tasks. Santiago is pushing for the first shipment to be sent over in a few weeks and I need you to make sure D-Neath has everything in place ready for it."

"You got it," Xeno responds.

The line goes dead, and Xeno lets out a long breath then curses Jeb all the way back to the Academy.

11

Pen

"THANK YOU FOR COMING, Pen. Please, take a seat," Madame Tuillard says, pointing at the chair when I enter her office the following morning. She clasps her hands on the desk in front of her and presses her mouth into a hard line. "I understand that you're aware of what's going on."

"Yes."

She nods tightly, staring at me for a moment as though trying to decide what's appropriate to say next. I don't envy her position and, honestly, I'm surprised she agreed to the drugs being delivered here at all. Then again, who am I to judge? We all do crazy things for the ones we love.

"I started this Academy because I love dance. It's my passion. It's what drives me. Like most of the students here, dance is my way to escape, to express myself. I was lucky enough to have a fulfilling career."

"Why are you telling me this?"

"Because when I see dancers as talented as you, I'm *excited*. There's something very special about you, Pen. Your audition was the best I've ever seen in all my time here. I see a bright future for you..." Her voice trails off and she sighs heavily.

"There's a but though, right?"

"I fell in love with Duncan before he went to prison. I met him at a nightclub that I'd snuck out to with my best friend. He was the cool kid, dangerous. I was the prim, middle class girl who was wrapped up in cotton wool by her parents and kept on a tight leash. Our attraction was immediate and explosive," she says almost wistfully.

"...Okay," I say, feeling more than a little awkward.

"Duncan said that you were friends with the Breakers as kids. Is that right?"

"We grew up together," I confirm, wondering where this conversation is taking us.

"You must have a very tight bond. Though, admittedly, that only seems apparent of late."

"We've had some issues to work through."

"I can understand that. When Duncan went to prison, I vowed to myself that I would never let another man hurt me the way he did."

"Hurt you?"

"*Emotionally*. He broke my heart. It's not a story I wish to get into, but I'm not stupid or blind, Pen. I see how you are with them. They hurt you too, didn't they?"

"Don't presume to know our relationship," I retort, feeling prickly.

She smiles softly. "I wouldn't dare. I guess what I'm saying is I *understand* the position you're in. When Duncan came out of prison and turned up on my doorstep, cap in hand, everything came flooding back. All those old emotions of love and lust that I'd felt for him before suddenly came hurtling back. I fought against them. God knows I tried. I didn't want to love him still..."

"You regret taking him back?"

Madame Tuillard shakes her head. "No, I don't regret it, but I'll never quite let him in the way I did before. Six months into our newly formed relationship, Duncan told me about this plan. He asked to use the Academy as a place for the shipment of drugs to be delivered to. Honestly, I felt used. It wasn't a good moment."

"But you're still with him...?"

"Ultimately, I chose to trust in *us*," she says with a rueful smile and a shrug of her shoulders.

"Was it the right decision? Trusting him, I mean."

"I guess only time will tell, but I want you to know that my focus *is* on the pupils at this academy first and foremost, even if that might not seem that way right now. I haven't made this decision lightly and honestly, Pen, I feel sick knowing that those drugs will pass through these doors, but I *trust* Duncan. He's made some poor choices in his life that I know he regrets. This is him trying to set things straight. To make amends. I have to believe in that, believe in him."

I nod, not answering because I'm not so sure about D-Neath. Granted, we've barely spoken more than a few words to each other, but there's a vibe about him that makes me wary. I don't know. Xeno said that he's proved himself loyal, but I'm reserving judgement for now.

"I don't mean to be rude, Madame Tuillard, and I apologise if I come across that way, but is there a point to this conversation?" I ask, feeling more and more uncomfortable as the minutes pass. I just want to get back to lessons. It's been hard enough getting my head around all this shit, and I respect Madame Tuillard for what she's done in her life, but I just want to get back to some form of normalcy, if only for a little while. She's the principal of this school, not my friend.

"I always love it when someone starts off a sentence that way, because we all know it's a prelude to being just that, rude." She grins then, leaning her elbows on the table and resting her chin on her crossed fingers. "That fight you have will put you in good stead for the challenges you're going to face in the future, both within a career in dance and in your personal life. I guess I just wanted you to know that we're in this together. That I *see* you, and I appreciate what you're going through right now. You're gifted, Pen. I would hate for your future to be ruined because you've been caught up in this. Just know when it's time to walk away, okay? That's my advice, for what it's worth."

Ah, there it is. A life lesson wrapped up in a compliment. For some reason that gets my hackles up. Funny how I can take advice from Grim, but not Madame Tuillard. I'm sure that says more about me than the woman sitting before me. "That's never going to happen."

"Just think—"

"Look," I say, holding my hand up and cutting her off. "I don't like what's happening any more than you do. I *hate* it. Do I wish that the Breakers weren't involved? Absolutely. But they *are* and that means so am I. I will never walk away from them. I did that once before and it almost destroyed me. I won't do it again. In fact, I want to be paired back up with Dax. River is a beautiful dancer and a great friend, but he and I just don't fit. I know that Dax can't stand Tiffany despite her efforts to fuck him..."

"He dropped you for her," she points out, hiding a smile at my jealous outburst.

"There was a reason for that. One we've fixed."

"I see," she nods, then focuses back on her computer screen, clicking a few buttons on her keyboard while I wait for her to mull over my request. "Well, I didn't agree to Dax's new partnership anyway. Duncan made that decision based on the troubles between you, not on what was right for the performance. Now that the issues are fixed, I see no reason why you shouldn't be dancing together. I shall break the news to Tiffany. I know you two don't get along and frankly it will sound better coming from me."

I nod. "I appreciate that..."

"You're welcome."

Madame Tuillard keeps her gaze fixed on the computer screen, content it would seem to allow the silence to stretch out between us. I sigh heavily. "I apologise if I've come across as a bitch. You've given me a huge opportunity accepting me here on a scholarship. I'm beyond grateful for that, you've no idea just how much." I say. "Dance is my passion too. It's what drives me, but those men...? They're my heart. I won't turn my back on them."

When she doesn't respond, and with nothing left to discuss, I get up and head to the door. As my fingers curl around the door handle, Madame Tuillard clears her throat.

"Pen—"

I turn to face her. "Yes?"

"The production company who will be filming the final show is visiting in a week's time. They want to film an advert for the end of year show. It will be aired a couple of months before the live televised event. Sebastian and Sasha will be coming up with a routine. I was going to ask Xeno, but he's already got enough on his plate. I had hoped to bring in an external choreographer, but Luka refused point blank."

"*Luka Petrin*, the ballet dancer?"

"Yes. We're old friends and he owes me a favor. This one was just too big for him to agree to," she says, refusing to elaborate further. I don't ask, it's not my business, but given he disappeared off the face of the Earth after his wife's death it's not hard to guess why he's not helping out.

"Wait, we haven't even learned the routine yet for this advert. Shouldn't we get started on rehearsals for it if they're coming next week?" I ask, wondering how the hell I'll fit it all in with the rehearsals we're already doing for the end of year show, dance classes, and working at Tales. Not to mention all the other *stuff*.

"Oh, no. The advert won't be filmed until after the Christmas break. The production team is coming in to record *you* dancing solo."

"Me?" I ask, pointing a finger at my chest.

"They wanted to put together some social media marketing for the end of year show and asked me to choose my favourite dancer to feature in this teaser. I'd like that dancer to be you."

"Me?" I repeat, sounding like a broken record.

Madame Tuillard levels her gaze on me. "Yes, *you*. That's one of the reasons I asked you here today. Pen, you encompass everything I'm trying to achieve here at the Academy."

"I do?"

"Why is that so hard to believe? Surely you're aware of just how much of an incredible dancer you are?" She cocks her head at me and frowns.

"Let's just say I've never really had the support I needed from those closest to me and leave it at that."

Madame Tuillard nods. "Use that. Use that disappointment and show whoever hurt you that despite it, *because* of it, you're the incredible dancer you are today. The track you will be dancing to is *Bird Set Free* by Sia. Have the routine ready for filming a week from today."

"You want me to choreograph it?"

"Like I said before, you're talented, Pen. I trust you to get this right."

"I've got a week?" I ask, my mind immediately going into choreographer mode.

"One week." Madame Tuillard nods. "I look forward to seeing what you come up with." And with that, I'm dismissed.

12

Pen

"YOU'RE GOING to smash it, Titch. Don't stress," York says later that day as he watches me go over a trickier part of the routine I've put together for the social media teasers. He's sitting crossed legged on the studio floor, tapping out a beat with his fingers whilst watching me sweat my arse off. "You got this." His attention is focused on me as I stumble over a portion of the routine I haven't quite got down yet. Beyond the studio, students move about the Academy completely unaware of my growing frustration.

"Easy for you to say, *Mr. Tap Genius*," I reply, swiping my forehead free of sweat. "You shit out tap routines without so much as breaking a sweat."

"Shit out? Fucking gross, I'm not sure I like that analogy," he replies, crinkling up his nose.

"You know what I mean."

He grins up at me, his appreciative gaze roving over my sweaty body. I'm wearing my usual dance gear of leggings, a crop top, and a loose t-shirt that's currently hanging off one shoulder, but despite being a sweaty mess he appears to find me a turn on. He doesn't look half bad himself in loose cargo trousers, high top trainers, a muscle shirt, and his hair a tousled, sexy mess. *Totally distracting.* I really need to focus.

"I can't help it that I'm this decade's version of Fred Astaire. What can I say? I'm blessed with talent and good looks. You're a lucky lady, Titch." Mischief lights his eyes as he smirks.

"Bigheaded much?" Zayn jokes as he steps into the studio with us and chucks his hoodie at York's head. "Hey, Pen."

"Hey," I reply, drinking him in. A slow, sexy smile pulls up his lips.

"Just telling the truth, man," York replies, pulling on Zayn's hoodie over his top.

"What the fuck are you doing?" Zayn asks, shaking his head.

"It's fucking mine now."

"Take it off, shithead."

"Nope." York zips the hoodie up and smirks.

Zayn rolls his eyes. "Fuck sake. You owe me a shit ton of clothes already."

"Stop grumbling. Either sit down, zip it, and watch Titch dance, or sod off. She's busy and doesn't need you distracting her."

I'm about to tell York that he's already distracting me, so one more person won't make a difference when Zayn cuts in.

"Listen, York, Xeno is fucking bossy enough, no need to take position as second in command," Zayn says, striding over to me and pulling me into a hug.

"What're you doing here?" I ask, accepting Zayn's hug and

laughing as he grabs a handful of my arse. The routine isn't exactly going to plan so I may as well enjoy this brief interlude.

"Getting my fix before the other tossers do. I've missed you," he says, jerking his head as Dax and Xeno enter the studio half a beat later.

"It's literally been twenty-four hours since we saw each other last," I reply, laughing.

"Twenty-four motherfucking long, *agonising* hours you mean?"

Zayn plants a kiss on my lips before Dax steps up and shoves him playfully aside. "Hands off, dickhead. My turn," Dax says, wrapping me up in his huge arms. I breathe him in, joy bubbling up my throat as laughter parts my lips like champagne bubbles. Zayn flips him off, then winks at me to let me know he's not offended by Dax's behaviour.

"What's this, some kind of intervention?" I ask when he finally puts me back on the floor. I flick my gaze from Dax to Xeno who shuts the studio door behind him, locking it. I raise my brows at that but don't say a word. I'm guessing he wants privacy.

Hmm, I could be down with that.

"Something along those lines," Xeno replies, undressing me with his eyes, just like I'm doing to my Breakers. All four are dressed in their version of dance gear, which is essentially sweatpants that sit low on their hips and loose tanks that show off their ridiculous muscles and stunning tattoos. They really are beautiful men, and as Dax and Zayn sit down on the studio floor either side of York, I feel my cheeks flush at the sudden energy in the room. It's both lighthearted *and* filled with an abundance of sexual tension. In other words, I'm screwed.

"Madame Tuillard told me you've got a routine to put together for the film crew coming next week, I figured you could use our assistance in getting it perfect," Xeno says, cocking his head to the side as he regards me, his flop of dark curly hair falling into his eyes.

"You don't think I'm capable of putting something together myself?" I ask haughtily, planting a hand on my hip and flicking my gaze to York who's grinning from ear to ear and watching us with amusement. He knows I'm playing.

"That is *not* what I said."

"I'm pretty sure I'm capable of putting together a great routine, thanks very much. Is this because you're a teacher now? Should I bow down to your greatness like all the other girls do?" I feign annoyance, when really, I'm just messing with him. It's been a while since we've had this kind of banter, any kind of banter for that matter, and I'm enjoying myself way too much to stop now.

"It *is* kinda what you said..." York points out, and I see the amusement glinting in his eyes.

"I fucking never," Xeno says, throwing him a scathing look.

"I mean, you can be a real fucking know-it-all bitch in rehearsals," Zayn adds, his face deadpan as he catches on and adds fuel to the fire.

"Me, a *bitch*? I am not a bitch." Xeno scowls, looking between us in that domineering way of his.

"What, too manly to be a bitch, is that it?" Dax adds, his brows raised.

I see the amusement in their eyes, and I try to hold my laughter inside and keep a serious face, but when York bursts out laughing, I can't help but follow. Zayn and Dax start laughing too. Xeno flips them the finger.

"Fuck the lot of you," he says, but I see the laughter in his eyes and grin, warmth spreading through my veins. Striding over to me, he draws me into his arms, that warmth flaring into delicious heat.

"So, you're here to *help* me, huh?" I ask, cocking a brow, both of us aware of his growing erection pressing into my belly. He chuckles, dropping his gaze to my mouth, a slow smile pulling up his lips.

"As a matter of fact, York texted us and said you were looking *finnneeee—*"

"Actually, I think my words were: Titch is ripping up the dance floor and I swear to fuck I'm about to come in my pants," York interrupts.

"I can't believe you just admitted that," Zayn says, shaking his head. "Do you have no shame?"

York shoves his shoulder. "I'm not ashamed of the fact that our girl turns me the fuck on." York looks at me, his eyes smouldering. I swallow hard.

"You also said that if we didn't get here quick, you'd be taking matters into your own hands and helping Kid to release some of the tension she was feeling," Dax adds with a challenge in his gaze.

Xeno grins devilishly. "That's right, so you can blame York for our sudden appearance, Tiny. I was *trying* to cover up the fact that we're all thirsty fucks and need a fix of our girl."

"Is that so?" I glance over at York who shrugs, running a hand through his tousled hair.

"What can I say. I'm too thoughtful for my own good. I could've kept you all to myself, but I didn't. Count yourselves lucky lads."

Dax rolls his eyes and Zayn shakes his head. "Stop trying to get brownie points."

"Is that why you locked the door?" I bite my bottom lip teasingly and Xeno groans, dropping his forehead to mine as his fingers curl into my hips.

"It's the middle of the day and there are way too many people about for us to take advantage of you right now."

"You wouldn't be taking advantage when I want it, want you all," I whisper against his lips.

He draws back, then slaps my arse lightly. "Focus! We are *not* here to fuck, Tiny. We're here to watch you dance."

"You're such a fucking spoilsport, Xeno," Dax grumbles.

"Fucking bitch, more like," Zayn adds with a grin.

"If you're not going to play, sit the fuck down, Xeno. I'm getting a fucking hard on watching you two together," York gripes, adjusting himself.

Xeno grins, happiness that I haven't witnessed for some time lighting up his green eyes. Today, the shards within them don't seem so sharp. "Let's see what you've got, Tiny."

"Okay, fine," I pout, pulling a face.

"None of that or I might just change my mind and fuck you against that wall whilst the boys here watch."

"Fuck yeah," York exclaims, earning him a dig in the ribs from Dax.

Heat rushes through me at the thought, but when Xeno stalks away, sitting down on the floor next to Dax, I decide now's not the time to get hot and bothered with any of the Breakers. I'm no prude, but the hallway is heaving with pupils moving between classes and even though the door might be locked, I'm not about to give anyone a show, even if it's an auditory one. I'm more than happy to be intimate with any one of my Breakers whilst the rest watch, but strangers? Not so much.

"Ignore these fuckers, Kid, and bench those thoughts for later. We want to see you dance," Dax says.

"Okay, it's still pretty rough, but I'd appreciate your thoughts."

Taking a deep breath, I stride over to the sound system, press play, then take up my position in the centre of the studio. As the piano intro begins, I draw in a deep lungful of breath and allow my eyes to rove over each of my Breakers in turn.

Then I dance.

※

"WHAT DO YOU THINK?" I ask, my chest heaving as I remove my t-shirt and swipe at the sweat beading on my forehead.

"Pen, that was... Jesus, fuck!" Zayn exclaims, shaking his head in disbelief.

"What this donut meant is that Madame Tuillard was right to choose you. Titch, you blow our motherfucking minds. Dax, you okay, mate?" York claps Dax on the back, gripping his shoulder.

"What York said," Dax mumbles, and I can't help but laugh.

"Oh, thank God. I was a little worried it was too simple. The song just kinda led me on this one," I say, running the t-shirt over the slick skin of my stomach. My sports crop top is drenched with sweat too, and without looking down I know my nipples are erect and are pushing against the material, given the way Xeno's gaze keeps flicking from my face to my breasts. I can't help it; my body reacts when I dance. Not only does dancing soothe me, keeping me sane when I need to work through my emotions, but at times like this, dancing lights me up. It turns me on, and when my four boyfriends are watching... Well, you get the picture.

"It was fucking perfect, Tiny. Just like you," Xeno says as he climbs to his feet and removes his top, baring his chest to me.

"What are you doing...?" I ask, allowing my gaze to trail over his beautiful body. Even the guys look surprised. Well, Dax and Zayn do. York just looks like the cat that's got the cream.

"Hell to the fuck, yes!" he exclaims, jumping up to remove his top too.

"What's going on?" I ask, bewildered. "Are you... Are we...?"

"...About to fuck," Xeno says, finishing my sentence for me. We lock gazes and I nod.

His grin widens as he brushes past me, his fingers grazing over my skin. "Stay right there, Tiny. I think you'll enjoy this," he says, as he strides towards the sound system and swaps out my mobile phone for his own.

"Enjoy *what* exactly?"

"Come on lads, it's been a while since we've danced to this track," York says, giving Dax and Zayn a look that I can't quite interpret. "The last time we did, Titch nearly had a heart attack, though she would never have admitted it at the time. I'm pretty sure that was the moment when she fell in love with our sorry arses."

"Ohhh! I see where this is going." Dax smirks, climbing to his feet, giving Zayn a look that has my insides turning to mush and my lady parts begging for attention.

"Fuck, yes!" Zayn jumps up and rips his top off. When Dax follows suit my cheeks flush an even deeper pink.

"Oh, shit..." I exclaim, the penny finally dropping as the track begins to play. I recognise the song instantly and my cheeks flush a furious red. I know exactly where they're going with this. The memory of that night when we were kids instantly returns and I grow hot, feeling embarrassed for the girl I was. Second to the 'tickle my pickle' conversation, that night was cringeworthy not because of what the guys did, but because I had no idea how to handle the way they'd made me feel. We'd been drinking in the basement of Jackson Street, and *Take Your Shirt Off* by T-Pain had come on. The guys had danced for me, teased me with their dance skills and their hot bodies until my knickers had become wet and my skin as heated as it is now. They'd been oblivious to my reaction to them at the time. Not anymore.

"Sit," Xeno demands, placing a chair behind me. He steps in front of me, close enough so that the backs of my legs hit the seat. Pressing his mouth against my ear he says, "That night, when we danced for you, I *knew* how turned on you were. I wanted you then, Tiny. So fucking much."

Then he rests his hand against my shoulder and pushes me into the seat before dropping into a crouch before me, placing his hands on my knees. "We're all grown up now. No need to hide how we feel, right?"

"Right," I reply, biting my lip as he slides my legs open on the next beat, rises upwards and curls his fingers around the chair back, then gives me a motherfucking lap dance.

Instantly, my skin prickles with desire and my clit throbs as he slowly undulates his body before me in a sexy-as-fuck body roll. I watch with parted lips as his muscles ripple beneath his taut, smooth skin and I automatically raise my hand to his chest, wanting to touch him.

"No touching, Tiny. You know the rules," he whispers, echoing the words he'd said to me as a kid. He'd teased me then, and he's doing the same now. Fucker.

When I drag my gaze away from his crotch and up to his

smiling face, I can't help but lick my lips. He grins, dips down and quickly kisses me before stepping back and striding away. He high-fives Dax who is currently busting out moves alongside York and Zayn, the three of them grinning.

Jesus, I'm so fucking happy I could burst.

Dax strides towards me, his grey-green eyes ablaze with love and laughter. He stops a few feet away, turns his back to me, and I hold my breath because I remember this damn move. As a kid I literally forgot how to breathe. My reaction is no different now. With one final look over his shoulder, Dax winks then drops to one knee before flipping over into a backward roll, his legs wide before he straddles my legs, his arse grinding over my lap, the muscles in his arm and back flexing as he dances.

York whistles in encouragement, and Dax stands, turning to face me. "Hey, Kid," he says, his voice low, deep. A sexy smile plays about his lips as he straddles my lap once more, his thick arms on either side of my head, his hands grasping the back of the chair as he gyrates his hips. Automatically, my hands press against his thighs, and unlike Xeno, he doesn't tell me to stop. "This is harder for me, than it is for you."

I laugh, because I can see just how *hard* it is as I glance at his cock that is thick and erect beneath his joggers. "Fuck," I whisper out, my whole body on fire with lust.

Dax winks then leans back, dropping both hands to the floor before raising his right leg, his foot gently brushing against the back of my head as he grinds his hips.

Zayn hollers and I let out another laugh. This is really fucking happening.

Kicking his leg over, Dax twists away from me and stands, then strides towards York, bopping fists with him. York meets my gaze, and I don't need to look at his crotch to know he's as turned on as I am. Like Xeno and Dax, he straddles me, standing this time, then as the music flicks onto a slower more sensual track by some unknown singer, York grabs the back of my chair and lowers me to the ground so that I'm lying on the floor beneath him.

"This is new," I whisper, my clit throbbing at the pure sexiness of the dance, and my virile Breakers. He winks.

"I spent a lot of time replaying that night. You were too young, too innocent, but you're not that girl anymore. You're a woman, and this is fair game after that torture you just put us through," he says, then steps away out of my line of sight. When he returns, he's sliding across the floor on parted knees stopping only when his crotch is directly above my head. From where I'm lying, I have a perfect view of his sweat pant-covered crotch and the erection he's sporting. With his hands clasping the chair legs, he pulls the chair towards him so that my head and shoulders slide beneath his parted legs. My heart thumps loudly in my chest and I bite on my lip at view. York undulates his body, and I can't help but let out an appreciative moan. Leaning over, York grasps my hips and lifts me up so that my thighs are over his shoulder and my crotch is pressed up against his face in an upside-down reverse cowgirl style move, the chair abandoned on the floor. My arms automatically wrap around his waist, my head dangling between his legs.

Fuck. Me.

On the next beat, he adjusts me in his arms, lifting me up so my stomach is pressed against his shoulder. I can't help myself, I press a hot kiss against his abdomen, savouring the taste of his skin. His muscles contract beneath my lips and he swears under his breath. I giggle.

"Oh, Titch, now you're really gonna get it," he warns, and my clit throbs in excitement at his guttural words.

With my heart pounding loudly in my ears, York lifts me from his shoulders and places me on my feet. Standing before me, he leans in and kisses me, his tongue sweeping into my mouth hungrily before he steps away leaving me panting as Zayn approaches, a wicked glint in his eyes. Grasping the back of my head with one hand, Zayn grins before crushing his lips against mine and lowering me to the floor. One minute we're kissing, the next he's gone.

Around me Xeno, York and Dax are grooving to the beat, as they fix the heat of their gazes on me, successfully distracting me until Zayn kneels between my parted legs facing away from me. I watch in curiosity as he wraps his legs beneath my raised ones.

"What the....?" I begin, but the question is snatched from my lips as he leans forward onto his hands, tightens his legs around mine, and flips me over onto my stomach. All the air whooshes out of my lungs, and before the laughter can even escape my lips, Zayn is above me once more, straddling my arse and fisting my hair. I let out a surprised laugh that's swallowed quickly by a moan, as he pulls my head back and runs his teeth against my exposed neck.

"You're killing me," I whisper, crazy with lust and full of laughter.

"Now you know how we feel every time you dance, Pen," Zayn replies, letting my hair go, then jumping to his feet and grasping me under the arms, pulling me up with him. When he presses his chest against my back and places his hand between my breasts, I let out a shuddering breath. "See how your heart races, how your pulse dances, your skin flushes and your clit throbs..."

"Yes," I pant, barely able to stand up straight, I'm so turned on.

"This is what you do to us, every fucking minute of every day. I walk around with a hard dick twenty-four seven. But when you dance like you just did, Pen. Well, fuck me..." Zayn lowers his lips to my neck and sucks. My skin tingles as my gaze fixes on the flaming darkness of Xeno's gaze, then flicks to Dax and finally York. Their expressions are ones of lust and love and I swear my knees get even weaker.

"You're gonna want to file this one away in your spank bank, Titch. I know I will," York says with a wink just as the door to the studio flies open and Sebastian walks in, keys in hand.

He takes one look at me and grins. "Rehearsing, are we?"

"Yep, rehearsing," I squeak, unable to hide my flaming cheeks as Zayn steps away from me, sporting a semi, and Dax, Xeno and York grab their shirts, pulling them back on.

"Well, find another studio to rehearse in. I've got a lesson to teach," Sebastian replies, striding over to the front of the studio, hiding a smirk the whole way.

I puff out a breath and almost die of embarrassment as Dax flings his arm over my shoulders and guides me from the room, the rest of the Breakers following behind.

13

Pen

"PEN SCOTT, YOU SNEAKY BITCH!" Clancy grins, pulling me into a hug later that week. It's Friday already and we've literally been in a whirlwind of classes and rehearsals. I've barely had time to think, let alone spend any quality time with her or any of my boys since they gave me the best fucking lap dance of my life at the beginning of the week. I've been permanently turned on since that moment, with no relief. We've all been so caught up.

"Hey, girl." I grin, wrapping her in a hug and feeling immediately guilty that we haven't been able to catch up. Both of us have been too exhausted at the end of the day to do much more than send each other a couple of texts and pass out in our separate rooms before starting all over again the next day.

"You didn't tell me that you and Dax were duetting again.

Tiffany is fucking fuming! I would have laughed if it wasn't for River. He's a bit put out."

"Ah, fuck. I was going to tell him the news myself..."

"Tiffany got there first," River says as he enters the studio, dumping his bag on the bench. He gives me a hurt look, and I immediately feel like the worst human on the planet.

"I'm so sorry, River. Dax and I... Well, we kinda sorted out our differences... I didn't get a chance to tell you with everything going on. I've been mad busy."

River sighs, folding his arms across his chest. "Yeah, I get it. Dax and you fit. I'd be lying if I said otherwise." He cocks his head, then smiles. "Clancy told me about you being chosen by Tuillard to dance for the social media teasers. That's fucking awesome!"

"Thank you! It's why I haven't had a chance to speak with you properly. I've been practicing every spare chance I get. I think I've got the routine down now. I hope so anyway, given they're filming Monday. I really am sorry."

"I get it. Honestly, I'm cool, Pen."

"You sure?" I pull a face, knowing he hates Tiffany as much as the rest of us do.

"I'm man enough to know we weren't right dancing together, but fuck am I pissed to be paired up with Tiffany again. Jesus Christ, she's a fucking nightmare." He scrapes a hand through his hair, then jerks his chin. "Speak of the devil..."

Behind us Tiffany storms into the studio, her face red with anger. She strides over to me and shoves her bony fingers against my shoulder. "You. Fucking. Bitch!" she snarls with every jab, her beautiful face getting more and more twisted up. I laugh, I can't help it. When the shoes on the other foot and all that... I look from her finger still digging into my skin and slowly drag my gaze up her arm to her face.

"You might want to take your hand off me," I warn her.

"Or what? You going to hit me, *street rat?*"

I smile leisurely. "That's exactly what I'm going to do. So, unless you want your pretty little nose broken, I suggest you back the fuck up." Frankly, I'm done with the bitch. She's meddled in my business way too much and given what I know, I'm not sure her threat of me getting kicked out of Stardom for punching her is gonna wash anymore.

Tiffany laughs as though she has the upper hand then has the audacity to get in my face. "I'm going to see to it that you get thrown out of here on your arse," she warns, and I can't help it, I tip my head back and roar with laughter.

"Yeah, not gonna happen," I reply, slapping Tiffany's hand away and stepping back. I could punch her in the face and get some satisfaction out of it, but honestly, I'm so bored of the bullshit. I can be the bigger person, I suppose. "Listen, you're pissed off, I get it. Dax is an amazing dancer, but you and him just don't gel."

"You don't know anything," she retorts.

"Tiffany, just give up. You're starting to act like a fucking stalker. Just face it, you don't have what Pen has. None of them are interested in you. Stop acting like a slut and start appreciating what you have. River is a *phenomenal* dancer," Clancy says, giving River a gentle smile which he returns with a wink.

"Don't tell me what to do," she hisses.

"Tiffany, just deal with it. I am," River says, sighing heavily. "I don't want to fucking dance with you either, but here we are, so suck it the fuck up. We've got a great routine, and if you put half as much effort into learning it as you do chasing after something you can't have, then Madame Tuillard might even consider our duet for the show."

"Shut up, you dick. Just because you're shag—"

Tiffany's tirade is interrupted by Xeno and the rest of the Breakers as they step into the studio, their gazes immediately resting on us. Dax frowns and York eyes widen with glee, the arsehole loves a good bitch fight. Xeno, however, is gritting his jaw and Zayn is glaring at Tiffany, like he wants to knock her out. My heart warms at seeing them despite the tense situation. We haven't all been together since Monday. I've missed hanging out with them.

"Everything alright?" Xeno asks, as they all take a spot in the studio. He strolls to the front of the class, plugging his mobile into the surround sound system.

"It's fine," Tiffany snaps, glaring at me whilst simultaneously trying to smile at Xeno. Her face is all twisted up in her effort to cover up her nasty attitude.

"It better be." He gives her a scathing look, one which can't be interpreted any other way. She bristles, not used to his change in attitude towards her.

Clancy laughs then squeezes my hand. "Girl, I'm so fucking jelly right now. You need to get yourself beneath that hunk-a-chunk like asap." With that she strolls off to an empty spot in the studio chuckling.

I mean, she's not wrong there... Thing is, I already have.

Tiffany huffs and just as she's about to walk off, I grip her by the elbow and lean in close, whispering in her ear. "And for the record, a man as built as Dax really does have a beautiful *big* dick to match. He certainly knows what to do with it, that's for sure."

Tiffany hisses at me through her teeth, but I just give her a sweet smile then find a spot in the studio and start warming up, at least I would have if Xeno hadn't caught my eye.

"Pen, a word," he says, cocking his head.

"Sure," I say, passing the guys and smiling at each of them in turn, my heart swelling with love. This weekend, I'm staying over at their flat and I can't wait. This whole week we've tried to keep our newly formed relationship on the downlow, which hasn't been all that hard considering how busy we've all been. Xeno has kept me at arm's length in his lessons, Zayn and York have continued to meet me for lunch but have otherwise kept their hands off me and Dax has been busy teaching those kids I met a few weeks back. Apparently, they've asked about me, and I plan on dropping in on a lesson soon to see how they're getting on. Other than that, we've barely had time to catch up and spend time with each other in a more intimate way, let alone discuss important matters.

When I reach the front of the class, I notice Sophie sneak into the studio and rush straight over to Tiffany. Before long they're both glaring at me and talking in whispers. Fuck their petty shit, I really don't give a fuck. I've got what they'll never have, *my Breakers*.

As long as I have them, I can deal with anything.

"What is it?" I ask, lowering my voice. I'm standing next to Xeno, side-eyeing him as he looks at his clipboard. My arm brushes his, and he visibly shudders. Whenever I'm near him there's this kind of electricity that sparks between us. It's the same with all my Breakers. Our connection is so strong, so intense, that it would be impossible for others not to notice.

Flicking on the music, he gives me a serious look that belies the lust billowing in his eyes. *Tip Toe* by Jason Derulo featuring

French Montana starts to play and I cock my brow at his choice of music.

"I've missed you," he whispers, making my heart flip in my chest.

I lean in closer, peering over his arm and touching the sheet of paper, my fingers skating across his. "I've missed you too. So fucking much," I say, internally cursing our situation and the fact that Jeb has needed them for *Skins business* every damn night this past week.

"I'm sending a car to pick you up at eight tonight. We've got a lot to discuss..."

"I've got work at Tales," I say.

Xeno shakes his head. "Grim isn't opening up the club for a while. She's taken the opportunity to give it a facelift. We, however, are invited for a meeting tomorrow night at Tales. Hudson and D-Neath will be there to go over the plan," he explains, his voice low. "I want you there too."

Behind us Zayn is keeping everyone busy running through a series of warm-up steps, allowing us to talk, but I'm well aware of certain jealous bitch's eyes on us and the need to keep our voices low.

"Of course, but I need to stop by and see Lena this afternoon. I was hoping to go after this rehearsal. I want to check if she's okay. We haven't talked for a while, and I haven't been back to the flat since I left home."

"Absolutely, I'll get Dax to drive you. He's not teaching the kids tonight."

"I'd appreciate that."

"Be sure to make your excuses with Clancy, and pack enough for the weekend because you're not going to be available for the next couple days," Xeno says, his eyes darkening with lust.

"Is that so?"

"Yep. You're staying at our flat." His green eyes glitter with all sorts of promises that make my heart flutter and my core tighten.

"She's my best friend, and she's far from stupid. I'm not sure how long I'm going to be able to keep things from her," I whisper under my breath.

"What does she know?" he asks me, pointing at the clipboard in his hand to cover up the fact that we're not talking dance.

"She knows that we were once friends..." I chew on my lip. "She's open-minded when it comes to relationships. I trust her."

Xeno frowns, and I know he finds it difficult to comprehend that I have a friend outside of the Breakers. Now that we're back together again, his possessiveness is rearing its head once more. But my friendship with Clancy and River is non-negotiable. They both mean way too much to me to leave behind.

"She's been a good friend?" he asks.

"The best. She's a rare find."

Xeno looks into the mirror, watching her as she dances. York is currently winking at her and she rolls her eyes, laughing at his cheekiness. "I can see that. York likes her, and he's the best judge of character."

"He is," I agree.

"Okay, keep her in the loop about us, but not about the real reason why we're here. She doesn't need to be dragged into this. It's safer that way."

"I had no intention of telling her about any of that."

Xeno nods. "I'll let Dax know the plan and once you've caught up with Lena, he'll bring you home."

"*Home?*"

"Yes, our home. Yours too...If you want it to be one day, that is," he says softly, keeping his face free from emotion but I feel it, nevertheless. God, do I feel it.

"I do."

The electricity crackles between us as we lock eyes and I swear to fuck if someone gave me a lightbulb to hold right now, I wouldn't be surprised if it lit up brighter than Leicester Square on New Year's Eve.

"Good," Xeno says loudly, his voice rising just enough to be heard over the music. "Get back to it. I don't want to have to call you out on this again, Pen. I expect *complete* cooperation. No more slacking. Got it?!"

I have to smother a smirk at his attempt to cover up our conversation with a telling off. "Sure," I respond. "You've got my complete and utter cooperation," I say sweetly, before turning on my heel and joining the rest of the dancers.

The rest of the rehearsal is spent practicing our group dance. Zayn's choreography is shit-hot and despite Madame Tuillard's suggestion of bringing in some external choreographers, that hasn't materialised, so we've continued to practice the epic routine Zayn has put together for us all.

***

"LET ME GET THIS STRAIGHT, you're seeing all *four* of them at once?" Clancy asks, her cherry-red lips widening as she smiles. She's sitting on my bed watching me pack a weekend bag. I've no idea what to take so I've put in a selection of casual and semi-smart outfits. Tales won't be open tomorrow night, but I figure I should make a bit of an effort at least.

"That's about the sum of it, yep," I confirm, my cheeks heating as I pop my wash bag into the holdall.

"Well, fuck me." She squeals, then jumps up, throwing her arms around me. I stumble a little, laughing.

"Stop it, you lunatic."

"I can't help it, you are literally living my best life," she replies letting me go with a wide grin.

"I'm not."

"You bloody well are! Do you know how jealous every woman will be of you."

"I'd rather we keep this between us," I say, frowning.

Raising her pretty eyebrows, Clancy laughs. "Hey, you won't catch me gossiping, but do you really think people won't start noticing? You've already kissed York in front of everyone in tap class. Zayn has made it perfectly clear he's got the hots for you and anyone with a lick of sense can see Dax and Xeno are fucking crazy for you."

"Is it that obvious?"

Clancy shakes her head, her pretty curls bouncy around her face. "Err, yes. It is now. All that I-hate-you-but-I-love-you sexual tension has been replaced with I-loved-you-all-along-and-now-we're-fucking-like-goddamn-rabbits."

"Shit," I say, wincing.

"Girl, just fucking embrace it. You've got a harem of your very own. I'm so jealous I could puke!"

"A harem?"

"A *reverse harem* to be precise. Come on, tell me you've heard of the phrase..." Clancy screws up her nose at my blank look, then bursts out laughing. "Jesus, you need to get educated. Here you are living the dream and you've no idea. I've got some incredible romance books you could borrow if you want?"

"There are romance books about harems?"

"*Reverse harem*," she corrects me, and I pull a face. "Oh, Jesus. You really have been living under a rock. Remind me when you come back from your sex-fest weekend and I'll loan you a few. You've seriously never heard of a reverse harem?"

"I've heard of a *harem*. One dude with loads of women. Normally some kind of Sheikh or whatever."

"Precisely. Except you're the male equivalent, so to speak. Hence a *reverse* harem. Girl fucking power and all that! It's about time you got your freak on. I can live vicariously through you."

I laugh. "Well, when you put it that way."

"You're literally living a polyamorous life. It's like the best of all worlds. You've got four fit guys in love with you and they're totally cool with each other being in your life as well. All those cocks. Hmm... but only three holes..." She tips her head to the side, actually thinking about the logistics. My cheeks flame. I hadn't even considered that. I mean individually, yes, absolutely of course. Even being with two of them at once, because I've already explored that, but all four...

"Girl, that would be so damn hot."

Shaking my head out of the gutter, I jab her in the arm. "It's not just about sex, and it's not as simple as that..."

"Of course it isn't, but nothing good ever is." She winks and then cups my face in her hands and smacks a warm kiss against my mouth. "You know, if you ever fancy adding another harem member, you know who to call." With a wink and a slap on my arse, she swivels on her feet and walks to the door, swaying her hips provocatively. Opening it, she turns and gives me a huge grin. "Now I'm going to fuck River within an inch of his life and then try and figure out how I can persuade him to join my harem."

"You haven't got one," I say, giggling.

"Not *yet*."

"You're incorrigible."

"Abso-fucking-lutely. Now, I'm off, but the moment you're back I want a blow-by-blow of *everything*."

"Sure," I respond, my cheeks heating at the thought of what's to come. I know I should be more worried about the bigger picture and this whole thing with Santiago and Jeb, but I have to admit the thought of being alone with my Breakers once again is more than a little distracting. Tonight can be about us, tomorrow we can worry about the next steps in the plan. For a few hours at least I want to put aside everything we've got to face and just be happy with the men I love. Maybe we can even dance together again, just the five of us?

"Don't do anything I wouldn't do," Clancy says, interrupting my thoughts.

"Oh, I plan to."

"Atta girl!" Clancy gives me the biggest, most heartfelt smile, then gently closes the door behind her. My heart warms, and for the first time in forever I begin to feel like perhaps things will work out for all of us.

14

Pen

"I APPRECIATE you coming with me. I know you probably have better things to do than act as chauffeur," I say, smiling over at Dax as he drives us towards my mum's place. I haven't seen or spoken to her since I moved out, and it's not an experience I'm looking forward to. Not that I plan on speaking with her, I just want to check in on Lena.

"Kid, I would've come regardless," he replies, indicating right and merging onto the motorway in one smooth movement. Pressing his foot on the accelerator, he shifts lanes like a pro racer or something. I feel a tingle run down my spine at the sheer confidence he has cutting through the traffic at such a high speed. The last time I was in this Bentley I was a wreck and Dax was far less accommodating. This time I get to appreciate what an incredible car it is and just how sexy Dax looks driving it.

"Thank you," I say a little breathlessly, my gaze drifting to his thick tattooed forearms, the muscles tensing and flexing as he drives. Why are forearms so sexy? All my Breakers have gorgeous arms, but Dax's take the cake. He's just so... so *male* in all the ways that matter. Sometimes I feel a little overwhelmed in his company. He's like this force of nature but in a quiet, watchful way.

"You okay?" he asks me.

"Uh-huh..."

Currently he's dressed in a pair of smart black jeans that hug his firm arse and thighs, and a grey roll neck sweater with the sleeves pulled back to the elbows, showing off his beautiful tattoos. He's looking particularly delicious tonight and I have a feeling he's dressed up for me.

"Stop doing that," he grins suddenly, glancing over at me, his grey-green eyes sparkling with mirth.

"Stop doing what?" I ask, my tongue running over my bottom lip as I take my fill of him.

"*That*. Staring at me like you want to eat me. It's... *distracting*." He shifts in his seat, a rueful smile playing over his lips as he drops his gaze to his crotch briefly.

"Oh," I say. "That must be distracting." Stifling a giggle, I allow my heated gaze to rove over his growing erection. "Perhaps you should've worn looser jeans?"

"Hmm, perhaps," he takes his left hand off the steering wheel, and covers my hand with his, then places it on his cock. My cheeks flush with heat as I run my palm over his hard length.

"Dax, is that a gun in your pocket or are you glad to see me?"

"Cute, Kid. Cute..."

His voice trails off as I rub him through his jeans, and if I weren't so confident in his driving ability, I wouldn't be having so much fun teasing him right now. With every stroke, my knickers grow wetter and Dax grows bigger.

"Fuck, Kid. Perhaps this wasn't the best idea I've ever had..." he chokes out. I can see he's fighting the urge to pull off the motorway so that we can find somewhere to finish this off. Then again, we're in central London, there isn't really anywhere we can go park that won't be surrounded by pedestrians, not to mention the fact I'm not into dogging.

"You really shouldn't start something you can't finish," I whisper, popping open his fly one button at a time.

"Kid..." he warns, his voice low, gravelly.

"Shh, just concentrate on driving, let me do the rest."

"Fuck!" he exclaims as my palm finds the opening to his boxer shorts and wraps around his beautiful cock.

"Luckily I have small hands. That's quite a tight fit," I say breathlessly, my own excitement obvious as I free his cock and start stroking him in that way I remember he likes.

"Kid, seriously, I might crash the fucking car if you carry on."

"Then I should make this quick..."

"Quick—?"

Unbuckling my seat belt, I lean across the central divide, thanking the Lord Almighty this is an automatic, and wrap my lips around the bulbous head of his dick, humming when I taste the salty precum.

"Fuck! Fuck! Fuck!" Dax swears, the car jerking forward suddenly as his foot hits the accelerator pedal a little too hard. "You're fulfilling... *Fuck*... one of my.... *Fuck me*... fantasies right now."

I'd laugh in glee if my mouth wasn't so full of him. Dax winds his fingers in my hair and gently presses against the back of my head. I take him in a little further, grasping his thigh with one hand to support myself as I suck him off.

"Hold on, baby, I gotta take the next exit," he says after a minute of cursing and moaning. Releasing my head, he takes the wheel in both hands and I lick him from base to tip, and back again. "We'll be at your mum's in five," he warns, more curse words flying out of his mouth as he drives us, and I drive *him* wild.

A couple of minutes later, he's coming in my mouth as we pull up outside the block of flats I grew up in. Swallowing down his cum, I lick my lips provocatively as he parks the car and tucks his cock away. The second he's decent, he leans over, grabs me by the back of my neck and kisses me until I'm panting and needy.

"I'll deal with you later," he says, lust billowing in his eyes as he pulls back.

"Deal with me?"

"Yeah, deal with you. You took off your seatbelt. Fucking dangerous, Kid. I'm gonna spank your arse for wilfully putting yourself in danger like that," he says, before jumping out of the car and striding around to open my door like a true gentleman. "After you."

"Why, thank you," I say with a huge grin, already imagining what a spanking would feel like at the hands of Dax. He smiles wickedly, crowding me against the closed car door.

"Do you know how much I wanted you the last time I had you up against this car?"

"No, how much?" I ask, having a pretty good idea.

His knee presses up against my core, as he boxes me in and whispers against my ear. "So. Fucking. Much."

"Rah, look at that Bentley. Nice fucking ride, man!" A boy of about fifteen appears out from behind the garages. He's smoking weed and his red-rimmed, glassy eyes focus, or at least try to, on the car. "She's fucking insane. What I'd do to drive that baby."

Dax groans, then pushes off the car and turns around slowly. The boy's eyes widen a little when his gaze finally focuses on him.

"Where's the rest of them?" Dax asks, causing the boy to cock his head. I'm pretty sure that such a simple question uses more than a few brain cells to answer.

"The rest of them?"

"Yeah, the fuckers who're gonna try and steal my car, or at least my hubcaps."

The boy splutters whilst I chuckle. "I ain't gonna steal nothing, man. I swear it."

Dax folds his arms across his chest. "Yeah, and my name's Robin fucking Hood."

"What?"

"Never fucking mind. Just tell your boys not to fuck with my car. Got it?"

"What's in it for me?"

Dax scowls, noticing a few shady looking kids lingering on the street corner. All of them are eying up his car and taking a great interest in our conversation. Having grown up on this estate we both know that Dax is correct in his assumption that they'd try and steal his car the second our backs are turned.

"I need to deal with this. Meet you up there?"

"Sure thing. See you in ten?"

"I'll have this sorted in three."

"Go easy, they're just kids," I say.

"The Breakers were once kids too and look how we turned out."

"Fair point."

"LENA, ARE YOU HOME?" I call out, stepping into the hallway, pocketing my keys as soon as I'm inside. The first thing I notice is the familiar smell of cigarette smoke and the cheap potpourri mum puts out to try and mask the smell. Fucking gross. What this place needs is a good airing. Better still, mum needs to give up her nasty habit and stop slowly killing her daughter with secondhand smoke.

"Pen?!"

At the end of the hallway, Lena steps out of her bedroom and squeals, rushing towards me in a flurry of pink fluffy pyjamas, face mask and wet hair. She throws herself into my arms and hugs me.

"Hey, Lena," I murmur, holding her close, not caring that her strawberry face mask has rubbed off onto my cheek. "Nice pyjamas. Haven't seen those before."

"What are you doing here?" she asks, grinning that gorgeous smile of hers. It's only been a couple weeks since I saw her last, but even in that time she's changed. She's growing up fast and is already towering over me. I definitely got the short gene, whilst she got all the legs. Lena is what I'd call a natural stunner and the total opposite of me in more ways than just our looks. She's a lot more trusting and open than I am, that's for sure.

"Can't I check in on my baby sister every once in a while?"

"Well sure, but haven't you got, like, work to go to tonight or something?"

"Nope, not tonight."

"Does that mean you're staying over?" She looks so hopeful that guilt riddles my chest.

When I don't answer straight away, she plasters on a fake

smile, grabs my hand and drags me towards the kitchen. "Let me make you a cuppa. Mum went shopping yesterday so we've got food in. Are you hungry?" she asks me.

"No. I'm good, but a cup of tea would be nice."

"Sure." She busies herself making tea whilst I take a look around the kitchen. It's really clean, and despite the stale smell of cigarette smoke, the whole kitchen and living room is a lot tidier than it ever was when I was living here.

"The place looks... tidy," I say, because whilst it's certainly clean, it's hardly the Ritz.

"Yeah, Mum's been a bit better about tidying up after herself," Lena explains, wrinkling her nose. I watch her as she scratches the tip, removing some of the face mask as she does so.

"How *are* things with mum?" I ask tentatively.

Lena hands me a mug of tea with plenty of milk and a dash of sugar, just the way I like it. "Good..." she hesitates, chewing on her lip.

"What, Lena?"

"Nothing."

"Lena!" I warn.

She sighs and rolls her eyes. "She's kinda sobered up a bit."

"Sobered up a bit? You say that like it's not a good thing?"

"I mean, she's sobered up *a lot*."

"Did she get a visit from the social, is that it?" I ask, putting Mum's sudden change of attitude down to the fact that someone must've threatened to take Lena away.

"No, she didn't. I swear one day she was pissed and lying on the sofa out of her head and the next she's cooking homemade meals and cleaning the house up."

"Fuck," I say, as shocked as Lena is.

"Don't get me wrong, she's been a bit rough the last couple weeks. I'm guessing her body needed to adjust, but I swear it's like she's a new woman."

"Yeah, I'll believe that when I see it." My eyes trail to the coffee table and the half-dozen cigarette butts sitting in an ashtray.

Lena follows my gaze. "She still smokes but believe it or not she's got a nicotine patch on her arm and has cut down from thirty to twenty cigarettes a day."

My mouth falls open in shock and Lena laughs. "I know, right? She's a changed woman. It's weird."

The front door opens, and Mum calls out Lena's name. It's a strange feeling hearing the brightness in her voice and not the usual husky slurred speech from smoking and drinking too much. "Lena, who are you talking—?"

"Hey, Mum," I say as she steps into the kitchen, surprise written across her face.

"Penelope, you're home."

"I just came to see Lena," I explain. *Not you.*

She nods, understanding what I don't say, but rather than coming back with a nasty retort like I expect her too, she steps into the living room and places her coat and bag on the sofa. "Are you staying for dinner? I was going to make a stir-fry."

Lena's eyes widen as she looks between me and our Mum. Clearly she was expecting a different reaction to my appearance too. I swallow, a tight feeling in my chest forming. "No, I can't. I really was just popping in for a quick visit and a cup of tea," I say.

For a brief moment I see disappointment flash across my mum's face, and it floors me a little. Not once in my whole entire life has my mum ever looked at me like she wished we spent more time together. Not once.

"That's a shame. Maybe another time. You could tell us about the Academy and how you're getting on."

My mouth pops open, then slams shut. Even Lena is suddenly at a loss for words. "Yeah, maybe," I respond noncommittally.

"Okay, well, I'm just going to grab a shower. It's been a long day at work."

"Work?" I ask, flicking my gaze between her and Lena.

"Yes, I got a new job at a really nice hair salon in the high street. I could get you a discount if you ever wanted to tame that hair of yours," she says, reaching up and pushing back a strand of hair back off my face. I flinch, stepping back, a lump in my throat forming at her sudden affection. Her hand falls away and she gives me a half-smile before stepping out of the kitchen and into the bathroom down the hall. I let out a long breath, feeling shaky and weird.

"What the fuck was that? Has our mum been body snatched or something?" I question, trying to cover up this sudden rush of unwelcome emotion with humour.

"See, I told you she'd changed." Lena cocks her head and smiles sadly. "Sorry, Pen," she whispers.

"What for?"

"For mum never being the person you needed her to be. I know it's too late now."

She's right, it is, but for Lena's sake I'm glad she's turned over a new leaf. I just hope it lasts. "Come here," I say, holding open my arms. Lena steps right in and I hug her tightly. "I'm so glad mum has sobered up, but you remember I'm still here if you need me. Any hour of the day or night, I will come. Okay?"

"Yeah, okay," Lena replies.

A knock at the door has us parting and I step out into the hall to answer. I know who it is, and I don't want Pen getting a shock at seeing Dax on the other side.

"Everything good?" Dax asks me the second I open the door. He peers down the hallway and smiles.

"Oh, my fucking God, is that you, Dax?" Lena asks, her voice getting higher with every syllable out of her mouth as she approaches.

Dax chuckles. "Hey, Squirt," he says, referring to her by the nickname he used when we were friends before.

"Fuck me. I *bet* you've got better things to do than working tonight," she titters as I glare at her over my shoulder. "Hi, Dax. Don't you look... *big*." Her eyes work their way up from his feet to the top of his head.

"I could say the same for you." He smiles warmly and I swear my heart melts into a puddle. "How're you doing?"

"Yeah, I'm good. Thanks for the package. I love these PJ's."

"Package?" I look between them both.

Lena pulls a face, chewing on her bottom lip as she glances between me and Dax. "The Breakers have been sending me stuff for a while now."

"Sending you stuff? What stuff? Why didn't you say anything?" I ask, flipping my gaze between them both, my voice rising.

"Shit, chill. I mean I only realised it was the Breakers and not some weird arse stalker when Xeno dropped off these pyjamas and other nice stuff the other week. It's just things mum can't afford. Nice shampoo, make up, perfume, that kind of thing. I came home from school and he was here, having a chat with mum... Oh, shit," she exclaims, coming to the same conclusion as me.

Our mum's sudden sobriety makes perfect sense now. I'm not

sure whether to be grateful that he's gone behind my back and has been taking care of Lena or pissed off that he never thought to tell me.

"I have literally no idea what to say." I look at Dax, not sure what to make of it all.

"And your mum, how is she doing now?" Dax asks, his assessing gaze taking everything in as he subtly tries to change the subject. I narrow my eyes at him.

"She's taking a shower, right now. Wanna come in for a bit?" Lena asks.

"No, can't tonight, Lena. Dax and I have a duet to practice," I lie quickly before Dax can take her up on his offer. I want to get back to the flat and speak with Xeno, he's got some explaining to do.

"Oooh, a duet. I'd like to see you in action... I mean, you both. Together. *Dancing*. Yes, dancing... a duet. Sorry, that sounded a bit perverted, didn't it?"

"Jesus, Lena," I mutter.

"You take care, Squirt," Dax grins, finding her fumbling cute.

"I will."

Dax takes my hand in his and Lena practically squeals when she notices.

"I'll call you in a couple days," I say.

"You betcha!" She winks, watching us both with glee as we walk down the hallway.

Once outside, Dax bursts out laughing.

"What?"

"She reminds me a lot of you when you were young. So innocent..."

I scoff. "Believe me Lena is *not* that innocent," I reply, remembering our conversation in the café about Teddy Smith's nine-inch cock and how her best friend gave him a blowy on their school trip to the Isle of White.

"So that whole awkward conversation about *tickling pickles* never came up with your sister then?" Dax laughs and I smack him on the chest, internally cringing at the younger more innocent version of me.

"No, no it didn't. Besides, don't change the bloody subject. Spill!" I order, wanting to know more about what Xeno's been up too.

"No way. That's a conversation you'll be needing to have with Xeno. I'm not getting involved. I told him you'd be pissed when you found out."

"I'm not pissed. At least, I don't think I am. I'm confused. Lena started getting all this stuff a couple weeks before I auditioned at Stardom Academy. I was worried she was either stealing it, she had a sugar daddy, or worse, had gotten involved with the Skins. Looks like I was partially right."

"Xeno's a mercurial bastard, that's for sure. I didn't find out about what he'd been doing until a couple days ago—"

"Wait, *he* was sending the stuff, not all of you?"

"Yep."

"I don't understand."

Dax stops by the Bentley, resting his forearm on the roof of the car. "Lena has always been your priority. Xeno knows how much you love her, worry about her. I'm no psychologist, Kid, but I think it was his way of taking care of you without admitting that he still loved you. But if you want an honest answer, you're going to have to ask him."

"Then I guess I'll have to do just that."

15

Pen

"SO THIS IS NICE," I say from my position on the floor, taking a huge bite out of my slice of pepperoni pizza. It's been a long day of dancing and rehearsals, so being here with the guys in their own flat is just what I needed, especially after seeing the body snatched version of my mum this afternoon and finding out Xeno has been sending my sister care packages. I still haven't brought it up with him yet, but now seems the perfect time. My mum's new attitude might've floored me, but Xeno's involvement does even more so. I'm not convinced she's turned over a new leaf, but for my sister's sake I have to hope she has.

"Nice?" Dax drops down on the floor beside me, placing three beers on the coffee table. He wraps his arm around my shoulder then leans over and gives me a kiss on the cheek.

"Yes, I've missed being with you like this. It feels so normal, natural. I've missed hanging out with you all."

"We've missed you too, Kid. So fucking much," Dax replies, his voice gruff with emotion and I know he isn't just talking about this week.

I snuggle closer into his side, breathing in his scent as my fingers trail across his chest, rimming the V-neck of his t-shirt. He smells so fucking good, and the skin on his chest is smooth and hair free. I'm pretty sure he waxes. For all his rugged good looks and manliness, he's quite the metrosexual man. I love that about him. Opposite, Xeno leans over and grabs a beer, chucking another crust into the empty pizza box. He swallows down a mouthful, peering at us both as he does so. He's thoughtful this evening, quiet in a way that's unsettling.

"Xeno, can I ask you something?"

"Sure."

"Lena told me something interesting today..." My voice trails off as I try to broach the subject.

"Is this because I paid your mum a visit?" he asks me, resting his beer back on the table.

"Yes, that and the fact you've been sending Lena care packages."

"Ah, those." He flicks his gaze to Dax. "You told her?"

"No, Lena did," Dax replies.

"Why?" I ask him. "I mean, I'm grateful that you've been looking out for her, but why do that?"

He blows out a breath, his green eyes glinting with emotions I can't decipher. "Because I wanted to do something right. I wanted to make sure she was okay."

"But she started receiving stuff just before I auditioned for Stardom," I point out, confused, and honestly a little hurt. The fact he sent her gifts and not me stings a little, not because I wanted those things, but because of the thought that went behind it.

"It was because..." Xeno swipes a hand through his hair, the curls bouncing back the second his hands pass over the strands.

"What, Xeno?" I press, trying to understand. Beside me Dax remains quiet, not giving Xeno an out by stepping in, despite how tense this conversation is getting.

"I saw Lena with her friends in the high street a few days after we came back to Hackney. She was mucking about, skipping school actually," he explains, a tiny smile of amusement lifting up his lips.

"Bunking off school...!"

"Don't be pissed. She's just being a kid. We did a lot worse, remember?" Dax reminds me.

"You might be right, but she doesn't know that. I want her to get an education," I retort, feeling prickly about the subject because Dax is right, we were worse, *a lot* worse.

"I decided to stick around and check out what she was doing. I watched her go into a store with her mates then a few minutes later come out with a rucksack full of stuff she'd nicked."

"What? She was shoplifting?! I'm going to murder her!" I exclaim.

"Yeah, they went into a café after and she divided up her haul between her mates. She didn't notice me grabbing a coffee. Anyway, I figured I'd send her stuff so she wouldn't need to go nicking." He shrugs as though that's enough of an explanation.

"But that doesn't explain *why*. She's not your responsibility, Xeno."

"Lena's a good kid. I didn't want her getting into shit."

"Xeno... Fess up," Dax says, locking gazes with Xeno. "Come on, man. Tell her."

He sighs. "At the time I convinced myself I did what I did because I wanted to keep Lena out of trouble, and that's still true..."

"But?"

"But I did it because of you," he admits eventually, staring at me. "Even when I'd convinced myself I didn't love you, deep down I did. I understand that now. I sent Lena those care packages because I knew it would kill you to know your sister was stealing stuff. I wanted to look out for you and Lena."

"And my mum..." I ask softly, untangling myself from Dax's arms before shifting around the coffee table, so I can be close to Xeno. My knees press into the side of his thigh as I reach to cup his cheek and encourage him to look at me.

"...Needed to hear some home truths. More importantly, I needed to make amends for treating you so badly, for abandoning you, for believing that you wanted to hurt us when you walked away when really you were trying to protect us. You did what you did to protect Lena, to protect us. It's my turn to do the same for you."

"What did you say to her?"

"That's not important. What's important is that she's sobering up. She's getting counselling for her addiction and is having therapy."

"How? She can't afford that."

"I'm paying for it."

"You're paying for it...?"

"Yes. I want her to sort out her shit. I want her to make an effort with you. I want *her* to make amends for how she's treated you, Tiny. At the very least, she needs to be a good mum to Lena. Counselling and therapy will help her to do that."

"I don't... This is... I'm..." I stutter, unable to find the words to express how I feel. I appreciate his efforts, for caring about me enough to try and fix what's broken between my mum and me, but it's not as simple as that. I'm not sure we can be fixed. I don't like my mum, let alone love her... I just. I don't know. My eyes fill with tears and my insides swirl with emotions that I can't unravel in the moment.

"I've done the wrong thing, haven't I?" he frowns, swiping a thumb across my cheek to capture the tear that's fallen.

"No, you've done something wonderful and I'm so glad Lena will benefit from this, I'm just not so sure I ever will. Too much has happened between me and my mum. I can't forgive what she's done. It hurts too much."

"I'm sorry," Xeno says gruffly.

"Don't be. Don't ever be sorry for doing something good out of love and affection. Don't be afraid to express your love with me, *however* that looks," I say, meaning every word, just like I did that night we made love for the first time. "But no more secrets. We can't rebuild *us* if we're still hiding stuff from each other."

Xeno nods then pulls me into his arms and holds me close. "I'm so fucking glad you're here. I've missed you so fucking much."

"I know."

Just as I'm relaxing into his hold, Xeno's mobile beeps with a message. A frown creases his forehead when he reads it.

"Is something wrong?" I ask him.

"Zayn has been called into Rocks," he replies, flicking his concerned gaze to Dax.

"What for?" Dax tenses.

"A member of Dante's Crew was caught selling cocaine in SE1."

"Dante's Crew is still about? I didn't realise," I say, remembering that night at Rocks when we were kids. That was when Frederico propositioned me and talked about me like I was some kind of slut, causing Dax to beat the shit out of him. It was also the night that Dax and I kissed for the first time. The resulting fight in Abney Park Cemetery was the last time I saw Frederico and his crew.

"Yeah, they are. Frederico now runs an arms business," Dax explains.

My mouth drops open. "An *arms* business?"

"Small fry, mostly knives, occasionally handguns. He's not international, or even regional, but he's getting cocky," Dax informs me, scowling. There's no love lost there, that's for sure. "Moving in on the Skins' territory is fucking stupid."

"Agreed. Jeb won't let that stand."

"What's going to happen?"

A look passes between the two and Xeno sighs. "Over the years our crews have crossed paths, but Frederico has always backed off when it came down to the wire. He's usually too chicken shit to try anything like this."

"Usually?"

"Yeah, looks like he's getting too big for his boots. Jeb's gonna be pissed."

Xeno nods. "My best guess is that Frederico has someone backing him. This isn't something he'd try on his own."

"Why would someone back him?" I ask.

He shrugs. "We're not the only ones who dislike Jeb. Besides, it kinda goes with the territory. This ain't the first time another gang has tried to move in on the Skins' patch, but this isn't Frederico's usual style. He's too much of a pussy to make a move on his own. Which is exactly why I think someone else is behind it."

"I see, so what happens to people who try and move in on the Skins' patch?" I ask, having a pretty good idea what the answer is going to be but ask anyway.

"They're taken out," Xeno says, his expression void of any emotion.

"The Skins take them out...?"

Dax shakes his head. "No, *we* do it. We're the Breakers, remember?"

"Fuck," I whisper.

"Dante's Crew is based in West London," Xeno goes on to explain. "They're small fry, and really no threat to the Skins. Selling knives to street kids really doesn't affect Jeb's business plan, but moving in on his patch with drugs... *That's* an act of defiance that can't be ignored."

"Zayn's going to have to fight, isn't he?"

"Yeah, he is," Xeno confirms, sighing.

"Frederico?"

"No, the poor fucker caught selling the drugs. Frederico will be running scared," Xeno explains.

"And Jeb's entertaining this? Isn't he usually a shoot first and ask questions later kind of arsehole?"

Xeno glances back at his phone, another text message coming in. "Normally, yes, but Jeb's going to make an example of this man whilst making money from the fight. He knows Zayn won't lose."

My mouth suddenly goes very dry, and I grab one of the beers, knocking back a mouthful.

"What if Zayn does lose? What then?"

"Losing isn't an option. Zayn *will* win," Dax says, watching me carefully.

"And what construes a win in a knife fight, Dax?"

"Whoever falls first from either too much blood loss or a lethal stab wound—"

"What?!"

"Like Dax said, Zayn *will* win." The darkness in Xeno's eyes glitters with everything he's had to bear witness to over the years.

"Jesus," I whisper.

"It's what he has to do to survive, Kid. What we've *all* had to do to survive. It is what it is."

I feel them both watching me as the weight of their words sink in. I know that they've hurt people, killed people in the name of the Skins. I'd rationalised the firefight at Tales as self-defence. They were *protecting* me. Besides, not being awake to witness any of it helps, but this is something different altogether. This is premeditated. This is two men fighting to the death, or at least until their opponent is so injured they can no longer fight back. My stomach churns and I suddenly lose my appetite.

"Can't you stop this? Can't you do something?" I ask, my voice betraying me.

"This is the world we live in, Kid."

"... And the world we're working on being free from," Xeno adds firmly.

"Is there no other way?"

Dax shakes his head. "No. Zayn will fight. He'll win, and we'll be here for him when he does. That's how we get through. That's how we've always gotten through."

Xeno's phone rings then and he takes the call, striding off to the kitchen area for a little privacy.

"I hate this."

Dax opens his arms to me, and I crawl into his lap, finding comfort in the sheer size of him as he envelops me in his hold. "If I could somehow protect you from this I would, but I can't, Kid. I can't. This is our reality right now."

Xeno ends his call a minute later and grabs his coat. "I've asked York to come home. I'll meet Zayn at Rocks. Jeb doesn't give a fuck who tags along and I'd rather it was me. York should be here with you, Tiny. You'll need him."

Honestly, I don't understand what he means by that. I need *all* of them, not just one or the other. Unwinding myself from Dax's arms I get up and approach Xeno. He's holding himself stiffly and I see how he's shutting down, mentally preparing himself for what's to come. "Are you okay?" I ask. It's a stupid question because of course he isn't. None of us are.

"I can go," Dax cuts in, seeing how worried I am about Xeno.

"No. York's on his way back here now. I want you both to stay with Tiny. *I've* got this."

"Xeno, man. I can deal. You know that. It doesn't always have to be you." Dax gets up from the floor and claps his hand on Xeno's shoulder.

"Your place is here with Tiny. I need you here with her."

Dax sighs. "Xeno..."

"No!" he says firmly. "I've got this." Pulling on his jacket, Xeno fires off another quick text. As the seconds pass his whole demeanor changes and the softer, more vulnerable Xeno I've seen glimpses of over the last week or so disappears before my eyes. "Don't expect us back before dawn."

"I'll look after Kid until you return." Dax squeezes Xeno's shoulder before giving us both a moment as he tidies up the pizza boxes, carrying them into the kitchen.

"This is what you do, isn't it?" I ask quietly when Dax is out of earshot. I rest my hands on Xeno's chest, needing to feel the thump of his heart, needing to know that he's still human and not this cold, distant person he's turning into now.

"Do?" he asks, canting his head, his curls falling across his forehead.

I reach up and push them back. "Take everything on."

"If I were doing that then I'd be killing that guy for Zayn. This time I can't."

"This time?" I whisper, my fingers brushing over the stubble of his chin.

"I kill so they don't have to." Xeno's expression is blank, his eyes a void. It scares me, the numbness I see.

"Xeno..." My voice breaks and I swallow hard. I fucking *hate* this. I hate what they've had to do, what they've become. It's a physical pain that tears me up inside.

"Don't, Tiny. We chose this life, and we *have* to do this. I need you to be that girl who can face any damn thing and survive it. Just be here when we get home. Be here and be strong. He's going to need you."

Cupping my face in his hands, Xeno brushes his lips against my own. I can sense him pulling away and I curl my hands around his wrists, clinging on to him. "I'll be here. I'll be strong," I promise him.

"I'm counting on it," he replies, pressing the most heartfelt kiss against my lips. It's a kiss that's different to those we've shared before, and I suddenly feel the need to hold him in my arms and never let go. Of course, we can't always get what we want.

"I have to go."

"Be safe," I whisper against his lips, releasing him. "Bring Zayn home in one piece."

He nods, then leaves.

16

Pen

"THAT'S IT, bro. I'm all Fred Astaire'd out," Dax groans when York reaches for the control and hunts Netflix for another black and white dance movie. It's way past two in the morning, but none of us are tired. Well, maybe tired of York's choice of movies. I love Fred Astaire as much as the next person, but I switched off two movies ago, my mind elsewhere. With every passing hour my anxiety has grown.

"You don't know what you're missing," York protests. "Look, they've got *Swing Time* too."

Dax throws a pillow at his head. "Enough already!"

Chuckling, York flicks off the TV. The screen goes black, throwing us into semi darkness. This whole evening he's been the joker, the lighthearted one. He's kept us preoccupied with his wit and charm. I love and appreciate his efforts, but I'm feeling restless past the point of distraction.

"So what now?" he asks, and I feel the heat of his stare as I get up and walk to the window.

"It's such a beautiful view," I say absentmindedly as I look out onto the cityscape beyond the window.

"It is," York agrees, stepping up behind me. He wraps his arms around my waist and rests his chin on top of my head. I get a whiff of his signature CKOne perfume and it immediately takes me back to our childhood.

"Have you heard anything yet?"

"They'll be home soon, Titch. Try not to worry."

I let out a broken laugh. "How can I not worry about them, about *all* of you?"

York turns me around in his arms and I tip my head back to look up at him. "Because we're badasses, that's why."

"You mean arrogant?" I laugh, but it comes out choked. "No one's invincible, York."

"Zat is vhere you are vrong, my pretty morsel. I'm a vampire, and *I'm* invincible, mwa-ha-ha-haa!" he replies, tipping his head back in a mock Count Dracula impression.

"You're such a dick," Dax says, throwing another cushion at York's head. It bounces off him, messing up his already disheveled hair so it sticks up all over his head in white-blonde spikes. Despite his cuteness, I can't seem to crack a genuine smile. I'm too worried.

"Seriously, York. This isn't funny." I frown, trying everything in my power to be the strong person Zayn needs me to be and feeling as though I'm failing. It's hard work being strong all the time. York presses his forefinger against the crease in my brow, sliding it gently over each eyebrow in turn. Then looks at me in that disarming way of his.

"I know what you need," he says, wiggling his eyebrows.

"I'm not in the mood..." I mutter. As much as I want him, the last thing on my mind is sex. I won't settle until Zayn and Xeno are back, and whilst I have to believe Zayn will win the fight, that doesn't mean to say he'll be okay when he returns, physically or emotionally. Fuck, maybe he won't be affected at all. I'm not sure what's worse.

York presses his hand against his chest in mock horror. "Fuck, Titch, you sure know how to burst a man's ego."

"I didn't mean to—"

"Stop it, I'm just messing with you. Come on, let's dance this out."

"Dance?"

He grins. "Are you tired?"

"No—"

"Then let's dance." Grasping my hand in his, York pulls me towards the door in the corner of the room that leads to their dance studio. "You coming, *big boy*?"

Dax rolls his eyes, but gets up and follows us both anyway. "You keep calling me that, York, and I'm gonna think you fancy me."

"Hey, man. I just appreciate a decent sized, platonic-cock."

"Platonic-cock? Fuck, man, I seriously worry about you sometimes."

York laughs loudly, flicking on the light to the dance studio. "You need to lighten up. Women appreciate other women all the time. Just because I think you've got a decent sized dick; doesn't mean I want to suck it."

"Decent sized dick? Suck it? Fuck me," Dax grumbles and I can't help but grin.

"Any song preference?" York asks as we step into the studio. He winks at me, loving that his ribbing is making Dax uncomfortable. It's certainly helping to lighten my mood.

I shake my head. "You choose."

York kisses my knuckles then wanders over to the sound system. I feel Dax's hand rest on my lower back. "How does he do that?" I ask, referring to York's ability to remain so fucking positive.

"We all have our roles to play, Kid. York's the optimist. During times like this he keeps us distracted with his banter and his stupid fucking jokes. That's why Xeno swapped places with him. He knew you'd need the distraction, and you already know that Xeno is a moody motherfucker."

"Yeah, I can see that now. So, what's your role then?"

Dax shrugs. "I'm just the big guy who can fight."

"No way, man," York says, overhearing our conversation and suddenly becoming very serious. "You're the one we can count on to be there no matter what. You're the *only* one who can keep Xeno in check. You're the fucking rock."

Dax laughs. "First you're giving my cock a nickname and now this? Anyone would think you love me, York."

York plants his hand on his hip and gives him a sassy smile. "Of course, I fucking love every big, alpha-hot hole, inch of you."

"Shut the fuck up, dude, and choose a damn song."

"Ohh, I love it when you talk dirty to me," York retorts, and I can't help but smile. I've missed this banter between them. It warms my heart like nothing else. Xeno was right, I needed York here tonight.

"Jeez, alright. Don't get your knickers in a twist, *big boy*."

I swallow a laugh as York attaches his mobile phone to the sound system, resting it on the table. He doesn't press play straight away. Instead, he pushes against a panel in the wall that I hadn't noticed the last time I was in this studio, given I was preoccupied with Dax. It opens up to reveal a cupboard. He grabs two pairs of tap shoes from a built-in shoe rack and turns around grinning.

Dax groans. "I ain't tap dancing."

"These aren't for you," York says, handing one pair to me whilst he puts on the other.

"When did you—?"

"I bought them a week or so ago. Couldn't have Zayn one-upping me..." he jokes, his gaze softening when he sees the look on my face. "I wanted to buy something nice for you too. These are the best money can buy. They're made out of the softest Italian cowhide leather. I think it's all the pasta those Italian cows eat on the daily."

"Err, genius, cows eat grass." Dax chuckles.

"Pasta, grass, whatever. I swear it's like dancing on air."

"I don't know what to say."

"You don't have to say anything..." York takes my hand, looking down at me. "Dance with me, Titch?"

"Of course I'll dance with you." Rising up onto my tiptoes, I plant a quick peck against his lips, but when I pull back, he captures my head and deepens the kiss.

"York," I mutter against his mouth, wanting so badly to lean into him, to forget about what's going on this evening, but I can't. I can't. I pull away, my cheeks flushing with heat.

"Don't stop on my account," Dax rumbles, a lopsided smile

pulling up his lips as he strolls over to a bench pushed up against the mirror and sits, watching us both. My heart stutters and I'm reminded of that time together on Xeno's bed when we were kids.

"Another time?" I say softly, because as much as I love York and Dax, that's not the kind of distraction I need, not whilst the other pieces of my heart are doing dangerous things in the name of the Skins.

"You better believe it, Titch," York responds. Stepping back, he swipes a hand through his hair, blowing out a long breath.

"Blue balls ain't a good look on you," Dax says, cracking up.

"Fuck off," York mumbles, but he's grinning too.

Pulling on my new tap shoes, I perform a quick ball shuffle change, testing them out. "They're perfect."

York turns to Dax. "Are you sure you ain't up for some tap dance?"

"Nope." Dax shakes his head, and leans back against the mirror, his long legs stretching out in front of him. "Ain't my style."

"Don't knock it until you try it... Then again, it takes some *skill* to dance like this," York states with a cheeky wink before he starts tapping a series of impressive steps that make me dizzy just to watch. He's a genius, there's no denying that.

"Fucking show-off," Dax grumbles, folding his arms across his chest. "Come on then blue balls, let us see what you got. Stop pissing around and turn the damn music on."

York presses play, and a familiar tune starts playing out over the speaker.

"No. Fucking. Way." Dax laughs raucously. "A very nineties tune, mate. You know you really were born in the wrong fucking era."

"It only came out the year before I was born, so it *is* my era, sort of. I fucking love this song."

York steps into the middle of the studio and starts to tap, grinning the whole time as *You Get What You Give*, by the New Radicals plays. He's beaming, his feet tapping perfectly in time to the beat. It's just what I needed. Something uplifting. Something to put a smile on all our faces.

Picking up his jaunty vibe, I join York in the center of the dance floor, copying his sequence of tap steps then interspersing them with some of my own.

"This song is making my ears bleed!" Dax shouts out over the music.

"You wouldn't know good music if it punched you in the face!" York replies, giving Dax the finger. "Let's show the fucker what he's missing." He takes my hands, twines his fingers with mine, and brings me around to face him, tapping with a lightness and a joy that I can't help but smile at. I concentrate on his footwork, overwhelmed by his gift. There's no way I can keep up.

"Your feet are ridiculous," I mutter.

"Eyes on me, Titch," he says, lifting my chin with his fingers and pinning me with his glacier-eyes. I'll never get used to how he takes my breath away every time he looks at me. "Let your feet do the talking. It's just me and Dax. Shake off your worries, Titch. Don't think too hard."

"But what if Zayn doesn't—"

"No. Zayn *will* come home, Xeno will make sure of it. Now fucking move your feet!" he demands with a squeeze of my hand and a determined grit of his jaw. Jumping back, he flings his arms wide and sings along to the song as he taps with lightning-fast feet. For a moment, I watch him, awed by his talent. But this isn't just about showing off, this is so much more than that. This is his way of relieving his stress, his worries. This is York funnelling all his fears and turning it into something uplifting. He dances as though every step will ensure Zayn's safety, *believing* that Zayn will come home unharmed.

There's a power in that, in his belief.

It rubs off on me.

Behind us, Dax is bopping his head, watching York with respect and love. He catches my eye and winks, encouraging me. God, my heart feels so full despite the circumstances.

I feel the absolute love they all have for one another, for me. I feel their hope for our future, and all of a sudden, I'm that fourteen-year-old kid again. I'm that courageous girl following her heart and believing in four boys who brought sunshine and happiness to her life at the moment she needed it most.

My Breakers. My whole fucking heart.

Right then and there I make a decision to trust in the Breakers, in *us*, and I sure as fuck won't give up. Jeb can go fuck himself. David can rot in hell. The Masks can try and do their worst. And Santiago Garcia, he's going down.

Grinning, I dance as though Zayn's life depends on it.

I *feel* the music. I *hear* the beat. I *trust* in their belief.

With every sequence of steps a feeling of hope fills my chest, giving me the strength to face an uncertain future head on. We dance with abandon, with impact, with positivity and a determination to let go of our fears so that we can be there for Zayn when he returns.

He's going to need us. He's going to need *me* to be strong.

"That's it, Titch, move your damn feet!" York yells.

The song tells us all not to give up, to feel the music, to dance. So, I do.

I dance until my worries are beaten into the floor beneath my feet and I'm the woman Zayn needs me to be.

Strong. Fierce. Determined.

17

Zayn

"NEED ANYTHING?" Xeno asks me as we step into the flat. He eyes me carefully, waiting to see how I'm going to react to the fact I've just murdered a man. I blink back the image of blood and staring, blank eyes.

"No."

He grabs my arm, his fingers curling around my bicep. "Do you need anything?" he repeats firmly. I know he's worried I'll lose my shit in front of Pen, that the remnants of this evening will rub off on her. I get it. I don't want our shitty fucking life to scar her the same way it's scarred us, and that's why I made a promise to myself to bury what happened tonight, to forget about it. I've done it before; I'll do it again. He fucking knows that.

"I *said*, I've got this."

Xeno drops my arm. "Good."

"I'm gonna take a shower."

The flat's quiet when we head inside, which doesn't surprise me given it's almost dawn. Wincing, I place my hand against my newly stitched up wound that sits just below my left pec. Fortunately for me, it's a shallow cut and will heal quickly. I can already tell it will only leave a faint scar. My opponent wasn't so lucky. A knife through the heart is pretty fucking permanent. The serrated edge of my saw-tooth knife carved through his flesh, muscle and bone like fucking butter. He didn't stand a chance, not against me.

Jeb knew that. Tonight he made his point. Frederico, and whoever he's working for, would've received a very firm message. Fuck with the Skins and you're dead.

Swallowing down the nausea I feel, I head towards my bedroom. I need to wash away this shitty fucking night, take a sleeping pill and fall into the oblivion of a dreamless sleep they afford me. I sure as fuck don't want to relive this evening's events or any other I've had to endure for my piece of shit uncle.

When I reach my bedroom door and push it open, I find Pen curled up on my bed with a blanket thrown over her, one bare arm and leg showing. "Fuck me," I whisper, so engrossed at how fucking stunning Pen looks lying on my bed in her sleep shorts and tank that I don't notice Dax sitting in the armchair in the corner of the room. He raises his finger, pressing it against his lips, then stands.

"She wanted to stay up and wait for you but eventually passed out on the sofa... I carried her in here."

"Why isn't she in your room?" I ask. In his position, I would be wrapped around Pen and made sure she knew how much I fucking loved her.

"You need her more than I do right now. I ain't feeling selfish tonight," he shrugs.

"And York?"

"In his room dealing with blue balls."

That draws a smile from me. "I bet," I say, glancing back at Pen who is so fucking tempting right now. "Thanks, man," I say, meaning it, because he's right, I do need her. I need her so fucking badly. All I want to do is curl around her, press my face into her hair and fucking hold her.

"I got you, bro," Dax says quietly, giving me a nod before stepping out of the room.

Kicking off my shoes and placing my jacket over the armchair, I step up to the side of the bed and look down at the girl I've loved for seven years now. She looks so peaceful with her bare legs drawn up and her mouth slightly ajar as she breathes softly. The fact that Dax was able to just sit there and let her sleep whilst she's wearing this sexy little outfit blows my damn mind. The guy's got next level restraint, that's for sure.

"Look at you," I whisper, wanting desperately to touch her, to lie down beside her, but I force myself to step into the bathroom and take a shower first. Even though I washed the blood from my hands and changed at Rocks, I don't want her to wake up next to a man-made filthy by his actions. I'm well aware that having a shower can't wash away my sins, but at least my body will be clean for her even if my soul isn't.

After showering and changing into a loose pair of grey joggers and a t-shirt, I climb into bed behind Pen. Shifting closer, I wrap my body around hers, my arm snaking around her waist as I bury my nose in her hair. I instantly relax, knowing she's in my arms, this girl I fucking adore.

"Zayn?" she murmurs sleepily. "Is that you?"

"Hey, Pen. Yeah, it's me. Go back to sleep."

She turns in my arms, her eyes hooded and a little unfocused as she reaches up to cup my cheek. I can't help but lean into her hand. She's so fucking warm and soft. "You're back."

"I am."

"Are you hurt?" she asks, the sleepiness in her gaze replaced with concern as her brown eyes widen.

"It's just a scratch," I say, pulling her closer and brushing my lips against her forehead.

"That's what you said before. Let me see," she demands, fully awake now. She sits up, pushing me flat onto the bed and lifts up my t-shirt. I shudder at the feel of her fingers as they slide over my skin. Her gentleness unsettles me, the violence of the past few hours brought starkly to light with her soft touch.

"I'm good, Pen, seriously," I lie.

"Don't do that," she bites out. Anger blazes across her face as she straddles me, her knees pressed to either side of my hips.

"Do what?"

"Lie to me. You're not okay. *This* isn't okay," she exclaims.

"I'm not lying. It really doesn't hurt." My dick, however, that's hurting right now. It's straining against my joggers, desperate for a little respite as my body instantly reacts to her despite my exhaustion. She wiggles on my lap and my dick grows bigger. I watch her skin flush, but she just frowns, too preoccupied with my injury.

"It'll scar, just like all the rest," she whispers, her gaze trailing over my ruined chest before resting on my face. There are so many questions in her eyes, so much pain and regret that for the first time in my life I feel fucking helpless in a way that makes me uncomfortable. What the fuck must she think of me? I'm a murdering bastard. I took a man's life tonight all in the name of the Skins, some piece of shit gang headed up by my poor excuse of an uncle. I'm doing this for a man I hate and a gang I want out of. Actually, that's no longer true. I'm doing this for the Breakers, for Pen. We have a goal in sight, and now that Pen is back and ours once more, that goal is even more important. We've all got to carry on as usual until the time comes when we can take back our fucking freedom. Reaching up I brush her hair back off her face, my fingers trailing through the silky strands.

"I know what you're thinking."

"I'm mad, Zayn. So fucking mad. Furious, in fact."

"I did what I had to do, Pen."

Her nostrils flare, the concern in her gaze falling away, replaced instead with the anger she speaks of. "All of this is because of him. You're scarred because of *that* fucking man!"

"I'm scarred by the choices *I* made."

"That's bullshit. That boy I knew wasn't a fucking murderer. *He* made you that way. I know you, Zayn, you're not this man!" she cries, her fingers curling into my shoulders as she looks down at me. I see her battling with herself, with her love for me and her disgust at what I've done. I don't envy her position. I couldn't love me either given the circumstances.

"But I *am,* Pen. Tonight I killed a man. I fucking watched the life bleed out of him. I saw his fucking soul snuff out right there in his eyes. I made sure I watched. Not because I'm a sick fuck who takes enjoyment in ending someone's life, but so I can never fucking forget what I've done. I have to live with that."

"You had no choice," she says, grasping at excuses for me when we both know that there is *always* a choice.

"I could've said no and suffered the consequences. I could've stood back and let him win. I didn't. I chose to live. I chose *us*, I chose the Breakers. I will choose you and my brothers every fucking time. So, if I have to fight a thousand men to get to that place we're all dreaming of and blacken my soul whilst I do it, I fucking will. This isn't just about me. This is about *us*."

Pen grits her teeth, and although her eyes are misty with tears, she refuses to let them fall. I'm grateful for that, because her tears will undo me, and right now I'm trying so fucking hard not to fall apart. Pen was always the one who kept us grounded, out of trouble. Without her we would've joined the Skins a lot earlier. She gave us a reason to be good. When she left, we had three years of embracing the violence with no one to remind us that what we were doing was wrong. Now that she's back and ours again, we have to adjust. It's not gonna be easy to face our crimes beneath the spotlight of her love.

"Zayn's right," Xeno says, from the open doorway. I hadn't even noticed he was standing there and by the look of surprise on Pen's face, neither had she. "Every single thing we do from now on is about the five of us. Every decision is with *all* of us in mind. Zayn needed to be that person tonight. If he'd refused to fight, if he hadn't fought back, Jeb would've known something was up and you'd better believe that cunt would've put a bullet in his brain. It doesn't matter to him that they're related. The only person Jeb cares about is himself."

Pen's shoulders drop and she nods, studying Xeno closely. "That's why you went wasn't it, to make sure if that happened, you'd be there to shoot the bastard first?"

"Partly, yes, but I really did think you'd need York tonight. Did he help to distract you?" he asks, crossing his arms and leaning against the door frame.

"Yes."

"Good. I knew he would. York has a way of making you see the bright side of life even when it's mostly fucking dark."

"Is it...?" Pen asks him.

Xeno frowns "Is it what?"

"Dark... *for you?*"

Xeno fixes his gaze on Pen. "Yeah, it has been for a long time, Tiny."

Pen swallows hard, accepting his truth before turning to face me. "And you?"

"Sometimes it's so fucking dark I think I've gone blind," I admit.

She doesn't say a word, instead she cups my face in her palm and holds her hand out to Xeno, offering us both solace in her arms. I hold my goddamn breath, but he doesn't move even though I know he wants to. I can *see* how much he fucking wants to.

"Are you really gonna stand there just like that stubborn seventeen-year-old kid you once were? There's no need to be a fucking martyr, Xeno. Let her fucking *love* you."

He narrows his eyes at me, and I swear to fuck if looks could kill, I'd be dead right now.

"Are you *trying* to piss me off?" he asks, stepping into the room and closing the door behind him. He leans against it scowling, but I see the tremble of his hand, and the way he watches Pen like he wants to fucking bury himself inside of her. Xeno ain't fooling anyone. He wants her. He wants *this*.

I smile. "That wasn't so hard, now was it?"

"Don't fucking push me, Zayn."

"You know as well as I do that I can't make you do a damn

thing, Xeno. But I am giving you a choice. You can be a chicken-shit and leave—"

"Or—?" he cuts in.

"Or you can join in," Pen finishes. Her smile is soft, warm, welcoming. Still, he hesitates.

But I won't.

When Pen turns her attention back to me, her eyes lighting up with love and lust, I reach up and cup the back of her head with my hand and pull her down for a kiss that blows every other kiss we've shared before out of the motherfucking water. I suck on the plumpness of her bottom lip, my teeth sinking gently into the flesh before I sweep my tongue into her mouth, consuming all the air within her lungs and setting fire to every last shred of doubt between us.

Wrapping my arm around her back, I haul her closer to me so she's pressed tight against my chest. My pulse thunders and she kisses me as though wanting to erase my memory of the past few hours. She kisses me knowing what I've done and loving me anyway. With every stroke of her tongue, every brush of her lips, and every gentle moan of enjoyment, the image of the man I murdered is replaced with the woman I love, with Pen.

Her smell.

Her taste.

Her touch.

Her sighs and moans.

Her voice.

Her.

"Zayn, I love you," she mutters, raining kisses all over my face.

This woman is everything. She's the stitches to my scars. The balm to my pain. The hip to my goddamn hop. The fucking light in all this bullshit darkness.

"I love you, Pen. *Fuck!* I'm so in love with you I can't think straight."

She laughs softly, her lips brushing over mine. "Then don't think. Just do."

Sliding my hands up and under her vest top, I palm her tits, my cock jerking as she groans into my mouth. We kiss for long minutes like two fucking teenagers making up for lost time. My hand slides under the waistband of her sleep shorts and grasps her peachy arse. She rolls against me, her pussy rubbing over my cock.

Fuck, I really need her to be naked right now.

Pulling back, I glance over at Xeno who's watching us both intently. He's leaning back against the door, his hands tucked into his trouser pockets, but it doesn't hide the fact that he's as hard as I am.

"We've been here before, Xeno. Why torture yourself?" I ask, shaking my head at him before removing Pen's top. Her hair falls over her chest, and I stroke my fingers over the strands, brushing her hair aside so I can palm her tit and suck her nipple into my mouth. She grasps my head to her chest, grinding against me, and I swear to fuck, she tastes like all things sweet and sinful. Like chocolate covered strawberries sprinkled with the purest cocaine. I feel fucking high.

She blows my damn mind.

"I'm not torturing myself," Xeno replies, and in my periphery I see his hand lower over his cock. "I *like* to watch. I like to watch Pen. *That* turns me the fuck on. So, do me a favour Zayn, shut the fuck up and make love to our girl."

"Then you watch, mate. Knock yourself out, because I'm

gonna love our girl enough for the both of us," I say, turning my attention back to Pen.

"I'm counting on it," Xeno responds, resting against the door as he watches me wrap her hair around my fist and tug. I don't understand the look on his face, as though he's in pain, but I can't think past this moment enough to figure it out. There's a conversation that needs to be had, but right now isn't the time.

Instead, I love our girl whilst Xeno gets his rocks off.

My gaze flicks over to him between kisses, and a huge part of me is turned on by *him* watching *us*. My best mate, my ally, my brother, watches as I slide my lips across Pen's shoulders, up her neck and along her jaw. He fixes his gaze on Pen as she gyrates her hips against mine, her pussy rubbing against my cock. Unzipping his fly, Xeno stares intently as I flip Pen over and tuck my fingers under the waistband of her sleep shorts. He mutters curse words as I yank them down her legs and throw them across the room at him. He fists his cock as I push her legs apart, my finger sliding along her glistening, pink slit.

"Fuck," he exclaims as I grip her thighs and bury my head between her legs, tasting her sweetness with my tongue. She's so goddamn ripe, so fucking delicious.

When I pull back, replacing my tongue with my fingers I glance over at Xeno and catch him pumping his cock as Pen writhes beneath me.

Xeno locks eyes with me. "What the fuck are you doing, Zayn? Don't deny our girl what she deserves."

He jerks his chin and I grin, lowering my mouth back to her sweet pussy, loving how she tastes, how she writhes beneath me. Pen comes a few minutes later, a scream ripping out of her throat, her legs shaking, her cunt pulsating around my fingers. As she comes down from her orgasm, I grab a condom from the bedside cabinet and slide it over my dick. The whole time Xeno's gaze is fixed on Pen as he pumps his hand up and down the length of his cock. Our eyes meet and Xeno nods, silently giving me his approval as I climb above Pen and slide into her with one firm thrust.

He watches me fuck our girl.

He watches as I bury myself deep inside her wet warmth.

He watches as I love Pen with every firm stroke, with every kiss, with every single cell in my motherfucking body.

I fuck her with a full heart, a damaged soul and my best friend looking on.

If I could crawl beneath her skin and stay there, I would. Fuck this world and all the shit in it. I would die a happy man buried deep inside this beautiful woman.

"I fucking love you," I grind out, smothering Pen with kisses as I slow down my thrusts into a more even tempo. I want to savour every second of this. I want to imprint the memory of her beneath me into my soul. I want this to last forever. I never want it to end. Drawing back, I pull my dick out to the tip, loving the way Pen whimpers and grasps at my arse, urging me to slide back in.

"Zayn," she whimpers, her voice breathless and needy as she pulls me down for a kiss. It turns me the fuck on that I have this affect on her, that I can make her this wet.

She's finally mine. She's finally in my arms.

"What, beautiful?" I ask, clasping her face in my hands, my thumbs rubbing over her cheekbones, as I sink inside of her inch by blissful inch.

"Zayn, please," she begs, clawing at me. Her eyes roll back in her head, her back arches and her nipples pebble, scraping against my chest. "I need to…"

"Shh, I got you," I whisper, my whole fucking body trembling with the desire to slam into her like a teenage boy fucking for the first time. Withdrawing to the tip once more, I slide back into her in one slow, torturous stroke. I continue like that, teasing us both with intense pleasure until I'm almost fucking blind with it.

"Zayn, I need to come," Pen pants, her fingers digging into my skin, her teeth finding my shoulder as she bites down on me.

"Soon, beautiful," I say, shaking now with my determination to hold back, to draw out this moment until we both come harder than ever before. I don't want fireworks; I want an atomic fucking bomb. This has been three years in the making and you bet your arse I'm gonna make sure she comes harder than ever before. I want to give my girl the world, but for now I'll make sure she has an orgasm that blows her fucking mind.

"Zayn, now!" Pen snaps, her hand flying up as she grips my jaw and pulls me down for a rough kiss. She's mad, and greedy, and I'm fucking here for it.

"You heard her," Xeno grinds out, his voice guttural as he steps closer to the bed. Pen's eyes snap open as she looks from me to Xeno. Her pupils are blown wide, her skin is flush, and her lips parted. "Make her come," he orders.

Bossy, motherfucking bastard.

"Do it, right the fuck now."

"Gladly," I respond, sliding balls deep inside of Pen, slamming into her as Xeno watches us both with heavy-lidded eyes and a heavy, straining cock fisted in his hand.

She screams my name as I fuck her, as I *love* her without restraint. We kiss messily, our hands roaming over one another.

Pen's internal muscles tighten around me like a fist with every hard thrust, and as she orgasms, I vow to never let her walk away from us again. I vow to protect her, to hold her close, to dance with her every fucking chance I get, but most of all, I vow to love this woman for the rest of my motherfucking life.

"I love you," Pen whispers to us both.

I come with her words filling my head, Xeno following shortly after, and for a few bliss-filled minutes the world ain't so fucking dark anymore.

18

Pen

"WELL, you look all kinds of beautiful, sweetheart," Beast says, whistling as I step into Tales.

"Thanks," I reply, grinning. I'm actually funneling a mix of Grim's, Clancy's and my own style by pairing black skinny jeans with my favourite heeled biker boots and a red, corseted top. I feel both sexy and stylish. My boys sure appreciated my efforts, each one of them kissing me until I was breathless before we left the flat.

Xeno snarls, putting a possessive arm around my waist. "Eyes up, *motherfucker*," he grinds out, even though Beast is being a perfect gentleman and hasn't lowered his gaze from my face.

"Xeno, don't start a fight. We've only been here ten fucking seconds," York mutters under his breath in warning. Though to be fair, he's also giving Beast daggers. It's kind of amusing because I know Beast is winding them all up. The guy is so in love with Grim it's not even funny. He's not interested in me, not in that way.

"I reckon the four of us could take him," Zayn remarks, stepping into the club behind us. He doesn't even bother to lower his voice. Despite everything that happened at Grim's last weekend, he's still pissed about Beast dropping me back to the Academy a few weeks back, it's kinda sweet in a macho, chest-bashing, kind of way.

Dax cocks his head, giving Beast a once over. "Maybe if his hands are tied," he suggests with a grin. He's the first to offer Beast his hand to shake. Beast takes it, slapping Dax on the shoulder before levelling his gaze at Xeno.

"Number one, *mate*, you call me motherfucker again and I'll deck you. Number two, Pen is a beautiful woman and deserves to be told that often, and number three, in case it's escaped your notice Grim is *my* woman and no one comes close to how I feel about her. No offense, Pen," he says to me with a wink.

"None taken," I reply, resting my palm against Xeno's chest, both in reassurance and in warning. He really doesn't need to start a fight here tonight. I agree with York in that respect.

"And lastly, the four of you couldn't take me on even if my hands *were* tied. Though maybe if Pen was added to the mix you might be able to get a one up on me. She's feisty, and *very* distracting."

Dax grins, glancing over at me. "She sure is." Pride fills his gaze followed by a heavy dose of lust as his gaze roves over me appreciatively. "Our Kid can be very, *very* distracting," he adds, and my cheeks flush at the memory of me giving him a blow job whilst he was driving the Bentley.

"I fucking bet," Beast says, smirking at the look each one of my Breakers give me right at that moment. "Man, I'm glad Grim ain't into ménage à trois. I would go mad with fucking jealousy."

"Reverse harem," Dax corrects him.

My mouth falls open. "What the fu—"

"Clancy lent me a couple books," Dax interjects with a sly grin, "She said it would be good research. She wasn't wrong. I read one last night whilst you guys were..."

"I'm gonna *kill* Clancy," I say, my cheeks heating.

"Why? They're good books," he counters with a wink.

Beast frowns, shaking his head. "Well, props to you guys, but it ain't my kind of thing. I'm not sharing my missus with no fucking one."

"Just as well, mate, because we're not sharing Kid with anyone else either, and I have it on authority that you ain't her type," Dax quips.

"What, you mean fit, tatted, with wit, charm and a big cock? I think I'm *every* girl's type. Come on, I'm a fucking catch."

Dax snorts. "Yeah, that and *old*. I know a guy who can help with erectile dysfunction. Isn't that a common occurrence in men over fifty?"

"You little shit. I'm not that fucking old," Beast retorts, cuffing Dax around the back of the head none too gently. Dax swears, giving him a shove back only for Beast to wrap his arm around Dax's shoulder like long lost pals. I'm stunned into silence honestly. It wasn't so long ago that Beast was threatening to shoot Dax dead. Now look at them.

"Nothing like beating the shit out of each other to help a friendship blossom," Xeno grumbles under his breath. If I'm not mistaken there's a little jealousy there too.

"Right lads, now that we've got the male posturing bullshit out of the way and cleared the air where our women are concerned, let's get some drinks in. Grim has gone to pick up Hudson and will be here in ten. D-Neath should be here a little while after." Beast explains as we follow him to the corner of the warehouse where the bar is located. At the moment, Tales is cleared of all furniture apart from a large circular table big enough to seat us all, and of course the fighting cage, but even that looks like it's had a new canvas fitted. I'm glad, the blood stains from the fights were bad enough to dance on.

"Where is everything?"

"We had to do a deep clean. Blood stains are a motherfucker to get rid of. The cleaners finished up this morning. We'll be good to open up again soon."

"The cleaners?" I ask, frowning. The place doesn't look all that tidy. Just empty.

"Not those kind of cleaners, sweetheart," he responds with a dark chuckle. "More... specialised."

"Ah, I see," I respond, catching his meaning. Come to think of it, the place certainly smells like a mixture of chlorine, industrial bleach and something close to paint thinner, not exactly products used in general household clean-ups. I shiver at the thought of what this place must've looked like last weekend.

He gives me a wry grin. "If you ever need to get rid of dead bodies and a shitload of blood, you just come find me and I'll hook you up."

"I'll keep that in mind."

"Good. Oh, and if you want to use the girls again in another routine, just let me or Grim know and we'll arrange for them to be here when you need them," Beast adds as an afterthought.

"Despite the bloodshed, the punters still wanna come back for more. You've certainly made a name for yourself."

"What name, the *harbinger of death*?" I joke, when really, it's not fucking funny. Beast seems to think so though, even if my boys don't. He laughs, then gets serious when no one else joins in.

"Listen, none of that shit is on you. Besides, as soon as I shot Malik's brains out of his head, the place cleared pretty fucking quickly. It ain't unusual for shit to go tits up at Tales. Most of the fuckers live off the excitement. If anyone's the harbinger of death, it's me. I got this name for a reason and I'm more than happy to take the title."

"Well, in that case, can I swing by sometime this week after I've finalised the choreography? I'd like to run through a few things with the girls."

"Sure thing. Give me a call when and I'll come pick you—"

"No the fuck you won't," Xeno cuts in. "One of *us* will bring her. Your days as chauffeur are over."

Beast grins. "Whatever you need to make you feel in control, mate. Now, what can I get you all to drink?" he asks, heading behind the bar whilst we all take a seat at the table.

"Titch would like a Malibu and Coke," York says, pulling out a chair for me so I can sit. I smile up at him and he brushes a kiss against my cheek, then sits in the chair to my left seeing as Xeno has taken the one to my right and has thrown his arm over my shoulders possessively.

"Pen?" Beast asks, checking that's good with me.

"Yep, like York said. Malibu and Coke please."

"I'll have an Irish cream over ice," York adds.

Beast cocks a brow. "Sweet tooth?"

York smirks. "Yeah, something like that," he says, leaning over and burying his nose in my hair before he presses a kiss against my temple.

"Brandy for Xeno, and a whiskey for me," Dax cuts in, sitting on York's left.

"And I'll take a beer," Zayn adds, flanking Xeno's right.

"Coming right up." Beast prepares our drinks and by the time he's added another four drinks to the tray—presumably for Grim, Hudson, D-Neath and himself— a door to the left of the bar opens.

"Good evening," Hudson says, letting in a blast of cold air as he enters. This time he's not wearing a suit but dressed down in dark jeans and a black jumper. He gives me a smile that would be disarming if I wasn't still pissed at him.

"Evening," Dax and York respond. Xeno gives him a nod and Zayn jerks his head in greeting.

Behind him Grim steps into the club.

"Hey," she says with a quick smile, passing us by and striding straight over to Beast.

Leaning over the bar, she kisses Beast passionately before taking the tray of drinks and placing them on the centre of the table. I hold back a laugh at the look of shock on Beast's face as he steps out from behind the bar.

"What was that for?" he asks her.

"Can't a woman kiss her man when she feels like it?" Grim takes a seat at the table opposite us whilst Beast hands out our drinks to muttered thanks.

"Babe, you know you can kiss me whenever you fucking like, I ain't ever gonna say no, but you're not usually so... open with your affection."

She shrugs, her gaze flicking to me. I frown. I hope this isn't her staking her claim on Beast because I'm seriously not interested in him. I'm about to say exactly that but Hudson steps in with a comment of his own as he sits at the table opposite Dax..

"You should've seen the kiss she gave me on the way over. The driver nearly crashed," he jokes, winking at Xeno who smirks.

Beast's hand hovers over a pint of Guinness and for a minute I think he's gonna lose his shit, but when he barks out a laugh, passing the drink to Hudson, I relax. "Now I *know* you're lying. Louisa would cut your balls off," he says, pulling out a chair for Grim. She sits, and he settles beside her opposite us.

Hudson raises his glass of Guinness. "Yep, she certainly would," he confirms before taking a sip of the black liquid. They both crack up laughing whilst Grim pulls out a packet of cigarettes and lights one up. The tip glows a fiery red, sizzling with the inhalation. She seems tense.

"Well, now we've got that all cleared up. Let's get started, shall we?"

Beneath a cloud of smoke, her gaze flits between Xeno and I as she takes in our body language. I'm leaning into his hold, my hand resting against his chest. I know what she must be thinking, that I've given in too easily. Whilst I appreciate her concern, I don't need her judgement. She might've made Beast work for her love and affection, but I'm not going to waste one single moment more playing games. Xeno's fingers stroke absentmindedly over my bare arm as he takes the sudden silence as an opportunity to speak.

"Beast tells us that you're reopening soon."

"Yeah, just as soon as we get the place sorted. It's getting a makeover first," she confirms, before glancing my way. "I'll let you know when we need you back, but if you need the girls to practice, let Beast know."

"Yeah, Beast said. I will swing by this week sometime..."

She nods. "Good."

"What have you done to secure Pen's safety?" York suddenly asks, squeezing my thigh. "Because we were close to losing our girl last week and not one of us is willing to put her in danger again."

"We've beefed up our security by double and have put in more stringent checks on any new members joining. No one's getting close to your girl again. Not on my watch," Beast assures me with a wink, before looking at each of the Breakers in turn.

"Has the new security been cleared? I need guarantees, not half-baked promises," Xeno growls.

Grim cocks her head, tapping the ash from her cigarette into an ashtray. "Yes, they've been cleared. What do you take me for? You're not the only one with somebody to lose."

"Babe, I appreciate your concern, but I don't need protecting. Never have. We all know I'm bulletproof," Beast says with a grin.

He reminds me a little of York, another man who thinks *Lady Luck* is on his side. Maybe it's all just bravado, and I suspect it is a little with York, but Beast really does seem to believe he's untouchable. I can tell by the easy way he holds himself and the frustration in Grim's eyes. She takes a sip of her champagne and twists in her seat to face Beast.

"That kind of arrogance will get you killed. Don't talk stupid. I need you to be smart and stay the fuck alive until we can deal with this situation."

Zayn leans forward, his elbows resting on the table. "No disrespect intended, Grim, but you didn't check out the crew who brought in Malik's man thoroughly enough. If you had, then we wouldn't be in this position now. You also knew that Malik wanted Pen and yet you *allowed* him back in your club. So, forgive us for not trusting your word. Like Xeno said, we need guarantees."

"Now listen to me, dickhead—!" Beast starts, glaring at Zayn. Grim holds her hand up and shakes her head, silencing him.

"You're right. I *didn't* do my job thoroughly enough, and for that I hold myself completely accountable. Which is why I've made sure that this time we've got Tales and everyone who works within it, protected by the best." She sighs heavily, looking directly at me. "I allowed Malik Brov back into my club for selfish reasons, but I didn't for one second think he'd dare try to kidnap you from beneath our noses. I underestimated him and that is something I'm going to have to live with, to *learn* from. I was arrogant, certain of my position. I thought I was untouchable. I'm not. None of us are. Reputation only gets you so far, but there will always be people who will test your limits. Who will try and steal what you have."

"Selfish reasons... you mean money, right?" I ask, fixing my gaze on her.

"Yes. Like I've always said, I'm a businesswoman and old habits die hard. Malik paid a lot of money to be seated closest to the stage. My greed and arrogance put you in danger and I'm sorry for it."

"Looks like I wasn't the only one who fucked up that night then," Xeno remarks.

Grim cuts him a look. "I guess not," she concedes, giving him a slight smile. "I give you all my word that I won't be complacent again. These men and women we've hired were handpicked by Hudson's head of security. Every single one has experience in the military and protective services. They're completely off grid. The best of the best."

"Completely off grid? No one's completely off grid. You can't take a shit these days without some motherfucker knowing about it," Xeno says, looking pointedly at Hudson who managed to find out about the money they were saving and their plans to live abroad.

"They're *ghosts*," Hudson says.

"Ghosts?" I question.

"For all intents and purposes, they *don't* exist. The same rules we live by simply don't apply to them."

"Then why didn't you ask these *ghosts* to help deal with Santiago? Why risk *my* men?"

"Pen's got a good point there," Beast says, earning him a glare from Grim.

"Because I needed people who were already on the inside. People who were familiar with his businesses, who could gather information in plain sight without raising suspicion," he explains.

I level my gaze with Hudson. "I understand your reasoning, but that doesn't mean to say that I agree with any of it. Frankly, I wished you'd never approached them." I'm very aware of everyone's eyes on me, but I ignore them. I'm still pissed off with the whole thing, and I didn't get a chance to voice my opinion fully the first time I met Hudson. Hence the verbal diarrhoea now.

"Even if that meant you never seeing them again?" Hudson asks me, pinning me with his penetrating green eyes.

"At least they'd be safe from harm."

"That's a falsity and you know it. Life expectancy for gang members is drastically lowered. Most don't get to see their thirtieth birthday."

"Hey, I did," Beast exclaims rather proudly.

"You are the exception to the rule, Beast," Hudson replies, then fixes his eyes back on me.

"And what you're doing now isn't life threatening? They might not get to see their next birthday, let alone their thirtieth," I point out, refusing to concede the point.

"This is something they *can* control. I've given them the chance to get back what was taken from them. They wouldn't have agreed if it wasn't worth the risk," he counters.

"He's right, Titch. No point in arguing over something that we chose. Let's just move on, yeah?" York says, squeezing my thigh.

"Fine," I mumble, picking up my drink and draining it.

"Okay, so whilst Pen is working here, she'll be protected by the ghosts—" Dax says.

"Err, who the fuck am I?" Beast remarks.

"And Beast," Dax adds with a smirk.

Xeno rolls his eyes. "Outside of Tales she has *our* protection. David has already asked Tiny to get close to us, and now Jeb has suggested we allow her to do the same, so there'll be no issues on that front."

"Good, that makes everything a hell of a lot easier," Grim says.

"But how are we going to deal with David? He's going to be calling Pen soon, and when he does, we need to give him something," Zayn says.

"What exactly did he ask of you?" Grim asks me.

"David isn't a fool. He knows that the Breakers aren't at the Academy to further their career in dance. He wants to know what they're up to. He's pissed at Jeb for keeping secrets," I explain. "He said that when the time is right, he's going to kill them—"

"Cocky fucker. I'd like to see him try," York growls.

"He said that as long as I find out what the Breakers are up to at the Academy, he won't hurt Lena. That's about the sum of it."

"Okay. We're all in agreement that David is a huge problem

that needs to be permanently resolved," Grim states, watching me carefully. "He's your brother..."

I shake my head. "He might be my brother, but he's not family. I just share the same DNA," I reply, making my point.

"So you want him dead?" Beast asks.

"I didn't say that..." I bite my lip. I don't want to be responsible for anyone's death. Even my brother's. Murder, even if it isn't by my hand, is a surefire way to stain a person's soul. I'm not sure I'm strong enough to bear the marks of such an act. "I just don't want him to hurt the people I love anymore."

Grim leans across the table and reaches for my hand, squeezing it. "When he next calls, you don't tell him shit, Pen. In fact, whilst you're on the phone why don't you tell him to go fuck himself. I'm pretty sure you've been wanting to do that for years now."

"What?" My mouth drops open in shock, and the built-in fear I've always had when it comes to my brother begins to show. I press my shaking hands flat against the table.

"I'm not sure that's the best idea," York counters, looking over at me. He knows what David is capable of. They all do.

"Lena is *safe*, she has guards protecting her around the clock, but I'm gonna add two ghosts to the team looking after her as well," Grim says, looking at Hudson who nods.

"Done."

"Even if he was able to follow through with his threat personally which, by the way, I highly doubt, neither he nor anyone else will be able to get close enough to Lena to hurt her. I guarantee you. Besides, telling him nothing, *provoking* him, might just work in our favour," Grim points out.

"How so?" Dax asks.

"David is egotistical and narcissistic, not to mention bat-shit crazy," Hudson says, seemingly picking up on Grim's thoughts. "He will hate that you're not afraid of him anymore and it will make him question why."

"I'm still afraid of him," I admit.

"Yes, but he won't know that. It will have him worried, perhaps enough to force his hand into doing something drastic."

"Drastic, like killing the people I love?"

"That's a given," Hudson says. "No, I mean drastic like going against Jeb."

"Why would he do that?" I ask.

"He's built quite a business in Mexico for Jeb and ultimately Santiago. If he believes a deal is being made without his knowledge, which it clearly is, then that's going to dent his pride. Your brother won't let that slide. He's going to have to take matters into his own hands."

"You mean take out my guys?"

Xeno laughs, hauling me closer and pressing a kiss against my temple. "Tiny, we are more than capable of looking after ourselves. He can't take *us* out."

I throw Xeno a scathing look, not impressed. "A bullet doesn't care about your confidence, Xeno, it'll kill you regardless."

"David is due to call you after the drugs are delivered. By that time, he'll make his own assumption about what's going on. The same assumption we want him to believe..." Grim says.

"That Jeb's fucking over Santiago..."

"David has always wanted what Jeb has," Xeno confirms, glancing at me. "He's played the long game. Jeb is too fucking stupid to see it."

"Your brother is power hungry," Hudson says. "Like Xeno

said, your brother has always wanted the Skins and what we're doing will give him the perfect opportunity to sow the seeds of doubt with Santiago. Once the drugs are delivered and the placebo placed amongst the mix, it won't take long for word to get out that the drugs are duds. David will hear about it too, and guess who he'll blame..."

"Jeb," I respond.

"Precisely, playing right into our hands," Grim says with a sly smile. "And all you need to do to confirm his ideas is refuse to tell him a damn thing when he asks."

"He'll run back to Santiago, who by then will have heard something's up with the shipment too. Jeb will be panicking and looking guilty as fuck. Things will begin to unravel, and Santiago will have no choice but to intervene," Hudson says.

"It's a perfect plan." Grim smiles and leans back in her chair. "When he calls, you tell him nothing. Then you tell him to go fuck himself."

"Tell who to go fuck himself?" a familiar voice asks.

"Ah, Duncan, perfect timing. Come and join us," Hudson replies.

D-Neath strides across the warehouse, acknowledging everyone at the table with a jerk of his chin, then pulls up a chair and sits next to Hudson. "So, what did I miss?"

19

Pen

BY THE TIME we return to the flat it's the early hours of Sunday morning and I'm dead on my feet. Wrapping my arms around York's waist, I lean into his hold as we stand in the kitchen whilst Dax prepares everyone a drink. Water for me, tea for York and coffee for the rest of them.

"How do you feel about everything?" Xeno asks me. His eyes are shadowed with dark circles, and I see the weight of what we've spent the last four hours discussing sitting heavily on his shoulders.

I rub my temple. "Like my head's about to explode."

"Yeah, I can relate," Zayn says, giving me a rueful smile.

"It's a lot to get your head around, but we're nearly there. D-Neath will be taking the shipment of *Dancing Shoes* in a couple weeks' time."

"I can't believe that's what they've named the drug," I say. "It turns my stomach."

"Yeah, it's pretty fucked up. The ballet shoes are a nice touch," York adds sarcastically.

"Once the shipment arrives at the Academy and part of it is successfully replaced with a placebo drug, things will start moving quickly," Xeno continues. "It won't be long before word on the street gets out that Jeb is distributing poor quality drugs to the various crews around the country, but more importantly, that Santiago can no longer be trusted as a supplier."

"Yeah, shit will hit the fan pretty quickly. People pay good money for a high, and when they don't get what they're promised there'll be hell to pay," Zayn says.

"Why not swap all of the drugs out?"

Xeno cocks his head and scrapes a hand over his jaw. "Because it would be too obvious. We need Santiago to question the whole supply chain. Right from the factory where the drugs are made and packaged up in Cuba, all the way through to the people selling them on the street."

"But if you're right about David, then he'll lay blame firmly on Jeb," I point out.

"Either way, Santiago will have to deal with the issue," Xeno says with a shrug. "It doesn't matter what gets Santiago over here, just that he *does* get over here. As Hudson explained, Santiago's reputation is extremely important to him. As much of a cunt he is, he prides himself on providing quality drugs. We mess with that; we mess with his whole business plan."

"Makes sense, but the fact that Interpol is allowing a large proportion of the drugs out into the general population surprises me," I admit, rubbing at my head. Even York's gentle kisses are doing nothing to ease the growing ache.

"I get it, but if we swap out all the drugs it will be too obvious. The key to this whole plan is Santiago losing faith in the supply chain. Everything we've put into place will eventually lead him right to Jeb's doorstep, or if we're right about David, he'll get Santiago there quicker. Santiago won't tolerate that kind of betrayal, and his pride won't allow him to send someone else in to punish Jeb," Zayn explains.

"*Kill* him, you mean," York points out, holding me a little tighter.

Zayn nods tightly. "Yeah, exactly."

I frown. "And if he doesn't come?"

"Then we go to Plan B," Xeno says.

I frown. "Plan B? Grim and Hudson didn't mention a Plan B."

Xeno watches me closely. "That's because we've not discussed it with them."

"What do you mean you've not discussed it with them?"

"We've worked with Hudson for the last year to ensure that *this* plan works. Hudson and Grim strongly believe we'll be able to draw out Santiago this way, and that when he confronts Jeb on UK soil, Interpol will sweep in and they'll both be arrested..." Xeno explains.

"But you're not convinced?"

He shakes his head. "I'm a realist, Tiny. There's a good chance Santiago *will* fall for the trap, and if he does, then fucking perfect. Like a lot of criminals, he's arrogant, and he's been in and out of the country before without getting caught. Most likely he has help. There are as many dodgy police in the UK as there are in the rest of the world."

"And yet, you've got a Plan B just in case."

"Always gotta have a Plan B," York quips, grinning down at me. He might be smiling, and pretending to be all chill, but his eyes are telling me a different story.

"What *is* this Plan B?" I persist, not liking the way all four of my men are looking cagey as fuck. "Xeno?"

"I'll kill them both."

"What?!" I snap.

"And after I put them down, I'll pay a visit to your brother and put a bullet in his head too."

For a second I just stare at him open mouthed. Then the reality of this stupid fucking Plan B sinks in. "No. No way. That's suicide and you know it!" I shout, my voice betraying me.

"Titch—" York begins, but I shove out of his hold and within two steps have my fingers pressed into Xeno's chest.

"Don't you even think about it! That's the stupidest idea I've ever fucking heard. They'll kill you!"

"Not if I kill them first," he shrugs, smiling down at me like this is all some big fucking joke.

"Xeno, it isn't funny. Are you insane?"

"No, just really good at assassinating people." This time he doesn't smile, and a shiver tracks down my spine at the implication of his words, at the confidence in his gaze. He's done this before.

"Then Plan A *has* to work," I say, stubbornly. "No matter what."

"That's the idea," Xeno replies, capturing my hand in his and kissing my knuckles. I step forward into his arms and drop my head against his chest. A moment later he wraps his arms around me and hauls me close. "We got this, Tiny."

I groan in his arms; my headache feels like little knives stabbing into my brain. "I'm not feeling so great," I admit.

"Here, take these," Dax says, passing me the glass of water and some painkillers, before kissing me on the temple. He looks at Xeno, then back at me. "You need to *sleep*."

"I agree. We can discuss anything else once you've had some rest," Xeno says, taking the proffered mug of black coffee from Dax.

"That sounds like a really good idea, actually," I reply, beginning to see stars from all the pain.

"Go and get some rest," Xeno orders.

"Aren't you going to bed?" I ask, looking between them all.

"I wanna go over a few details of the plan with Zayn. There are a few things I want to smooth out and he knows Jeb the best."

"Don't you need York and Dax too?" I ask.

"Nope," he responds, a look passing between them all.

"Guess that means we should go to bed then," York says softly, wrapping his arm back around my shoulder and brushing his lips across the top of my head.

"To sleep," Dax adds firmly, giving York a look.

"To sleep," he agrees.

༞

I WAKE up several hours later, with a thick, tattooed arm laying across my waist and the covers tangled up around our legs. Dax is still fast asleep, his breath tickling my skin. He looks so peaceful, not to mention completely delicious. I reach up and brush my fingers across the crease in his brow. He mutters in his sleep, snuggling closer.

"You know, he *is* pretty fucking adorable when he's asleep," York remarks softly, a twinkle in his eyes when I turn to face him. He has his head propped up on his hand as he looks down at us both. My heart stutters in my chest at how fucking beautiful he is with his white-blonde hair flopping over his forehead and bare chest covered in his oak tree tattoo. Laughter lights in his eyes.

"What?" I whisper, lifting my hand to trail my fingers lightly over the lifelike trunk. I feel his heart beating fast beneath my fingers, especially when they trail lower over the roots of the tree, disappearing beneath the waistband of his joggers.

"You didn't even flinch at his morning breath," he replies, swallowing hard, his joke lost beneath the lust swirling in his eyes.

"Stop it. He doesn't have smelly breath," I retort, smothering a laugh as I shift in Dax's hold so that I'm on my side facing York.

York wrinkles his nose. "You love him that much you're willing to forgive his stinky breath, huh?" he asks, his hand coming up to rest between my breasts, just above the spot where Dax's arm is still thrown across me. I suck in a sharp breath as the edge of his hand rests against the curve of my breast and his fingertips run across the neckline of my vest top.

"Stop being mean," I whisper. Behind me Dax lets out a mumble of incoherent words. "Just count yourself lucky that I love you enough to forgive *your* morning breath."

"I don't have morning breath," he counters, showing me a beautiful white, straight-toothed smile. "I just cleaned my teeth thank you very much."

I shake my head and pull a face, covering my nose. "Are you sure?" I joke, holding in a laugh as he huffs a breath into his cupped hand.

"Not funny, Titch," York grins, his hand rising from my chest to cup my jaw. He lowers his head to rest on the pillow beside mine, then runs the tip of his nose over the bridge of mine. It's a really sweet, affectionate move that makes my heart swell. "Do you know how beautiful you are?"

"I could say the same to you."

He smiles, stroking my face with his fingers as he watches me closely, his gaze sliding over my face, pausing on my lips for a moment before rising back up to look in my eyes.

"I want to ask you something," he says, serious all of a sudden as he tucks a stray piece of hair behind my ear.

"Sure, go ahead."

"Am I your favourite, is that why you've saved the best 'til last?"

For a moment I think he is actually being serious, but when his lip starts twitching and a laugh bursts out of his mouth, I shake my head giving him a shove. Behind me, Dax mutters in his sleep, disturbed by our laughter. "Shh, you'll wake Dax up."

"Uh-huh," York responds leaning in close again.

"What do you think you're doing?" I ask, licking my bottom lip. I know full well what he's about to do and my heart hammers at the anticipation of his kiss. I feel warm and safe. Being here, sandwiched between two of the men I love seems completely natural, just like it had when I'd made love with Zayn yesterday and Xeno had watched.

"Proving that you've saved the best for last," he says, before kissing me with a peppermint tongue.

I smile into his mouth as he slides his hand over my thigh and hip and presses the length of his body against mine. He's hard, I can feel just how hard through the thin material of my sleep shorts and his soft flannel pyjama bottoms which, incidentally, are surprisingly sexy on him.

I hook my leg over his so that I can rub against him. "Hmm," I hum, loving the feel of him against my aching core.

"Fuck, Titch," he mumbles against my lips, his hips grinding against me as we dry hump and kiss with muffled moans, Dax's arm still trapped between us.

"Shit, well that's certainly something to wake up too," Dax chuckles sleepily as he shifts closer behind me, his open mouth pressed against the spot where my neck meets my shoulder.

"Hands off my cock, *big boy*," York retorts, pulling back to look at Dax behind me before dropping his gaze lower. He's grinning and the love I feel emanating from him makes me go all gooey inside.

"Wait, that's your cock?" Dax exclaims in mock horror.

"Well it certainly ain't yours, mate."

Even though I burst out laughing at their playfulness, my cheeks heat. "Oh my God, you two!"

"Want to let it go now?" York chuckles.

"Gladly. I've got better things to hold onto anyway," Dax quips, his large hand cupping my breast gently as his mouth lowers back to my shoulder. The sensation of his hot mouth, teeth and tongue sliding over my skin sends sparks flying down my spine. With heavy-lidded eyes, and my hips grinding against York's cock, I arch my neck allowing Dax better access. He doesn't disappoint me, and I let out little mewls of appreciation as his large hand cups my jaw and he smothers me in kisses.

"Keep making those noises, Titch, and I might just come in my pants right now. It's been agony keeping away whilst these other bastards had their wicked way with you," York says roughly as he reaches for the waistband of my shorts and slides them down my legs, leaving me bare below. Gently his finger grazes over my slit and he growls when he finds me wet and wanting.

Dax chuckles, shaking his head. "Don't you dare, motherfucker. Our girl needs to come at least twice before you do."

"Damn right," York smirks, reaching for my top and helping me to remove it. Now I'm completely naked and at the mercy of these men.

"Fuck, Kid. I've been dreaming about fucking your pussy with my tongue again," Dax groans, sliding down my body and positioning himself between my legs. "Look at that, York, can you see her pretty little cunt, all pink and wet for us?"

I watch Dax as his tattooed hands grip my thighs gently as he settles between them. York smiles languidly, his hand snaking beneath the waistband of his joggers as he watches Dax part my pussy lips with his fingers. "Beautiful," he grinds out.

"Eat her out, Dax. Fuck our girl with your tongue. Make her come," York encourages before lowering his mouth over my breast and sucking my nipple into his mouth.

"Gladly," Dax replies, licking me from core to clit in one firm stroke.

"Fuck!" I cry, my hips jerking, one hand curling into York's hair, pulling him close against my chest, whilst the other cups the back of Dax's head and my hips rise to meet his mouth. Heat builds within my core as I throw my head back and writhe beneath them, a long groan curling out of my mouth like smoke from a cigarette.

"Look at you," York cries, pulling back and staring at me as his fingers slide between my legs beneath Dax's lips and tongue. I can't tell where his fingers start and Dax's tongue ends. I just feel heat, a blazing beautiful heat as these two men love me with their tongues and their lips, their words and their hands.

"Watch, Titch. Watch how we love you," York demands, sliding his arm beneath the pillow I'm resting my head on and lifting me up slightly. My eyes trail downwards, my elbows digging into the mattress as I attempt to hold myself upright. I meet Dax's grey-green gaze, the whole bottom half of his face buried between my legs as his tongue plunges in and out of my core.

"Look at my fingers on your clit and Dax's tongue deep inside your pussy. Do you like that, Titch?" he asks me.

"Yes," I pant as they work in tandem, York's fingers alternate between circling my clit and gently holding my pussy lips apart as Dax licks me between his parted fingers. It's so fucking hot and I feel the familiar swirling sensation in the pit of my stomach as an orgasm builds.

"I'm going to come," I pant, throwing my head back and letting out a lust-filled cry as my legs begin to shake, my nipples pebble, and my skin flushes. Prickles of sensation slide down my spine as York groans and Dax talks dirty to me this time.

"Watch me fuck your sweet pussy. Watch us fucking *love you*," Dax urges.

I lift my head back up, my chest heaving as I do as he asks.

I watch with lust and love as Dax pushes two thick, tattooed fingers inside of me.

I watch with my heart fucking racing as York's thumb circles my clit over and over again.

I watch with a cry trapped in my throat as Dax locks eyes with me then sucks York's glistening fingers into his mouth.

Into his mouth.

The sound that releases from their throats has me quaking, and my core gushing as I come.

I come as Dax deep throats York's fingers.

I come so hard that my arms give way and I fall back onto the bed, my spine arched, my toes curled into the bedsheet, a guttural moan ripping out of my throat.

Did I just imagine that? Did Dax just suck my cum of off York's fingers?

"Fuck! Oh Fuck, that was so... so..." I cry, unable to articulate how turned on I am. How fucking sexy it was to watch.

"Now that is how you tickle a pickle," York chuckles before leaning over and kissing me roughly. When he finally pulls back, Dax is lying to my left, stroking his large hands over my breasts.

"Do you do that often... Are you...?"

"Gay?" York laughs, then shakes his head. "No. I mean, I love this fucking brute, and I appreciate a good looking guy, but it's you who makes me hard, Titch. We love *you*. You're the centre of our fucking universe and we just want to turn you the fuck on. Did that turn you on?"

"Yes," I admit. How could it not? I briefly wonder what else Dax would be willing to put into his mouth and my cheeks flame at the thought.

"Tell us what you want."

"Right now, I want you to make love to me, York. I need you to do that," I reply, not brave enough yet to express my deepest fantasies.

"Then that's what he'll do," Dax says, running his lips over the shell of my ear. "And I'm going to watch York fuck you, Kid. I'm going to stroke my cock whilst he does, and when you're about to come I'm going to slide my finger in your arse. I'm gonna fill you up until you beg us for release, then I'm going to spill my seed all over that beautiful arse of yours," Dax rumbles between nips and kisses on my neck and ear.

"Oh God," I blurt out.

York's gaze darkens. His pupils are so wide that I can barely see the blue that I love so much. "Fuck me, mate, you sure have a way with words," he jokes, but his voice is thick with lust.

"Zayn's not the only smooth talker," Dax replies, grasping my chin before kissing me deeply.

"Hmm, a Titch sandwich. Just what I wanted for breakfast. Which side are you gonna be?"

Dax grins. "I thought I made that clear. I'm *bottom*."

We quickly undress each other until Dax and York are as naked as I am. When we've been kissing and caressing and exploring each other for what seems like hours, I straddle York's naked body and position myself above his sheathed cock. We lock eyes, and there's no question of how York feels for me. None.

His love is unmistakable, and I bask in it.

"That's it, Kid. Wrap your beautiful pussy around York's cock. Fill yourself up," Dax grinds out as he settles behind me, between York's parted legs.

Grasping York's cock gently in my fist, I slowly lower myself over his thick length until he's fully seated inside of me, my internal walls fisting him tight.

"Fuuucckkk!" York exclaims, his head rolling back, the veins in his neck popping beneath his skin.

"Don't blow your load just yet," Dax chuckles, his large hands finding my hips as he helps me to slide up and down York's cock. "Keep moving, Kid. Keep fucking York just like that," Dax encourages me, his hand running over my stomach and his fingers sliding between my legs as he plays with my clit from behind.

"Fuck, Titch, I'm so close," York blurts out, his gaze is heated and full of love, his fingers gripping my hips as I move above him.

"Me too," I whimper, my palms pressing against York's abs, my fingernails biting into his skin. When I'm close to coming, Dax swaps hands and presses his wet fingers between the crack of my arse cheeks. When he rims my arse gently, I let out a cry, jerking at his touch. It's surprisingly sensitive and I push back against his finger, saying without words what I want him to do.

"That's it, baby," he says, his voice guttural as he gradually presses his finger into the tight hole.

With a cry I lean forward against York's chest, my clit rubbing against his pelvis whilst his cock slams into me and Dax's finger remains seated in my arse. With every thrust of my hips, I'm closer to the edge, I'm chasing that high, and when York's arms wrap around my back and he sinks his teeth into the tender skin of my neck, I come apart.

Not long after, so do my men.

20

Pen

THE FILM CREW triple check their equipment that's placed about the auditorium whilst I stand just off centre stage and try to calm my racing nerves. This is the first time I've actually been inside the auditorium since starting at the Academy. Tucked away at the back of the building on the ground floor, it's surprisingly large and can seat a couple hundred people comfortably.

Seated in the last row of seats in the stalls are the Breakers, as well as Clancy and River. Unsurprisingly, neither Tiffany nor Sophie came to watch me dance. Not that I give a flying fuck about their absence. I'm pretty sure if Tiffany could get away with it, she'd have tried to sabotage my performance today. She's a spiteful bitch like that. Clancy already told me she had some pepper spray ready just in case. I fucking love that girl.

As the director, Scott, talks to Madame Tuillard on the other side of the stage, I go through a series of warmups to ease the tension and nerves in my body. I know what I've choreographed is good enough, but that doesn't stop me from doubting myself. Old habits die hard and all that.

"We're going to start filming in five minutes, Pen," Scott says, giving me a thumbs up.

"Sure," I reply, shaking out my hands and the tension I hold there.

Out of the corner of my eye, I see movement down the aisle, but as the stage is so lit up the rest of the auditorium has been thrown into semi-darkness and I can't see who it is until they step onto the stage. Expecting one of my guys, I'm taken aback somewhat when I'm faced with D-Neath.

"Alright, Pen?" he asks, striding across the stage towards me.

"Why wouldn't I be?" I question.

"No reason," he replies, something flickering in his gaze, something that makes the hair on the back of my neck stand. Why do I feel creeped out around him? "I just wanted to wish you luck..."

"You want to wish *me* luck?"

"You sound surprised."

"I am," I reply bluntly. The fact of the matter is, this is the first real conversation we've had since I started here, and since he referred to me as *'that short snappy bitch'*, when he spoke with Xeno after I caught him talking on the phone to Jeb that time a while back, I *know* he dislikes me. I guess the feeling's mutual.

"I ain't been too forthcoming. A lot on my mind. You know how it is," he says, giving me a gold-toothed smile that's a little too salacious for my liking. Fucking creep.

"Uh-huh." I pointedly flick my gaze to Madame Tuillard then back at him, raising my brows as I do. "I *see* how it is," I reply, reading this situation perfectly well. He's a player. I'd bet my life he cheated on Madame Tuillard and that's what she'd referred to when we spoke before.

"Anyway... break a leg?" He winks, allowing his gaze to rove over me in a way that is clearly sexual. I lift my chin, looking down at him even though he towers over me in height.

"The only thing that will be breaking is your face if you keep looking at me like that," I reply quietly so only he can hear. He opens his mouth to respond, then obviously thinks better of it. Plastering on a fake smile, I cock a brow and wait. "Was there something else?"

He gives me a once-over, then shakes his head. "Nah, nothing else."

"Duncan?" Madame Tuillard calls out from across the stage, drawing his attention away from me. "Come and meet Scott." She gives him a wide grin and my heart sinks for her. It wouldn't surprise me if he's been shagging students at this school. What a player.

As he walks away, I let out a breath I hadn't realised I was holding, the arrow on my internal cunt-o-meter hitting the red zone. D-Neath doesn't give me the chills like my brother or Jeb, that's not what I'm feeling. Apart from his clear disregard for Madame Tuillard's feelings and player bullshit, there's something else about him that I can't quite put my finger on. Shrugging off the feeling of disquiet, and benching those thoughts for another time, I bend over and touch my palms to the floor, stretching out my hamstrings whilst mentally going over the routine in my head.

"Alright, Pen, let's start shooting. Are you ready?" Scott asks after another couple of minutes.

Straightening up, I stride over to my mark on the stage and

nod. "I'm ready."

The auditorium quietens, and the lights on the stage shut off. For a moment I'm pitched into darkness, nothing but the faint red light coming from the camera recording. My skin prickles as I

focus my thoughts, centering myself as I wait for the music to start. I remind myself in the few moments of quiet who this dance is for. I've no idea if Madame Tuillard knows anything about my history, or my brother, but the moment she told me I would be dancing to this song I knew how I wanted to perform to it. I wanted to tell a story with this song, but it isn't just a lyrical piece. This is me acting as much as I'm dancing. I'm merging the two disciplines to get my point across. My body might move to the music, but the expression on my face will have power too. I'm fully aware that there's a chance my brother is going to see this video, and as such the message within it is for *him*.

This is the one and only time I will dance for my brother.

I want him to see this performance and fucking rage. I want him to know that I won't be *beaten* down anymore. I won't be *held* back by him. I won't be *repressed*, afraid, fucking terrified. I won't let the fear eat me alive. This is me showing him I'm fucking done.

This is me saying I'm fighting back.

Come get me motherfucker. Come and fucking get me.

As the opening piano sequence begins, I stand in my black shorts and matching crop top, barefoot in a pool of dim light. My head is bowed, my hair falling forward in a shroud, my feet hip-width apart and my hands loose at my sides. I breathe in deeply through my nose and as I draw in a deep lungful of breath, the first line of the song begins to play.

Just like that, a flip switch's inside of me. I feel the rage in my limbs as my fingers crawl up my body, clutch my face and grip my hair. Pulling at the strands, I tip my head back and scream silently. I remember how David used to take great pleasure in grabbing my hair and yanking out clumps of it when he used to beat on me. There were so many times he dragged me across the floor by a fistful of hair as I clawed at his hands, as I twisted and fought for him to free me. If he watches this, he'll understand. I know he will.

Stepping forward a few steps, I punch out with my fists, I lash out with my legs. I fight back with every enraged step just like I did as a kid. Sia sings about being worn down, about struggling beneath someone's abuse.

He wore me down. He beat me. He hurt me. Abused me. Was cruel. Vindictive. Vile.

I was a child with no one to protect me. No one. All I had was myself. I was just a fucking kid.

But I never once allowed him to destroy my soul. He might have beat me black and blue. He might have torn the hair from my head. He might have kicked me, slapped me, punched me, but he never, *ever* broke me.

Dance saved my life as a kid.

Right now, I'm using it to express everything I was never able to say.

Digging deep, I put every unspoken word into my dance. Every movement I make with my body is a *fuck you* to the man who hurt me in the worst possible way.

As I dance, I imitate the way I'd fought him as a defenceless kid. My body is all hard edges and sharp angles, turning it into a weapon as I try to fight back. Lifting my leg up, my knee bent, my foot raised, I kick out. I follow through the movement with a raised fist, my face twisting up in agony.

But he was always too strong.

I drop to my knees, my hands reaching upwards for that invisible tormentor, as I claw at the memory, my face twisting in agony. He fucking wore me down. He pushed me to the ground. He bruised and clawed. He punched and kicked. Right here on the stage I curl up into that ball. Trying to make myself small, hidden, invisible.

I curl up wanting to disappear.

NO!

This dance isn't about being small, suppressed. This is about fighting back. This is about getting back up every time I've been knocked down. This is about finding strength. Courage.

Tears stream down my face as my fingers claw at the floor, as I lift my shoulders up, my forehead pressed against the wooden boards of the stage. My right leg straightens as I kick out to the side. Pointing my toes, I push up onto my hands and look directly into the camera then I slam my fist against the floor repeatedly before sliding out my left leg so that I'm now sitting in the splits, my legs horizontal to the floor. With the next beat, I bring my legs together in front of me. Reaching up, I punch at the air then lie back, place my hands above my shoulders and kick my legs up and over my head in a backwards floor flip, landing on my feet with grace and ease.

Swiping at my eyes, I flick my gaze to the spot in the auditorium where I know my Breakers and my friends are sitting. I jerk my chin at them and I fucking smile. I can hear nothing but Sia's voice sounding out over the speakers, but I know I have their support, their love. I can feel their energy. It gives me the fire, the fuel to keep dancing.

Focusing back on the camera, I reach out with my hands and claw my fingers, imitating how my brother would wrap his around my throat. Then I grab my wrist with my hand and yank it down, stamping out my anger before throwing my arms wide, and twisting away in a pirouette.

That's the moment I let go. My feet practically fly across the stage as I dance just like a bird set free, just like Sia sings. My wings are no longer clipped. I'm no longer broken. I'm no longer beaten to the ground. I'm no longer silent.

Dancing is my voice, and by God, it's fucking loud. I'm screaming at the top of my lungs with my movements. I'm roaring, fucking hollering. Every step is a word that I yell.

For so long I let my fear rule me. I held it all inside.

Not anymore.

Running across the stage, I jump upwards into a straddle split leap, ripping through the air. I fucking soar, my legs wide, my arms flung out, a brilliant smile spreading across my face.

When I land, I immediately spin out into a series of pirouettes until I'm back at the spot on the stage where I started. With a heaving chest, I throw my arms wide then tip my head back in another silent roar.

Then I use all that strength, that courage and I funnel it back into the second half of my routine, into hip-hop. Stepping into the *Superman* move, I throw my arms up and kick back with my legs before changing tempo and transitioning into the *Stick and Roll*, jerking my elbows back as though I'm pulling on a rope whilst my knees turn inwards. With every step, I draw on the dance I shared with my Breakers when we were kids, using it now.

I dance for that kid who fought for her life and made me into the woman I am today.

I dance with strength, courage and fierceness.

When the song finishes, the final chords playing out over the auditorium, I stand covered in a sheen of sweat. I feel that rush of power I always get when I dance and funnel all of that energy into my eyes as I look directly into the camera.

This is for you David. This is the one and only dance you shall ever get from me.

Fuck you.

Fuck you, David.

Then the spotlight flicks off and I'm pitched back into darkness. Silence greets me, and for a moment all I can hear is my heavy breathing and the pulsing rush of blood in my ears.

Then the clapping starts.

Followed by cheers.

Whistling.

Stamping of feet.

When the lights turn back on, every single person in the auditorium is on their feet for me. My gaze automatically goes to my Breakers at the back of the studio, only they're no longer there. Instead, one by one they step up onto the stage, looking at me like I'm the most precious person in the world. They look at me with adoration, with love, with understanding, kindness, and a fierce protectiveness. Xeno swallows hard and I see the emotion leaking from his gaze as Dax puts an arm around his shoulder. York and Zayn are grinning, their love and affection obvious.

"Kid," Dax murmurs. "Come here."

I run to them, to my boys, and I throw my arms around Dax's waist, pressing my tear-stained cheek against his chest. Just like that, they wrap me up in their love, gathering around me. They don't give a flying fuck what anyone thinks.

This is us.

Fuck you, David.

21

Pen

THE SHIPMENT of drugs arrives almost two weeks to the day after our meeting at Tales.

According to Xeno, the drugs crossed the British Channel via a shipping company delivering, amongst other things, dance wear and equipment. One of the containers held a couple hundred boxes. All of them, bar one large box, were filled with dance related items. Interpol's undercover officers, who were conveniently working at Southampton port at the time, unloaded the container onto the back of a lorry which was then driven to a warehouse in Hackney. The large box marked 'Dancing Shoes' in bold letters was separated from the shipment, by an unsuspecting worker, and labelled for delivery.

Another couple of hours later, a million pound's worth of *Dancing Shoes*— the new drug made and developed by Santiago

Garcia's scientists back in Cuba— arrives at the door of Stardom Academy just as Clancy and I pass by the reception desk and head into the canteen for lunch after a long week of dance classes and rehearsals.

"Did I tell you that Tiffany has been acting up for River in their duet, the bitch is treating him like shit. I fucking hate her, she really just needs to get over herself..."

"Uh-huh," I reply absentmindedly as I pull out my mobile phone and type off a quick message to the Breakers, letting them know the shipment has arrived.

"You alright? You seem a little distracted," Clancy asks me, her pretty eyebrows drawing together in a frown. They're like two strikes of lightning, and the same bright orange colour as her hair. She's so pretty, but just like a lightning storm, unpredictable too. I love that about her.

"Shit sorry, my ballet lesson was brutal today," I explain. It's not a complete lie, Sebastian had us going through a particular section of a routine repeatedly and now my toes are bruised from the footwork. Even with the beautiful pointes Zayn bought me, I haven't come out unscathed, and will need to soak my feet as soon as I get a chance.

"River said that he's a cool guy, but a hard taskmaster."

"Yeah. I really like Sebastian too. He's down to earth and non-judgmental, not to mention a really beautiful dancer," I say, taking a tray from Clancy and loading it with tuna salad, a bread roll, and a bottle of water. Clancy helps herself to a slice of pizza, an iced doughnut and a chocolate milkshake. My girl loves her junk food. Not that it matters, we burn off the calories as soon as we consume them, but after years of eating junk food because it was cheap, I choose to eat healthily now.

"Hey, I'm sorry Tiffany's giving River shit," I say, nudging her and jerking my chin at River as he enters the canteen looking thunderous. "Poor guy has his work cut out for him with that bitch."

"You did hear me then," Clancy replies with a wink. "Oh fuck, he looks pissed off. I think he was supposed to be meeting Tiffany for a rehearsal this lunchtime. Looks like he's been stood up. Why am I not surprised?"

River spots us in the queue and gives us a little wave, but another female dancer starts chatting to him, preventing him from coming over right away. Clancy makes a little growly noise, like a puppy practising to be a guard dog. "Who the fuck is that, and why is she pawing at my man?"

I laugh. "Ease up, Clancy. Pretty sure River only has eyes for you."

She huffs, folding her arms across her chest and narrowing her eyes. "Don't tell me to ease up, Pen, you know as well as I do that you'd scratch out her eyes if she were doing the same to one of your guys."

"Yeah. Point well made."

In my pocket my phone vibrates with a new message. I pull it out, and quickly open my group chat with the Breakers. Next to me Clancy's attention is fixed on River and his new admirer.

Xeno: We've been called to Rocks tonight.

Me: About the delivery?

Zayn: Yep, Jeb wants to make sure everything's in order.

York: Cocksucker

Dax: I've checked the delivery. It's all there.

Xeno: And the placebo?

Dax: D-Neath's swapping the required amount as we speak. I'll package them up and call Hud. He'll send a courier to collect them and hand them over to Interpol to bag up as evidence.

Zayn: Good. We'll deliver the rest to Rocks tonight as planned.

York: Has Hudson been informed?

Dax: Called it in just now. I've let Grim and Beast know too.

Xeno: Good, and so it begins.

I read the exchange with trepidation. I knew this was coming, but the reality is so much harder to stomach. This is dangerous and I'm scared. Clancy looks from River, who is still chatting to that chick on the other side of the canteen, to me.

"Please tell me you're having a sext chat right now. I bet those Breakers are dirty as fuck!" she says, trying to peer over my shoulder. I press the phone to my chest.

"It's private!"

She pulls a face but doesn't push me to show her. "Spoilsport," she counters.

"But you still love me, right?"

"Yep, like a shitload." Then she turns away and gathers second helpings of everything on her tray, presumably for River. My attention flicks back to the messages on my phone.

Me: Please be safe.

Dax: Always.

Xeno: Tiny…

Me: Yes?

Xeno: We're going out tomorrow night. I'll pick you up at 7pm.

Me: Isn't there gangster shit you need to be getting on with? Besides, I have a dress rehearsal at Tales tomorrow night before the reopening next week.

Zayn: We settled it with Grim already.

York: Yep. Rehearsal tonight, tomorrow night you're ours.

Me: Okay, I'll call a cab to get me to Tales.

Dax: Beast is picking you up. I squared it with him.

Xeno: The fuck he is.

Dax: Chill man. Beast loves Grim. Besides I'd rather it was him looking out for Kid than some dodgy fucking cab driver.

The three bubbles seem to turn over forever, and someone behind me in the queue mutters "Hurry the fuck up," under their breath.

"Patience is a virtue," I snap, catching up with Clancy who's moved a few feet further along in the queue.

Xeno: Fine. This time only.

Dax: Dress up.

Me: Dress up?

York: Yeah, tomorrow night. Dress up. Della is singing at Jewels.

"What the fuck?" I squeal, slamming my mouth shut when Clancy gives me a curious look.

Me: Don't joke.

Zayn: No joke, Pen. Della is gonna be singing.

My heart races and I have to stop myself from doing a happy dance. I'm going to hear *Della* sing in the flesh! She grew up in Tottenham in the borough of Haringey, a stone's throw from Hackney. Another kid who made good on her dream.

Jesus fucking Christ.

"Oh man, here he comes," Clancy says, nudging me with her elbow. I glance over at River who's now striding towards us looking stressed as fuck, and my heart sinks a little. He's had it rough these past few weeks, and it makes me feel guilty.

Me: Can I invite Clancy and River? Tiffany has been giving them shit.

I hold my breath and wait, half expecting the answer to be no, but I care about River and Clancy a lot and they deserve a night out after everything Tiffany has put River through recently. Not to mention Clancy who's had to deal with the bitch most of her life.

York: I don't see why not.

Xeno: Sure.

Me: Thank you. Thank you. Thank you. Thank you!!!! Can you tell I'm excited! Argh!!! I love you all. Be safe tonight, okay?

Zayn: Right back atcha Pen.

York: Love you too, Titch.

Dax: Love you, Kid.

Xeno: Everyone delete this message.

I smile at Xeno's abruptness, my thumb hovering over the delete button when three floating bubbles appear once again.

Xeno: I love you.

I smile, then press delete.

"I'm telling you, Clancy, I'm gonna knock your sister out one of these days. She's being a complete fucking bitch!" River complains the second he's within hearing distance.

Clancy pulls a face. "What has she done now?"

"How about not turning up for any of our goddamn rehearsals for a start. Today's the last fucking straw. She no longer has a partner in me. I'd rather concentrate on the group dance than be fucked over by your sister one more time. She can go fuck herself. After lunch I'm going to speak with Madame Tuillard and explain my situation."

"Oh shit, I'm so sorry, River," Clancy replies, pressing her hand against his chest.

"It's not your fault. You're not responsible for her actions. She's a spoiled little bitch and you're the complete opposite. You're my little tapper." His eyes soften as he looks at her.

My little tapper? I hold in a giggle at the affectionate nickname. I mean I can hardly talk. I'm known as Kid, Tiny and Titch....

"You keep talking sweet to me like that and a girl could get used to it," Clancy replies, her cheeks blushing pink. He grins at her then meets her lips with a kiss as she pushes up onto her tiptoes.

"Oy, oy! You two wanna get a room?!" Someone in the canteen jeers as their kiss deepens. I flick my gaze away from their public display of affection whilst Clancy lifts her middle finger to whomever called out and then jumps up into River's arms, continuing to kiss him passionately. I chuckle. There she is, my little exhibitionist. By the time they pull apart, all flushed cheeks and lust-filled eyes, the whole canteen is cheering.

Clancy smiles broadly, and so does River.

"I'm sorry about the whole Tiffany situation," I say to him.

"Hey, it's not your fault. You were always supposed to dance with Dax anyway. Besides, I'm still a winner. I've got my little tapper right here." He grins at Clancy who presses another kiss against his mouth before he lowers her back to her feet.

"Come on, let's eat. I'm bloody starving," Clancy says.

We pay for our lunch then find a seat in the canteen. Ten minutes later, with a full belly and a grin spreading across my face at the affection between my two pals, I mention Jewels nightclub.

"Wait, you know the location of *Jewels* nightclub? Fuck me, that's like the best kept secret in the whole of London."

"Yep, I do."

"How..." She narrows her eyes at me, then widens them suddenly. "Wait a minute, *that's* where Zayn took you on the date wasn't it? You were cagey as fuck about where you went and now I know why. That's like THE MOST exclusive club in London ever. The rich and famous party there," she explains to River, happiness flooding her face as she bounces excitedly in her seat.

"Cool," he replies, shaking his head and laughing at her enthusiasm.

River isn't the type of guy to be easily impressed by exclusive clubs or famous people. He's the type of guy who takes people at face value regardless of their background or baggage. I love that about him. He's not judgemental in the slightest. River is one of the few people at the Academy purely here for dance and doesn't give a flying fuck about fame and fortune.

"I wasn't being cagey about it," I protest with a smile, and a roll of my eyes. "Just because I didn't want to give a blow-by-blow account of what went down doesn't mean I was being cagey.

"You so were!" she retorts with a huff, then waves her hand in the air and squeals in excitement. "I can't believe that you're going to Jewels nightclub tomorrow night. You lucky bitch. Who are you going with? Zayn took you the last time, so I reckon it won't be him again." She taps her chin thinking hard. "Ooooh I bet it's gonna be my partner in crime, Yorky baby. That sneaky little bugger has been cagey all week. Plus, the guy is like a bitch in heat... Oh, wait, what's the male version of that?"

"I've no clue," I reply.

"It doesn't matter," she says, waving her hand in the air again, and batting the rogue thought away. "I bet he'll be ramming his dick inside you the second he gets a chance."

"Clancy!" River exclaims, shaking his head at her crudeness, but smiling through it all. He looks at her just like my Breakers look at me. There's no doubt he's in love with her. My heart warms.

"What, River? She's dating all *four* of them. The whole bloody Academy knows that just the same as you. I just want to know who's drawn the lucky straw tomorrow night, that's all." She grins mischievously and River rolls his eyes in mirth.

"We're all going together," I reply with a grin.

"All four of them are taking you on a date to *Jewels* nightclub. Oh my god, girl. I'm so jelly."

"Yep, and by all, I mean you two as well—"

"Wait, what?" Clancy sits up straight, her curls bouncing around her head as she moves. "Girl, you better not be pulling my leg!"

"I'm not. You two have been working as hard as the rest of us and putting up with Tiffany's shit more than anyone. You deserve a night out. It's going to be amazing!"

Clancy squeals then throws herself across the table, pulling me in for a hug and kissing me like an overzealous mother would a toddler who's just managed to piss in a potty. "Oh my GOD! I fucking LOVE YOU, girl!" she cries, dropping back in her seat and turning her enthusiasm towards River who is shaking his head and chuckling.

"And that's not the best part of it," I say, unable to hide my own excitement now.

"What's better than this?" Clancy asks.

"Della's going to be singing."

"Shut the back door!" Clancy screeches loudly, capturing the attention of a few of the dancers sitting at tables close by. She stands upright, her chair scraping across the floor noisily as she starts doing a little tap sequence.

"Shhh, keep it down," I say, placing my finger over my lips and tugging at her arm so she sits back down. "This is a speakeasy club, totally exclusive and there are *rules*," I hiss, grinning mischievously.

"Rules?" she asks, her eyes wide and her smile growing.

"Yep. You can't tell anyone the location, it's top secret. It remains exclusive because everyone signs a non-disclosure agreement when they enter..." I lie, loving how gullible she is as she nods her head and promises not to tell.

"Well shit, now I'm even more excited."

"Is that even possible?" River says dryly, winking at me when she elbows him in the side.

"Shut up," she whispers. "Della is my idol. I love her."

"Since when," River replies.

"Since forever! Just because I haven't told you that yet, doesn't mean it isn't true."

"Well, you know what this means?" Clancy says, her smile widening even further.

"What?"

"A shopping trip. We need new outfits, girl!"

River groans. "Count me out. The last time I went shopping for clothes with you I ended up with leather hotpants."

Clancy bursts out laughing and throws her arms around his neck, planting a kiss on his cheek. "Don't even pretend you don't like them."

"I didn't say that. I'm just not coming this time." He presses a kiss against Clancy's mouth then untangles himself from her arms. "I'm going to go see Madame Tuillard. Catch you later?"

"Sure, babe," Clancy replies, waving him off before turning her attention back to me.

"So motherfucking Della, huh?"

"Yep, motherfucking Della."

22

Pen

"THANKS FOR DROPPING ME BACK, BEAST," I say, leaning my head against the headrest as Beast drives me home to the Academy. My muscles are aching from the rehearsal, but in a good way. The girls were amazing, and we've got the routine down.

"Grim told me your boys are at Rocks tonight with that prick, Jeb."

"Yep. He's got them there on *business*," I reply, finger quoting the air. "I fucking hate him so much."

"Yeah, I bet. He's always been a prick. The little cocksucker needs to be put down, but now ain't the time apparently."

I nod my head, glancing over at Beast who is gritting his jaw and looking a little less cocksure than normal. "Everything alright?" I ask him.

He glances over at me, giving me a wink that is as fake as his smile. "Yep, fine and fucking dandy."

"You sure about that?"

"Actually, I could use a drink. Fancy a quick detour?"

"Are you sure that's a good idea? I mean, the guys..."

"Pen, not being funny, but you're your own person, right? I'm your friend. I've also made myself perfectly clear to your Breakers that I only have eyes for *my* missus. Frankly, she's all I can manage." He grins then, winking at me.

"Yeah, but how would Grim feel about you grabbing a drink with me? I really like and respect Grim. I do *not* want to piss her off."

"I may act like an idiot sometimes, but I ain't stupid. I already said I was gonna grab a drink with you. Grim's cool with it."

"She is?" Something in my voice must sound uncertain because Beast chuckles.

"Yep, she is. Grim is normally pretty fucking possessive, but the fact that she's okay with us being friends says a lot about you. She trusts you, *likes* you. That doesn't happen very often."

"I like her too."

"Besides, Grim has been best friends with a rich, good looking, millionaire for years now. She often goes out for drinks with Hud and I don't bat an eye—"

"Woah, I'm not being used as some kind of pawn in your tit-for-tat game!" I exclaim, raising my eyebrows at him.

"Chill, Pen. I'm not a man who plays games. Truth is, I needed an excuse to visit this pub tonight..."

His voice trails off and I give him a quizzical look. "What's up?"

"Nothing, I hope. Just crossing the t's and dotting the i's."

"Should I be worrying?"

"Nope. Got it all in hand."

"Got *what* in hand?"

Beast glances at me and rolls his eyes like I'm making a big deal out of nothing, but I'm not an idiot, I can see how tightly he grasps the steering wheel. Something's up.

"Beast?"

"There's been some whispers about The Masks. I wanted to check in on some acquaintances, see what they've heard. They're in town tonight."

"Shit."

"Don't fret it, sweetheart," Beast says, indicating left before he takes the turn. Two minutes later, he pulls up outside a small Irish pub just off Hackney's main high street. I raise a brow at the dirty looking pub. "I know the owners. The O'Briens and I go way back."

"It's past one in the morning, aren't pubs supposed to close at midnight?"

"Like I said, I know the owners, and I happen to know they've got a lock-in going on tonight."

"Cool. I guess we get a drink then?"

We jump out of the car and head into a side entrance of the pub. Inside of *The Noble Arms* is just like the outside. Frankly, it could use a lick of paint and a thorough cleaning, but the half a dozen men who are still inside the pub don't seem to mind as they sit at a round table playing a game of what looks like Blackjack.

"Beast, how are ye?" A heavily accented voice says from the table. The beautiful Irish accent belongs to a middle-aged man with thick black hair and deep blue eyes.

"Good. Are you doing well, Col?"

"As well as can be expected," he replies, before returning to his game. None of the other men even bother to look up from their cards. I'm not sure if that's an insult or a compliment. Around us the air hangs thick with cigarette smoke that only adds more of a yellow stain to the mustard-coloured walls. The stale smell of beer, with an undercurrent of dried blood, makes me want to choke. I cough into my hand and Beast looks down at me, pulling a face.

"We won't be long, promise," he says, guiding me over to the bar. Ever the gentleman, he pulls out a bar stool for me to sit on. Standing up from behind the bar an older man in his late forties, with salt and pepper hair and the brightest blue eyes I've ever seen, surprises me.

"Shit!" I exclaim, almost having a heart attack as he gives me a quick once over before he flicks his gaze to Beast and clasps his outstretched hand, giving it a shake.

"Good to see you, Beast!" the man replies with a heavy Irish accent.

"And you, Tom. Is Arden here yet?"

"Downstairs. I'll fetch him in a bit. What can I get you?"

"A drink for my friend. Whatever she wants," Beast says.

"Coming right up. What would you like to drink, *álainn*?" Tom replies, giving me a once-over. I shift uncomfortably on my chair at his assessing gaze. "It means beautiful."

Beast notices how uncomfortable I am and steps in. "This is Pen. She's a friend of mine *and* Grim's and she's taken, so stop with the flattery."

Tom grins. "You can't help a man for trying."

"Pen is working at Tales as our new dancer, you might've heard of her...?"

Tom turns his attention back to me, his assessing gaze turning into one of mirth. "Well, shit. *You're* the girl that's got everyone in a tizzy, huh?"

"A tizzy?" I reply, holding in a nervous laugh.

"Believe me, Tom, this one gets *every* man with half a cock in a tizzy. She's like one of those *Aos Sí* you fuckers are always going on about."

"Aos Sí?" I ask, bewildered.

"Fairies," Tom explains, pointing to a brass fairy sitting above the row of bottles behind him. "They may be small, but they sure are mighty and not to be fucked with…"

"*Exactly*," Beast replies, dropping his hand on my shoulder and squeezing. "Pen ain't no wilting flower, that's for sure. She's got *a lot* of people looking out for her too. Catch my drift?"

Tom nods, getting the message loud and clear. "So, what can I get you to drink, Pen?" he asks me.

"Just a lemonade, please."

"And I'll have a pint of Guinness," Beast adds.

"Coming up. It's good to see you, Beast. Connall's missed you."

"The fucker is back? He didn't fucking mention that," Beast says, a little prickly.

"Yep, yesterday. I reckon he's balls deep in Siobhan right about now, so you can cut him some slack," Tom replies with a chuckle.

Beast laughs. "Yeah, okay. Point taken."

I look between the two, bewildered by their conversation. I've no idea who these people are. Then again, I don't need to know. These are Beast's friends, not mine. I take a sip of my lemonade and sit patiently whilst they chat for the next few minutes like a couple of housewives with nothing better to do. My phone buzzes and I take it out, clicking on the message.

Xeno: You home yet?

Me: Just went on a quick detour.

Xeno: Detour. WTF, Pen?

Dax: Err, what?

York: If that fucker tries anything on…

Zayn: We should've booked you a cab.

Me: STOP! I'm fine. I'm at The Noble Arms pub. Beast said that he's heard some whispers about The Masks. He's waiting to speak with someone named Arden…? He might know something apparently.

Xeno: The fuck! Arden?! I'm gonna kill Beast!

A moment later my phone rings. "Shit, Xeno's calling," I say, pulling a face.

Beast and Tom glance over at me. Tom pushes back from the counter, knocks back a finger of whiskey then heads towards the end of the bar. "Let me go fetch Arden for you. He's downstairs with Carrick and Lorcan. I'm guessing you need to make this quick?"

"Grand," Beast replies, slipping into an Irish accent that makes me almost choke on my lemonade before turning to me and snatching my phone from my hands. "I'll deal with this."

"Beast, I'm not sure…"

Too late. I pull a face as Beast scolds Xeno.

"Calm your tits, Xeno. Pen is safe. Arden and the O'Briens are friends. Don't get your knickers in a twist. I'll have her safely home in half an hour max."

"Beast, give me the phone back," I hiss, trying to snatch it from him, but he just winks at me and moves out of my reach.

"I'll fill you in on what I find out. Just deal with your shit, and

I'll deal with mine. Alright? Here's your girl," he says, then hands me back the phone.

"Pen. Call me the second you're out of the pub. Got it?!" Xeno snaps out in a rush.

"Got it. Jeez stop being dramatic," I whisper-shout into the mouthpiece.

"I'm not. Arden isn't someone you fuck with—"

"I wasn't planning on fucking with anyone," I retort, with probably a little too much sass given the delight in Beast's eyes and the growl coming from Xeno.

"Just call me. I gotta go!"

"Fine. Bye."

"I love you," Xeno snaps out in a rush, then the line goes dead.

"He loves you, eh?" Beast says, raising an eyebrow.

"You heard that?" I ask, tucking the phone away.

"Hard not too when he practically roared it down the phone. Did no one teach him how to woo a woman the right way?"

"You're such a plum," I say, and he nudges me playfully with his rather large elbow, then focuses his attention on the guys playing Blackjack by studying them in the mirror behind the bar. The laughter dies in his eyes and he seems to tense up just a little.

"Ever heard of the O'Briens?" Beast asks me, his voice low.

"No? Should I have?"

"Tom's family owns this pub. He's an O'Brien and the eldest of five brothers. His other four brothers have pubs dotted around London. The guys behind us are Tom's men."

"His men?"

"Yeah, they work for him. Keep Tom and his young family safe."

"Safe, from who?"

"Their rivals. The O'Farrell's. They've a long history of bloodshed. Ain't pretty."

"Do the O'Farrell's own pubs in London too?"

Beast shakes his head. "Nope. They're back in Ireland. Kilkenny. The O'Brien's moved here when the O'Farrell's took their land and their business in a bitter war over a hundred years ago. They've been enemies ever since."

"Shit, that's a long time."

"Yep. Every now and then things blow up between the families. Last time was twenty years ago. Tom's younger sister, Aoife, fell in love with Niall, who happens to be the oldest brother, and leader of the O'Farrell's. He got her knocked up, then married her and hid her away on his estate in Ireland. Four years later the families clashed in an epic fight."

"What happened?"

"Aoife was killed in the crossfire, leaving their daughter motherless. Both sides have been wanting revenge ever since, blaming each other for Aoife's death. Fucked up if you ask me," he mutters.

"Poor kid."

"Not a kid anymore. She's gotta be around twenty-three now. According to the whispers she's a rare beauty but damaged. She witnessed the bloodshed. Is mute. That's about as much as I know."

"Fuck! So how *do* you know so much about their story?" I ask, sipping on my lemonade.

"Connall, Tom's younger brother, is my best mate. Though I ain't seen him for a few months. He's been dealing with business abroad."

"Ah! So your best mate, Tom's brother, is the one currently balls deep in Siobhan?" I ask, smirking a little.

"I don't blame him. If I was away from Grim for that long I'd be doing the same."

"Okay, so who's Arden? Is he another friend of yours? Xeno wasn't too happy that I'm here under the same roof as him. Should I be worried? Is he the one who might have heard something about The Masks?"

Beast regards me. "Full of questions tonight, ain't ya?"

"Just making sure I know what's going on. You can hardly blame me. I'm already deep into my own shit, I don't really need any more."

"Arden Dálaigh is a member of the Dálaigh family. They're Irish travellers. Tough, fierce and *not* to be fucked with. The O'Briens and the Dálaigh family are tight. Arden is well known in the underground fight scene and his best mates, Carrik O'Shea and Lorcan Sheehan, fight alongside him. They come as a trio. Travel together all over Europe. They *know* things. Have seen the darkest parts of this world and survived them. Even for my standards those kids are legends."

"Kids? How old are we talking exactly?"

"No more than twenty-four. Though I swear to fuck, you look them in the eye and those fuckers are older than time itself. Everyone respects them. *Everyone*. The O'Farrells included."

"And you it would seem?" I say, surprised by the flicker of fear in his eyes.

"I might mouth off, Pen, but I know when I've met my match."

"Fuucckkkk!" I exclaim. These guys must be fierce if Beast thinks they're his betters.

"They're known as *The Deana-dhe*."

"What does that mean?"

"It's an Irish term for butterfly," a velvety smooth, Irish accent responds.

Butterfly? I almost laugh, then swallow it down when my gaze settles on the man with eyes so piercing, they rival York's. Except where York has fire within his icy-blue depths, there's nothing but ice in this man's amber orbs. His gaze flicks to me then Beast as he brushes his thick black hair back off his forehead.

"Arden. Good to see you again," Beast replies, twisting in his seat and holding his hand out for him to shake. Standing either side of Arden are two men, both of whom are extremely attractive in a lethal kind of way. Lethal like a panther before it pounces, or a shark before it bites. All three have a large butterfly tattooed on the front of their necks, the colourful wings wrapping up and around their Adam's apples but that's where their similarity ends.

Arden takes Beast's hand and shakes it. "These are my brothers, Carrick and Lorcan," Arden says, presumably more for my benefit than Beasts, given he already knows who they are.

"I'm Pen," I reply, looking between them.

"The girl who dances for Grim?" the man to Arden's left responds, Carrick. He's taller than Arden by an inch, broader and his eyes are darker than Zayn's. So black they look almost demonic. He cocks his head to the side, his light-brown hair reaching his shoulders. "We've heard a lot about you."

"That's right," Beast confirms, and I can't help but notice how he angles his body slightly in front of me.

"You killed The Collector for this one...?" Lorcan asks, he looks at me unimpressed, his strange grey eyes flicking over me briefly. The colour of his eyes matches his silver hair. I can't work out if it's dyed or natural, either way I don't fucking like him. Any of them actually. They've got a weird vibe.

"Yes."

"And you want to know what we've heard?"

"Tom told me you were in town. I figured if anyone knew about what they're up to, you would."

Arden nods, accepting a drink from Tom who's returned to his spot behind the bar.

"The Masks haven't left the castle, that I do know," Arden confirms.

Beast's shoulders relax. "Good."

Carrick snorts knocking back a three-fingered shot of something dark brown, rum maybe? "The Masks *never* leave their castle. Doesn't mean to say you're safe. Far from it. I suggest you keep your head to the ground and eyes sharp. Watch your backs. The Masks are their father's sons, after all."

"Got it," Beast replies, his jaw clenching.

Lorcan settles his stormy grey eyes on me before flicking his gaze to Beast. "Don't underestimate The Masks, they'll steal from you what you hold dear the most." A prickle runs down my spine at his words, at the look he gives us both.

Silence stretches out between us, until finally Tom speaks. "Well, it's probably time you got Pen home, yes?" he says pointedly.

Beast nods, reaching for me. He places a hand firmly on my lower back. "Yeah. Thank you for your time. I appreciate it."

We leave the pub and get into Beast's car. I turn to look at him, my mouth popping open. "I have so many questions."

"None of which I can answer, but I can tell you this. *The Deana-dhe* are legends in the Irish community. Some would even say they're gods."

I snort. "Gods? I'm pretty sure they're humans like the rest of us. Made of flesh and bone."

"That's not something I'd like to test out," he mutters.

"They seem to know a lot about The Masks..."

"They know a lot about everyone. Grim and I included."

"Do you believe what they said?"

"Every word," Beast replies before putting the car into drive and pressing the accelerator.

"Should I be worried?"

"No. *You* shouldn't. It's me and Grim who need to keep our eyes open and our ears to the ground. I shot Malik after all."

"Beast—"

"Pen. We got this. It's gonna be cool, okay?"

"Okay," I mumble, not convinced in the slightest as I pick up my mobile phone and call Xeno as promised.

23

Pen

"HERE WE ARE," Xeno says as he parks outside the pawn shop, which fronts Jewels nightclub, the following evening. I smile over at him as his hungry gaze slides up from my killer heels, along my bare legs and up my deep purple, floaty dress, finally resting on my face. "You look beautiful, Tiny."

"Thank you." My cheeks heat under the scrutiny of his stare and the dangerous edge of his love. Whenever Xeno looks at me this way, I feel like a glacier melting under the intense heat of the sun. Tonight he's wearing a sharp, dark grey suit, an open collared white shirt, and black and white brogue shoes, the kind gangsters would've worn back in the 1920's and 30's. His curly hair is slicked back with wet-look gel and he's cleanly shaven. I've never seen him look so handsome. I shift in my seat, pressing my thighs together.

"You okay?" he asks, his eyes flicking downwards, a knowing smile lighting his emerald eyes.

I raise my hand and brush my thumb over his bottom lip, my fingers sliding along his jaw. "I'm more than okay. You look amazing, Xeno."

"As much as I'd love to watch you two get it on, I kinda want to hear Della sing first," Clancy says, laughter in her voice.

River chuckles. "I dunno, I reckon Pen and Xeno would put on quite the show."

"One you'll never be invited to watch, my friend," Xeno replies with a wink. He bites my thumb playfully then hops out of the car. A couple of minutes later we're sitting down at a large circular table right next to the stage.

"Where are the guys?" I ask.

"They'll be here soon," he replies, motioning for the waiter to come over as we settle into our seats. Xeno orders a bottle of Dom Perignon and a bottle of Cognac.

Clancy grabs my hand beneath the table, leans over and squeals excitedly in my ear, successfully distracting me from the fact that Zayn, Dax and York aren't here yet. "Dom Perignon! That stuff costs a bomb!"

"Fifty pound a glass, apparently. I've no idea how much that bottle costs."

"Shit on a stick. I do not have that kind of money..." she hisses under her breath.

"You've been good friends to our girl. We appreciate it. Tonight's on me," Xeno says gruffly, before turning his attention back to the waiter who's still hovering nearby. He motions him back over and talks in a low voice. After a moment the waiter nods, then tips his head at me and disappears into the club, presumably to get our drinks.

"Everything okay?" I ask Xeno, still feeling unsettled that the others aren't here yet.

He rests his hand on my thigh, squeezing gently. "You're stressing out. Don't. They're on their way."

"But—"

"How did last night go with the rehearsal?" he asks, changing the subject.

"Shouldn't I be asking you how last night went? Jeb rubbing his hands in glee yet?"

"We're not talking about him tonight, okay? I'll fill you in on everything later."

"Fine. You're right."

"So the rehearsal?"

"It was great. The girls are getting better and better with every routine I teach them. Grim seemed pleased, and I guess that's all that matters."

Xeno nods. "Anything you put together is incredible. You're a beautiful dancer, Tiny. Grim's lucky to have you even if I hate you working there. As soon as this is over, your obligation to Grim will end."

"It's not an obligation. Despite everything that's happened I like working there. I want to cont—"

"No. Absolutely not," he counters, shaking his head. There's a finality to his tone, and it puts my back up instantly. I give him a look which he meets with a stubborn one of his own. "I'm already pissed at Beast for taking you with him to meet *The Deana-dhe*. I've never met them, but I've heard the stories."

"Exactly, *stories*. They're humans like the rest of us."

Xeno's jaw tightens. "Yeah, I don't believe in those fairytales either, but that doesn't mean to say they're not fucking demonic in every other sense of the word. I don't want you rubbing shoulders with the likes of them and you will if you continue to dance for Grim. That's *her* world, it's not yours, Pen."

"We'll discuss this later," I say, trying not to let this moment ruin our night. There's a lot of sense in what he's saying, but I'm not some little woman Xeno or the rest can push around. I need to make my own choices, and my own mistakes.

Xeno gives me a curt nod. "Agreed."

"OhMyFuckingGodThisPlaceIsUnreal," Clancy blurts out from beside me, running her words together in her excitement as she pulls my attention away from Xeno and starts pointing at the stage. The curtains have been pulled back to reveal a stunning grand piano, the smooth dark wood glinting in the overhead lights. The club is large enough to house a couple dozen tables and a large dance floor, but the decor is stylish and the lighting soft, giving the impression of a much more intimate space.

I smile. "It's pretty impressive, isn't it?"

"Urgh, it's surreal. So, *this* is how the other half live, is it?"

Laughing, I nod. "I guess it is." Little does she know that the *other half* she's referring to includes Xeno and the rest of the Breakers who own this place.

"You look gorgeous by the way, and totally fit in."

"Thanks! I *do* feel sexy." Clancy grins, then leans in close. "River actually said he'd rather spend the night fucking me in this dress than come to the club. So, I know I must look good."

"I'm not surprised."

"That's not quite what I said..." River pipes up. "I said that I'd really love to fuck you all night long in that dress."

"They'll be plenty of time to fuck all day tomorrow," Clancy counters, biting on her crimson lip seductively. The colour matches perfectly with her slinky, low cut, dress. The second I saw it; I knew she'd look killer in it. Paired with a pair of strappy black heels and her shapely dancers' legs, she looks hot. The flickering candlelight at the tables and subdued lighting throughout the club picks up the golden lights in her red hair perfectly. River really is a very lucky guy, and by the appreciative looks she keeps getting from other patrons, I'm not the only one who thinks that.

"I'm happy to be here. It's a pretty cool place..." River's voice trails off as his attention is drawn to someone on the other side of the club. "Is that *Burnzy?*" he asks, his eyebrows lifting in surprise. For someone who isn't usually impressed by famous people, he's looking pretty starstruck right about now.

"Yep. Burnzy and Della are good friends. They're regulars here. It wasn't long ago when they performed together on the stage," Xeno says like he knows them both intimately. Perhaps he does.

"Sir, your drinks," the waiter says, interrupting the questions that I just know Clancy is desperate to ask, given the wide-eyed look on her face. Xeno nods his thanks to the waiter who places a bottle of Cognac on the table with four crystal cut glasses then takes the champagne cooler and glasses from a fellow waiter and adds those to the table too.

"Champagne or Cognac," Xeno asks us.

"Champagne for me and River, please," Clancy replies, taking the glass from the waiter when he hands it to her.

"And for Madam?" the waiter asks.

"Champagne too, please."

Once the waiter has poured me a glass and Xeno a double shot of Cognac, he leaves us to enjoy our drinks.

River takes a sip of his champagne, watching Burnzy greet some friends a few tables over. "I got to admit, I love his music."

"*You* love Burnzy?" Xeno asks, looking at River above the rim of his glass.

"What, because I happen to be a ballet dancer, I can't enjoy Grime music?"

"He's got a point," I say.

"You don't seem the type, that's all... I don't give a shit either way," Xeno shrugs, taking another sip of his Cognac and focusing on the stage.

"Well, I'm glad we got *that* cleared up," River mutters.

Clancy pulls a face and fidgets nervously in her seat next to me. This is the first time outside of the studio that our respective boyfriends have socialised. Neither one of us wants it to go tits up.

Xeno glances at River, lowering his glass to the table. "That was rude. I apologise. I'm not a cunt, at least not all the time."

"Just a cunt in rehearsals, to people you don't like, and when deciding who should or shouldn't like Grime music, then?" River counters with a smirk.

Xeno doesn't respond immediately, and for a minute I think he's going to pull a gun and point it at River's head. He doesn't, thankfully. Instead, he chuckles. "That's about right."

River shrugs. "Hey, at least you're man enough to admit it."

"I've got Tiny to thank for that," Xeno says, sliding his gaze from River back to me.

For the next half an hour we sit and talk, enjoying each other's company, until Xeno gets up and excuses himself. I capture his hand, looking up at him. "Should I be worrying?" I ask.

He shakes his head. "Nope, five minutes and the guys will be here. I just need to check in with Jasper, the Maitre d'. I won't be long."

"Okay." I frown. He's acting cagey and I'm not sure I like it.

Xeno presses his finger against the crease in my brow, then strokes slowly down my nose before bending down, cupping my face and kissing me breathless. By the time he finishes I'm too flustered to call after him as he strides away. "No fair," I finally manage to mutter.

"You really are a lucky bitch," Clancy says, chuckling.

Just when I'm about to go look for Xeno, the lights dim in the club, casting us all into darkness. A familiar tune begins, the piano chords sounding out around the club as it descends into silence.

"Oh. My. God. This is it!" Clancy whisper-shouts under her breath. She grasps my hand on the table and squeezes. "I love this track. I might cry!"

I'm about to respond when Della begins to sing, and the stage is slowly illuminated to reveal her sitting behind the piano, her fingers moving expertly over the keys. She looks stunning in a simple white blouse and wide-legged black trousers, her hair up in a sleek chignon and her make up perfect. The audience falls into raptured silence, and my skin breaks out in goosebumps at her beautiful voice, but it isn't her singing that has me gasping.

It's my Breakers.

"What. The. Fuck?" Clancy exclaims, her fingers squeezing mine in a death grip. "They're *dancing*!"

My mouth drops open in shock, no words forming as I watch York, Xeno, Dax, and Zayn spin out onto the stage in a series of side-split leaps. They jump so high that Della smiles and the crowd gasps.

My heart... it fucking gasps with them.

Bare chested and wearing loose white trousers that sit low on their hips, showing off their beautifully defined muscles and stunning tattoos, my Breakers dance. They move fluidly around the grand piano, with light, graceful steps that are full of emotion and feeling. The only dance I've ever seen them do together is hip-hop, so I'm stunned by the gentleness, and the absolutely stunning expression of *longing* and *love* that fits perfectly with the lyrics.

They're just so... so beautiful.

"This is for you. You know that, right?" Clancy whispers, her voice choked with tears. "Jesus. I can see why you love them so much. I think *I'm* in love with them all a little."

"Me too," River adds softly.

I can't answer. I can't seem to do much more than breathe, and even that is difficult. My hands begin to shake, my throat tightening, clogging with heavy tears. Every step they make, every move across the stage, every word Della sings and the incredible conviction of their dancing, it does something to me. It gives me *hope*. Hope that despite our mistakes, despite our bad decisions, despite our circumstances, despite the people trying to destroy us, we have a chance to be happy. Really, really happy.

We were lost for so long. All of us wrapped up in our own pain, afraid to move forward, afraid to forgive, afraid to love again. Now we've found a way back to each other. Through dance, we found a way to *see* each other once more. To see who we really are beyond the various masks we all wear to protect ourselves from the world.

Right now, they're not the Breakers, they're not gangsters or members of the Skins, they're not the owners of this club, they're not even my guys. They're *dancers*. They're their own true selves.

They're the men they were always supposed to be and it's a beautiful thing to watch.

Xeno dances with a freedom I've never seen before. He's usually more guarded, more protective of who he truly is. But I see more of his heart than ever before as he launches into the air in a front flip and lands on light feet. His chest heaves as he looks out into the audience, at me, and even though he must only be able to see darkness and the faint glow of the candles flickering, I feel the connection, it zings across my skin as I break out in goosebumps.

"Holy fucking shit," Clancy mutters.

Xeno steps back into the shadows and Zayn steps forward, grinning, then he throws himself into a series of hip-hop moves that astound the audience with a display of his genius. Zayn transitions from a *head slide* into a *windmill* then a *turtle* before flipping upwards and finishing up with *happy feet,* reminding me of a time when things were so much simpler, even though it didn't feel that way at the time. It reminds me of when we were young, when life was less complicated. He throws a smile into the audience, winking sexily and I know it's just for me.

"These guys..." Clancy mutters, and those tears I was holding inside begin to slide down my face. This is their way of expressing their love. It's an apology for the three-year absence, for the hurt and the longing. This is forgiveness. This is... *everything.*

"I know..." I whisper, utterly entranced as Zayn steps back and York steps forward, high-fiving as they swap places.

York's dance is a mixture of joy, grace and exuberance. There's a freedom to the way he tap dances that is impossible to replicate, and a power that comes from a place deep inside, from his soul. Every step, every shuffle-ball-change, every stomp, every flare of his arms, every fucking droplet of sweat is York giving himself to me.

"I swear York is Fred Astaire reincarnated," Clancy says, as enraptured as I am. "Wait, actually more like Bill 'Bojangles' Robinson. He's in-fucking-sanely good. I'm in awe, Pen."

"Me too," I whisper. "Me too."

The spotlight falls on Dax next, illuminating him in a soft yellow glow as he performs a series of pirouettes, spinning on the spot with his right leg extended then bent as he turns, moving so fast and with such elegance that there isn't one person in the club who isn't astonished by his gratefulness. Finishing with a side split, his left foot flat on the floor, his right toe pointing to the ceiling and the material of his trousers leg sliding down to his hip revealing even more ink, the audience goes nuts. They cheer and clap, in awe of this huge, muscular, tattooed man performing ballet with such dexterity and finesse.

"Fuck me!" Della exclaims, saying what everyone else is thinking.

With a heaving chest and a wide grin, Dax lowers his leg and looks out into the crowd, his eyes searching until a second spotlight falls over me. He smiles and raises his hand, jerking his head as the rest of the Breakers step back into the light. All four of my guys look at me just as Della takes the mike and stands.

"Pen, care to join us?" she asks, laughing in that dirty-sexy way of hers at my clear shock.

"Oh. My. God!" Clancy blurts out, nudging me with her elbow.

"I can't..." I murmur. This is different to dancing at Tales with the girls. This is *Della*, the hottest UK singer around. These are my guys. This is too personal. My heart is pounding so loud I'm afraid it's going to give out.

"You bloody well can! Slide off those heels and go dance with your boys. If you don't, then I will!" Clancy encourages with a laugh.

A different beat begins to play and another, male voice starts to sing, breaking only to speak. "Get yo arse up here, Pen!" Burnzy shouts, stepping out onto the stage and winking at my Breakers.

"Hell to the fuck, yes!" River exclaims loudly, jumping to his feet as he starts to dance to the music that begins to play. All four of my men grin as Burnzy and Della begin singing their version of *Own It*.

"Oh, what the hell," I exclaim, kicking off my shoes and striding towards the stage.

The club erupts with cheers and whistles as I step up onto the stage and fucking *own it*, dancing with the men I love.

24

Dax

KID SLIDES her hand into mine, grinning as I place her in the centre of the semi-circle we've created just for her. Stepping back to stand beside York, the four of us watch her intently. Her eyes are glassy with emotion, her cheeks flushed, but her expression is one of pure joy and a deep, heartfelt love. Like my brothers, I feel her love like the force of a motherfucking truck ploughing into my chest. She takes my damn breath away.

"Dance with us," Xeno says, his voice gravelly and dripping with unspoken words as Burnzy sings.

Kid looks at him, grooving to the beat as she bites her lower lip. Electricity sparks between them, hitting me in the gut, but I'm not jealous of their attraction, I never have been. What we have is unique, special. These guys are my fucking brothers, and Kid is *our* soulmate. I knew it the second she walked into the basement of number 15 Jackson Street wearing her bruises like armour. That tiny, courageous little girl became my Kid. Our lucky penny. Our motherfucking world.

With flushed cheeks, she stares at us one by one, setting us alight without even touching us. A slow, sexy smile spreads across her face as she lifts her arms above her head and rolls her body, lowering to the floor then back up again. In return we let loose, grooving to the beat with fire and lust in our eyes. Turning around, Kid throws one last sexy look over her shoulder before she slides her hands down her thighs, cups her knees, widens her legs then starts to twerk in time to the beat. From our position, the skirt of her dress lifts, showing off the tops of her thighs, and revealing the slip of white material that covers her pussy. My cock fucking jerks in my pants.

Fuck. Me.

She motherfucking *owns* it. Just like we knew she would.

Without thought, I freestyle to the beat, focusing on her sexy body and complimenting her steps with my own. Right here and now, she is *fire* and I'm more than fucking willing to burn up in her flames.

I know the guys feel what I feel, this gut-churning, soul-squeezing, cock-clenching, ball-tingling, motherfucking *love*. She makes me feel like I can rule the goddamn world. She makes me feel like a fucking king, and when she dances it's as though we're the only ones in existence. Every other fucker fades away. All our problems disappear. All the hurt dissolves.

This girl has the power to reset time, I swear to fucking God.

"Fuck me," York mutters, voicing my thoughts out loud.

I glance at him, he's practically salivating, and I would've fucking laughed if I wasn't doing the exact same thing. Just like Zayn and Xeno he freestyles, moving in time to the beat. We dance, complimenting each other's steps without even having to think about it, because just like Kid is ours, we are each other's too. We belong together, the five of us. We always have.

I'm not a religious man but I swear that there's something spiritual that happens when we dance together. We might be mere mortals, but Kid, she's a motherfucking goddess.

Nothing compares to her.

Not one damn thing lives up to her and the way she makes us feel.

She is the motherfucking centre of our universe and there isn't a thing that will change that.

Fuck, I'll dance every goddamn day for the rest of my godforsaken life until my feet are nothing but bloody stumps, if that's what it takes to keep her happy. I'll worship her. I'll protect her. I'll love her until my heart stops beating, and then love her even more in the afterlife.

Kid jerks her body, her feet stomping to the beat, her thighs and calf muscles flexing with every step. I watch her, practically salivating as her tight little arse moves beneath the silky material of her dress. She clutches the hem, lifting the material with hands, as she interjects some latin steps into her dance that has my balls tingling.

I could come just watching her dance. One day I want to test that theory.

Zayn lifts his fingers to his lips and whistles, breaking me out of my lust-crazed thoughts. She throws him a sexy smile over her shoulder then really sinks into the dance, changing style completely and dropping some Azonto steps, a native dance to West Africa. Xeno's eyes nearly pop out of his head as she bends her knees, swings her arms and jumps back and forward in time to the beat. Of course, none of us can resist the call of such a tribal dance as we imitate her steps, adding our own personal flare. Soon she switches pace and transitions into street dance, beads of perspiration sliding over her skin as she dances. Always one to keep us on our toes, her flare for creating incredible choreography rivals that of Zayn.

The spotlight follows her as she moves around us, dancing with each of us in turn. Zayn presses his front against her back, taking her outstretched hands and with her knees pressed together, she corkscrews downwards, before rising back up again. He presses a kiss against the curve of her neck then lets her slide into Xeno's arms as he gets down and dirty with her. She grinds against his thigh that he's slid between her parted legs, then bends her over backwards, the tip of his nose running up from her belly button to the dip in her throat as he lifts her back up. I watch the electricity spark and crackle between them as Kid rises up onto her tiptoes and brushes her lips against his mouth before she spins away into York's arms.

York grins so fucking wide, I'm sure his face is about to split in half. The love he shows her in that one look as he wraps an arm around her waist is combustible. He's mad for her, just like we all are. Bringing Kid to his side, they tap a sequence of steps that ends up with Kid sliding into a split that has the crowd losing their shit.

With a cheeky peck to York's cheek she rises up onto her tiptoes, then dances towards me. I nod once and she picks up speed, launching herself into my arms. Kid steps onto my bent knee and I lift her off her feet, throwing her up above my head. Flipping her legs out horizontally, I catch her as she falls. It's a lift we've been practising for our duet and she pulls it off perfectly.

It really doesn't matter what style Kid dances—tap, contemporary, lyrical, hip-hop, ballet, freestyle—our girl owns every damn one. Just like she owns me. Just like she owns us.

A possessive growl rips out of Xeno's mouth, as I lower her slowly down my body and kiss her deeply before letting her go. I wink at Xeno then turn my attention back to Kid. We all watch her with lust crazed eyes as we freestyle to the music, our blood pumping, our hearts beating, our bodies vibing. We dance without inhibition, and for the first time in a very long fucking time, I feel real joy. It's like the sun finally shining after years and years of surviving the night.

Like Burnzy sings, she's on fire and all we can do is bask in her blinding light with the knowledge that she's ours once again.

Throwing a look over her shoulder at us, Kid grins, then recreates our winning dance from that fateful night all those years ago. She shreds the stage with her passion, with her determination, and I watch with fucking pride as she holds up a metaphorical middle finger to the mistakes of our past, to Jeb, to David. If I were a betting man, I reckon those cunts' ears are burning. That wherever they are right in this moment, they feel a shift in the air; they sense that there's a day of reckoning coming soon…

With passion firing in our veins, with love pumping in our hearts, with courage in our lungs, strength in our bones and fight in our muscles, we rip up our history and shred the past with our steps. With perfectly synchronicity, Xeno, York, Zayn and I gather around our girl and fucking dance like we've never danced before.

The energy between us is indescribable, palpable. It's fierce, fucking powerful. Right here, right in this moment, we kick arse and take names, and just like that, Kid resets time. She gives us another chance to start over.

We take it. We take this chance to be happy.

Unafraid. Fucking whole again.

25

Pen

FOR THE NEXT week and a half we exist in a state of blissful happiness. It might be a fragile kind of happiness, a happiness that can be ripped away from us at any given moment, but we grasp hold of it with both hands. I make sure to spend time with each of the guys in and out of the dance studio, cementing our bond with every passing day. We've slowly got back to the comfortable way we were with each other when we were kids. The ease of being in each other's company has returned, and our relationship has strengthened.

I love my Breakers, completely and wholly.

It isn't just my love life that's been going well either. My performance at Tales over the weekend was well received. Despite how I came to get the job, the fact that I'm earning a decent living dancing makes me insanely happy. Grim and I are becoming good friends and no one's more surprised by that fact than I am. I've even been home twice in the last week to visit Lena and even though I'll never feel comfortable around my mum, or even find it in my heart to forgive her for how she's treated me over the years, I can see the difference in her already, and I can also see how happy that makes Lena. I guess that's all that matters, when all is said and done. I don't need a relationship with my mum, but I'm glad Lena has one.

As I dance in the studio with Dax, it's easy to convince myself that things will be okay, that the plan will work and someday soon the Breakers will be free from the Skins, and I'll be free from my brother. It's easy to convince myself we'll have the life we've always wanted, easy until my phone rings and a familiar name appears across the screen.

"Fuck!"

"What's up?" Dax asks me, picking up his towel and wiping the sweat off his face. We've been working on our duet for the last couple hours and we're just packing up.

"It's David," I say, my hands trembling as I look up from the screen.

Dax strides over to me and takes my free hand in his. "We knew this day would come. You got this, Kid. I'm here. We're here. Lena's safe. You're safe."

I nod, answering the call.

"Fucking *finally*, what were you doing, Penelope? Did you have your mouth filled with cock, you dirty little whore."

"What is it, David?"

"Don't take that tone of voice with me, bitch! You know full well why I'm ringing."

"You're right, I do."

"And?" he snaps, reacting with even more anger to my cool, steady voice. I look up at Dax who gives me a nod and squeezes my hand.

"And nothing, David. I have no information for you."

"YOU FUCKING WHAT!" he roars, loud enough for me to pull the phone away from my ear. Dax's nostrils flare, his eyes gleaming with rage. I lower the phone back to my ear and wait for him to finish his tirade.

"I don't have the information you want, but what I do have are *my* Breakers and I've got you to thank for that."

"You stupid bitch. Do you really think that because you've opened your legs to those pricks that you're safe? Neither you nor Lena, or those cunts are safe. Mark my words, Penelope, you're going to regret ever fucking me over!" he sneers.

I can't help myself; I laugh. I laugh so hard that tears stream down my face. Dax looks at me with concern, but I wave it away. Maybe I *am* a little hysterical, maybe this *is* years of pent-up emotion finally tumbling out of me. Either way, it feels good to laugh in the face of my biggest tormentor.

"Just get it all out, David," I say as patronisingly as possible. A deathly silence fills the line and I grit my teeth.

"Tell your Breakers and that cunt Jeb that I know all about what they're doing. Going behind my fucking back. Thinking I wouldn't find out. I'm a part of the Skins! Fuck, *I'm* the fucking brains behind the goddamn outfit and Jeb has the fucking gall to leave *me* out of the loop!"

"I don't know what you're talking about."

David laughs. He knows as well as I do that I'm lying. "Just know this, Penelope. I'm gonna kill your precious Breakers, then I'm going to kill Lena and *then* when you've lost everyone you love, I'm coming for you. When that day comes, there will be no one left to protect you."

"That's a threat I've heard a million times before, David. I'm not scared of you anymore. You don't have the power to hurt me. Do you hear me? I. Am. Done."

On the other end of the line David starts shouting incoherently at me, but I block out the steady stream of abuse, concentrating instead on Dax who gives me a look so filled with love that I find the strength to say what I've always wanted to say to my brother, but had never been brave enough to.

"Do you know what David—"

"What, *Penelope?*" he sneers.

"Go. Fuck. Yourself!"

Then I end the call, drop the phone and throw myself into Dax's arms. He hauls me against his chest and presses a kiss to the top of my head. "I'm so proud of you, Kid. God fucking knows I want to kill that cunt for speaking to you the way he did."

"He won't let this go, Dax," I reply, knowing with absolute certainty that he'll follow through on his threat, or at least try to. Despite that, I'm not alone anymore. I don't need to kowtow to his cruelty and brutality. It's time to stand up to my brother.

"You're right, he won't, but what the fucker doesn't realise is that I won't let him hurt you ever again. You hear me, Kid. *Never again*," Dax says vehemently. Then he cups my face in his palms and kisses me until I forget my brother's threat and all the years of abuse I've endured by his hand.

"Come on, let's dance one more time," Dax says, taking my hand in his. He picks up his mobile phone and selects a song, bluetoothing it to the speakers before tucking it back into his back pocket. *Rise Up* by Andra Day starts to play; it's the song we've chosen to choreograph a duet too and the words mean a lot to the both of us.

Dax understands how I feel more than most. He understands what it's like to live with abuse daily. He understands the pain, the self-hatred, the disappointment, the bitterness and anger. He understands the fear and the rage. We will rise up above our past abuse. Together we will overcome all of the heartache and sadness because all we really need is each other, just like the song suggests.

Pressing his palms against mine, we raise our hands slowly upwards. Dax smiles down at me, his chest heaving as I slide my right leg out to the side, sweeping it behind me and drawing an imaginary half-circle with my pointed toe. Placing all the weight on my back foot I walk backwards as Dax moves forwards, our hands still pressed together.

"We'll get through this," he says, sliding his hands down my arms and torso in a sensual sweep, until finally resting them on my waist. "Your brother is a black stain. He's discoloured your life for too long now. It's time to fight back, Pen."

"I know that," I respond, lowering my hands to his shoulders. "I'm done being scared."

Dax nods, his fingers curling tighter around my waist as he presses a lingering kiss against my lips. On the next beat he lifts me up on straightened arms, the muscles flexing with tension beneath his skin as he holds me aloft. You would think I weigh nothing, held up like this with my thighs pressed against his torso and my hair falling in a shroud around us both, but Dax is strong, both physically and mentally. He's my protector, my dark knight, and one fourth of my beating heart.

"I love you, Kid. I'll keep you safe, no matter what," he says, a fierce protectiveness blazing in his eyes as he bends his arms and legs then throws me up in the air, just like we've been practising. I throw my legs out, twisting my body so that it's horizontal to the floor and just for a brief moment my heart stops beating in fear that he won't catch me.

But he does.

Every single time he catches me when I fall.

As soon as I land in his arms, I fling my arms above my head and point my feet before he flips me so that my stomach is pressed against his and I'm wrapped around his waist, my knees against his lower back, my arms reaching for my calves. Pressed against him this way, his skin hot against mine, his muscles firm, *strong*, as he holds me, I feel safe.

"I won't ever let you go, Kid. Trust me to keep you safe," he mutters, and I feel his strength encircle me as he bends his knees and curls over my back until we're joined together like two interlocking chains, separate from each other but part of a whole.

For the next few beats of the song, we remain joined together this way until he slowly lifts his torso and I unfurl from around his waist, rolling my body so that my back hits the firmness of his thighs and he helps me to stand.

With his hand curled in mine, we turn back-to-back, my head resting against his spine. I feel the thump of his heart, sure and strong. I feel the heat of his body pervade mine. I feel the intention in his movements as he rolls his body, then bends at the waist, leaning over to the side as his tattooed arm slides over my stomach. I mirror him, leaning to the side, my arm sliding across his abs. The love in his eyes as I twist my head to face him, takes my breath away. His fingers press against my skin as we straighten up. My hand falls away from his torso and Dax steps around me, so that we're facing each other.

"You have me forever, Kid," he mutters, pressing his forehead against mine and resting his hands against my hips. He kisses me then, a tender brush against my lips before he spins away and waits for me on the other side of the studio. I move towards him, every sway of my hips, and point of my toes, every twist and turn, every goddamn step full of meaning, intention, *love*.

He's a fighter, just like I am.

A goddamn survivor.

Then I run, closing the gap. Power surges through my veins as I step up onto his bent leg and he wraps his arm around my thigh, lifting me up onto his shoulder in one smooth move.

It's a precarious hold, but I'm not afraid.

I trust him.

I trust our bond.

I trust that somehow, we'll *rise up*.

That we'll get through this. That'll we'll find stability and safety eventually.

Dax moves across the studio with me sitting on his shoulder, with every step he takes I trust in his strength, in his ability to be my safety net. My Dark Knight carries me as though I weigh nothing, as though I am a part of him, an extension of his body.

And when I tumble to the side, my leg rolling off his shoulders, he catches me once again.

He makes sure I land safely.

Locking eyes with me, Dax nods. He smiles his beautiful, heart-stopping smile before he spins away from me in a series of barrel turn leaps. I mirror him, and we synchronise our movements across the studio floor. The humid air rushing over our skin. Both of us are covered in a sheen of sweat as we dance with the music flooding our veins, with hope pumping our hearts, with trust and love moving our feet and feeding out movements.

When I dance with Dax, I stop feeling afraid.

I don't hurt anymore.

I can breathe again.

I'm no longer alone.

My skin flushes with heat. Every single part of me lights up with a deep sense of happiness, of belonging. Our bond grows with every twist and turn, with every touch, every lift, every movement, every glance.

We dance like we make love, and it is the most beautiful, exhilarating experience.

It's uplifting.

It mends the broken parts, fusing them together with every step.

When I dance with my Breakers, I feel whole again. Individually, or together as a group, it doesn't matter. David can't take that feeling of belonging away. I won't let him.

I fucking refuse.

26

Pen

"THANKS FOR LETTING me tag along, Pen," Clancy says the following Tuesday. "I've been dying to get a look inside the infamous Tales fight club". She grins at me, her curly red hair wild about her head as she practically bounces up and down with excitement.

York rolls his eyes, indicating right as we turn into the industrial estate that houses Tales. "Seriously Clancy, you need to chill. Grim doesn't do well with girly girls."

"*Grim's* going to be there? I'm gonna meet the badass bitch owner of Tales?"

"Yep, that's right," York confirms, giving me a look in the rearview mirror. I know what he's thinking, that it's a mistake to bring along Clancy. She's like a puppy, and a badly behaved one at that. I love her regardless. Besides, the dance is flamenco inspired, and second to tap, Clancy is pretty badass at it.

"Fuck. I'm about to meet a real-life, in the flesh, gangster. Will her boyfriend be there too? I gotta say, he's fucking beautiful. I wouldn't mind climbing his pole."

"Whatever you do, *do not* say that in front of Grim," York warns. "I've seen her beat the ever-living shit out of a woman who dared come onto her man. She's an exceptional fighter and will not tolerate anyone flirting with Beast."

"Yessss! I love her even more now. Urgh, why can't I have a gangster partner? Like, it's sexy as fuck."

"You've got River," I remind her.

"I do, and fuck is he good in bed. Ballet dancers are flex-i-ble," she says, her eyebrows waggling. "Then again, I bet you know that already, York, seeing as our girl rocks ballet too."

"No comment," York replies, winking at me in the rearview mirror as he pulls up to a parking space outside Tales.

"Spoilsport," Clancy mutters, grinning. She leans over and prods me in the hip with her finger. "You know if you're ever up for spicing up your sex life, I'm still open to joining your harem."

York switches the engine off and turns in his seat. "The fuck, Clancy! I'm not sure what I should be more pissed off about, the fact you think Titch needs her sex life spiced up—which, by the way, she does not—or that you've come on to her."

Clancy winks at me then grins at York. "Don't worry, York, she turned me down anyway."

"Ignore Clancy, as much as I love her arse, I don't love her arse *that* way."

"A crying shame." She grins then pulls me in for a hug, smacking a kiss against my cheek.

"Well thank fuck, because I can't be dealing with another person vying for Titch's attention. I can barely cope with the three fuckers I call my best friends," York quips with a shake of his head. "Come on, Clancy, let's introduce you to Grim and Beast, and for the love of God, keep the flirting to yourself. Okay?"

Grim notices us enter and holds her finger up indicating she'll be with us in a minute. Today she's dressed down in a pair of cut-off black denim shorts, Ramones t-shirt, and chunky biker boots with her legs bare. Her assessing gaze immediately lands on Clancy, and even though I already told Grim she was coming today to help me with the choreo I have planned, she still regards her with an edge of disdain.

"Oh fuck, did you see the look she gave me?"

"She's like that with everyone. Just remember what I said about Beast and you'll be good," York says.

"Will she warm up a bit?"

"Nope. Not unless she likes you, and right now the only girl she happens to like is Pen."

"Well then, we have something in common," Clancy retorts, pulling back her shoulders and lifting her chin. You gotta love her.

"Just be yourself, minus the flirty banter. It'll be fine," I reassure her.

"I want this place set up by this evening. Get to it people! I don't pay you to sit around and chat. Move it!" Grim shouts, pulling her gun from the back of her jean shorts and pointing it at a couple of blokes who are taking a cigarette break in the corner of the warehouse. I've never seen two people move as quickly. Beast chuckles, pressing a kiss against her cheek, and gently pushes her towards us.

"Fuck! Did she just pull out a gun?" Clancy hisses under her breath. "I mean, I can take a verbal bashing but a bullet through the skull is pretty fucking final."

York smirks. "I wouldn't put it past her..."

Clancy's skin flushes as she looks over at me, her eyes wide. "Fuck! She really *is* a badass, isn't she? I've got a girl crush."

"Do you ever stop?" I mutter under my breath, fighting to hold back a giggle.

"Hey, Pen! Good to see you. The girls will be out in a second," Grim says, pulling me in for a brief hug the moment she's close enough. She nods at York. "So, you're the chauffeur today."

"Yep, looks that way."

"And you must be Clancy," Grim asks, turning to face my best friend. She cuts her a look that could be interpreted a number of ways. Clancy clearly takes it as a challenge to impress her and holds her hand out to shake.

"Nice to meet you."

Grim's eyes drop to Clancy's proffered hand. After a beat she takes it. "I'm not sure anyone has ever said that it's nice to meet me."

Clancy smiles, and I can see the sexy way she cocks her hip. I groan internally. "There's always a first."

Grim lets go of her hand and nods. "I'm not into women," she says, pinning Clancy with her stare before turning her attention back to me. Clancy's cheeks flare and York stifles a laugh. "I'm looking forward to seeing what you've got planned for this weekend. Do you want to go change? The girls are out back doing the same."

"Sure thing."

"Great. I've got shit to be getting on with in the meantime—mainly trying not to shoot these lazy cocksuckers—so I'll catch you in a few," Grim says, walking off only to stop a few paces away. "Oh, wait. I forgot to say—"

"What?" I ask her.

"I saw your dance on Instagram—"

I pull a face. "*You* have Instagram?"

"I have a private account under a completely random name. It's quite a useful tool to keep an eye on people. Anyway, I saw your dance." She grins at me, giving me a look of solidarity. "You fucking told him, Pen. I'm so fucking proud of you." With that she turns on her heel and walks away.

Clancy blows out a breath. "Well, fuck, I might be in love."

The three of us burst out laughing, and I'm pretty sure I can hear Grim joining in too.

FOUR DAYS LATER, Clancy and I are in the changing room at Tales putting the last-minute touches to our outfits for the show. "Thanks so much for standing in for Sophia tonight. I appreciate it," I say, passing her a glass of champagne, which she downs in one long, thirsty gulp. It's Saturday night and this is the second performance of the routine Clancy helped me to choreograph.

"Girl, you know I'd do anything for you," she replies with a wide, red-lipsticked grin before throwing her arms around me, a cloud of Chanel Number 5 perfume engulfing us both.

The rest of the dancers bar Sophia—a pretty blonde who called out with the stomach bug—are also getting dressed. There's a lot of laughter and excitement, we're all hyped for the show given it went so well last night. It's a mash-up of tap, flamenco and a little bit of street added in. As usual, the girls picked up the routine with ease and Grim was more than happy with what I put together with Clancy's help. Not one of the dancers have been worried about a repeat of the bloodshed of a few weeks ago. I'm guessing working at Tales, surrounded by criminal men and women on the regular, gets you used to the violence. Or perhaps it's the extra security around the place. The new hires might be *ghosts* but they have an air of badassery that makes us all feel a lot safer in their presence. Contrary to their namesakes, they're very much a visible presence.

"Well, just know that I'm happy to return the favour at any time," I say, passing Clancy the black wig and purple lace eye mask. She pulls the wig on, adjusting it until it falls over her shoulders just right. Then adds the mask.

"I look hot!" she states, twirling in a circle and showing off the black long-sleeved bodysuit, purple stockings and silk, and a see-through, ankle-length skirt. Paired with black, sparkly heeled tap shoes and she looks gorgeous.

"You do!" I agree, pulling on my own wig and mask. The rest of the dancers do the same; dressed like this it's difficult to tell us apart, which was purposeful on my part. I want the audience to focus on *all* of us, not just me. The beauty of this dance is the synchronicity, not the individualism of each dancer. I don't want to be in the spotlight, but a part of the whole.

"Seriously, though," I say, placing my hands on her shoulders. "I'm grateful you stepped in. The routine wouldn't have worked with one dancer missing."

"Hey, you're welcome. Besides, I got to witness Beast beat the shit out of that dude tonight... what was his name again?"

"Jefferson Sloane, but on the street, he's known as *Mad Dick Magenta*. He's the best fighter the Callous Crew has," Grim says, stepping into the changing room. "Not a bad fighter, actually. Just sloppy. The kid is far better at parkour. I've seen him leap from the top of a five-story building onto a window ledge two floors below just to spray paint his tag. He has no fear. None. In fact, all of the members of the Callous Crew are fearless."

"Parkour and graffiti. Cool," I say.

"Well he was no match for Beast's left hook. I thought Jefferson's head was going to rip clean off his shoulders," Clancy remarks, her cheeks flushed pink with excitement. "It was such an exciting fight. All that blood!"

Grim glances at me, then shakes her head. "Your friend is quite the bloodthirsty little thing."

"She's special, that's for sure," I reply with a chuckle.

"Uh-huh... Anyway, enough of the chit-chat. Are you ready? I'm just giving you a ten-minute warning—"

"Oh, I should go pee! I get nervous as shit before a performance," Clancy says, interrupting Grim. Pulling an apologetic face, she rushes off to the toilet.

"She's a good person. She's been a good friend," I say, wanting Grim to see what I see. She doesn't have to like her, but it would be good if she stopped looking at her like she's someone I should be wary of.

"Seems like it..." Grim cocks her head to the side, studying me.

"What? Why are you looking at me like that?" I ask.

Grim jerks her head. "Come on, I need to speak with you in my office for a second," she says before turning her attention to the dancers. "Frank will escort you to the cage in a few minutes. Make sure Clancy is with you."

"Sure," a dancer named Lola replies. She's a beautiful, voluptuous black woman with the prettiest brown eyes and long, lean legs. I've been particularly impressed with her dancing this week. She picked up the routine really quickly and has a natural flare for flamenco.

"What's up?" I ask Grim the moment we step into her office. Beast is lounging on the leather sofa in the corner of the room, nursing a glass of whiskey. He looks like he's just taken a nap, rather than fought in the cage. There's not a split lip or bruise in sight. The fact that Dax managed to fuck him up when they fought has got to indicate how good a fighter he is. Beast seemed to think so, given he's been training him between Dax taking lessons at the Academy, teaching the local kids and doing nefarious criminal shit.

"You're supposed to be out there mingling," Grim says, her annoyance clear.

"Babe, I just came in here to change and grab a drink. What's up, you looked stressed," he remarks, sitting up.

"It's fine," Grim replies, waving away his concern.

"Okay," he frowns then looks at me. "Hey, Pen. *You* good?" He knocks back the drink, placing the empty glass on the low table before him.

"I think so," I reply, giving Grim a confused look. "Is this about Clancy?"

Grim sits on the edge of her desk. "Fuck, no. I can see why you like her. She's a little nuts, but harmless."

"Oh Jesus, thank fuck. I thought you were gonna drop a bombshell," I reply, letting out a sigh of relief.

"She checks out. Her dad works at the law firm that got D-Neath's sentence shortened. Although Interpol had more to do with that than the law firm did. Otherwise, there's nothing nefarious about Clancy, apart from the fact she flirted with me the other day. But I'll let that pass." She shrugs, her lips lifting up in a smile that doesn't reach her eyes. I frown, something's up but I'm prevented from asking when Beast bursts out laughing.

"Shut the fuck up! That little redhead rocket flirted with you?" Beast exclaims, his eyebrows shooting up so high they're almost lost in his hairline. "I would've liked to have seen that. She's got some balls, that's for sure. What did you do?"

"I told her I wasn't interested in girls..."

Beast laughs. "That's because you've got *me*, baby."

"Yeah, you're all the *girl* I need." Grim winks at me, then lights up a cigarette. I can't help but notice that her fingers are trembling a little as she takes a drag then lets out a stream of smoke.

"Babe, this cock is better than any strap-on out there. Fuck the Rampant Rabbit, I got everything you need right here," Beast boasts, gripping his cock over his jeans.

Grim frowns, ignoring him and focusing on me instead. "So... you wanted to talk to me about that *thing*."

"That thing?"

"Uh huh." Grim gives me that look, the ones girls give each other when they need you to pretend you know what the fuck they're going on about.

"Oh yeah, *the thing*. Maybe now would be a good time to discuss it considering the guys aren't about..." I look pointedly at Beast.

He points at his chest. "Ohhh, right. You're gonna do that girl-talk shit. This is my cue to leave, yeah?"

Grim silently thanks me with her eyes. "Pen just needed some boy advice, that's all."

Beast gets up and plants a kiss on the top of Grim's head. "Babe, do you know how proud I am of you?"

"Proud?" Grim frowns.

"Yeah, proud of you for making friends. I'm happy for you, I know it ain't easy having me as your best friend."

"I think you'll find that's Hud."

Beast clutches his chest. "Fuck, babe, you're killing me," he jokes before grasping the back of her neck and kissing her deeply. By the time he pulls back, Grim's face is flushed and I'm looking anywhere in the room so long as it's not at them.

"You've haven't got long before you're on stage, Pen" Beast reminds me. "Make this quick."

"Shit!" Grim exclaims the second the door closes behind him. She stubs out her half-smoked cigarette in an ashtray on her desk and starts muttering under her breath. I've never seen her like this. Whatever's troubling her, it must be big.

"Grim, what's the matter?" I ask tentatively, my eyes following her as she starts pacing back and forth in front of me. "Is it Lena? Something to do with Santiago? Have The Masks finally made a move?"

"No. Fuck, no. Nothing like that."

"What then? What's the matter?" When she starts wringing her hands, I begin to panic. "Seriously, Grim, you're starting to freak me out."

"I'm such a fucking idiot. I should just get rid—"

"Get rid? Of whom, the ghosts?"

"Fuck. This is such a bad fucking idea. I don't know why I'm even entertaining it."

"What's a bad idea? Is there something wrong with the plan? Are the Breakers in trouble?"

"I mean it's not as if I'm going to be any good at it anyway..." she continues, rambling now.

"Good at what?"

"Fuck, I've had to build a fucking fortress around Christy and she's not even my child. What business do I have even entertaining this...? I'm normally so careful."

"Entertaining what... Wait, who's Christy? What are you talking about?"

She stops pacing and turns to face me, pinning me with her stare. Since meeting Grim I've not once seen fear in her eyes. Right now, I do. "She's my little sister, Pen."

"*You* have a younger sister?"

"Half-sister, my dad was basically a man-whore. God knows how many brothers and sisters I have out there. Ford and Christy are the only two that I know of."

"Does Ford know about her?"

"No, and it's going to stay that way. I'm trusting you with this. You can't tell anyone, not even the Breakers."

"Grim..." I begin, not wanting to keep any more secrets from them.

"I know what I'm asking of you, but please Pen. I need your word. No one must know about her."

"Shit, okay. I won't say anything. Promise."

"I only found out about Christy when my father died. He included her in his will. I was nineteen when I took over Tales, she was twelve. She was his best kept secret, and now she's mine."

"Wow, that must've been a shock."

"It was a bit..." Her voice trails off as she chews on her lip. "She's a good kid. Well, not much of a kid anymore. You're around the same age. You remind me of her, actually."

"Yeah, how so?"

"She's a dancer like you, ballet. She's pretty fucking good."

"That's great."

Grim nods, heaving out a sigh. "Beast is the only other person who knows of her existence, aside from you now."

"So, this is about Christy? Has something happened to her?"

"No, she's well hidden, but she's just an example of *why* I shouldn't even be considering this. Fuck, how could I be so stupid, Pen?"

"Grim, I can't help you if you don't tell me what's up."

Sitting down heavily in her seat, Grim blows out a shaky breath then lifts her chin and straightens her spine. "I'm pregnant."

"You're *pregnant*?" My eyes drop to Grim's hand that, consciously or not, is pressed protectively over her stomach.

"Yes," she nods, reaching for her packet of cigarettes, then thinks better of it and screws up the packet, dropping them in the bin. Grim's eyes turn glassy like she's about to burst into tears. "See!" she shouts, "I'm not fit to be a mother! I've been poisoning my baby with cigarette smoke."

Then the tears fall, and the woman who seems as tough as any man in the criminal underworld crumbles.

27

Pen

AN HOUR LATER, after I've finished my performance, Grim looks up at me from behind her desk, a determined look on her face. "I'm going to tell Beast as soon as we're alone," she confesses.

"Good. You shouldn't make such an important decision on your own," I say gently, leaning over and folding my hand over hers. I've changed out of my performance outfit and am nursing a Malibu and coke.

"Yeah, I know..." Her voice trails off as she picks at the skin around her nail.

"What?"

"This was never the plan, Pen. I never wanted to bring up a child in this environment, and yet..."

"Yet?"

"Yet now that our baby is growing inside of me, I can't... I don't want to..." her voice cracks and she swallows hard, gritting her teeth.

"Then don't, Grim. Keep the baby."

Leaning back in her seat, Grim covers her face for a moment. Her shoulders start shaking and muffled sobs leak out from behind her fingers. Seeing someone so together, so strong, break apart like this kills me. There's a softer side to Grim, and it just proves that no matter how strong anyone appears to be on the outside, we're all just covering up our own heartbreak and insecurities on the inside.

"Grim, it'll be okay..." I get up to give her a hug, but she holds her hand up, swiping at her face and ruining the newly applied mascara she'd just put on.

"No, don't. It'll just make me worse. I won't be able to stop if you hug me," she sniffles, dabbing at her eyes with the sleeve of her top.

"It's okay to cry, Grim. It's probably got a lot to do with the hormones too."

"No, it's *not* okay. Not for me. I can't afford to be seen as weak. I can't afford to have any vulnerabilities. It's bad enough loving Beast, but a child...? If I keep this baby, then it will be targeted, just like Lena has been for you. Just like my sister would be if anyone knew of her existence. Women like me can't have children or a family and run a successful, *illegal* business. This changes everything, Pen."

"So you're *not* going to keep the baby?"

"The honest answer is that I don't know. Fuck, I could really do with a stiff drink right now."

"How far along are you? Have you seen a doctor yet?"

"A doctor?" she replies incredulously. "Fuck, I only took the pregnancy test this morning, so I'm not that far yet. I haven't had a proper doctor for years."

"Don't you ever get sick?"

"Rarely, and if I do need a doctor for something, Joey normally sorts me out. Most prescription drugs can be bought on the black market."

"That quack? You need a *proper* doctor, Grim, not some dude who knows nothing about women and pregnancy."

"I know, you're right, but it's not as simple as that for me. I trust very few people, Pen."

"What about Hudson? He's got kids, why not ask him?"

"He'll want me to keep the baby...."

"You don't want the baby?"

Tears well in Grim's eyes, and she looks down at her hand resting on her stomach. "I love Beast. Fuck, I love that brute so fucking much. How can I even consider killing a part of him, a part of me? I'm a horrible fucking person."

"You're *scared*, Grim. Your fears are warranted. I understand that for a woman in your position this isn't a decision you can make lightly. I understand this all too well, you know I do. There is no judgement from me. Whatever you decide, I'm here for you."

"If this was you, Pen, what would you do?"

"Do you want my honest opinion?" I ask her.

"Yes."

"I would keep the baby. No questions."

"And what about the fact this baby would be a target for the rest of its life because of what its mother chooses to do for a living, and the enemies her father has made over the years?"

"Grim, when we first met, this club was filled with dozens of crews. Every single one of them respected you and Beast enough not to start a war."

"Because I have armed men watching their every move..."

"Out of *respect*," I counter.

"Yet, Malik Brov—"

"Was the exception to the rule."

"Jeb? Santiago?"

"Will be taken care of before you're even showing, right?"

"Right."

"So my point is, you have more allies than enemies, and the enemies you do have can be dealt with..."

Grim regards me for a moment. "But what if I'm just not cut out to be a mother? What then?"

"Are you serious? Look at what you've done for me. My sister is *safe* because of you. Not to mention the fact that you looked out for me. You made a deal with Jeb to save my arse, you gave me this job," I remind her.

"You're good for business," she retorts, determined to prove what a horrible person she is and how unfit a mother she would be. "Don't pretend I'm a good person, Pen."

"Rubbish. If you were a bad person, you would've allowed Malik to buy me that first time he tried. You didn't. You looked out for me, and from what I've heard you looked out for Asia too. You'll make an exceptional mother. I know it," I say fiercely.

"Who'll make an exceptional mother?"

Grim's eyes widen, her face draining of colour as Beast steps into the room swiftly followed by Dax, who's come to pick me up tonight. "Beast...." Her gaze flicks from me to Beast and back again.

"I'm so sorry," I whisper.

"Wait, what are you saying here?" Beast asks, his gaze dropping to Grim's hand that's still resting protectively over her stomach. She doesn't respond right away, she simply stares at him whilst he stares back, this long, silent conversation going on between them.

"Grim?" he questions, his voice low, wary.

"We're having a baby," she says, holding Beast's gaze as his eyes snap up.

Behind Beast, Dax's mouth drops open. "Fuck me," he mutters, glancing my way. I shake my head, willing him to keep his opinion to himself. Grim has a short temper at the best of times, but fuelled by hormones and panic, she could be very dangerous to anyone who pisses her off.

"Grim, did you just say... *baby*?" Beast kind of stumbles sideways, shock rendering him speechless for a moment.

Dax reaches for him and Beast leans into his hold, completely oblivious to the fact that Dax has his arm wrapped around his waist. It would be comical if this wasn't such a touching moment. I can't imagine such a fierce, powerful man like Beast ever needing anyone to hold him upright before.

"It's alright, mate," Dax says, giving me a look. I know what he's thinking, because I'm thinking it too. This is a private moment, and we've no business being here.

"I should go," I say, standing.

"No, wait," Grim says, stopping me in my tracks, before focusing back on Beast.

"This is what you were discussing earlier when you chucked me out?" he questions, a look of hurt crossing his face.

"I... I was going to tell you after we closed tonight..."

Beast stares at Grim for a long moment, and I swear I don't

breathe the entire time. Then he kind of shakes himself and a surprised laugh breaks free from his lips. "I'm going to be a dad!" he exclaims. The joy on his face is undeniable as he strides towards Grim and hauls her into his arms, enveloping her in a tight hug. "Babe, you don't know how happy I am. This is fucking unreal! I'm going to be a motherfucking father!"

"You are," Grim replies, her shock and fear replaced with a moment of pure joy as they both just laugh and hug each other, allowing themselves happiness in the moment. It's beautiful to watch. That kind of joy is hard to find given the environment they both live in.

Dax steps up beside me, his arm circling my waist. "We should go," he whispers into my ear before releasing me.

"Yeah, we should," I reply, sliding my hand into his.

As we reach the door, Grim calls out, "Wait!" Stepping free from Beast's hold, she says "Don't forget your wages." Opening the top drawer in her desk she pulls out a small manilla envelope, holding it out to me.

"Thank you," I say, taking it from her.

"No, thank you. You were incredible tonight, and not just the routine you performed. I appreciate everything," she says softly.

"You ever need a friend, you call me," I reply, offering her the hand of friendship that she extended to me the first night we met.

She nods. "Speak soon?"

"Yeah, of course."

"So, Grim's pregnant?" Dax asks after we say goodnight to everyone, and head out into the carpark to wait for Clancy.

"Yeah, but you need to keep this quiet," I reply under my breath, flicking my gaze to Clancy who's striding towards us, a huge grin on her face. "Grim doesn't need anyone knowing the news just yet. It's not our business."

"Fair enough."

"Hey, so I'm gonna head to Chastity's Nightclub. River's already there, and Lola said she wanted to come along too," Clancy says, her eyes lighting up with mischief.

"It's already two in the morning. Shouldn't you be heading back to the Academy? I can give you a lift," Dax offers.

Clancy laughs. "Sleep is for the weak. Besides, I'm on a promise." She turns to glance over her shoulder at Lola who gives her a wave and a sexy smile. "Lola's driving us."

Dax pushes off from the Bentley and opens the door for me. "Have a good one."

"Will do!" Clancy replies, leaning in to give me a hug before skipping off towards Lola. I watch them pull away before I climb into the Bentley.

"So, do you wanna go clubbing?" Dax asks me, a smile pulling up his lips.

"Not even a little bit," I reply with a shake of my head. "Let's go home."

Dax pulls out his mobile phone from his jacket pocket. "Sure thing. I just need to text the guys to let them know I'm dropping you back off at the Academy," he says a little distractedly as he frowns at his phone.

"Oh, I meant... seeing as it's a Saturday night, I thought maybe we could go back to your place—"

"Fuck!" Dax exclaims, cutting my sentence short as he presses play on a message and lifts it to his ear. The expression on his face changes as the seconds tick by.

"What is it?"

He passes me the phone and puts the car in drive. "Buckle up, Kid. Something's going down at Rocks. We gotta go!"

The car's back wheels spins and as he releases the handbrake we fly forward. "Dax, what's happening?" I ask, alarmed by his panic and the multitude of voicemail messages on his phone, not to mention text messages.

"There's been a retaliation to the fight Zayn had with that guy from Dante's Crew. Shit's going down."

"Oh fuck!"

"I had my motherfucking phone on silent, Kid! I'm a stupid fucking idiot!" he exclaims, taking risks as he drives recklessly through the streets of London. It's a miracle we don't get pulled over by the police.

"It's not your fault this happened."

"It *is* my fault. I should've put Frederico down years ago."

"You tried," I say, recalling the night Frederico beat the shit out of Dax, using two of his crew members to hold him down because he was too pussy to fight him one-on-one.

"Well tonight we're ending that cunt once and for all," Dax promises, pulling into a side street not far from Rocks in record time. He turns to me, handing me the car keys, then pulls out a revolver from the glove compartment. Popping the magazine, he checks the bullets before clicking it back into place, then presses a hard kiss against my lips.

"Come back to me," I demand.

He nods, getting out of the car. "Lock the door. Do not open it for anyone except us. If I'm not back with the guys in ten minutes, I want you to get the fuck out of here and wait at our place. The key to the flat is on that bunch," he says, then slams the door and rushes off before I can even respond.

Fifteen minutes pass and I'm still waiting for his return. I know he said ten minutes. I know I'm disobeying him, but fuck, I can't seem to move my damn arse. The street is like a graveyard with no one around, and a feeling of disquiet travels down my spine. I consider calling Beast or Grim, but given everything that's gone down tonight, I decide against it. My Breakers will be okay. They have to be.

"Fuck, where are you?" I whisper, looking for the millionth time in the rearview mirror, but this time instead of being greeted with an empty street, I notice four familiar figures running towards me. Unclipping my seatbelt, I open the car door, a mixture of relief and fear flooding every fibre of my body.

"TINY!" Xeno roars, just as an arm slides around my waist and something cold and sharp presses against my throat.

"Hello, Penelope, long time no see," a familiar voice says.

28

Pen

"LET ME GO, FREDERICO," I bite out, trying to control the fear in my voice.

My fingers tighten around the bunch of keys in my hand, the teeth biting into my palm as the Bentley's internal lights switch off and the central locking system flicks on.

Frederico's lips press against my ear, and I bite down hard on the inside of my cheek. My nostrils flare as I smell the metallic scent of blood and feel the wet warmth of it as he presses his cheek against mine. "Hmm, I can see why those cocksuckers are so fucked in the head over you, Penelope. I bet you taste just as good as you smell." His grip tightens around my waist, making it even harder for me to breathe. "Fuck, and the way you move... You're fucking famous now. Over a million views of your dance, and here

I am holding your life in my motherfucking hands," he says, then licks me.

He fucking licks me.

"Fuck you, arsewipe," I bite out through my teeth. I will not fucking scream. I refuse to give him the satisfaction. Instead, I concentrate on my Breakers and take comfort that they're alive. That they're here.

"Let her go!" Dax snarls as the four of them come to an abrupt stop a few feet away.

Frederico laughs and just grips me tighter. His fingers bite into my upper arm, bruising me as he presses the knife harder against my throat. I can feel the sharp sting of the knife's edge as it slices into my skin.

"They'll kill you," I say through gritted teeth.

"That's where you're wrong, Penelope. These fuckers won't kill me as long as this knife's pressed against your pretty little throat... Do as I say and maybe you'll survive the night."

"Take your motherfucking hands off her now, cunt!" Xeno roars, Dax, Zayn and York flanking him. All three have the cold glint of their rage focused on Frederico, and it's scary as fuck. They have death in their eyes and blood on their hands. Not one of them has come out of the fight at Rocks unscathed, even Dax has a rapidly swelling cheek, and all of them are covered in blood. It's splattered across their clothes and skin, the savagery of what must've happened in Rocks reflected in the wildness within their eyes.

"Fuck you, prick. Me and Penelope here are gonna take a little ride in your Bentley," Frederico counters, stepping sideways and dragging me with him.

"You aren't going anywhere in my car, and you're a fool if you think we'd let you take our girl," Dax says, the vein in his forehead popping as he raises his gun and flicks off the safety.

"Don't even think about it!" Frederico growls, pressing the knife tighter against my throat.

York takes a step closer, a baseball bat gripped in his hand and a crazed look in his eyes. A trickle of blood runs down my skin and this time I can't help but let out a whimper of pain.

"There's no way out of this, Frederico. There's four of us and one of you. Drop the knife and we'll let you go unharmed," York negotiates, the calmness he displays is just a cover for the rage he's feeling. I see it in the ticking of his jaw and the curl of his lip.

"You heard him. Let Pen go and we'll forget this," Zayn adds, lowering the bloody knife he's holding to his side. I watch as crimson droplets slide from the blade's edge.

Drip. Drip. Drip.

Xeno remains fiercely quiet, like a volcano on the verge of erupting, and I know it's because the lie won't fall as easily from his lips. He will kill Frederico the second he gets the chance.

"You really are fucked up over this piece of trash, ain't ya?" Frederico sneers, his free hand reaching for the car door. He tries the handle, but it's locked. If he'd paid any attention, he would've realised that already. "Unlock it, bitch!"

"No."

"Unlock it right the fuck now or I will slide this knife across your throat so quickly your Breakers won't have a chance in hell of saving you. Imagine how they'd feel when the life in your eyes fades away."

My eyes fill with tears, but I blink them back, refusing to shed one for this bastard. I don't want to give him what he wants, but I also don't want my Breakers to witness my death. It will ruin them. They'll be lost forever.

"Don't!" Xeno snaps, fixing his gaze on me.

"Do it!" Frederico growls.

I press my thumb on the key fob. The car door unlocks.

"Good girl."

"Fuck you," I mutter, stiffening in his hold as Frederico bites my earlobe, then sucks it into his mouth.

Dax looks down the barrel of his gun. "You motherfucking bastard!"

I hear the grin in Frederico's voice and see the rage burning across my Breakers faces. With the knife still pressed against my throat, Frederico doesn't open the door straight away, instead his hand circles my waist and moves upwards. I know what he's about to do and it makes my stomach turn over. "Look at you all going insane over this trashy bit of pussy. I never understood the draw. She ain't even that pretty."

"I swear to fuck, you move another fucking inch and I'll put a bullet between your eyes," Dax says through gritted teeth. His focus remains on Frederico, his arm is steady, his aim sure, but Frederico isn't stupid, he uses me as a human shield. Dax won't be able to get a clear shot. We all know that.

"Try it, dick, and watch your girl bleed out within seconds. All you'll have left of her is a corpse... Then again, I heard you're a bunch of twisted fucks these days. Do you want me to kill her so you can fuck her dead body?"

"You piece of shit. I'm gonna have fun gouging your motherfucking eyes out!" Xeno shouts.

Frederico lets out a laugh that verges on hysterical, then grabs my breast over the top of my hoodie and squeezes hard. I cry out again and Xeno roars, jerking towards me. Zayn reaches for him and wraps his arm around his torso, pulling him back as he urgently whispers into his ear. I swallow hard, trying to decipher what he's saying. Whatever it is, it has the desired effect. Xeno stops struggling. Instead, he eyes Frederico with a calm resolve. The darkness in his eyes grows and for the briefest of moments his gaze flicks behind us before he looks back at me. I see how his fingers unfurl a little, some of the tension leaving his body. I realise then that we have company. Someone else is here and Frederico has no idea.

"Oh, this is so much fucking fun," Frederico leers.

Xeno flicks his gaze from mine to Frederico's. "Believe me when I say this, there will be no mercy. You hurt her; you will die a long, painful death. You've heard the rumours and now you've seen with your eyes what we can do. Your crew is all dead. There's no one left. Every fucking surface inside of Rocks is covered with their spilt blood. Your friends, the boys *you* grew up with, they're all fucking gone because you dared to make a move against us. Dante's Crew no longer exists. You're the last man standing."

"There are plenty of Skins dead too, or have you forgotten that part? I'd say the Skins ain't looking too good either right about now."

"Do you really think you'll survive this, huh?" Xeno asks, ignoring Frederico's attempt to enrage him further.

Frederico squeezes my breast harder and I grind my teeth together so that I don't scream and risk my throat being slit. "I'm planning on doing a lot more than surviving," he retorts, dropping his hand and reaching behind us. He jostles us both a few steps to the side so that he can open the car door behind him. Then pulls us both into the open space.

"If you let Pen go and drive away right the fuck now, we'll give you a head start," Xeno promises, his gaze flicking to mine then to York, silently telling me to look at him. I do.

"So, what, now you're suddenly willing to let me go without repercussions? I ain't a fool," Frederico says to Xeno with a sneer. Despite his bravado, I can smell his fear. It's pungent.

"We're willing to give you the chance to get away with a head start. If you're smart, you'll take it, because maybe we won't hunt you down, maybe we'll let you live a life elsewhere, but that's *only* if you let Pen go," York says before glancing at Dax. "Put your gun down," he urges. A look passes between them and Dax nods. He slowly lowers his gun to the ground, placing it on the floor before rising back up slowly. Beside him York drops his baseball bat, the sounds of it hitting the pavement is loud enough to make me jump. More blood slides down my neck and I bite back the sting of tears.

"It'll be okay," he reassures me. "Now close your eyes, Titch."

I do as he asks, trusting him.

Three things happen at once.

The knife falls away from my throat as Frederico shoves me forward roughly, kicking the back of my knees, unbalancing me further. As I fall the sound of a gun being fired rips through the air, and I swear I can feel the bullet lift the strands of my hair just above my head.

"Kiiiddddd!" Dax roars, and my eyes snap open as I throw my hands out. The pavement comes at me in slow motion, but before I hit the ground there's a blur of movement and I'm caught in a pair of strong arms, lifted off the ground and carried away from the fighting. Dax pushes me up against the brick wall of the building we're outside of, pinning me with his body.

"Are you okay?" he asks urgently, lifting my chin gently to

inspect the cut on my neck. He must be satisfied it's a superficial wound because his fingers roam over my face as though he's checking that I am, in fact, still breathing.

Behind us a blood curdling scream rips through the air. I push his hands away and try to look around his huge frame. "Dax, who was shot?!" I scream. Visions of one of the Breakers bleeding out on the pavement run through my head and I begin to shake violently.

Dax grips my face in his palms. "It's Frederico. Beast shot Frederico. The boys are okay, but we need to get you out of here."

"Beast?" I question, my eyes welling with tears. "How can Beast be here?"

"I messaged him. He came."

"Oh God!"

"Jeb is on the warpath, Kid. Rocks is fucking carnage. I should never have brought you here," he says, dipping his head low to peer at me. One of his eyes is bloodshot, the capillaries broken and blood seeping into the white making him look like one of those scary fucking zombies from that film 28 *Days Later* that scared the shit out of me when we watched it as kids. "I don't want you involved in this. Beast will take you home. But you need to go, right the fuck now."

I suddenly feel all the air leave my lungs, and a second later I'm gasping for air, like a fish out of water. My chest heaves as I try to draw in precious oxygen.

"Kid, I need you to breathe. Look at me, okay?" he insists.

I nod my head, trying to make sense of everything that's happening. Behind Dax I can hear Frederico's screams and the sickening sound of bones breaking, blood spurting, and skin splitting. "They're going to kill him, aren't they?" I whisper, my legs feeling like blocks of concrete.

"Not before they find out who sent him. Can you walk?"

I shake my head. Right at that moment I can barely stand. Without a moment's hesitation, Dax picks me up into his arms, carrying me bridal style. "Don't look," he demands, but of course I do. What I see will be forever imprinted on my soul, captured like a batch of grainy polaroid photographs. I blink against the violent snapshots, adding each one to the dusty, mildewed photo book that holds all my worst memories.

Blink. York lifts the baseball bat above his head then smashes it over Frederico's kneecap, breaking his leg in two from the force.

Blink. Frederico screams in pain, his back arching, blood spurting from his lips.

Blink. Zayn presses a knife against his neck, the serrated edge cutting into Frederico's skin, blood oozing from the cut.

Blink. Xeno crouches over Frederico, pressing two fingers deep into the gunshot wound in the dying man's chest.

Blink. Blink. Blink. Blink

Right before my eyes the men I love become the monsters of my nightmares. York's white-blond hair is splattered with blood, his lips dripping crimson. My vampire comes to life in the starkness of violence and rage. No longer beautiful. Zayn is the shadowy-faced slasher in all those horror movies we loved to watch as kids, the knife his murder weapon of choice.

Xeno is the twisted beast with his claws buried in a man's chest, ready to pull him to pieces to feed the animal within. And Dax, Dax is my captor. Monstrous in size, covered in blood and ink and gore.

"Talk, prick, or I make your death even more painful!" Xeno

snarls, snapping me out of my morbid thoughts and bringing me crashing back to reality.

"Ahhhhhhhhh!" Frederico cries out, blood bubbling up his throat and dripping out of his mouth as he struggles to scream, struggles to breathe.

Xeno leans over Frederico, getting in his face. "Who the fuck sent you?" Every last drop of compassion and empathy I'd begun to witness these past few weeks disappearing as quickly as the blood seeps from Frederico's body. "I asked you a motherfucking question!"

In response, Frederico just coughs up more blood through a spiteful pain-filled smile. I watch it splatter against Xeno's face as he struggles to form words. Even though his skin is deathly pale as death waits in the wings, ready to drag him into hell, I realise that he'll take this secret to his grave just to piss the Breakers off. I have to do something.

"Wait!" I say to Dax, gripping hold of his shirt in my fingers. "Put me down!"

"Kid, this ain't for you," he retorts.

"I said, put me down!"

"I need to get you out of here."

"No. Put me down, right the fuck now!" I shout, shaking and angry, scared and determined.

Willing my body to obey me, I stand on trembling legs. Dax keeps his hand fixed firmly on my elbow to steady me. Despite feeling as though I'm wading through mud, I step towards Frederico as Beast slides out from the Bentley and tucks away his gun into the back of his jeans.

"Hey sweetheart, look who came to save the day," he says with a wink and a smirk.

"How did you...?"

"Fucker was too preoccupied getting into the car that he didn't notice me sliding in on the other side. Soon as he let you go, I fired. By the way, he's got about five minutes until he bleeds out. Whatever the fuck you need to know, you'd better find out now."

I nod, my whole body shaking as I kneel next to Frederico. Xeno sits back on his haunches, his gaze a mixture of respect and anger. "You need to get out of here," he says.

"You need to let me do this," I counter, concentrating on the dying man before me, a mixture of hate, sympathy and horror fucking with my emotions.

"Why?"

"He's *dying*, Xeno."

"He deserves it."

I press my eyes closed briefly, swallowing hard, then fix my gaze back on Xeno. "He won't tell you what you want to know. Let *me* try."

"He *will* fucking tell me," Xeno growls, pressing his fingers deeper into the wound on Frederico's chest. Frederico mumbles incoherently, his gaze going in and out of focus.

"Xeno, stop," I whisper, placing my hand over his and feeling the wet warmth, sticky and viscous against my skin.

"He'll bleed out quicker if I remove my fingers now," he says. There's no sympathy in his voice, just cold, hard facts coming from a man whose eyes hold nothing but contempt and hatred for the man painting the concrete scarlet with his blood.

York's hand rests on my shoulder. "You've seen enough," he says, the baseball bat discarded now as he looks at me with haunted eyes. I glance down from York's blooded hands to Frederico's smashed knees and swallow hard. This is the first time since we were kids that I've witnessed their violence. I've heard about it, sure. They've each warned me what they're capable of, but I haven't seen it for my own eyes and it's not a sight I can easily swallow or will ever forget. The four of them are almost unrecognisable and nothing like the men who danced with me at Jewels nightclub a couple of weeks ago.

"You can't hide who you are from me, not anymore," I say before leaning over and cupping Frederico's cheek in my hand. He feels cold. Too cold. "Can you hear me, Frederico?" My voice is soft, cajoling, and I try to keep any signs of hate from it.

Frederico's eyes focus on my face, a single tear sliding down his cheek. He coughs some more, and I remove my hand from Xeno's arm and gently wrap my fingers around Zayn's wrist. "Take the knife off of his throat, Zayn. He can't talk with it there."

"Pen..."

"No. This needs to happen."

He hesitates but when Xeno nods, Zayn releases the pressure, pulling the knife away. Blood, so dark it's almost black, slides from the slit in Frederico's throat, joining the growing pool that's now seeping into my jeans. I try not to look too hard at the parted, jagged cut across his flesh beneath the weeping blood.

"Frederico, I need you to tell me who sent you," I say, gently stroking his face, like a mother would to comfort her child.

"He doesn't deserve your kindness," Beast mutters from behind us. I ignore him.

This man could've killed me. He could've slit my throat. He didn't. Right at the last moment, he chose to let me live and in doing so forfeited his own life. I'm choosing to hold onto that split second decision, that precise moment, in order to get me through. I've hated Frederico ever since that night when he beat Dax before my eyes in Abney Park Cemetery, then tried to rape me. That hasn't changed, and there's a large part of me that's glad he's dying, relieved that there's going to be one less arsehole in this world, but there's also a part of me that recognises that this could easily be one of my men. The line between good and evil is a thin one. I've placed my Breakers on one side of the line because of my love for them, but I *know* they've walked the other side of the line for a long time now. I've just witnessed how far over they've stepped. There was a time Frederico stood on the other side of the line. Knowing that he wasn't always an evil bastard helps me to do this, to show a scrap of kindness even if it's to get what we want.

"Who sent you, Frederico?" I persist, softly, my thumb rubbing over his cheekbone.

"He's fading fast," Dax mutters, but I focus only on the dying man before me.

"Mum," he murmurs, his eyes looking beyond me to someone else. More blood keeps leaking from his lips and I hold in the cry of frustration that I feel rising up my throat. I have to hold it together. I have to.

"I'm here," I say, hating myself for pretending to be his mother and knowing it's the only way to get him to speak.

"Mum?"

"Shh. It's okay." Leaning closer, I swipe at the tears trickling from his eyes, and stare right into the dying embers of his life. "Who sent you, Frederico? Who was responsible for sending your friends to their deaths tonight?" He mouths the word, his voice struggling to break free from the choking hands of death. "It's okay, I'm here." My voice cracks as I twist my head to the side and rest my ear just above his mouth. I feel sick about what I'm doing, but still I continue because now I'm a monster too. I'm the harbinger of death dressed up as an angel. I should be calling an ambulance, instead I'm pretending to be his mother and allowing him to bleed out.

"Jesus fuck," Beast mutters, and I can hear the discomfort in his voice. I don't suppose someone he's killed has ever experienced the same kindness in their final moments, even if it is pretend. It's easier to disconnect from an act of violence if you feel justified in your actions. Providing sympathy, empathy, makes the victim more human. It shines a light on what you've done. I feel the tension from my Breakers, but I persist. It's the only way.

"Frederico, please," I whisper. His mouth presses against my ear, and the response that falls from his lips strikes like a poisoned arrow to my heart.

"He saw your dance..." I pull back in shock and watch as blood gurgles up his throat, pouring out of his mouth. He fixes his gaze on me, cruelty flashing in his eyes as a slow smile spreads across his face. "You... provoked... the monster." More blood pours as his light dims.

"Who? *Who* saw me?" I insist, my stomach bottoming out because I see the answer in his eyes. I know. I know who's coming for us.

"David..."

My brother.

This was *him*. Of course it was.

Black spots blur my vision, but I blink them back, forcing the nausea away. Sitting back on my haunches, I stare at Frederico and the vacant emptiness in his eyes, feeling oddly calm. It's as though I'm having an out of body experience, and much like when I was a kid, my conscious mind seems to separate from the horror and the fear allowing me to function in the moment. I know the shock will hit me later, but right now all I can think of doing is pressing the pad of my thumb and finger against Frederico's eyelids, closing them. Not one of my Breakers speak, though I feel their concern for me. It doesn't make me feel any better, not when the weight of this violent night and all the ones yet to come weigh heavily on my shoulders. It presses down on me and with every passing second, I feel myself sinking into a place I haven't been in since that night David forced me to choose between the Breakers and my sister. I brought this upon us by facing my biggest fear. This is on me.

"What did he say, sweetheart?" Beast asks, breaking the silence. "Who's the fucker we gotta kill next?" He cocks his head to the side as I meet his gaze, blinking back the shock.

"My brother."

29

Pen

"WELL, well, well...isn't this fucking cozy..."

"Fuck!" Zayn hisses.

We both look up to find Jeb stepping out of an alleyway a little further down the street. He's holding a gun and has it aimed directly at me, a crazed look on his face.

"Fuck!" Zayn exclaims under his breath. I meet his gaze and swallow hard at the fear blazing in his eyes. He has his back to Jeb so can't see that he's holding a gun, but just like I'm familiar with the nuances of a madman's voice, so too is Zayn. Zayn reaches for his knife which is on the ground beside Frederico's still body and slides it up the sleeve of his hoodie. This isn't going to end well.

"Tell me, Penelope, why would your brother send Dante's Crew into *my* club to fuck with the Skins?" Jeb asks as I turn my attention to him now. I recognise the look in his eyes, it's one of distrust and blind rage. He smells a rat, and guess who he thinks is at the centre of it all... *me*.

Xeno stiffens, his eyes widening slightly, but he hides his surprise quickly and flashes a look at York next to me. Tension rises, thick and cloying as we all climb to our feet, Frederico's still warm body prone beneath us. York takes my elbow, pulling me gently so that I stand wedged between him and Dax. Zayn steps over Frederico to stand beside Xeno. Out of the corner of my eye I see Beast reach for his gun.

"Don't even think about it, Beast!" Jeb snarls, focusing on him now. "Place your gun on the ground and kick it towards me or I'll blow your motherfucking brains out!"

"Fucking chill, Jeb. Don't get your knickers in a twist," Beast retorts, slowly removing his gun from the back of his jeans and placing it on the concrete, he kicks it to the side, and it slides to a standstill between us. "It's been a stressful night, ain't it? Let's go back to Tales and grab a drink. How about that? We can sort this shit out there. I'm sure Grim will be more than happy to accommodate you all. She can send her clean-up crew around in a jiffy. Before you know it, it'll be like this night never fucking happened."

"Don't fucking patronise me, you piece of shit. I know Grim has something to do with all of this. Has she hooked up with David, is that it? Are the pair of them planning a fucking takeover? Did they persuade you fucking fools to join in?" Jeb accuses.

"You think Grim has joined forces with that piece of shit David? She wouldn't touch that first class prick with a bargepole," Beast replies with a lip curl. "She's got bigger fish to fry than fuck you over or side with *that* degenerate."

"Don't try and bullshit me. I'm no fool," Jeb counters, swiping his arm over his lip that's bleeding from a cut.

"What do you mean Grim has something to do with this? What are you talking about?" Xeno asks carefully, playing the bluffing game. He keeps his focus trained on Jeb and only him.

Jeb narrows his eyes. "My *club* being attacked, genius. My *name* being dragged through the motherfucking mud because someone," Jeb glares at Beast, "Has fucked with the supply of Dancing Shoes."

"And you think that's Grim? Are you slow in the head or something? *David* sent Dante's Crew in to take you all out. Not Grim, you muppet. I think you need to take issue with him," Beast replies, still trying to salvage the situation, even though his insults are only making matters worse.

"Then how do you explain my own fucking men turning on me?"

"No one's turned on anyone. We just took out Dante's Crew for *you*, Jeb," Zayn points out. "If we wanted to turn on you, we would've helped them. You need to calm down and think straight."

Jeb's hard stare lands on Zayn just as a dozen men step out of the alley behind him. All of them are armed with knives, though the only one who appears to be holding a gun is Jeb. I recognise a few of them from my time working at Rocks. They're all members of the Skins. Most of them are covered in bruises and blood just like my Breakers are, and more than a few of them are looking confused by the unravelling events.

"Don't tell me to calm the fuck down. Too much has happened recently and all of it seems to circle back to Penelope here, who you all seem very fucking protective of. Including *Grim*," Jeb says, jerking his gun in my direction. Zayn steps sideways, putting himself directly in front of me and in the line of fire. Jeb's eyes narrow at Zayn's attempt to protect me. He laughs. It's a cruel sound, loud and full of violence. "You fucking care about her still, don't you? I fucking *knew* this piece of trashy pussy would worm her way back under your skin. You were always soft, despite my fucking efforts. Fuck!" Anger pours out of him as he flicks the safety off. "Fucking move aside right now or I'll put a bullet in your brain. Blood or not, Zayn, you'll fucking die tonight if you don't."

"No!" I shout, lunging towards Zayn.

Dax grips my arm. "No, Kid. He won't shoot him. We've been here before," he says urgently under his breath. What the hell does he mean by that? How many times has Jeb threatened Zayn's life like this? Then I remember the scars criss-crossing his chest.

"You're paranoid, mate," Beast says as he pushes off the car and stands beside Zayn, almost blocking my view entirely. "I can assure you Grim has no interest whatsoever in your crew or your businesses. You and I both know that if she did, she would've taken you out a long time ago. As for the Breakers, I'd be thanking them if I were you. Who gives a fuck if they're interested in this bit of pussy."

"Shut the fuck up!" Jeb's lip curls up in distaste as he points his gun at Beast. I draw in a panicked breath. Maybe Dax is right, and he won't pump a bullet into Zayn's chest, but there's nothing stopping him from doing the same to Beast. Given the tension oozing from the men I love, they realise that too.

"Now that ain't very nice considering I helped your boys out tonight. That little dickwad, Frederico, is dead because *I* loaded a bullet in his back," Beast says, not even flinching.

Jeb barks out a laugh, the sound like sanity hanging on by a thread. "I find it very interesting that you're here, *Roger*. Wanna tell me why, or do I need to send someone around for your precious Grim?"

"Oh, fuck," York mutters under his breath.

Roger? Is that Beast's real name? I feel a hysterical laugh rise up my throat, but I choke it back. Now is not the time nor the place, but if we ever get out of this alive, I know my men are going to have fun ribbing him. God, I hope we get out of this alive. I hope they can take the piss out of Beast for the rest of their damn lives.

"The fuck?" Beast's whole demeanour changes and his voice lowers menacingly. "You need to be very careful what you say, *mate,* because I don't do well with threats to my woman as you well fucking know. But I *am* willing to let that go seeing as it's been a pissy fucking night for you so far. So, lower your motherfucking gun and call your boys off. What's left of them, anyway."

From my position, I can see Beast lowering his hand behind Zayn's body. He moves his fingers in some form of sign language or something. When I look up at Dax, he's concentrating on Beast's hand, then he looks across to York, jerking his chin and flicking his eyes downwards.

"What's going on?" I hiss. Neither answer as Beast continues to try and talk Jeb down.

"When Pen called to say she was in trouble. I came," Beast lies, because it wasn't me who called him but Dax. "We protect our assets unlike some dumbasses around here."

"That girl is fucking poison. I should've put a bullet in her head a long fucking time ago," Jeb counters furiously. "First Malik Brov gets his brains blown out coming after her, then Dante's crew make a move on my fucking patch because of her brother's orders, not to mention the fucking issue with my shipment of fucking drugs! You all have something to do with this. I fucking know it!"

"For fuck's sake, man. Stop making up movies in your head," Beast says, his agitation growing alongside the tension that's stretched as thin as my courage.

"Beast's right, Jeb. We're not your enemy," Xeno says, holding his nerve.

"Did David promise that bitch, is that it?" Jeb continues ignoring them both. "Take me out, and you get to fuck that cheap arse pussy for the rest of your days?" He laughs hysterically, unaware that Zayn is slowly lowering his knife that he'd hidden up his hoodie sleeve. "You should know by now that David's *obsessed* with the whore. He'll never let you have her, no matter what he's promised. This is his way of saying as much. Now she's going to fucking pay for his bullshit."

"David's a fucking psycho, sure, but you've known that all along. As far as Pen is concerned, like you said, she's just a piece of pussy we occasionally fuck around with, like *you* wanted us to, remember?" Xeno says, disdain in his voice that's so convincing I almost believe him.

"Yeah, is that so? So why the fuck are you all surrounding her like she's your goddamn queen, huh? If she's just a pussy to play with, then hand her the fuck over and let me send a message to her cunt of a brother. Maybe then I'll be convinced you're not all in on this!"

"Because, dipshit, she belongs to Grim who *you* made a deal with. You kill Pen, and all fucking bets are off. Believe me when I say that I will have no fucking issue ending this charade right here, right fucking now. Yet again, your boys are stepping in and saving your motherfucking arse. So do the right thing, put your limp dick away, back the fuck up, and I'll forget your threats against my woman."

I cringe knowing that Beast has just lit the match paper beneath Jeb's ire. There's no way he'll back down now and given the secret message Beast just gave York and Dax, I'd put money on the fact he's counting on it.

"What the fuck did you just say to me?" Jeb counters, spittle flying out of his mouth as he rages.

"He said back the fuck up, Jeb. It's over," Zayn interjects, his voice low, menacing in a way I've never heard before. It runs through me like a ghost through a graveyard.

"*It's over*? What the fuck is that supposed to—"

I'm not sure what my brain registers first, the whoosh of a knife as it slices through the air or the sound of a gunshot cracking like thunder overhead. Chaos ensues and just like earlier I capture the violence, adding it to the ever-growing photo book of memories in my head.

Blink. Beast is thrown back violently as a bullet enters his shoulder.

Blink. Zayn's knife pierces Jeb's chest, buried up to the hilt from the force. He falls to the ground.

Blink. York throws himself on top of me. My cheek pressed into the concrete.

Blink. Xeno dives for Beast's discarded gun.

Blink. Two members of the Skins drop. Blood, tissue and brain matter exploding from their heads.

Blink. Dax picks up his gun and fires more shots. He takes out three more men.

Blink. The rest of the Skins scatter.

Blink. More gunshots. *Blink.* More deaths. *Blink.* More blood. *Blink. Blink. Blink. Blink.*

Then screams. Sirens. Flashing lights.

"Get Tiny and Beast the fuck out of here!" A voice shouts. Xeno's, I think.

I'm lifted off the ground and hauled into the backseat of the Bentley by York who fixes the seatbelt around me then slams the door shut. Beast climbs into the car from the other side. His face pale, his hand pressed against the bullet wound in his shoulder.

"I'll be good. Nothing that can't be sewn up," he states with a tight smile before resting his head back, all the colour draining from his face.

I don't answer. I can't. I'm not even sure I can move.

Dax gets into the driver's seat and starts the car. "What about the others?" I manage to blurt out. My gaze focuses on Xeno, York and Zayn as we pull away from the curb.

"They need to stay. They'll be questions," Dax explains.

"They'll go to prison." My voice rises in panic.

"No. No they won't, but Beast will if he stays. We're keeping you both out of this."

Questions burn my tongue, but words don't form. All I can do is twist in my seat and stare out at three pieces of my heart standing amongst the carnage, the ground littered with bodies around them.

Blink.

30

Pen

WATER from the shower slides over my back as I sit on the tiled floor, hugging my knees to my chest. I can't seem to move, let alone feel.

Every time I close my eyes, I see York bringing his baseball bat down on Frederico's knees. I see Zayn and Xeno crouched over him, one with a knife pressed into his throat, the other with his finger shoved deep into the gunshot wound in his chest. I feel Dax's arms tight around me and smell the metallic scent of blood, violence and revenge in the air. It doesn't matter how many times I wash myself; I can't rid myself of Frederico's cries or the light leaving his eyes. I can't turn off the sound of his voice as he struggles to speak.

"*David...*"

I can't stop seeing the blood or the bodies as my mind flicks through the photo album of tonight's events. It doesn't matter if my eyes are open or shut, those memories are crystal clear as though playing out in front of me right now. So here I remain, hugging my knees to my chest in the bottom of Dax's shower, waiting for the numbness in my body to infect my mind.

"Kid?" Dax enters the bathroom. his voice sounds far away, lost beneath the screams of dying men.

"I'm fine," I mutter, unfurling my body slowly as I push upwards to stand on stiffened legs, my muscles tight from the cold.

"Jesus fucking Christ, the water's freezing! Your lips are turning blue!" He leans behind me, turning the shower off.

"It is? I hadn't noticed."

"Kid... Fuck..." A moment later a warm, fluffy towel is wrapped around my shoulders as he eases me out of the cubicle. Like me he's scrubbed tonight from his skin, but despite the fact he's no longer covered in blood, I still see the stain reflected in his eyes. "Come with me, Kid."

I follow him without argument, too numb to do anything else. He guides me back into his bedroom and eases me onto the edge of the bed. "Let me see your neck," he says, lifting my chin.

"It doesn't hurt," I reply, my words empty, hollowed out like all those dead bodies seeping blood.

"It isn't a deep cut... It shouldn't take long to heal."

"I guess that's something," I reply.

"Fuck, we could've lost you. I shouldn't have brought you along. Why the fuck did I do that?" He cups my face and presses his lips against my forehead, then sits on the bed next to me and wraps his arms tightly around me, but even his hug isn't enough to comfort me this time.

"Are they back yet?" I ask, pushing out of his hold, and pulling the towel tighter around me. It's been almost two hours since we drove away, leaving the rest of the Breakers behind to deal with the carnage, stopping only to drop Beast back at Tales to a furious Grim who threatened to kill him herself for daring to get shot.

Dax shakes his head. "Hud called, he's with them now. They're debriefing."

"Debriefing?"

"Yes." Dax chews on his lip as he regards me. It's a nervous tick, one that I've not seen in a very long time.

"What aren't you saying?"

"Being an informant has its perks, Kid, but I ain't sure that murdering a small army is one of them. There will be a lot of red tape to cut. It's gonna take a bit of time getting them out."

"Out?"

"Of custody. There were a lot of dead bodies, Kid."

"Yeah, I know. Don't remind me."

Even to my own ears my voice sounds empty, like an abandoned building with cracks in the walls and all the windows smashed in. I'm in shock, I know that, so processing what happened tonight is going to take time. Right now, I'm caught between being fervently on the side of my Breakers and disgusted by what I witnessed. Logically, I know it was a 'them or us' situation but that doesn't mean I am comfortable with any of it. Violence is something I've tried to avoid at all costs. Growing up with David, I've lived under the constant threat of it; I've spent my entire life avoiding it where I can and seeking comfort in dance. Having to witness the men I love embrace that side of themselves has well and truly shattered the illusions I built. Yes, they may have gotten into fights as kids but nothing like this. It's easy to turn a blind eye when you're in love, but to have part of their natures revealed in such a shocking way... it's hard to stomach. At least for me it is.

"If it makes you feel any better, violence isn't something that comes naturally to Zayn. York either," Dax says, reading me expertly.

"That's not how it looked tonight."

"What you saw tonight was the men who love you doing everything in their power to protect you. Nothing more. Nothing less."

"You don't need to cover for them. I saw the look in their eyes. I'm a big girl," I say.

Dax sighs. "I'm not protecting them. It's just the truth. I've always had anger inside of me, you know that. Growing up with my dad the way it was makes it all too easy to slip into violence. York and Zayn have had to embrace it to survive. It hasn't been easy for either of them. I've seen them battle every fucking day with the things they've had to do."

"But it's *easy* for you?"

"Maybe that's not exactly the right word to use. Not easy, not at all, just easier. I don't think about the person in front of me. I just think about—"

"Your dad?"

"Yes. If I allow myself to think anything else... Put it this way, I wouldn't be standing here today."

"You mean...?" I shift slightly, so I can get a better look at Dax.

"On my darkest days, I've thought about it. That makes me a coward, right?"

"No. Jesus, no. It makes you *human*, Dax," I choke out, tears forming like a stone in my throat. The thought of Dax even considering taking his own life has me all twisted up inside.

"What about Xeno?" I ask.

"Xeno uses violence as a way to cope."

"To *cope*? With what?"

Dax frowns. "I've never really been certain. He hasn't let any of us in enough to explain. I was hoping one day you'd be able to find out. Though I reckon it has something to do with the numbness that takes over after a kill. There's a certain kind of peace to be found there... At least for him."

Considering how numb I feel right now, I can understand that. I didn't kill Frederico but I sure as hell didn't try to save him either, so that makes me as guilty of his death as the rest of them. Maybe that's the real issue here, my own guilt. "And how do you deal with a night like this, Dax?"

"I shut myself down. Sometimes I dance. Sometimes I drink myself into oblivion. Occasionally, like Xeno, I'd find a woman to fuck..." His voice trails off as he tips my chin up and gently pushes a few strands of wet hair off my face.

"What?" I whisper. It might sting a little, but I'm not upset. I know they've slept with other women before me. My jealousy seems trivial now. It has no place here.

"It never meant anything. No one ever came close to how I feel about you. I know it's the same for the rest of them."

"You don't need to justify yourself to me, Dax. I just hate that you *had* to find a way to cope because of the things you did."

Dax presses his thumb and forefinger against his eyes, rubbing them. He looks as exhausted as I feel. Dark shadows rim his eyes, and his cheek is turning a deep shade of purple, matching the night sky that edges the horizon as dawn begins to rise.

"You were really brave tonight, Kid. So fucking brave. What

you did..." Cupping my cheek, he strokes his thumb across my cheekbone. "I'm so fucking sorry."

"You can't protect me from the violence. Not anymore. I've lived on the fringes of it since I was a kid. This is your life... and now it's mine." My voice breaks as I try to keep my shit together. I can't afford to break. I won't. It's not as if I haven't seen a man killed before now, so I don't know why I'm taking this so fucking hard.

"It's a life we live *for now*. It's not a life we'll be living forever. I promise you that," he says vehemently.

"You still believe that the plan is going to work after what happened tonight?"

"It already is.... The drugs have been in circulation for a couple of weeks now. There have been whispers building on the street that *Dancing Shoes* is a dud drug. We expected some kind of backlash, just not exactly this."

"Do you think David and Santiago know about what you're doing with Hudson?"

"No, I don't. Believe me, if they did, things would be a hell of a lot worse right now. I think David believes *Jeb* screwed over Santiago and that we were in on it too. It makes sense that he sent in Dante's Crew to take us all out as a way to prove his loyalty to Santiago. Not to mention send you a message. Kill two birds with one stone and all that."

"But Jeb believed it was you guys, David and Grim..."

"Precisely, and he was only partly wrong. He believed we'd done it to set him up and take over the Skins... I don't think he would've come to that conclusion, at least not this quickly, if he hadn't seen how we reacted to Frederico's attempt on your life.

The second he walked out of the alleyway we all knew he had to die. It was him or us."

"Now that Jeb's dead, where does that leave us?"

"By killing Jeb, David and Santiago will believe one of two things... Either we killed Jeb because we found out *he* was screwing Santiago and wanted to show our loyalty, or because Jeb found out that *we* were. It doesn't really matter what story they choose to believe, though knowing your brother, he's already persuaded Santiago that it was us all along, given how this is going. We just have to up the ante now, lure Santiago to the U.K so he can sort us out."

"By sort, you mean kill, because that's what he'll do, right?"

"He'll almost certainly try, but the key is he'll be on U.K soil and we'll be ready for him."

"Just like you wanted."

"Yeah, just like we wanted," Dax replies with a tight nod.

My jaw begins to chatter as Dax kneels on the floor at my feet and begins rubbing my thighs over the towel to dry me off. His hands are warm, and I see the intent in his eyes as though he's trying to rub away the events of tonight with his sheer will. But he has to know I've already scrubbed my skin raw of the blood. The terror and the violence aren't so easy to rid myself of.

"Don't."

"Don't what?" Dax asks, his hands stilling.

"I can dry myself."

Swallowing hard, he nods, then climbs to his feet. I feel tears clogging my throat, but I refuse to let them fall. Fuck that. I survived years of my brother's abuse. I'm strong enough to get through this, whatever it is that I'm feeling right now.

"When will it happen?"

"That I don't know, but we have to be ready for anything."

I meet his gaze and nod. "I'm scared," I admit. I'm fucking terrified.

"I know, Kid,"

"So what happens now?"

"Now you get dressed. You're gonna eat some food and then we'll wait for news." Dax says as he strides over to the chest of drawers and starts rummaging around, looking for something.

"What about David?"

"As far as Interpol can tell he isn't in the country. There's been no sign of him entering the U.K. through any of the airports or shipping ports."

"He's doing this all remotely?"

"It looks that way."

"And Santiago?"

"Ah, here they are," Dax says, ignoring my question. He pulls out some clothes from the drawer and hands them to me. "I figured you'd need something comfortable here for when you stayed over." He hands me a pair of soft, grey, flannel pyjamas. I take them from him gratefully. "I cleared out the chest of drawers of my stuff and filled it with clothes you might need when you stay over. You should find everything you need in there."

"You bought these?" I ask him as I stand, allowing the towel to fall away.

Dax swallows hard, but like the gentleman he is, keeps his eyes firmly fixed on my face and away from my nakedness. "Yes. Are they okay?"

"They're perfect, thank you," I say quietly, my heart hurting in a way I can't describe as I pull them on. He watches me closely as he rests against the vanity unit.

"Kid—"

"You didn't answer my question about Santiago," I say, interrupting whatever he was about to say.

"Interpol has had no flags that he's entered the country either."

"Do you really believe this plan will work, that Santiago will settle this personally himself and walk into the trap?"

"You want my honest opinion?"

"Yes, please. I'd rather that than you lie to protect me."

"I think Santiago would happily use your brother to try and take us out first. Whilst he's known for dealing with betrayal and disloyalty himself, on this occasion I don't think he'll step foot in this country with your brother offering his *assistance*. That's why your brother's got to die, Kid. Only then will Santiago step in."

"Are you saying what I think you're saying?" I ask.

Dax swipes a hand over his face before looking back at me. "Xeno's moving on to Plan B, or at least part of it. He's flying out to Mexico. He's going to kill your brother."

For a moment I just look at Dax in shock, then fear expands in my chest, pouring out of my mouth in a rush of anger. "The fuck he is!" I shout. "When was this decided?"

"He called whilst you were in the shower. Gave me a heads up."

"This is bullshit!"

"Kid—"

"No! Xeno is not going to Mexico. This is not happening. It's a death sentence. You know that, right?" Dax clamps his mouth shut, refusing to answer me, but I can see he thinks the same. "I will not lose him now. I won't!"

"Kid, nothing you say will make him change his mind."

"I don't care. I'll fucking tie him to a chair if I have to. He's not doing this," I exclaim, storming out of Dax's bedroom and into the front room.

"What are you doing, Kid?" Dax asks as I sit down on the sofa.

"Waiting."

"They'll be hours at the very least. Maybe even days..."

"Then I'll make myself comfortable," I reply stubbornly, folding my arms across my chest.

Dax is wise enough not to argue with me. He knows as well as I do that I won't back down.

31

Pen

I'M on the phone with Clancy still spinning the lie about a stomach bug that's taken the five of us out when Xeno, York and Zayn finally return home. It's been three days since the events of Saturday night. Three days of worry, of barely eating or sleeping. I've endured nightmares, flashbacks, tremors and cold sweats. My brain has twisted that night up into something even more terrifying, and that fear I felt has grown like a weed, choking the love I have for my Breakers, constricting my heart. I'm a fucking mess.

"Do you think you'll be well enough to come back soon? Coz I'm telling you; Tiffany and her side-bitch Sophie are driving me up the wall. Plus, Madame Tuillard is stalking around the Academy like the wicked witch of the west and D-Neath is being cagey as fuck. He had some dudes in suits pay him a visit yesterday. Handsome fuckers..."

"I've gotta go—" I say, flashing a look at the hollowed-out versions of my Breakers as they enter the flat.

"But—"

"I'll see you at the Academy in a couple days, okay? Love you." I end the call, chucking my mobile phone onto the coffee table before standing to face them. There's a part of me that wants to throw myself into their arms, but how can I comfort them when I haven't even been able to comfort myself.

"Where's Dax?" Xeno asks, and the abruptness of his tone has me flinching.

"Taking a shower."

He nods, barely looking at me. "I should take one too."

"Xeno...?" My voice trails off at the coldness I feel emanating from him. It only serves to fuck with my head even more, as though he's becoming the monster my brain has twisted him into after Saturday night.

"I need a minute."

"Wait. We need to talk!" I say desperately. Moving around the sofa quickly, I grab his arm reflexively. He stiffens.

"Not now, Tiny," he bites out, the tension in his body whip-sharp. I drop my hand, stung by his reaction and that sudden feeling of dread creeping up my spine.

"What happened? I've been waiting for you to come home, going out of mind with worry. Are you okay?" I ask, forcing the jittery feeling away as I look between them all. "Zayn? York?"

"It's been a long few days, Titch. We're all just really fucking tired. We've barely slept a few hours between us," York says, scraping a hand through his hair. Some of the white-blonde strands have a pink tint to them that could only be one thing.

That's all it takes to send me hurtling back to Saturday night and the fucking trembling starts. *Again.*

Zayn steps towards me. "Pen, you're shaking."

I grit my teeth, holding my hands up as I blink the memories away and force myself to focus. They're home. They're safe. They're *my* Breakers, the ones I love, not the fucked-up version my brain has started to twist into monsters. "I'm fine. I'll be fine…"

"Said no woman, ever," York says, breaking out a smile that's as fake as my courage is right now.

I give him my own shaky smile, forcing myself to straighten my spine and lift my chin. "If you can deal with this, then so can I."

"You shouldn't have to deal with anything. You shouldn't be in the middle of all of this. You shouldn't have even been there Saturday night and you sure as fuck shouldn't have witnessed what you did!" Xeno snaps, looking at me as though I'm to blame for everything that went down. Given the circumstances, he's probably right. Now he's cleaning up the mess that is my psycho brother.

"You're going to do it, aren't you?" I murmur. "You're really going to fly out to Mexico and try to kill David?"

"Dax, that motherfucker. I told him not to say anything!"

"It's madness!"

"Tiny, this has to happen—" he begins, his jaw tight, his whole body tense.

"No, it doesn't," I cut in. "Plan B is *not* happening. You are not going to Mexico!"

Xeno shakes his head, his brown curls loose and unruly. In fact, every part of him seems wild, unhinged. "We need to take David out of the equation. This has to end. I'm done with all the bullshit."

"Even if you did get close enough to kill my brother then somehow get safely back home again, who's to say that Santiago won't just use someone else to take his place and do his dirty work for him?"

"Pen has a point," Zayn says tiredly. Xeno glares at him.

"Maybe he will, maybe he won't, but I will not stand back and wait for that cunt to try and take out the people I love again. I will *not* lose any of you. Do you fucking understand? I won't!"

"But—"

"No, Tiny. David won't stop until all the people I love are dead. He's using this as an excuse to do what he wanted to do years ago. You know that! This isn't just about showing loyalty to Santiago," Xeno exclaims.

"Xeno, we knew something like this would happen... We knew the risks when we took on this job," York says, edging closer to Xeno as though he's expecting him to lash out.

"That was *before* we got Tiny back," Xeno counters, his gaze snapping from mine to York's and back again. "That prick had a motherfucking knife against your throat. It may as well have been David standing there!"

"But I'm fine," I lie. Physically I'm okay, but mentally I'm far from okay. That's not something I'm willing to share right now though. If I do, it will only fuel Xeno's indignation. "You dealt with the threat, Xeno. I'm standing right here. You don't need to go running off on a suicide mission. Not for me."

Xeno strides forward and grasps my shoulders. "Not for you?" he seethes.

"Exactly," I reply stubbornly, gritting my jaw.

"What the fuck is that supposed to mean? You mean *everything* to me, Tiny! Don't you dare fucking insinuate that you're not worthy of our protection, that you don't deserve to be safe, to live a happy fucking life. You are worth it. I would die for these bastards here, but for you, Tiny, I will tear the world apart with my bare fucking hands to keep you safe. Do you understand me?!" he roars, the love in his eyes frightening in its intensity.

"Xeno, back the fuck up," York says, placing a hand on his shoulder. He grips him firmly, the veins in the back of York's hand popping. They stare at each other, both unyielding as I stand sandwiched between them both. My tremors return and I try not to have a fucking breakdown right here between them, as my nostrils flare and I suck in a much needed breath.

I'm not scared of the men I love. I'm not. I love them. They love me. I say repeatedly, over and over in my head until I'm feeling calmer.

"This ends now. I'll take them all out if I have too. Hudson can go screw himself. His revenge isn't worth your lives. It fucking isn't!" Xeno says, backing off. I let out a long, shaky breath.

"Believe me, Xeno, we all agree that David deserves to die," Zayn says, his voice even. "But on this I'm with Pen."

Xeno glares at both Zayn and York in turn before resting his gaze back on me. "I'm going to Mexico and killing that motherfucker like I should've done years ago. I'm not changing my mind."

"For fuck's sake," York curses.

Blinking back my tears of frustration and trauma, I watch Xeno stride off towards his bedroom, disappearing from view. "If he goes, I know he won't come home. I know it. I don't care how good an assassin he thinks he is. I know my brother. He'll take him out. Then he'll take each of you out one by one until there's only me left. There *has* to be another way."

"We'll talk to him when he's had a chance to calm down,"

Zayn says, tugging at the hem of his top in agitation. It's only then that I notice they're wearing joggers and t-shirts rather than the clothes they'd worn two nights ago. Which is probably just as well given they were covered in blood. I'm not sure I could've dealt with seeing that.

"Where are your clothes?" I ask.

"Evidence," Zayn answers. His voice raspy with fatigue. "We were stripped, questioned, and released pending investigation."

"Pending investigation? What the fuck does that mean?"

"It's standard procedure," York explains. "We might not be police officers, but we've proven ourselves enough times to gain some allowances. That's why we were able to come home."

"Allowances...? So that's what murder's called these days."

Zayn sighs. "The four of us have put our necks on the line for Interpol more times than I can count. The information we've passed to them about Santiago over the last year is enough to put him away for life. Whilst messy to clean up, this is nothing in comparison to what they'll gain from Santiago's arrest and incarceration. Besides, they still need us. It ain't over yet."

"Far from over," York adds, brushing his bloodstained hair back off his face. "Fortunately for us, we have immunity from the law. Xeno made sure of that when we made the deal with Hudson and the powers that be at Interpol..."

"Must be nice to know you can do whatever you want without any repercussions..."

York frowns, his icy-blue eyes searching my face. "We've never once taken advantage of that."

"Until now." My voice is neutral, steady, but of course York reads something in my expression, and it pisses him off.

"You're *angry*? Do you think we should be punished for what happened?" he asks, flinching.

"No. I'm *glad* you're home..." It's not a complete lie. Not a lie at all, in fact. I'm so fucking relieved that they're here. *Safe*.

"But..."

I press my eyes shut briefly, forcing away the memories and willing myself to forget the darker versions of the men I love. How can I explain how I feel? How can I tell them that the darkness I'd witnessed in all of them has haunted me these past few days? That I've woken up choking back the tears, barely able to draw breath from the nightmares. How can I explain that a small piece of me is afraid... of *them*? In all the time I've loved them, even when they returned, changed from the boys I grew up with, I was never afraid of them. *Never*. I don't know how to deal with that. Fear has no place in a relationship. It has no place in our love. Forcing myself not to have a fucking meltdown, I open my eyes. Both York and Zayn are staring at me with a mixture of hurt, confusion and disappointment.

"I'm scared," I say, forcing the words out of my mouth. "I'm scared of what I saw, what I feel. I'm scared that I'm going to lose you. I'm scared that we may never recover from everything that's happened even if we do all make it out of this nightmare alive..."

"Don't do that, Titch," York exclaims, dragging his gaze over me.

"Do what?"

"Pull away." He grits his jaw, and I can see how he battles with his emotions.

"Is this because I killed Jeb?" Zayn asks. "I did that to protect you, Pen."

"I know that..." *But.* Yet again, that silent word sits heavy between us.

"Titch, Frederico and Jeb threatened your life. That piece of shit had a knife pressed against your throat. Do you have any idea how fucking torturous that was?" York asks. I try not to flinch at the bitterness crawling into his voice. I get where they're coming from, I do, but it doesn't make this any easier to digest. When I don't answer York, when I look away and bite down on all the acidic words burning my throat, Zayn lifts my chin and forces me to look at him instead. His eyes are pitch black, not even the light reflected from the table lamp brightens them.

"I'll tell you what it felt like, Pen. It was as though our fucking guts had been sliced open and our insides ripped out. I don't regret cutting Frederico's throat and I sure as fuck don't regret killing Jeb. He's had it coming for a long time now."

"He's your uncle," I whisper, as if that should make a difference. It doesn't. Blood doesn't make family bonds, not in the way that counts. I know that better than anyone. Jeb was a cruel bastard.

"And David's *your* brother. Don't tell me that if you were faced with killing David to save Lena's life, that you wouldn't do it?"

"I would do *anything* to keep her safe..."

"Then why the fuck is this so hard to swallow? They're *dead*. Good fucking riddance!" he shouts, balling his fists and glaring at me angrily. "Don't make those bastards human when we both know they were fucking monsters. Have you forgotten how they both treated you before tonight?"

"No, I haven't. It's just..."

"It's just *what?*"

"You're..."

"Monsters too. Am I right?" York interjects, his eyes flaring with hurt.

My eyes fill with tears and my voice breaks. "No... No... that's *not* what I mean." What I *saw* was monstrous. It haunts me, but I know they're not monsters like Jeb or even Frederico. I *know* that. I do.

Zayn clutches his hair in frustration. "Then what the fuck do you mean? Why are you looking at us like that, Pen. *Why?*"

"What the fuck's going on?" Dax exclaims, striding into the room and coming to an abrupt standstill. He looks at me, his features softening. "Kid..."

"I didn't mean... I'm just... Shit!" I exclaim, the trauma of the past few days worming its way back into my psyche. Dax strides towards me as an ice-cold sweat breaks out over my skin and tremors begin to take over my body. I can't seem to get a grip on myself as I wrap my arms around my chest in self-comfort.

"Hey, it's okay," Dax says, sliding his arm around my shoulder. I flinch, hating myself in that moment for doing so because when I look up at his face, it's as though I've slapped him. Dropping his arm, he gives me space. Over the past few days, Dax has begun to understand that I've needed him close but not too close whilst I try to get my head straight. I'm so grateful he hasn't tried to push me.

"Titch...?" York frowns, his anger disappearing as he places his hand on my arm and searches my face. Right now, there's nothing I can do but let him read me. I don't have the energy to slip on a mask. "Tell me I haven't lost you," he eventually whispers.

"What you need to do, York, is back the fuck off. Kid's in shock and you arseholes haven't fucking helped the situation! Now get out of my sight before I break your faces!"

"No. Don't fight. This isn't what I want," I say, scared, frustrated with myself. "I just have to get my head around everything. I just need time."

York recovers first, his expression one of apology and regret. He looks at me like I'm a wounded animal who'll either die from fright or lash out to protect itself. Right now, both reactions are possible. "This is so fucked up. I'm sorry, Titch. I'm sorry you had to witness what happened. I'm not that man. Not really. Not deep down. You know that, right? I fucking swear it. I *love* you."

My eyes fill with tears, but I blink them back, forcing myself to be strong, and willing myself to stop shaking. To see York, my funny, lighthearted, Fred Astaire loving, best friend. "I know you do. I love you too. *I do.*"

York swallows hard and dips his head, but I see the apprehension in his gaze regardless. He sees the fear I hold inside despite my efforts to cover it up. "I'm going to go shower and sleep. We'll talk more in a few hours, okay?"

"Okay," I agree, biting the inside of my cheek until it bleeds.

"Zayn, are we good?" Dax questions, daring him to object.

"Fuck, yes, of course we are. It's been a fucked up few days. I'm not... myself."

"I know that. I'm not either."

"We'll be okay," he replies heavily, and for the first time since we've found each other again, I seriously begin to doubt the truth in that statement.

32

Xeno

"WHERE IS SHE?" I snap, entering the living room a couple hours after storming out of it. Dax sits alone nursing a glass of whisky, the tumbler dangling between his middle finger and thumb as he stares at the amber liquid lost in thought. "Dax?"

"My room, asleep."

"Zayn and York?"

"Out cold."

Spinning on my feet I head back the way I came. I'm a rude cunt, I know that, but I don't give a shit. I just need my girl. I need her so bad I can't fucking think straight. Dax follows me.

"Xeno, what are you doing?" he asks, clamping his hand on my shoulder and forcing me to stop. He moves in front of me, blocking my way along the hallway.

"What the fuck do you think *you're* doing?"

"You're not in the right frame of mind to see Kid just yet," he replies. "You need to get your head straight."

"Don't tell me what I need, Dax. You don't get to decide when I see my girl."

Dax grits his jaw and uses his considerable size to block my way. "*Our* girl, you fucker, and I won't let you near her when you're like this. You need to calm down, right the fuck now."

"I *am* calm."

"You're not calm. You know it. I know it. You're angry. I fucking get it. We *all* are, but you going in there like this isn't gonna solve a damn thing."

"We could've lost her!"

"I know that. We didn't."

"And we won't when I fucking kill that cunt David."

"Jesus, where's your head at, man? This ain't like you." Dax squeezes my arm gently, concern written across his face. "You know it's a suicide mission."

"I need him dead."

"Do you fucking hear yourself? You're the one who makes sure we don't lose our shit and go off the rails. You make sure we never do something stupid. You're the one who holds us together. You're the glue, man. Please don't come unstuck now. We need you to keep your head."

"Fuck!" My shoulders drop as I feel the weight of our situation sit heavily upon them. Dax is right, but I can't seem to control this fear inside my chest. We came so fucking close to losing Tiny and it almost brought me to my knees. Seeing that prick bleeding out was the only thing to stop me from losing my mind entirely. If Zayn hadn't taken out Jeb, I would've. Now all I can focus on is killing David. It's the only thing preventing me from losing my ever-loving mind. I *have* to take him out. I *have* to keep the people I love safe.

"Think about this logically, without all the emotion. David lives in a fortress over there. You've seen the intel on his place. He barely leaves the compound, and when he does, he's surrounded by at least a dozen armed guards. Jeb had no idea about how powerful David had become, but we do. *You* do. It's an impossible task."

I run a hand through my hair, grasping at the ends and tugging before meeting Dax's infuriated stare with one of my own. "The *only* thing getting me through is knowing that in a few day's time I'll be blowing David's brains out."

"Deep down you know that ain't how it's gonna play out, right?"

"I *know* he has to die."

"He does, I don't dispute that. You're good at what you do, Xeno, but you won't get close enough. It's a fool's errand and you fucking know it."

"I don't want to talk about it anymore. My mind's made up. I want to see Tiny..." I counter, stepping around Dax who just moves in front of me again. "Get the fuck out of my way!"

"No, Xeno."

"What the fuck do you think I'm going to do, huh? I *love* her, Dax!" I shout, and this time my voice fucking cracks like a goddamn pussy. "I *need* her."

Dax eyes flicker with sympathy. "I know you do, Xeno, but I also know you need to get your head right. Please, man. Do this for me, for Kid. Get some proper rest then come find her when you're feeling calmer. She's barely slept these past few days. I'll watch over her in the meantime."

"I fucking need her," I repeat, dropping my head.

"We *all* need her, Xeno. She needs you too, just not like this..." His voice trails off and there's no denying the haunted look in his eyes.

"What?" I snap. Dax draws in a shaky breath. Whatever he's feeling now is more than just him being pissy at me for losing my cool, not that I had much to begin with.

"She ain't coping well with what happened, Xeno."

I frown. "What are you saying?"

"Kid hates violence. You know that. She saw us covered in blood, tooled up, fucking raging. We killed men in front of her."

"We had no choice!"

"I know that, I believe she does too. Regardless, this ain't easy for her to swallow. We've lived this life for a long time. Kid has done everything in her power to stay out of it. She's fragile right now. She blames herself for what happened that night."

"This is *not* on her!"

"I know that. We all do." Dax sighs, scrubbing a hand over his face. "She chose to fight back. We encouraged her to do that. You know as well as I do that the dance she performed was for her brother, to show him that he hasn't crushed her spirit or her courage. She sent him a message, and he responded. The guilt is eating her up."

"She's stronger than you give her credit for, Dax. She's had to be."

"Sometimes even the strongest ones break. Give her some time. At least allow her to fucking sleep, *please*."

"And I suppose you're the one who's going to be there for her, picking up the pieces."

Dax sighs, running a hand over his head. "It ain't like that. I'm not keeping her from you. Fuck, you know I love you motherfuckers, that I love *us*, the five of us. You're my family, arsehole, but I *always* swore to protect her. I didn't. None of us did. We let her down. I owe her this, and the rest of you owe her the best men you can be. If that means me stepping in when you're all acting like pricks, then I fucking will," Dax retorts.

He's a stubborn fucker. He's also right. I tell him as much despite my pride.

"You're right. You always fucking are, but know this Dax, I'll be doing the same. When you lose your shit—and I know you, I see the violence brewing inside of you—then be prepared for me to step in, just like you are now."

"I'd expect nothing less," Dax nods, then squeezes my shoulder and enters his bedroom shutting the door behind him.

"XENO, CAN I COME IN?"

I jump out of bed, startled awake the moment I hear Tiny's voice.

"Hey," I say, opening the door. She looks up at me, her brown eyes limned in a sadness that makes my heart contract painfully. Fuck.

"I'm sorry if I woke you."

"I've slept enough. Is Dax awake?" I ask, looking over her shoulder and down the corridor. The door to his bedroom is closed as are York's and Zayn's.

"No, he's still sleeping. York and Zayn too, I checked."

"I'm not surprised, it's been a rough few days..." My voice trails off as she regards me, hovering in the hallway, uncertain.

Stepping aside, my heart pumps wildly as she brushes past me and I breathe in her familiar scent. Closing the door, I lean against it, taking my fill of her messy hair and flushed cheeks as sleep still lingers in the softness of her gaze and relaxed posture.

"What about you, have you slept?" she asks, frowning.

"I've had a few hours."

"Good..." Her voice trails off as she fiddles with the hem of her top. I can't help but notice the slight tremor in her hands and I'm reminded of what Dax had said. Being strong takes its toll. We all have our limits, and maybe this time, Tiny has hit hers.

"I'm glad you came. I wanted to talk to you, clear the air..." I begin.

"By talk, you mean *tell* me you're going to Mexico to kill my brother."

"Tiny, my mind's made up..."

"Don't our opinions matter at all?" she asks.

"I'm doing this for them as much as I'm doing it for you."

She steps forward, cocking her head to the side as she studies me with knowing eyes. "Don't do that, Xeno. Don't lie to me, not now. This is about *your* fear, *your* pain, *your* anger. You're not thinking about the rest of us," she retorts. Her voice might be low, soft, sensual in a way that rouses me, but anger still flares to life within it. "This is a selfish reaction."

"I'm protecting you," I counter in frustration. "I'm doing this so they don't have to. So *you* can be safe from that fucking monster."

"You're willing to die, for what? So my brother can have the satisfaction of killing the man I love."

"I wasn't sure if that was still the case," I say, meeting her gaze, wanting to be certain. It's a fucking needy thing to say, and fuck knows I've never been needy, but right now I want the truth.

"What, that I love you?"

"That you love *any* of us still."

"Do you think I would still be here if I didn't? God, you're so fucking infuriating!"

"I don't know. Maybe when this is all over, you'll walk away again?" It's a low blow and one I instantly regret, but instead of apologising like a decent human being, I fold my arms across my chest and press my lips into a hard line.

Tiny presses her fingers against her eyes, her small, delicate hands shaking. When she looks at me again there's determination in her stare, and her fingers are balled into fists, the fight I always knew she still possessed revealing itself to me. "That was a shitty thing to say, Xeno. I love you. All of you. That hasn't changed. Though you're determined to make it hard for me."

"But is it enough?"

"It *has* to be," she replies with a firm nod of her head. "What I'm feeling. It will pass."

Despite her conviction, I hear the doubt in her voice. It guts me like nothing else does. "We never lied to you... Not about what we've become."

"I know that but knowing who you are and seeing it with my own eyes are two very different things. It's... *a lot*."

I nod. "I don't deny that. It will be over soon."

"Sooner, if you have your way."

"I *will* kill David. That fucker has to die."

Tiny's nostrils flare as she draws in a frustrated breath. "There are other ways to gut a pig, ways that don't involve you leaving the country and taking this on by yourself," she counters.

"Fuck, Tiny. Why can't you trust me to do this? Have a little faith."

She shakes her head, her anger blazing now. "This *isn't* about trust or faith, Xeno. This is about *us*. They love you. *I* love you and we can't let you do this. I won't let you do this!" she says, fiercely, her whispered words, harsh. Her cheeks might be flushed, and her hair ruffled from sleep, but there's no softness left in her words now. This is an order, one that tightens a hold around my heart.

"Tiny, it's non-negotiable."

"*Bullshit*... I spent the last three years thinking about you all. Longing for you. Loving you, fucking *hating* you. I've only just got you all back and I refuse to accept a future without you in it! You stupid, stubborn bastard!" she exclaims, stepping into my space and jabbing her finger into my chest with every word.

"Tiny," I warn, gritting my teeth.

"No! He's *my* brother. Don't you think I'm owed retribution?"

"So that's what this is about? You want to be the one to put the bullet in his brain... I didn't think you had it in you," I reply, the words coming out harsher than I'd intended.

"I don't want to kill anyone. Fuck! I've seen what taking someone's life has done to you all. I want David to rot in jail for the rest of his life knowing that I'm on the outside living and loving and *happy* with the men I love. That would be worse than death for my brother. A bullet to the brain is too kind, too quick. I know that much, at least."

Her chest heaves with agitation as she curls her fingers into my top, glaring at me. Beneath her touch my heart beats wildly, enraged at her persistent need to fucking push me. I feel the familiar tightness in my throat and the sickness in my stomach that will only abate when I appease the beast within. I will see this through or die trying.

"Do you remember what you said to me after that night at Rocks? Do *they* even know what you said to me?"

"Tiny..."

"Because *I* do. I remember. You came to my house. You stood on my doorstep, looked me in the eye and said that I was *dead* to you. You broke what was left of my heart that night, Xeno, and I'll be damned if I let you do that again, not after everything we've been through to get to this point. I love you but I will *not* let you break me one more time."

"I was a kid. I was angry, Tiny. So fucking hurt. I was lost, insane with sadness. I wanted to hurt you—" I counter.

"—And you succeeded. This time you won't," she says adamantly. "If you leave for Mexico, if you do this despite everything we've said, I won't forgive you a second time even if you're lucky enough not to fucking die!" She lets me go, stepping back, her body shaking. We stare at each other, neither one of us wanting to back down, too stubborn in our anger.

"What's the plan then, Tiny?" I find myself eventually saying.

She looks at me with suspicion as I lean my head back against the door, fucking exhausted with it all. The fear inside my chest expands, and where once I would've used violence to appease the emotion threatening to tear me apart, all I can do is let that fear chip away at my defences. My fingers curl into my palms, my nails cutting into the soft flesh there as I seek out some form of release. I hate this feeling of being so out of control. The thought of putting a bullet in David's brain was the only thing keeping me sane. If I don't have that, what else is left to keep me in check?

"I need a coffee. We can talk some more," she says, lifting her chin stubbornly.

My gaze trails over her face, lowering to her neck and resting on the two-inch horizontal cut that's already crusted over. She won't scar, but that means shit. We're all fucked up from the wounds that have never healed inside. A familiar rage builds in my stomach and I know that I need to find a way to override it right this fucking second, that I need to find a way to work through my issues, and given violence isn't an option right now, the only logical way to do that is through dance.

My dance. Bachata.

"I'd rather dance."

"Dance?"

"Yes. Will you dance with me, Tiny?"

"I don't think that's a good idea right—"

Grasping her arm I pull her towards me. "Dance with me." It comes out as an order but really, it's a plea. Acting one way, feeling another. Typical fucking me. Earlier I had shown her anger when really all I felt was fear. Still fucking do.

"Are you trying to seduce me into submission? Is that the plan, Xeno?" she asks with a soft voice, her gaze landing on my hand wrapped around her arm. There's caution in her gaze, a flash of fear. I release her.

"I'm fucking this up..."

"Fucking what up?"

"I don't want to seduce you, Tiny," I say in frustration. "I just want to dance. Nothing more."

She holds my gaze for a long time and I'm fully aware that at this moment she's fighting her own demons. Eventually she nods her head, determined. "Then let's dance."

Pushing off the door, I grab my mobile phone, feeling the heat of her stare as she watches me select a track. *I Just Want You*, an instrumental bachata track by Marco Lopetuso, begins to play.

"What's this?" she asks, cocking her head as she listens to the song. Her long brown hair falls over her shoulder, and I have the urge to run my hands through the silky strands.

It's not a song I've ever played in my lessons at the Academy or shared with anyone else before today. It means something special to me. This is a song that I've invented countless routines in my head to but never shared, and that's because of the woman standing before me. I never wanted to dance to this track with anyone else but her. Deep down, hidden beneath the lies I told myself, it was always her.

My Tiny.

The girl who holds my beaten-up, broken heart in her hands and has ever since we were kids. The woman who tears me up inside because I love her so damn much, and don't know how the fuck to handle that. The dancer who makes my skin burn just to move with her. She's the one I'd die for above all else. She's the one I'll kill for without fucking question.

I'm a man of few words, yet I'm filled up to the fucking brim with intense emotions. Over the past few days, I've felt them all. I've been plagued by rage, shame, helplessness, guilt, insecurity, *love*.

Somehow this track allows me to express them without losing my ever-loving mind. When things get really bad and violence isn't an option, I dance to this track until I can breathe again. Now I want to share it with her.

"It's beautiful," she whispers.

"I've never danced to this song with anyone else before…" I

say, swallowing my nerves and ignoring the roaring, pulsing, rush of blood in my ears and the fucking heat the burns beneath my cheeks. Turning my back to Tiny, I pull off my sweater and t-shirt needing to relieve myself of the confines of my clothes, not because I want to seduce her, but because suddenly I can't fucking breathe. I push away the memory of Frederico holding a knife to her neck as I concentrate on the song.

"You're undressing?"

"It helps..."

"With what?"

"Me to breathe."

"Breathe?"

I swallow hard, itching to hold her and yet wanting to run. The building pressure inside of me grows. "I don't know how else to explain... Can we just dance...?"

"That's why I'm here, right?" she answers, waiting for me to make the first move.

Stepping close, I place my hand on the middle of her back and clutch her hand against my chest. Her eyes widen as I position my legs and press my thumb against her spine as the familiar beat kicks in on the track.

"This is bachata," she says.

"Yes."

"Why now? What's changed?" she whispers as our bodies mould together and we move to the distinct beat of the music. It's natural, the way we dance together. Instinctual. Like coming home. I knew it would be. Dancing with her at Tales, then briefly at Jewels gave me a taste of how it would be to dance bachata with her. I already know that I will never want to dance bachata with anyone else ever again.

"Does there have to be a reason?" I ask, dipping her backwards slowly, before lifting her back up again. My hand slides down her back, over her arse and under her thigh, hooking her leg over my hip. She grinds against me as I stare into her beautiful brown eyes. Eyes that seem to change shade with her mood. Right now, they're a deep brown. Sensual. Alluring. For a moment, at least, the anger and fear are gone. I swallow hard.

"Do you want to know what I think?" she whispers, her forehead pressed against mine, our lips grazing as she clutches the back of my neck and runs her fingers over my cheek.

"What, Tiny?" I reply, easing her leg down, and capturing her thigh between my own as we rock rhythmically from side to side.

"This dance is a goodbye. You're going to go to Mexico regardless of what I say. You don't believe you'll come back any more than we do, so it's easy for you to break our hearts when you won't see the repercussions of your actions."

Her voice cracks, her body trembles, but she doesn't stop moving; instead, she raises her hands to meet mine. We dance like this, our bodies parted, but our palms pressed together for the next few beats of the song. I see the emotion playing in her eyes. She's always wanted to dance bachata with me, and now she is. Right now, it's a dance of mixed emotions. Her fear, my pain. Her love, my determination. Her courage, my stubbornness.

"You're wrong..." I reply, releasing one hand, encouraging her to turn in a circle as I move behind her, keeping my distance for the next portion of the song. My gaze tracks the seductive sway of her hips, as she steps in time to the rhythm of the music. I'm enraptured by the way she moves and how fucking perfect she is.

"I am?" she questions as I step closer, lining myself up behind her. My chest, hips and thighs all pressed against her now; she fits perfectly.

"Dancing with you is helping to ease this feeling in my chest," I admit.

"What feeling?" she questions, turning her head to the side and looking up at me as I slide my hand upwards and rest it just below her breasts. I feel the delicious curve of the underside of her breast as she places her hand over mine, our fingers entwining. My cock jerks, and I will myself to keep dancing and not rip her clothes from her body and bury myself inside of her.

This isn't about sex. This is about so much more. Bachata is both sensual and controlled. The control is in the steps that are timed to the beat, but the sensuality is found in the closeness of our bodies pressed together, the building heat of cheeks brushing cheeks, lips grazing lips, fingers gliding over skin. It's a dance that speaks to my soul. I need passion and love, I *crave* it, but in a way that can be contained. Bachata allows that.

We rock our hips in time to the beat of the music, her arse pressed against my thickening cock. She hums, the soft sound vibrating through her back into my chest. I can't help myself; I lower my lips to hers, brushing over them softly. The pain beneath my rib cage expands. I nearly lost her. I still could. I will if David doesn't die.

"What feeling?" she persists, kissing me back. The edge of her tongue runs over my lower lip, teasing, stirring up more feeling, more pain.

"The rage. The pain. The love. It's too much," I admit.

For a second her step falters, but rather than stop dancing she spins around to face me, pressing her palm over my heart. "Too much?"

I concentrate on the basic count of the dance, the rising tide of the music. I use the familiar percussive beat to focus my mind and steady the bulging, rasping pain in my chest so that I can answer her truthfully. "I have to dampen every emotion. Love. Hate. Rage. Fear. Lust. Joy. I'm not normal, Tiny."

"Why did you never say anything?" she asks, as I grasp her upper arms and she rolls her shoulders, undulating against me. "I could've helped you."

"I didn't know how to love the right way. I still don't."

"Then let me teach you."

"It's not as simple as that…"

"It can be, if you let it. Will you let me help you?"

For a while I can't answer, not in words anyway. Instead, I guide her around my bedroom, the hugeness of the song and the intimacy of the space only serving to heighten the emotion further, not dampen it down like I'd hoped. I'm barely holding on.

"Xeno?" She reaches up to cup my face, her thumb dragging over my split lip and bruised cheek. Stepping into her parted legs, I rest my hands against her upper chest, holding her just beneath her armpits then lift my arms up, supporting hers on top of mine as I crouch into the hold, my hips rocking, encouraging her to do the same. Of course, she moves with me, and when I gently push her rib cage with my right hand, she knows what I mean to do and rolls her body with mine.

"I've already made so many mistakes when it comes to you, Tiny," I mutter against her cheek, my lips brushing over her skin. Her fingertips trail down my neck and across my pecs. Her touch feels like fucking fire.

"We've all made mistakes," she counters as I place my hand on her right shoulder and push gently so she spins under my arm, her hair whipping through the air as she moves. Reaching for her hip with one hand, and cupping her shoulder with the other, she lifts her leg and rolls her shoulder in one smooth motion. She fucking slays me. Dancing with her is as easy as breathing.

"I tried to make you choose because how could you possibly have a heart big enough to love all four of us when my heart was barely capable of loving at all?" I say, my thumb sliding down her spine and pinning her to me.

"Xeno..." her voice breaks, and the love she pours into her steps and the intensity of her stare almost floors me.

Digging deep, I concentrate on our movements, the beat, the count of our steps that intensify with every percussive beat. Tiny is a beautiful bachata dancer, a natural. Her expressive tendencies adding flare to her arm movements, and her perfect timing from years of dancing hip-hop ensuring she hits every single beat.

"I'm a man of too much. Too much hate, too much rage, too much fucking love."

"Too much is better than none at all. I'd rather have every last drop of your love, however you choose to express it, than nothing at all. I'd rather you live than die, Xeno."

"Fuck, Tiny..." My lips hover over hers, dusting her with softness when inside all I feel is this carnal kind of love, a savage possession, a turbulent need. It cuts me open.

"Keep dancing," she says, as though sensing the sudden change in me. "Concentrate on the steps, the beat. Let it soothe you, Xeno. Let's heal each other. It doesn't have to hurt."

In response, I pull Tiny against my chest, her torso resting against mine, her breasts pressed up against me as we move. With our hands still clasped together, I rest my cheek against hers as we dance in a tight circle to the beat of the song. Her thigh is tight between mine and she sways her body, her right foot rising with a cock of her hip. Every movement hits perfectly with the beat of the music and gradually, every step we take eases the ache as a flood of endorphins enters my system. It's a rush like no other. I instantly feel myself relax, and the rising, broiling tide of my emotion dies away.

"You're not alone, Xeno. You don't have to kill for any of us to ease your suffering. We'll find another way," Tiny says, pulling back, her eyes begging me to listen, her words promising safety and comfort.

The problem is I'm a product of my own making, and maybe if we didn't have this threat hanging over our heads, I'd be able to believe another way is possible. But it isn't.

Cupping her face in my hands, I press my lips against hers. She sobs against my mouth, her hands rising up and curling into my hair as she clutches me to her. I taste her salty tears and the metallic blood from my split lip. I feel her pain and fear, and as she scrambles up my body, wrapping her legs around my waist. I hold on for dear life. We kiss like two lovers who know their time is up. We kiss knowing this might be the last chance. I'm going to kill her brother, and Tiny will stick to her word just like she should. The song ends and I ease Tiny out of my hold and take a step away from her. It feels like an ice bucket of water has been chucked over my head.

"There is no other way. I leave Friday morning."

She gives me a heartbreaking look, then nods. "Then you leave me with no other choice."

33

Pen

"THANKS FOR COMING TO GET ME," I say, pressing my head against the cool glass of the window and watching the city lights blur against the night sky as we speed down the motorway.

"Hey, that's what friends are for, right? You don't need to thank me," Grim replies, squeezing my hand gently. Her fingers are warm against my chilled skin, and despite the warmth of the car and the heated seats, I'm still cold.

"Regardless, I appreciate it." My breath steams up the window, misting my view of the world. That's kind of how I feel right now, like everything's blurred. I'm finding it hard to distinguish between real memories and nightmares. Between what's the right thing to do and what's the wrong thing to do. Between love and fear. It's why I had to leave. Being with the Breakers right now isn't an option. I need to set my head right. Besides, I can't be there when Xeno leaves for Mexico.

"Will they hate me for this?" I ask, my voice quiet.

"They let you come with me, didn't they? I think they get what you need right now. You're not running away. You just need a little bit of time to deal with this."

"I'm not so sure. You didn't see how they looked at me. It was like that night all over again."

When my voice catches, Grim glances over at me. "If they give you a hard time, I'll break their fucking necks."

"I'm not sure that's helpful, Grim. I love them. I don't want them dead."

She glances over at me. "Yeah, I know you do, and despite this complete fuck-up of the last few days, they love you too. Enough to give you space and trust you'll return. Enough to take out two fucking crews."

"And David..." I mutter.

"What?" Grim asks

"Xeno's catching a flight to Mexico in a couple days. He's going to kill David."

"The fuck!?"

I swallow hard, blinking back my tears. "That's partly why I left. I couldn't stand to see Xeno leave. He's got it into his head that the only way to keep me safe is to kill David."

Grim is quiet for a moment. When she pulls off the motorway, following the sign to Hackney, a long sigh releases from her mouth. "I agree with him."

"With Xeno?"

"Yes."

"You knew about his plan?" I ask, my voice rising.

"No, but given what's gone down it doesn't come as a surprise. Though I have to admit, whilst I agree that David has to die, I don't agree that Xeno should be the one to do it."

"What do you mean?"

"I mean if anyone deserves to murder that fucking cunt, it's you..." She lets that statement hang in the air and when I don't respond after five long minutes, she pulls over onto a side street and parks the car before turning to face me.

"Pen. After Saturday night my opinion of your brother has changed. I thought he was just another bullshitter who barks and never bites, but he's proven that he's willing to do whatever it takes to take you and everyone you love out. He's played his first hand, and I'm betting it's only going to escalate, especially now that we suspect Santiago is sanctioning everything he does."

"So you *do* think Xeno should go to Mexico?" I ask in confusion.

"No, I think that's a fucking suicide mission, and the second we get home I'm calling Hud to intervene."

"So what's the alternative?"

"We draw David out, and when that day comes, you'll be the one to decide how he dies. Either by your hand, or by one of your Breakers. Hell, I'll even do it myself if that's what you want."

My eyes flick to her stomach. "No."

"No? You think being pregnant changes what I'm capable of?" Grim laughs, shaking her head. "If anything, knowing I have a baby inside of me makes me even more determined. I will protect my child until my very last breath."

"That isn't what I meant, Grim. I don't want David dead. I want him to *suffer*, and the only way that's going to happen is if he's rotting in prison for the rest of his life whilst I'm living mine freely with the men I love," I say, repeating what I said to Xeno just a few hours ago.

Grim considers me for a moment. "You're a lot like Hudson, do you know that? I think that's why I like you so much."

"How so?"

"He's smart, loving, kind, loyal and stubborn as fuck. Like you, he wants to see his arch nemesis rot in jail. It's kind of cute, actually. I would've had them both tortured." She grins then restarts the car, putting it into drive. "Okay then, prison it is. We'll get them both banged up together. Now we just have to figure out how to get the fuckers over here, because so far our plan ain't working out so great."

My mobile phone pings with a message from Clancy and I heave out a sigh. "Shit."

"What?"

"It's Clancy, she's expecting me back at the Academy tomorrow, but I can't face it right now... I'm going to get chucked out."

"The hell you will! I'll get Hud to speak to Tuillard. You'll go back Monday once you've had a few more days. Just text Clancy back and tell her that you aren't well enough yet. If she's as good a friend as you say she is, she'll understand."

"Thanks, Grim. I really do appreciate everything you're doing."

She glances over at me and nods. "Seems to me that you've spent your whole life looking out for everyone else, sacrificing your happiness so the people you love can be safe. Maybe it's time you let other people take care of you for a change, yeah?"

"Yeah," I reply softly.

"Beast is looking forward to seeing you. I think the stupid arse likes you." Grim winks, letting me know that she's cool with that.

"How's he doing? God, I haven't even asked about him, that's really shitty of me."

"Don't sweat it. He's fine, though his nose is pretty sore actually."

I frown. "His nose? I don't remember anyone punching him."

"That's because it happened after you dropped him home. The stupid fucker took a risk that could've got him killed. I am not about to be a single mother."

"I'm sorry."

"Why are *you* sorry? He can think for himself. Dax called; he came. Like me, Beast rarely likes anyone. He likes Dax, he likes you. I'm just pissed that he snuck off without telling me. He took advantage of the fact that this baby growing in my stomach makes me tired as fuck. I fell asleep in my damn office at Tales while he crept out and acted the hero."

"You know, he kind of was a hero. If it wasn't for him..."

"Yeah, I do know. That's the only reason I didn't murder his arse." Grim chuckles, shaking her head in amusement.

"How are you feeling, apart from the tiredness?"

"Put it this way, there's nothing like a baby growing inside your belly to bring out the mama bear in you. I'm feeling very fucking protective of the people I care about. You included, Pen. So, if those Breakers give you anymore shit, I'm gonna unleash *my* beast and I'm telling you, she's a lot scarier than Roger." She bursts out laughing and I can't help but join in.

"Is that really Beast's name... *Roger?*"

"Fucking awful, isn't it. Whilst Joey was digging out the bullet and sewing him up, Beast let it slip out that Jeb had called him by his real name in front of you all. That in itself is an act of war in Beast's eyes, regardless of all the other stuff Jeb came out with. If Zayn hadn't killed him, Beast would've just for that alone."

"Remind me not to call him Roger then," I say with a half-smile.

"Oh no, you'd better. He likes you too much to kill you for it."

We fall into companionable silence for the rest of the journey to Grim's place. Ten minutes later she drives down a familiar street in the posh part of Hackney. I sit up in my seat, my mouth dropping open as she pulls up outside number 15 Jackson Street. "Wait a minute..."

"Surprise," she says, with a hint of a smile playing on her lips.

"This is..."

"*Was* the Skins' headquarters. It's now mine."

"When? How?"

"Jeb found a new place a few years back, and I brought it for a steal from the family who owned it. I think they were grateful to finally get rid of it. It was a shit-tip, and now it isn't."

"But..." I shake my head, my eyes blinking back the shock as I take in the stunning home before me now. There are no broken windows, or missing tiles from the roof. The metal door that was supposed to keep squatters out, but never did, has been replaced with a large red door adorned with a lion's head brass knocker. The front drive is well manicured and lined with shrubs and plants, and the window frames are painted white. It's beautiful, and a far cry from the building I remember in my not-so-distant past.

"Home sweet home," Grim says, smiling proudly as she clicks a button on her key fob and the shiny black iron gate swings open, allowing her to drive straight in.

"This is unreal," I say, climbing out of the car. My gaze trails to the side of the building and the basement entrance that we used to use. I wonder if Asia's mural is still painted on the walls. My heart squeezes at the thought that it probably isn't.

"Come on, let's get you settled in," Grim says, winding her arm through mine and guiding me up the freshly painted front steps. She doesn't need to unlock the door because the second we reach the top step; Beast pulls it open.

"Well, hello there, sweetheart. How're you doing?" he asks, grinning at me with two black eyes and a plaster across his nose.

"Better than you by the looks of it," I joke.

"What, this?" he says, pointing at his nose. "I fell onto Grim's right hook."

"That's what she said." We all grin.

"Come on, it's bloody cold out here. Move aside, Roger, and let us in," Grim says with a wink. Beast swats her on the butt playfully as she walks past him. A laugh bursts from my lips but is soon snatched from my mouth as I step into the hallway.

"Holy shit!" I exclaim, my eyes widening as I take in the stunning hallway with wooden parquet flooring and artwork covering every inch of the walls. "Is that Asia's work?"

"Yep, the girl's got wicked skills," Beast replies.

"She's so talented," I say, my eyes drawn from the incredible artwork and upwards to the huge chandelier-slash-art installation hanging above the staircase. "Wow! Did she do that too?"

"No, it's awesome though, isn't it?" Grim asks, closing the door behind us and handing her coat and bag to Beast. He takes them and drops a kiss to her cheek. A look passes between them, and my chest tightens at their obvious love and intimacy. I look away.

"It's amazing. This place is... *gorgeous*."

"This is just the hallway, wait until you see the rest of the house," Beast says. "Grim has a good eye when it comes to interior design. She ain't just a pretty face."

Grim shoves his chest. "I'm *much* more than a pretty face and don't you forget it."

"Babe, I'll love you when your hair is thinning, your arse is sagging, and your tits are—"

Grim punches him in the arm. "Quit whilst you're ahead," she chides.

Beast turns to me and winks. "Come on, let me get you something to eat. Then we can discuss how hard I need to kick your Breakers' arses."

An hour later, after stuffing myself with a delicious ham, cheese and mushroom omelet and washing it down with a cup of tea, I climb under the covers of one of the most comfortable beds I've ever slept on and fall into a deep, dreamless sleep in the house that once held both my fondest memories and my darkest demons.

34

Pen

"YOU KEPT IT?" I ask, focusing on the mural in front of me. The colours are still as vibrant as they ever were, but that's the only part of the basement that's remained the same. Now there's a carpeted floor with underfloor heating, a massive floor to ceiling TV screen, and a huge purple cuddle chair situated at the back of the room that's big enough to sleep six let alone seat two people. There's even one of those posh wine refrigerators full of soft drinks and bottles of wine against one wall. Long gone is the musty, dirt-encrusted cellar filled with a moth-eaten sofa and a threadbare armchair. Now it's a perfectly indulgent mini-cinema with a downstairs shower room.

"Asia would've killed me if I painted over it. She said that one day it might be worth something. I'm sure she figures herself a

Banksy." Grim chuckles, but there's nothing but love and respect in her voice.

"She's just as good an artist," I reply, wandering over to the wall and pressing my hand against the mural. My fingers trace over the word Breakers and tears well in my eyes as a flood of memories come hurtling back. It'd been the best Christmas present I'd ever had, even if they did give it to me on New Year's Eve. I remember how they lit the room with fairy lights and candles, how we spent the night together just the four of us and I'd got drunk on Amaretto Sours that York had made for me. It had been the best night of my life then my worst when David turned up to ruin it, just like he always ruins everything. Pushing those memories aside, I plaster on a smile for Grim. She sits down on the cuddle chair, her hands stroking over the plush velvet material.

"When we bought this house, I had no idea that Asia did this. In fact, finding this mural was how we found out about Eastern's friendship with Dax. Hudson had been searching for a way to get close to Santiago for a long time, and when Eastern explained how this mural came to be, Hud and I knew that was the opportunity he was searching for. He just needed to persuade your Breakers to get on board."

"Funny how things work out..." I say.

"It is, isn't it...?" Grim blows out a breath, her eyes raking over my face. My stomach drops.

"What?"

"I like your bandana," she says, pointing to the one I'm wearing like a headband.

"Thanks, but this isn't about my bandana, is it?" I ask, knowing that the look in her eyes has nothing to do with my fashion choices.

She shakes her head. "No..."

"Grim, please. Just put me out of my misery."

"Xeno didn't fly out to Mexico this morning, Pen. He didn't take the flight."

"Wait, he didn't go?"

"No, he didn't go."

"Oh, thank fuck!" I blurt out, feeling as though a weight has been lifted off my shoulders. "The thought of him going through with it has had me tied up in knots these past few days. I've been worried sick."

"I know..." Grim's voice trails off and I look over at her.

"Is there something else?" I ask.

"I spoke to Clancy last night. She's stepping in for you this weekend at Tales and is more than happy to put a routine together at short notice. She's been at the club all day going through the routine."

"You didn't have to do that. I can go to work."

"No. You've had a shock. It's not every day you get a knife held against your throat and witness a bloodbath. I understand what that feels like to experience for the first time. I get what you're going through."

"You're talking as though it's something I'll get used to."

"I did," she shrugs. "Violence comes with the territory, Pen."

"I know that." Sighing heavily, I plaster a smile on my face. "I should ring Clancy. Thank her for stepping up."

"Yeah. She's a good person, Pen. She's also smart and knows that there's more to this than meets the eye. Do you trust her?"

"Yes, I do."

Grim nods. "Good. Trustworthy friends are a dime a dozen. Keep her close. You'll need her."

"I will. Thank you for everything you've done," I say, giving

Grim a hug. She pats me on the back, then leans back and squeezes my arm.

"You're all welcome to stay here this weekend. This cuddle chair doubles up as a bed but come Monday we go back to the plan. You need to get back to the Academy," she says, untangling herself from my hold.

I frown. "*All* welcome?"

"I invited your boys over. They should be here in about half an hour. I figured you'd want to see them now that you know Xeno hasn't flown to Mexico. You can sleep down here together. There's duvets and pillows in the cupboard over there and the cuddle chair is roomy enough for you all," Grim says, smiling knowingly.

"They're coming here *now*?! I exclaim. My stomach flips over, butterflies taking flight as I run my hand through my hair nervously.

"You want me to call them, tell them not to?"

"No, it's time. We've got a lot to discuss..." I've spent the past few days mulling over everything that's happened and no matter where my thoughts go, they always end up in exactly the same place; I love them. It's as simple and as complicated as that.

"That you do, girl." Grim tips her head to the side, studying me.

"Is this where you give me more advice?" I question, smiling a little so she knows I mean no disrespect.

"You've got something special with those boys, you know that, right?" She smiles gently. "Fuck me, I'm no expert in relationships, but I know *that* much."

"You really believe that?"

"I know what I said before about them but believe me those Breakers love you as much as Beast loves me, and that kind of love doesn't come around very often. It's fucking rare. Special. It deserves a chance."

"I thought you didn't like them?"

"I can be wrong. It happens." She gives me a wry smile. "They miss you. They've been calling and texting Beast like a bunch of lovesick puppies."

"Sounds like harassment to me," I joke.

"They're fucking insane for you, Pen."

"That's what I'm worried about. David is insane for me too..." My voice trails off as nausea rises up my throat again.

"This isn't the same, Pen. David's feelings for you are toxic."

"I know that." My gaze flicks back to the mural. It's been three days since I've seen or spoken to the Breakers and they've kept to their word and given me the space I needed to wrap my head around everything. "Being down here, seeing this mural again..."

"You've missed them too?"

"Yeah, so fucking much."

"Can I give you a piece of advice, Pen?"

"Sure."

"There will be times when your relationship will be tested to its limit. I don't pretend to know what it's like to be in a relationship with four men, but I do know what it's like to be with someone who doesn't fit society's idea of a *good* man..."

"Beast seems like a good man to me," I reply.

"He kills people, Pen. He does it without flinching. I've seen him in action more times than I can count. Beast truly is a beast, but *I* understand him. He is loyal and fucking brave. He's also dangerous. Cross him and die... But if he accepts you, then he'll have your back until the end of time. He will do anything to protect the ones he loves, just like the Breakers. I see that now."

"I hear what you're saying..."

Grim fixes me with her gaze. "At the end of the day, Pen, you're the *only* person who knows their hearts. They've killed people. News flash, so have I, but there's a difference between people who kill because they get a kick out of it and those who kill to keep who they love *safe,* to survive a life they never fucking asked for. Your brother and Santiago are psychopaths. They hurt people because it gets them off. They don't love, they don't even understand the concept, and the only person they look after is themselves. Your Breakers aren't like that."

"I know. I *know* that."

"Good. Well then..." Her voice trails off as she looks at me. Grim has been the kind of friend I never thought she could be, like an older sister I've always wanted. God knows she's shown more kindness to me these past few weeks than my own mum has my whole life.

"What?" I ask, softly.

"I'm not doing any of this because you're good for business, Pen. Though you really, really are. I'm doing this because I care. I just wanted to make sure you understood that."

I nod, the emotion wrapping around us both like a comforting blanket. "I do, and ditto.... One day I'd love to hear the story of how you and Beast got together," I say after a beat.

Grim laughs at that. "Ours isn't your typical love story. More like a *Brothers Grimm* fairytale honestly. I'm not sure it'll be your thing."

I raise my brows. "Are you kidding? I'm partial to the unusual. Everything else is boring."

She laughs. "Well, I suppose you have a point. Maybe when

this is all over, I'll tell you how that brute got me to fall in love with him. How about that?"

"I'd like that."

"I will warn you, though, it's kind of twisted. Beast's idea of wooing me was bringing me the hearts of my enemies."

When she doesn't burst out laughing, my mouth drops open in shock. "*What?* That's fucking gross." Not to mention insane, though I'm not stupid enough to mention that part out loud. I like Beast. I know he's got a reputation, but *shit*. It kind of puts everything I've been feeling into perspective. My Breakers might be violent when the need arises, but I'm pretty sure they don't go cutting out people's hearts and offering them up as gifts.

"It was a bit. The last heart he delivered was my father's. Most romantic thing he's ever done for me, though I didn't appreciate it at the time. Pretty sure I shot him for it actually," she replies with a shrug of her shoulders.

"What the fuck, Grim? He brought you your *father's* heart..."

"See? Told you, that's Grimm fairytale shit right there. I wonder whether my dad gave me the nickname Grim because somewhere in the back of his head he knew my life would end up like some twisted fairytale," she muses.

"I don't know what to say..." *Fucking hearts.*

"I told you Beast really is a beast, but he's *my* beast, and I have absolutely no doubts that he will be the best father to our baby. Though I already feel sorry for the poor fucker who falls in love with her..."

"*Her?*" I ask, blinking back my shock.

She pats her belly, her eyes lighting with love. "It's just a hunch, but I'd put good money on this little one being a girl."

"A little girl, eh?"

We both turn around as Beast enters the room. He's holding a cardboard box. I look from Grim to Beast and back again, my stomach tightening. "Please don't tell me that's a…"

Grim laughs so hard that tears spring from her eyes. "No, Pen. Beast hasn't brought me a heart since he stole mine. Isn't that right, Beast?"

Beast's eyes widen, and he looks over at me warily. "You told Pen about that? Way to make her fucking shit-scared of me!" Grim just laughs some more. "I don't make a habit of cutting out peoples' hearts, Pen. At least not anymore. Those were dark days and perhaps not a story for today. Yeah, my love?" Beast says, huffing out a breath as he strides across the room and places the cardboard box in the same cupboard that I changed my wet clothes in all those years ago.

"Definitely not a story for today," Grim agrees, taking his proffered hand when he offers it to her. "Catch you later, Pen, and remember what I said, okay?" Grim says, squeezing my arm before heading back upstairs with Beast, leaving me to wait for my Breakers in the place where it all began.

35

Pen

FLICKING on the massive TV screen, I scroll through the channels to find something to watch whilst I wait for my Breakers to arrive. Choosing a music channel that's playing *If You Want Love* by NF, I step into the open space between the cuddle chair and the TV screen and pull my bandana over my eyes, needing to dance with my heart and my memories, needing to centre myself. Letting the music wash over me, I let my mind go back to the first night I came here. I was so young, so fucking scared. When I really allow myself to think about that night, about what I went through, it makes me feel sick. I pity the kid I was. I feel so fucking bad for her. All she ever wanted was to be loved and instead she got a mother who resented her, and a brother who had an unhealthy obsession for her, still does.

Curling my fingers into fists and lifting my arms up as though

I'm about to start running, I step into the movement, my feet stomping to the beat of the song. My heart squeezes at the memory of that night. How he'd hurt me. All the fear and the fucking loneliness I'd felt. Back then I'd wanted to be free from him just for a little while. I needed to escape. I ran to find peace. I didn't want to feel afraid anymore.

Stamping my feet, I raise a fist, punching the air with every step as I work through the memory. Exaggerating the movements, I try to shake the stress free. I dance wildly, twisting my torso, kicking out my legs, sweeping low, then jumping high. I'm jerky in my movements, angry with my steps. So fucking angry. This is me working through that night, trying to make sense of it. With a heaving chest I let the music wash over me. Then as the verse hits, I perform a series of isolated arm movements. Folding them over my head, locking and popping, I imitate that cage I'd felt trapped in. The cage that was built on fear and violence, caused by my brother's hand. I recall the pain I'd felt, not the physical kind, because that's faded with time. I'm talking about the long-lasting pain that sits deep inside. The kind of pain that can only be healed by the men I love. My Breakers will be here soon and despite everything that's happened between us, despite what I've witnessed, I know that they're my safe place.

My solace.

My hope.

My future.

That night when I ran away from the abuse, I'd acted purely on instinct. Fuck, so many things could've gone wrong. I was fourteen, scared, alone, beaten and fucking bruised. I'd ended up at Jackson Street, a tiny part of me hoping that Zayn would be there.

I'd stood under the oak tree in the freezing rain feeling so fucking desolate, so *alone*.

Remembering that moment with such clarity, I stop moving, my arms rising up as I hug myself. The words wash over me as I think back, as I remember wanting so desperately to be loved. Then out of the shadows he'd appeared....

York.

He'd offered me the hand of friendship. He saw that I was in trouble and he'd acted on it. The second my hand slid into his, I knew. I *knew* I'd found someone special, just like I'd known it when Zayn had stepped into the playground and danced with me a few weeks before. Both times my shattered heart had sensed the good in them, the kindness, a kindred spirit. My heart had understood what I didn't at the time, that they were meant for me, that we were always supposed to *be*. That knowledge, that reminder, makes my heart lift, my spirit soar.

Lifting my right leg, extending it out to the side, I lean over in the opposite direction, I reach for that boy, that lifeline, but it's just a memory and it dissolves between my fingers. Drawing my leg and arms back in, I balance on one leg, my toes curling into the plush carpet as I hunch over myself. With the next beat, I feel the music rise up my chest and I absorb strength from it, from the words and the way they make me want to move.

Lowering my leg, and straightening up, I lift onto my tiptoes and dance through a series of ballet steps, moving from one foot to the other as I perform *adagio*. I dance a succession of slow, soft, lyrical movements, moving around the open space between the cuddle chair and the television, trusting my instincts and following my heart with every step.

For a few blissful moments I let everything go.

"Titch?"

York's voice reaches me over the music, but I don't stop moving or remove my blindfold, instead I spin around to face my Breakers. I don't need to see them to know they're all here in the basement with me. My heart, my fucking *soul* feels their presence. Without saying a word, I hold my hand out to York. I offer him friendship and hope, just like he'd offered it to me all those years ago. Beneath my bandana, tears spring to my eyes, but I refuse to let them fall.

Instead, I wait.

Just like I knew he would, York moves towards me and takes my hand, his warm fingers sliding over my palm as he steps close and pulls me against his chest.

"Don't be scared. I swear, no one here will hurt you," he says softly, drawing my hand up to his lips, and pressing a kiss against my palm. My throat closes over recognising the same words he said to me that first night we met. Pressing my cheek against his chest, I grip hold of him tightly as we sway from side to side and just like the song suggests, if I want trust, I need to give some away. So, that's what I do. I'm trusting my heart. I'm trusting him, *all* of them. For the next few beats, we just dance like two teenagers at a school dance, holding onto one another, our hearts racing and the attraction building until York's hands reach for my face and he kisses me, his tongue searching, the pads of his thumbs stroking my cheekbones. My fingers curl into his top and a sob rises up my throat at the emotion coming from him.

This kiss is a gift. It's love wrapped up in a heartfelt apology. It's hope. It's friendship. It's *everything*. With one last kiss to my forehead, York releases me, and I know he hasn't gone far. He's simply stepped back for one of the others to step forward. Zayn approaches next. He smells familiar, like home. His scent conjures up a more innocent time in our relationship, when dance, laughter and friendship was what mattered the most.

Dropping his head onto my shoulder, Zayn wraps his arms around my waist, and upper chest. He starts moving behind me, swaying his hips. Instinctively, I step to the beat with him. We move together as he holds me against his chest, as he peppers kisses against my neck.

"Zayn..." My voice cracks and I swallow back the agony in it. Fuck, I've missed him.

"Someone did a number on you, didn't they?" he whispers, and just like York, he repeats what he'd said that night. I can't help but give a sad smile at that, because he's right. Back then my brother had been responsible for my bruises. Now, some of the internal ones have been inflicted by the men I love, even if it has been unintentionally.

We sway to the music, Zayn's hips pressed against my lower back, his body curving over mine in a protective, *loving* embrace. Then his hands slide down my arms and wrap around my wrists before lifting my arms up horizontally to the floor, leaving me wide open, vulnerable, as he steps back. I know what he's doing, he's asking me to trust him. I did back then, and I do now. I trust him, *all* of them. Pressing a kiss against the curve of my neck, Zayn ducks under my arm and stands in front of me.

"I've missed you, Pen. So fucking much."

My chest rises and falls to the pounding of my heart at his heartfelt words. Still blindfolded, my senses are heightened as his fingers run along my arms and across my shoulders, finally meeting at the back of my head and curling into my hair. Tugging gently, he tips my head back, steps closer, then kisses me. My arms drop as his tongue parts my lips and we kiss. We kiss knowing that we can't change what's happened between us, but that we can move forward, we can forge our own path. Eventually, when I'm high on his love, Zayn steps away, leaving me open once more. With the butterflies in my stomach soaring, I wait.

"Hey, Kid."

"Hey," I whisper, cocking my head to the side as Dax steps closer, the heat of his body and sheer size making me feel small, yet *safe*. Placing his hands on my hips, Dax lifts me off the floor, and I automatically reach for his shoulders, wrapping my legs around his waist as he holds me against him, one hand cupping my arse, the other gripping the back of my neck.

"See a penny, pick it up, all day long you'll have good luck," he says against my lips, a smile in his voice, before he slides his tongue into my mouth and kisses me like a man who's done waiting. That brings laughter from both York and Zayn, but tellingly Xeno remains quiet. I try not to think about that too much. Right now, Dax is my focus and boy does he distract me. His fingers squeeze my arse, his mouth claims mine in a beautiful, bruising kiss.

"Alright, big boy, put Titch down before we all come in our pants watching you tongue fuck our girl," York says after a while.

"You're like a goddamn irritating gnat, you fucker," Dax grumbles, but despite that he lowers me to the floor, presses another chaste kiss against my cheek and steps away.

Clasping my hands in front of me, my heart in my mouth, I wait for Xeno to make his move. I could choose to still be angry with him, but right now this isn't about blame, or anger, it's about forgiveness, friendship and love. He's *here* after all. I can't do any of this without them.

"Xeno...?" I whisper, holding my hands out for him to take.

When long moments pass and Dax swears under his breath, I

assume Xeno has decided to turn me down once again, just like he did when we were kids. When I raise my hands to remove my blindfold, I suddenly feel Xeno's presence and I swear the room holds its breath. I know I do.

"Let me," he says, his fingers untying the knot at the back of my head.

Blinking back the sudden brightness, I allow my eyes to focus on Xeno standing before me and this time, when I look into his eyes, I *see* everything he's feeling. *Everything.* He brings all his emotions to the surface, allowing them to bleed through. Knowing that he trusts me to see the broken shards of him, knowing how vulnerable this must make him feel, reassures me in the strength of *us*. It makes me believe that we can get through anything.

"I'm sorry, Tiny. For not listening to you. For forcing you away again. *You* matter more than my need to appease the violence. We will deal with your brother together. However you want to do that."

"Thank you," I say, relief flooding through me at his honesty.

He swallows hard, looking over my head at his best friends behind me, before focusing his attention back to me. "But—"

"Why does there always have to be a but?" I ask with a smile in my voice and nerves in my belly.

"Because, Tiny, your safety comes first. Always," he replies fiercely. "If it ever gets to the point when I have to choose between you hating me and saving your life, I will choose your safety above all else. I know what you want, and if David comes here, we will try to make sure he's put away. That he serves the rest of his life in prison. However, we're *all* in agreement if he gets close enough to hurt you, we *will* put him down. No hesitation."

I breathe out slowly. Nodding. "Okay."

"Oh, thank fuck," Zayn exclaims, and I feel the tension leave him, all of them, as I agree with their decision.

If it was Lena in immediate danger, then I would do anything to protect her. Growing up, I made sure I was always the one who took a beating. He never touched her, mostly because mum protected her so fiercely, but there were times I caught him looking at her the way he looked at me and on those occasions I made sure his anger was focused on me, not her. So, I get it.

"What happens now?" I ask softly, looking up at Xeno under my lashes. The heat and sexual tension rising between us.

"Tonight, and all the nights for the rest of my fucking life, I'm going to love you even when it hurts. *Especially* when it hurts. My brothers will help me to keep doing that. York will keep me distracted with his stupid fucking sense of humour when the dark thoughts hound me," he says.

I swallow hard, as the others step closer, surrounding me. Dax is at my back, York to my right and Zayn to my left. "Will you do that York?" Xeno asks, and the vulnerability he shows brings tears to my eyes.

"You fucking got it, bro," York replies, squeezing his shoulder.

"I will lean on Zayn when I need to talk through how I'm feeling." Xeno looks at Zayn hopefully. "I'm counting on you to talk me out of my darkest moments when York's humour isn't enough."

"Every time, motherfucker," Zayn agrees with a light laugh.

"And when I go too far, Dax will step in and make me see sense," he says, glancing over my head at Dax, the group's rock and my dark angel.

"You bet your arse I will. I got you."

My heart swells. Xeno must've told them everything that he told me. Opening up like that is huge. It looks like I'm not the only one who's done some soul-searching these past few days. "And what about me?" I ask, leaning back against Dax's chest as I look up at Xeno, my body shuddering involuntarily as Zayn and York slide their hands over my abdomen, hugging me close, and Dax grasps my hips in his large hands.

"I will dance with you to work out these emotions," Xeno replies. Determined. Certain. "But more importantly... I. Will. Love. You. No. Matter. What." He grits his jaw, his eyes flashing with promise, with determination. "*We* will love you."

"Fuck, yes," Zayn, Dax and York respond simultaneously.

Xeno drops his gaze to my parted lips, watching as my tongue slides out and licks them. I really, really want to kiss him. I want to do more than kiss him, kiss them. I've no idea how we're going to do this, but right now all I can think about, all I *want*, is to forget my brother for one night and wrap myself up in the arms of the men I love.

"What do you need, Tiny?" Xeno asks me, his hands coming up to cup my face, as the rest of the Breakers hands rove over my body, their intentions clear.

"You. I want you. I want all of you. I want my Breakers to make love to me right here in the room where it all started. That's what I want," I hush out in a breathy, lust-fueled whisper.

"Hell, yes," York says, his hand rising up to cup my breast over my top, his thumb rubbing over my nipple.

"Pen..." Zayn says, drawing my attention to him. I look into his night-time eyes. They're sparkling with a galaxy of stars as he drinks me in. "We're going to fucking worship every goddamn inch of you. This night and every night from this point onwards."

"God, yes." I breath out, moaning as Zayn's hand slips beneath the waistband of my slouchy trousers and cups my mound over my knickers. I rock against his hand, already slick with heat, already needy with want.

"Not before I've spanked Kid's arse," Dax says, dropping his mouth to that sweet spot on my neck just beneath my ear. "I haven't forgotten what I promised, and I'm pretty sure these arseholes are happy to watch after I told them what you did. Fucking dangerous, Pen."

"Fucking *sexy*, you mean. I'm more than ready to get a blowy whilst speeding down the motorway." York growls, tweaking my nipple between his finger and thumb as Zayn presses his middle finger against my clit.

"Fuck... Me..." I exclaim, already breathless.

"Tiny, we're gonna *love* you... Because *not* loving you is a thousand times more painful than loving you could ever be," Xeno whispers against my mouth.

"We sure as fuck will," Dax agrees, sucking on my neck as Xeno's eyes flash with so much passion that my knees go weak.

"Jesus, stop with the sweet talk and kiss our girl before I do," York jokes, alternating between palming my breasts and rolling my nipple between his finger and thumb.

"Fuck you, dickhead," Xeno retorts with a grin, then leans over and presses his lips against mine, kissing me like he should've done when I admitted my feelings for them all on that other memorable night in this basement all those years ago.

36

Pen

XENO PULLS BACK, his fingers stroking over my cheeks, down my neck and across my collar bone. Through the TV screen *Heal* by Tom Odell plays and it couldn't be a more perfect song for this moment together. Xeno smiles gently, stepping back, then removes his jumper and t-shirt in one go. My gaze drops to his firm pecs and ripped abs, across to the tattoo on his forearm with the shattered heart and broken penny with my name on it. One day I'm going to ask him about it, but right now isn't that time.

"Take your clothes off," he says, his gaze flicking to Dax, York and Zayn behind me. It's a quiet demand that has my clit throbbing and my heart skipping a beat.

"So this is how it's going down," Zayn mutters with laughter in his voice. Xeno flicks his gaze to Zayn who gently removes his hand from between my legs then strips down to his boxers. I bite my bottom lip, unable to keep my eyes off him, my cheeks heating. Reaching up, I press my fingers against his scarred skin and meet his gaze with a steely one of my own.

"I'm glad he's dead," I say. "No more scars."

"No more scars," he repeats, his chest rising and falling beneath my touch as I step into his hold and he presses a kiss against my lips. The rising tide of the music lifts the emotion between us all. This is a song about healing, and right here, right now, this is what we're doing. Individually we've all been building up to this moment, but not together, not like this.

It feels right. How can a love like this, so fucking pure, so perfect ever be wrong?

Zayn's hands slide down my arm, reaching for the hem of my top. He pulls upwards, and I lift my arms, allowing him to remove my top. "Beautiful," he hushes out as his fingers trail over my bare flesh, his finger rimming my pale pink, lace bra. Sliding his hands around my back, Zayn tips me backwards slowly, his lips blazing a hot trail over the centre of my chest down to my stomach, then back up again. When he reaches my mouth, he nips my bottom lip with his chipped tooth, and I can't help but smile into his mouth. God, how I love him.

"You too, York," Xeno demands, and when I glance over at him, I can see the evidence of his desire. Like Zayn, his cock is rigid against his jeans.

"Hey, you don't need to tell me twice," York replies, chuckling. Zayn pushes gently against my shoulder, urging me to turn around and face York so I can watch him undress. My breath hitches with every layer of clothing he removes until he too stands before me in just his boxer shorts.

"York," I whisper, my gaze tracing over his oak tree tattoo and the branches that reach out across his shoulders and down his arms. It's so fucking beautiful. A work of art.

Zayn slides his lips over my shoulder, and we sway together, the heat of Zayn's body seeping into my back as York steps forward. I can't help but trace my fingers over his ink, loving the whirls and twists of the bark.

"Titch, you're killing me," York mumbles, grasping my hands in his as Zayn grasps my hips. He steps back, still holding onto my hands. Instinctively, I bend at the waist as York draws my top half towards him so that I'm bent over at a right angle, Zayn hands still firmly gripping my hips. I feel Zayn's firm cock slide against the crack of my arse, nothing but the thin layer of clothing separating us. Biting my lip, my gaze lands on York's erection, the tip of his cock peeping out of the waistband of his boxers.

"Fuck, look at you," York says, his voice rumbling up his chest as he releases my hands and

glances at Zayn. Before I can predict what's happening, York twists around, so he's crouching away from me on one bended knee. For a moment I'm mesmerised by the taut muscles of his back and arms as they flex beneath his pale skin. Then I remember. This is one of the moves we performed in our routine that night we won the competition at Rocks.

I know what I have to do.

Zayn lets me go and I reach forward, wrapping my arms around York's back, gluing myself to him. He rises up with the next beat, his arms reaching around behind him as I kick my legs out to the side, releasing my hold around his neck so that he can swing me around his waist, bringing me upright before him.

"You remembered," he says, his eyes lighting with happiness and love.

"Of course I did," I reply. "I never forgot, not that night or any of the ones before it. You're in my heart, York, you all are. I love you. All of you."

"I love you too, Titch," he says before dropping his mouth to mine and kissing me until I'm breathless.

"Take Tiny's trousers off, York," Xeno instructs, drawing us out of our passionate kiss and back into the room.

York grins, dipping down before me, his large hands sliding off my trousers until I'm left in my underwear. For a moment, York just crouches before me, his cheek pressed against my lower abdomen as I run my hand through his soft, white-blonde hair. My skin covers in goosebumps as we share this tender moment. Then York cups my arse, lowers his nose to my lace covered pussy and breathes in deep, humming all the while. I jerk in his hold at the feel of his nose against my clit and the eroticness of the moment.

"Fuck, man," Dax grumbles, removing his clothes before Xeno even has to ask.

Stepping up behind me, Dax wraps his arms around my waist and drops a kiss to my bare shoulder, then he lifts me. "Eat her out, York. Fuck our girl with your tongue," Dax demands as York slides my legs over his shoulders.

"Fuck!" I exclaim, my core weeping for his mouth.

"Titch, I'm going make you come with my tongue, then I'm gonna fuck you. I'm gonna fucking love you whilst my brothers watch," York grinds out then reaches up between us and rips at the flimsy string of my knickers, shredding them. I don't get to even register the brief, sharp sting of the material snapping against my skin before York pushes his tongue deep into my core.

"Oh my God!" I scream, bucking against him as heat bursts out over my skin, a shudder rippling down my spine.

"That's it, Kid. Fuck his face," Dax grinds out, kissing and licking my neck and ear, heightening the pleasure further.

With me supported in his arms, Dax steps back so that York can get better access and Zayn can join in. Taking my chin in his grip, Zayn kisses me roughly, his tongue piercing my lips as he unclasps my bra, pulling it off. I groan into his mouth as York laps at my pussy, his tongue flicking over my clit expertly. Dax cups my breasts, playing with my nipples until I'm a writhing, grinding ball of heat.

I'm so close to coming. So fucking close.

"Get in here, man," Dax orders, his voice rough, gruff. "It ain't the time to watch."

When I hear the sound of a belt buckle being removed, Zayn releases my mouth so that I can turn my head towards Xeno. Our gazes meet and his eyes flare with a ferocity that takes my breath away and makes my heart ache for him. Despite everything he's said tonight, this is hard on him. Containing how he feels is always going to be difficult, but if he's determined to not let it beat him, then neither will I.

"Xeno, come here, *please*. Trust us, trust this," I pant, my hips rocking against York's face as Zayn's hot mouth wraps around my nipple and sucks. My eyes shut as I arch my back, and when Xeno's mouth wraps around my other nipple and his teeth scrape against the erect bud, I let out a scream of ecstasy, my orgasm barreling out of nowhere.

With my clit spasming, my breath hitching, their hands, lips, fingers and tongues clasping, groping, pleasuring, fucking, I come. I come so fucking hard I go blind for a few seconds. For a few moments I leave the basement of number 15 Jackson Street and soar into the night sky a thousand feet above us.

When I come down, I'm laying on the centre of the cuddle chair, York straddling my body, his knees between my parted legs, his hands pressed into the seat either side of my head. Kneeling beside me is Zayn, his cock thick and long as he strokes himself.

With heavy-lidded eyes I look up at them both. They're both completely naked now, and York's rolling a condom onto his impressive dick. My mouth pops open, dirty words rolling around my mind like thunder in the sky.

"We're nowhere near done, Pen," Zayn says, a wicked glint in his eye as his thumb rolls over the slit of his cock before he gently rubs the bulbous head against my swollen lips. Automatically, I dart my tongue out to taste him and he pushes the head between my parted lips. He groans as I suck him into my mouth.

"Wait!" Xeno says, and Zayn pulls back, leaking precum.

My head snaps around as I look at Xeno and Dax who are both standing at the foot of the cuddle chair, gloriously, perfectly, naked. My core tightens, my muscles contracting at their sheer beauty, their masculinity. A lazy smile lifts up my lips as I gaze at each of them in turn. Dax and Zayn are stroking their dicks, but Xeno's gaze is fixed firmly on mine, the intensity makes me squirm.

"Tiny, York is going to fuck you now, okay?" he says.

"Yes," I agree on a hushed breath, widening my legs.

"Look at me," York requests, and I focus back on him as he lines up his dick at my entrance then slides inside me with one firm thrust.

"Oh God!" I cry, my eyes rolling back in my head as I grasp for him, clawing at his back.

York fucks me. He *loves* me passionately. We fuck until we're both slick with sweat and our skin is dusted pink. We love one another as Xeno, Zayn and Dax stroke their beautiful cocks.

"Suck Zayn's dick," Xeno demands, lust billowing off him. I meet his dark, glittering gaze over York's shoulder. I'm not afraid of what I see within it. I'm not afraid of the possessiveness, the hunger, the *yearning*. I welcome it.

York slows his pace, drawing out completely as he follows Xeno's orders. "On your hands and knees, Titch," he says, his voice gravelly with lust.

Flipping over onto my stomach, I draw up onto my hands and knees. York reaches for my hair, fisting it and drawing my head back gently so that Zayn can slide his cock between my parted lips.

"That's it, take Zayn deep," Xeno commands, just as York glides back into my swollen, slick pussy. I groan around Zayn's cock, licking and tasting him as he passes over my tongue.

"Fuuuuuuck," York and Zayn exclaim simultaneously as they seat themselves inside of me.

"That's it, now make each other come. I want to see you come," Xeno says, his voice guttural and full of fucking heat. Goddamn it, it's sexy.

We follow his commands willingly. I deep throat Zayn's dick whilst York fucks me from behind. Heat builds low in my belly, my pussy weeping as the taste of Zayn's precum explodes on my tongue. The gentle force of York's thrusts helps me to keep the rhythm while sucking Zayn's cock. In this position, I'm well aware how vulnerable I am. York could fuck me too hard, the force pushing Zayn's cock too deep into my throat, but I trust them to take care of me. We rock in time with each other until a wave of pleasure builds to breaking point. When Dax climbs onto the cuddle chair and slides beneath me, his mouth sucking onto one of my dangling tits, and his finger playing and flicking my clit, I come. Like a row of dominoes, my orgasm sets off York's and he cries out, his cock jerking within me as my pussy spasms around him.

"Fuuccckkk!" he cries, his fingers curling into my flesh as he bucks behind me.

Zayn follows shortly after, his cum hitting the back of my throat with a roar. I suck it down greedily, my head spinning as my orgasm rips through me. Wave after pleasurable wave washes over me as my eyes roll back in my head, my limbs feeling too heavy.

A few moments later York and Zayn pull back, sliding out of me and leaving me open, my release sliding down my thighs, my pussy glistening. I fall forward, my arse up in the air, my cheek and forearms pressed against the cuddle chair, with Dax chuckling beneath me. His large hand comes up as he strokes his hand over my spine.

"Fucking beautiful," York mutters, pressing a kiss against my arse cheek. He swipes two fingers through my folds then gets off the cuddle chair. I push back up, sitting on my heels, as I look over my shoulder at him. He smiles wickedly before turning to Xeno. "Open up," he says.

Xeno's eyes flash with surprise, but he does as York asks and I watch with bated breath as York slides his finger into Xeno's mouth. He hums, sucking my cum off York's fingers, not once taking his eyes off mine.

"Jesus Christ," I mumble, my clit throbbing once again as Xeno releases York's fingers, a dirty smile pulling up his lips.

"Careful, Xeno, York will be giving your dick a nickname too if you're not careful," Dax says, chuckling, as he props his head up on his bent arm.

"How do you know I haven't already, *big boy*?" York winks. We all laugh, and it feels so fucking good.

"I don't even want to know what you've called mine," Zayn mutters with a shake of his head.

York jerks his head. "You want a drink, *Lance of Love?*"

"Lance of Love?!" Zayn's mouth drops open, then he roars with laughter. "You fucking prick."

"It's kinda cute," I say with a shrug.

"I'll take a beer," Zayn replies, before leaning over and kissing me deeply. We break the kiss and Zayn grins. "You can call me anything you want, but I draw the line at Lance of Love." With one final kiss to my bare shoulder, he climbs off the cuddle chair and joins York. For a few seconds, I enjoy perving on them both as they help themselves to a couple of beers, their naked butts, strong backs and muscular legs a girl's wet dream.

My *very* wet dream.

Dax starts laughing. "Hey, Kid," he says from his spot beside me. "Your eyes are bugging out. Have you got your fill yet?"

I lock gazes with him and smile cheekily. "I feel thoroughly fucked, thank you very much." Over on the other side of the room, York and Zayn clink their beer bottles together. York smirks. "Of course you fucking do."

Smartarse.

"Not thoroughly enough," Xeno says, climbing onto the cuddle chair behind me. "I do believe Dax has a punishment to dole out?"

Dax grins, his grey-green eyes sparkling. "Fuck yes!"

"No!" I screech with laughter, jumping up and trying to escape. Xeno captures me, grabbing me around the waist as he pulls me back down.

"Where do you think you're going, Tiny? We ain't done with

you yet," he growls, bringing his hand up between my breasts, his hand wrapping gently around my throat before he clutches my chin and turns my head to the side. My laughter dies on my lips, replaced instead with burning, hot desire. "Ever been fucked by two men at once, Tiny?" he whispers against my mouth.

"No," I squeak.

"Good. Because *big boy* and me are gonna take that sweet cherry right the fuck now," he continues, brushing his lips against mine. There's laughter in his voice at York's nickname, and it fills me with so much love. "I'm going to take your sweet, tight arse and Dax is gonna fuck your slick pussy."

I let out a shocked noise, but he swallows it with a kiss that robs me of my breath and steals my heart. I'm not sure how long we kiss for but one second I'm melting into Xeno's kiss, the next I'm laying across Dax's lap and screaming out from a stinging slap against my arse, then moaning as he soothes away the pain with the gentle, reverent stroke of his fingers.

"That's for sucking my cock whilst I was driving. So fucking dangerous," Dax reprimands, his words coated with desire, as he slaps me twice more in quick succession. I cry out with every slap, the pain short-lived and countered with the gentle stroke of his fingers over the stinging skin that makes my legs tremble and my clit pulse. "And this is for sucking my cock whilst driving. So fucking sexy," he continues, spreading my legs and sliding his fingers through my folds. He pushes two fingers into me, and I cry out in pleasure as he pumps them in and out, his thumb circling the puckered hole of my arse, all whilst Xeno watches on, his own fist wrapped tightly around the base of his cock.

I writhe across Dax's lap, my pleasure leaking out over his

hand and between my thighs. He brings me almost to orgasm and just when I'm on the cusp of coming, he withdraws his fingers. "Sit on my face, Kid. Let me fucking taste your cum."

"This I gotta see," York states, and I glance over at him and Zayn who are watching us intently from the other side of the room. Both of them are hard again, both are watching us with lust that has only grown with every moment.

Pulling myself up on shaky arms, I climb across Dax as he lies back, very aware of Xeno as he watches us. "You want me to sit on your face?" I repeat, the words coming out husky and full of want.

"That's exactly what I want you to do. Come get filthy, Kid. Let me eat you up." Dax licks his lips, grasps my hips and pulls me towards his face.

Fireworks detonate behind my closed eyelids as Dax keeps his word and eats me the fuck up. His tongue is all up in my pussy, sweeping through my folds, sucking, licking, teasing, tormenting, and when Xeno positions himself in front of me and kisses me with the same fervour as Dax fucks my pussy, I come. Again. Screaming my pleasure into Xeno's mouth.

I get as long as it takes for Xeno and Dax to sheath their cocks with a condom before I'm seated to the hilt on Dax's cock. He fills me up, his pupils blown wide as Xeno settles himself behind us both between Dax's parted legs.

"Oh God," I cry as my swollen, too sensitive pussy presses against Dax's abs.

Xeno runs his teeth gently over my shoulder, clasping my breast from behind. He plays with my nipples, his tongue licking over my skin.

"Lean forward, Tiny," he says, his voice caught in the tightness of his throat. Releasing my breasts, Xeno strokes his fingers down my spine. "Kiss Dax but try and keep still. Let me get you ready. I don't want to hurt you."

I mumble out my response, nodding my head and leaning forward. Dax draws me in for a deep, passionate kiss, his tongue stroking mine whilst his hand clasps the back of my neck, and his fingers massage the base of my skull.

"Keep kissing, I'm going to loosen you up, okay?"

I groan my response, my inner muscles tightening around Dax's cock as Xeno reaches lower and slides his fingers through my folds and around the base of Dax's cock before rimming my tight hole. Gently, he slides a single finger into my arse, and I let out a moan, loving the feeling. Dax has already fingered me there, and it was a pleasurable experience.

"Jesus, you three are turning me the fuck on," Zayn exclaims through gritted teeth. York chuckles but I can't even respond as Xeno pushes another finger into my arse then starts moving them in and out gently, the slickness he'd collected allowing him to slide in and out easily. I try to keep still but when Dax groans into my mouth, I start shifting, pushing back against Xeno's fingers, my inner muscles tightening around Dax's cock. The tension builds once more, and I don't even know how I'm going to survive another orgasm. Yet my body welcomes it. When Xeno removes his fingers and presses his hand against the base of my spine, I beg him to fuck me.

"Please," I whimper, the growing orgasm winding up and up and up as I shift and grind on Dax's cock, my clit rubbing against his abs.

"Look at me, Tiny," Xeno demands.

I glance over my shoulder as he grips his dick and slides the tip into my arse. My mouth pops open at the slight burn, but he eases the head in slowly and waits for my body to adjust. Dax's hand strokes up and down my back as he whispers words of love and encouragement, his lips sliding over my ear and cheek with every caress.

"I love you. I love you so fucking much," Xeno says as he edges into me slowly, with care, affection and restraint. When he's fully seated, he stills, his hands caressing my hips and lower back as my body gives way to the most intense feeling of fullness.

I feel full of them. So fucking full. My heart, my pussy, my arse, my *soul*.

And when York and Zayn climb onto the sofa, their hands reaching for me and smoothing over my too hot skin, I close my eyes and just *feel*.

I feel Dax moving deep inside. I feel Xeno grow bigger, stretching me. I feel Zayn's kisses across my shoulder and York's gentle touch. I feel loved.

So. Fucking. Loved.

Later as I lay curled up in Xeno's arms—my head pressed against his chest watching Dax, Zayn and York laughing and joking as they pull on their boxer shorts and help themselves to some alcohol—Xeno brushes my damp hair off my forehead and breathes out a long, satiated breath.

"I once told you that you had to choose. I believed that the world wouldn't support our kind of love, *my* kind of love, so I turned my back on it. I was wrong, Tiny. What we have, the five of us, it's worth fighting for. You're our beating heart, and without you not one of us can survive. I can't promise you that we won't fuck up, but I can promise you that nothing and no one will come between the five of us again. Not Santiago, and certainly not your motherfucking brother."

"I believe you," I say, then press my lips against his and kiss him until our lips are bruised and our hearts begin to mend.

37

Pen

I WAKE up to the sound of my phone ringing whilst sandwiched between Dax and Zayn, both of whom groan in their sleep as I try to wiggle out of their arms. The phone stops ringing then immediately starts up again, causing anxiety to swirl in my stomach.

"What fucking time is it?" York groans, sitting up behind Zayn and rubbing a hand over his face. He's got a crease across his cheek from falling asleep on the zipper of a cushion. Given there's no windows in the basement, it's hard to tell what time of day it is. All I know is that we've spent hours hanging out, then making love, each of us finally falling asleep from an orgasm coma.

"I've no idea," I reply, gently removing Dax's arm from around my waist and gingerly standing between the sleeping pair, trying not to wake them. I step over Dax and then onto the floor, immediately searching for my phone, wearing nothing but York's shirt. Fortunately for me he's tall and it covers my naked arse as I crouch down and search through the clothes scattered about the room.

"Whose phone is that?" Xeno asks, stepping out of the shower room. He's got a towel wrapped around his waist and is rubbing another over his head as water drips over his smooth tan skin.

"Mine. Shit. I can't find it," I say, panicked by the fact that the second it stops, it immediately starts up again.

Grabbing up his jeans that were discarded by the fridge, Xeno discards his towel and pulls them on. "It's just past midday," he says, checking the time on his wristwatch. "Clancy perhaps?"

"Whoever it is, they're determined to reach me."

Xeno reads my concern and strides over to the couch. He shakes Dax and Zayn awake. York is already pulling on his clothes. "Get your clothes on, something's up," he says, saying out loud what I'm already beginning to feel inside.

Searching through the pile of clothes, I finally find my phone tucked into Dax's trainer. I swipe up, reading the screen.

"Fuck! Lena." She's called five times. When the phone starts ringing again, I immediately answer. I hear her sob and my heart fucking plummets. "Lena, shit. What's wrong?"

"Pen..." her voice cracks and she cries some more.

"Lena. Talk to me right now!" I put the phone on loudspeaker and frantically pull on my clothes.

"Pen, I don't know what to do. What do I do?" she cries out.

"Lena, take a deep breath and listen to me. I need you to tell me what's happening."

She keeps sobbing, unable to find the words. Glancing up at Xeno, I swallow hard. He's quietly giving the guys orders, and when I hear footsteps coming down into the basement, I already know it's Beast. He enters the room, dressed, a gun holstered at his side and a mobile phone pressed to his ear. Grim follows him in, still in her nightwear. I already know it's bad news when I see the look on her face. I look away, I can't afford to be weak now.

"She's... not... breathing, Pen," Lena says between sobs. "I don't know what to do."

"Who's not breathing?" I ask, my throat tightening, knowing already who she's talking about.

"It's Mum, Pen. I think she's... taken something..." More sobbing follows and I force myself to remain calm as I pull on my shoes even though my stomach is rolling over and I feel like I want to throw up.

"Where is she right now?" I ask, standing, sliding my arms into the sleeves of Zayn's hoodie that he's holding up for me. I zip it up quickly, grab my mobile, ready to go. My guys are already heading towards the stairs, knowing instinctively what I need to do.

"She's on... the... floor. Oh, God, I only went out for a little while. She was fine when I left," Lena sobs, hysterical now. It's obvious mum has overdosed, that selfish bitch. I push the anger down, lock it inside. It won't help Lena. Right now she needs me to keep calm.

"Tell Lena to let Gray in the flat. He's just outside," Beast says quickly. He nods, giving short one-word responses as he listens to, whom I'm assuming is Gray, on the other end of the line.

"Lena, we've sent someone to help you. His name is Gray. He's at the front door. Let him in."

"Who...? What...? How...?" she asks, her voice barely understandable, her confusion obvious.

"He's a friend. I've no time to explain. Stay on the line and let him in the flat. He will help you. We'll be there in ten minutes. We're leaving now, okay?"

"Okay," she manages to reply.

For a moment all I hear are her muffled movements and the low tenor of a man's voice talking to Lena. Beast flicks off his mobile and motions for us to follow him. "I'll drive," he says, before turning to Grim. "You stay here. I'll ring you when we get there."

"I'm coming," she replies.

"There's no time for you to change. Stay the fuck here, Grim," Beast orders, brooking no arguments. "Tennyson is on his way over."

"I don't need a babysitter," she replies.

"I don't give a fuck what you want, Grim. We don't know what we're walking into and you are not fucking going. He'll be here in two minutes."

Beast and Grim exchange looks and it's at that point that I suddenly realise this might be more than my mum having a relapse and an accidental overdose. Beast knows more than he's letting on right now. She nods, conceding to him in the moment. As I pass her by, she squeezes my arm in solidarity. She doesn't say a word. She doesn't have to. There are no words of comfort in a situation like this.

"Lena, are you still there?" I ask, rushing up the stairs and out into the cold morning air. The gravel of the driveway crunches underfoot.

"Yes."

"What's Gray doing?"

"He's giving mum mouth to mouth... Oh, God... Please...

Please... Please...!" Lena screams and I feel her pain cut right through my chest and bury itself in my heart.

"Lena, it's Xeno. I want you to go into your bedroom and lock the door," he says as we climb into Beast's seven-seater Mercedes MPV. "You're not to come out until we get there."

"Why?" she questions, her voice cracking.

Swallowing the rising nausea in my throat, I reiterate what he's said. "Lena, just do it, okay? Go into your bedroom and lock the door. We won't be long."

"Please don't let her die. Please..." she mumbles through the thickening sound of her pain.

"Lena. Are you in your bedroom yet?"

"Yes," she replies.

"Good. Now lock the door and wait for us."

"What? Why? What's going on, Pen?" she asks, her voice trembling with fear as well as sorrow. I can hear her teeth chatter, and I fist my fingers, my nails digging into the palm of my hand.

"We'll be there soon. Just keep talking, Lena. Let me know you're okay," I reply.

Dax grasps my hand, whilst Zayn and York take the seats opposite us and Xeno sits up front with Beast. We don't talk to each other for the whole journey, all six of us just listen to Lena as her heart breaks and mine goes numb.

It takes Beast six minutes to get to my mum's flat.

When I enter the flat, I head straight for Lena's bedroom, passing by the living room where Gray is still giving my mum mouth to mouth resuscitation. Flicking off the call and tucking my mobile into my back pocket, I knock on her door.

"Lena, it's me. I'm here now. Open up," I say gently.

"Pen!" she cries, yanking the door open and throwing herself into my arms, knocking us both backwards. She sobs into my hair, her legs giving way beneath her as we both collapse to the floor. I clutch her to me, stroking her hair and rocking her back and forth. Zayn and York stride towards me, and one look from Zayn tells me all I need to know.

"I'm sorry," he mouths, sorrow filling his eyes as he passes us by, a gun clutched in his hands as he checks the bathroom and my mum's bedroom.

York grits his jaw, love and sadness in his eyes as he crouches beside us both. "She's gone," he says gently, resting his hand on Lena's back.

"No!" she cries, yanking herself out of my arms and rushing down the hallway to the living room. Dax steps out of the doorway and clutches her by the shoulders.

"Sweetheart, I'm sorry," he says gently.

Lena screams, pounding her fists against his chest, the sound tearing through me. I stagger to my feet, barely able to keep myself upright as York wraps his arm around my waist and Dax hugs a sobbing Lena to his chest.

"Take Lena into the kitchen. Keep her there," Xeno says to Dax who nods, manoeuvring her into the room. He shuts the kitchen door, closing us out.

"The flat's clear," Zayn says, stepping out of my mum's bedroom as he looks at York, a silent conversation passing between them.

"What?" I say, forcing myself to remain upright. "What's going on?"

"Pen, you don't need to see this," Xeno says, blocking my path as I try to step into the living room.

"She's my mum, Xeno," I reply firmly. "If Lena has to live the rest of her life remembering what my mum looks like in death, then so will I. She won't go through that alone."

Xeno's eyes flick with sorrow but he nods, stepping aside.

Beast and the man I know now to be Gray are crouching over the prone form of my mum talking quietly. "This isn't an—" Beast says, his sentence cut short when he notices me. I watch as he lowers my mum's eyelids, shutting them so I don't see her blank staring eyes.

I swallow hard, pain swelling in my chest as I look at her. Apart from the discolouration around her lips, she looks peaceful. In death she looks healthier than I ever remember her looking in life, and something about that makes a sob rise up my chest. Pressing a hand over my mouth, I drop to the floor and run my shaking fingers over her cheek. She's cold.

"I'm sorry, Pen," Beast says, his voice gruff.

"She wasn't a good mum. At least not to me," I reply automatically, my voice void of emotion as I rip my hand back. I know it's not the right thing to say given the circumstances, but the words just fall from my lips regardless. I hate myself for them; for the bitterness, pain and lack of empathy they hold.

"What did she take?" I ask after a few minutes, dragging my gaze upwards to look over at Beast. He doesn't answer straight away, instead he glances at Xeno who's crouching beside me.

"Tell her," York says, stepping into the room with Zayn. Both look troubled.

"Tell me what?"

"This isn't an overdose, Pen," Beast says, looking at me carefully.

"What? How do you know that?"

"Look around you, there's no drug paraphernalia, no empty

bottles of alcohol to wash the pills down with. Nothing here suggests your mum has taken something to get high or even to kill herself."

I look about the room, taking in how spotless it looks. There isn't even the usual smell of cigarette smoke or any ashtrays filled with cigarette stubs, let alone what I've been used to seeing when I've found my mum passed out on numerous occasions over the years. Beast's right, she hasn't gone on a bender or tried to kill herself. My stomach churns and I swallow hard.

"Tell me," I demand.

Beast swipes a hand over his face, then points at the purple-blue tinge around her mouth. "This is from lack of oxygen," he says, then lowers the material of her turtleneck jumper. "She was strangled, Pen."

I see the finger shaped bruises around her throat, and I retch, reaching for the wastepaper bin tucked by the end of the sofa. When I've finished emptying my stomach, I look back up at Beast, wiping my sleeve across my mouth. "Please don't tell me that you're suggesting Lena..."

"No, of course not!" he exclaims, then turns to Gray who hands him a slip of paper. "This wasn't Lena, Pen. Gray said she returned home only a few minutes before she called you. Your mum has been dead for at least an hour, maybe a while longer. She was murdered whilst Lena was out of the house. It's why my men didn't pick anything up. They haven't been watching over your mum. I'm sorry."

With shaking fingers, I take the piece of paper from Beast and read the words scrawled in black ink across the surface.

Eenie, meenie, miney, mo.... Who's next, Penelope?

I look up, my heart thundering in my chest. There's only one person who knows the terror that line fills me with.

David.

He's back...

THE STORY CONTINUES IN FINALE. Available Now

ACKNOWLEDGMENTS

So what did you think?

If you're a member of my readers group on Facebook, *Queen Bea's Hive*, you'll know that I struggled with this book, not because of the story itself (though realising it needed a fourth book certainly helped my mojo) but because 2020 threw me into a head spin, like it did for many of us. 2020 was hard for so many different reasons, and we all have a story personal to our own experiences. What a year, eh?

Truth be known, there was a portion of 2020, whilst I was finishing Lyrical and starting Breakers, where my muse packed her bags and upped and left me for weeks on end. It was a *really* hard time, coupled with the stress of 2020 and managing my children's mental health in a time where their world was turned upside down, I buckled. It was a sunny Thursday afternoon in August and I remember it well. I don't want to go back there again.

So, as I step into 2021, nervous, hopeful, cautious, I bring one important lesson with me; *know your limits*. I'm ready for 2021 and the challenges and successes it's going to bring, and I have *so* many stories and new characters to share with you.

Lastly, as always I want to thank you for your continued support. This life I live would never have been possible without you all reading my books. Much love, Bea xoxo

ABOUT BEA PAIGE

Bea Paige lives a very secretive life in London... She likes red wine and Haribo sweets (preferably together) and occasionally swings around poles when the mood takes her.

Bea loves to write about love and all the different facets of such a powerful emotion. When she's not writing about love and passion, you'll find her reading about it and ugly crying.

Bea is always writing, and new ideas seem to appear at the most unlikely time, like in the shower or when driving her car.

She has lots more books planned, so be sure to subscribe to her newsletter:

beapaige.co.uk/newsletter-sign-up

ALSO BY BEA PAIGE

Grim & Beast's Duet

#1 Tales You Win

#2 Heads You Lose

Their Obsession Duet (dark reverse harem)

#1 The Dancer and The Masks

#2 The Masks and The Dancer

Academy of Stardom

(friends-to-enemies-lovers reverse harem)

#1 Freestyle

#2 Lyrical

#3 Breakers

#4 Finale

Academy of Misfits

(bully/academy reverse harem)

#1 Delinquent

#2 Reject

#3 Family

Finding Their Muse

(dark contemporary reverse harem)

#1 Steps

#2 Strokes

#3 Strings

#4 Symphony

#5 Finding Their Muse boxset

The Brothers Freed Series

(contemporary reverse harem)

#1 Avalanche of Desire

#2 Storm of Seduction

#3 Dawn of Love

#4 Brothers Freed Boxset

Contemporary Standalone's

Beyond the Horizon

For all up to date book releases please visit

www.beapaige.co.uk

Printed in Great Britain
by Amazon